PROPHECY OF ASHES:
A SUPERNATURAL PSYCHIC THRILLER

WRAITH HUNTER CHRONICLES: BOOK 1

By John R. Monteith

I0536846

Prologue

Diane dreamt of a human figure burning on a cross, blood pouring from the blurry apparition's chest. Time stopped, accelerated, and slowed again as the surreal nightmare unfolded.

An unseen wind flapped a milky gown over a ghost of feminine form who spoke with a young woman's voice. "Heed my warning."

In her ethereal vision, Diane responded with her human voice. "About what?"

"Suffering."

"I don't understand."

"You will see horrors born of mankind's deepest evils, and you will suffer with the victims."

Flashes of stabbings, beatings, and mutilations assaulted Diane's mind. "Why's this happening?"

"Merciless savagery."

"No. This can't happen."

"Only you can stop it."

"What should I do?"

As the apparition faded, she whispered. "Avenge me."

CHAPTER 1

Jacob finished his memorized recitation to his Master spirit and unsheathed the dagger. His anxious stench mingling with the scent of his prisoner's fear, he squeezed the handle and held his breath while creeping towards the kill.

Bound to a wooden cross, the virgin squirmed, and restricting ropes abraded her wrists. The cellar's cold stone walls swallowed her gagged and muffled screams, and her horrified, pleading eyes probed him for solace, which he met with practiced indifference.

Born human, he retained his full suite of emotions, but he compartmentalized the weak ones. The young lady's protesting muscles expressed betrayal and anger, but he'd insulated himself from shame and compassion long ago.

Her writhing feminine form tempted his touch, but the sacrificial ceremony marked the one night his lording spirit commanded his chastity. His Master denied his lust for her body but indulged his greed for her years.

The dominating spirit ordered him forward, through the circle of candles, towards the woman whose death would renew him. Hanging on planks he'd set in concrete, she shuddered and whined, and tears streamed down her flushing cheeks. As he bit back distant echoes of an empathy he'd long ago learned to forget, he aimed the knife at his victim's chest.

Before he could bury the blade, concussion grenades blew out the upstairs windows. He cringed, and the realization scared him.

Those who sought him had arrived.

Recalling the defenses he'd deployed throughout the French millhouse and its surrounding garden, he calmed himself.

Grenades, incendiary devices, tripwires, and spike traps protected him.

Those who hunted him were smart and relentless. But they weren't suicidal. Aware of and honoring his traps, they'd move slowly, and he'd finish before they could stop him.

His Master's prodding resonated throughout him, compelling him onward against the pursuing threat, to finish before the sacrifice's window of opportunity closed.

Spurred forward by fear, greed, and habit, he raised the knife. Running his free fingers down her supple flesh, he counted bony contours from the virgin's collarbone, turned the blade sideways to fit under her fourth rib, and aimed it at her left ventricle.

He slid the metal into her heart.

Like flame, pulsating crimson light shot from the blade, and the killer bathed in its oscillating glow.

Then, a dizzying rush of euphoria overcame him as he ingested her life.

Success. "Thank you, Master."

He avoided his sacrifice's fading eyes. Instead, he stared at the knife and watched dark blood pour over it and down the woman's tattered gown. The dying body warmed the dagger as stolen life flowed from the victim, through the handle, and into him.

His strength grew, and a youthful torrent of vigor, bordering on invincibility, pervaded his cells.

The dagger's light receded, yielding the cellar to tiny dancing flames, and Jacob withdrew it from the corpse.

Another concussion grenade exploded above, and dust billowed from the floorboards over his head. With cracking thunder, he heard the hunters bashing the millhouse's main oaken door.

He retraced his steps to the center of the candlelit circle, knelt, and pushed the knife into its sheath. He slipped into a cloak, and then he stood to inspect himself.

Around his waist hung a rope, which cinched his relic dagger against his waist, and a belt with his holstered Beretta pistol. His pockets held a flashlight and a wad of French cash.

He stepped from the circle, grabbed a candle, and trotted behind the cross. Having avoided the woman's lifeless face, he felt a twinge of relief. Humanity's weaknesses remained engrained in his soul, exposing him to emotions detrimental to his cause. Pity, regret, and remorse were enemies to keep dormant, and invoking them by an accidental connection to his victim was intolerable. From behind, the corpse seemed inhuman, safe.

Focusing on his escape, he splashed a staged cup of oil on the dried branches he'd piled under his offering's bound ankles. After tilting the candle into the glistening tinder, he watched the flame spread, dance, and touch dead flesh.

Fire shot up the crucifix, and as the ceiling planks ignited, he heard the millhouse's main door crumble.

The hunters were breaking in.

He turned towards the rear wall, shouldered open a creaky portal, and ducked into a tunnel. He flicked on his flashlight to verify its conical beam, and then he shut the door.

He placed his hands to his knees while coughing smoke from his lungs, and then he stood straight and rubbed his stinging eyes.

Stone walls swallowed his artificial light as he marched down the descending path. Small puddles cooled his bare feet, and the muddy footing slowed him, but his renewed life and adrenaline powered him forward.

Sheathed and holstered weapons bouncing off either hip, he accelerated to a trot. After covering a football field's length, he finished a gentle turn that revealed his barred exit. But before he could lift the staged key from the ground to work the padlock, he needed to disarm his trap.

To prevent intruders from using the tunnel, he'd wedged a grenade between heavy rocks and had secured its pin to a fishing wire tied to the gate. He withdrew his dagger and clutched the fragmentation weapon. He cut the glimmering wire and sheathed the knife. Quick work with a key then freed him to crawl into high marsh grass under Southern France's winter moon.

As he sniffed the living river, his pounding heart reminded him of his replenished vivacity. He wanted to sprint to the water, swim across, and dare his pursuers to catch him. But his seasoned wisdom warned him.

After each prior kill, his Master spirit had seemed to enjoy lording a fleeting and fictitious feeling of invulnerability over him at his moment of greatest exposure.

A glance over his shoulder showed orange and yellow lights dancing in the millhouse's windows, but the burning house on the hill hid the hunters. Though unable to see his adversaries, he reminded himself of their relentless tenacity in seeking him while he continued his stealthy crawl.

He knew they were coming.

After a long and patient minute, he saw mist rising from the Gardon River into Anduze's cool winter air. Laboring but invigorated, he churned his knees and elbows through more muck until he reached the water's edge.

He untied his rowboat from a sapling and slid over the vessel's edge. Beside him lay a survival bag containing clothing, food, and his rifle, and an oar pinched his ribs.

Rolling to his knees, he inspected the growing fire again, but this time he saw the movement of human silhouettes. He crouched and held his breath. As his eyes adjusted, he saw the hunters facing away, searching for him near the structure's exits.

He exhaled.

Letting the current carry him, he grabbed the oar, jabbed it into the mud, and pushed the boat into the river's flow. Wanting to exploit his eternal vigor, he considered rowing hard, but patient wisdom guided his choice to assure silence and let the water propel him. He also resisted the urge to withdraw his rifle from his bag, trusting time and his overseeing spirit to deliver him.

A gentle steer of the rudder angled him through a bend and hid him behind tall reeds. Ablaze, the house on the hill became an orange orb on a receding horizon, and the ritualistic theft of life became one of many necessary sacrifices in his history of survival. Confident he'd distanced himself from beyond hearing, he mounted his oars and rowed.

A vision appeared above the bow in which an unseen wind flapped a milky gown over a female frame. The young lady, exposed and pierced when he'd killed her, was now a ghost, clothed in dignity and unblemished in the afterlife. Her eyes became black orbs, and her voice carried deep, haunting tones that chilled him. "Why did you kill me?"

"I had no choice."

"You betrayed me. I will be avenged." She disappeared.

They always disappeared.

He snuck a peek at the full moon and snorted. Mankind was on its way to walking on its surface, and with his centuries-long witnessing of inventions, he expected human ingenuity to succeed. But the pending lunar landings which fascinated most men taunted him with a reminder.

As humanity improved its technology, it also found better ways to hunt. Tracking and killing tools worked against him, and he would need to get smarter. His pursuers had somehow connected him to the millhouse, and this escape had been his narrowest.

But he'd succeeded.

They hadn't seen him, he'd left no clues, and his hunters had learned nothing to use against him next time.

And the next time would come. It always did, every fifty years. On schedule, predictable, and following the rules of his Master spirit.

Instead of worrying about the next ritual, he entertained visions of his continued pursuit of hedonism.

Women and drink were on the menu as always, but perhaps he'd explore the synthetic opiates or the psychedelic hallucinogens romanticized in revolutionary rock music. Once relocated to a new country with a new name, he would apply his excessive wealth, enduring youth, and ancient wisdom to exploring and indulging new appetites for the next half century.

And that was plenty of time to bury deep within his decaying soul any fears of the hunters killing him before he could sacrifice his next victim.

CHAPTER 2

Diane revealed the final tarot card on the tablecloth.

The Tower.

Burning. Bodies plummeting.

Across the covered second-hand maple dining table, her client gasped.

The elderly Iraqi woman wore excessive clown-like makeup and oversized rings and bracelets, but Diane expected such glittering gaudiness from the matriarchs of Michigan's Christian Chaldean community who provided half her fortune telling clients.

Scouring her memory for the complete definition of the Tower, the harsh major arcana card, the tarot reader sought an optimistic spin. She reminded herself this was a performance more than a prophecy, and her acting and storytelling paid the bills. She invoked an empathetic but authoritative voice. "The Tower has a lot of hidden upsides."

Blue mascara mocking the gesture, the woman raised her eyebrows. "*Wulla, habibi*! About my granddaughter's wedding?"

Diane scanned the preceding nine cards, seeking a story to placate her vital income source. While concocting a believable tale, she pondered the old woman's historical attitude.

Three years of weekly readings had revealed a bitter, jealous, and judgmental elder, and Diane saw the problem. Sometimes, the cards uncovered nasty truths.

Her eyes flitting over the images, she sought a foundation upon which to answer the question about the pending wedding that culminated in the card showing flame and people dropping to their deaths.

Saving her, an earlier card caught her attention.

Reflecting the querent's subconscious mind, the sixth card in the cross was the Chariot. Control, assertion, victory.

Her client wanted to control her granddaughter's wedding, and from the perspective of her dominating desires, disaster loomed. If not disaster, then upheaval and revelation.

Someone–a daughter, a granddaughter, or other courageous family member–was standing up against the manipulating old woman. To advise the aged schemer to stop meddling while keeping her as a client, Diane followed her proven habits. Flattery and misdirection. "The cards are telling us a complex story. The sixth card tells us about your deepest concerns. Today, the Chariot symbolizes your determination to look after your granddaughter's well-being. It means you have a strong desire to protect her."

The insight calmed the woman, who furrowed her brow and pursed her lips before responding. "Of course, I do. I'm so glad you see it. Her mother says I try to control her, but what sort of grandmother would let her granddaughter be with men from the wrong families?"

As a business practice, Diane kept current with social media. Her twenty-something Chaldean colleagues posted enough content to predict the immigrant generation's gossip. The wedding included a half-Iraqi, half-not-Iraqi groom, and she surmised the mix infuriated her traditionalist client. "I've known you long enough to know that you mean well. Have you tried talking to your granddaughter about your concerns?"

The woman looked away and flicked her wrinkled fingers. "*Silla*, no. Her mother screamed at me when I suggested it. The newer generations have no respect for the old."

"I understand. That's frustrating, of course. I see that you want to talk to your granddaughter to make sure she knows she's doing the right thing, but her mother thinks you're going to just tell her to break off the engagement."

The old lady's face lit up. "*Ba'ad!* Yes. I have a right to make sure she gets good advice. She's too young to know on her own.

I need to get to her, but her mother won't let her visit me."

Predictable, the comment played into the tarot reader's finale. "I'm confident the tower means that you'll run into problems if you keep trying to go through her mother."

"What can I do? I've asked all the brothers and sisters of my generation on her mother's and father's side to talk to her, but her mother's stopping them, too."

Since it helped her through the difficult readings, Diane remembered the structure of her client's extended family. The target of today's discussion was the granddaughter's uncle. "We have a reversed three of swords in the eighth position. Let's focus on that. It means you'll have to play the peacemaker."

"How can I make peace if I can't talk to anyone?"

Diane frowned, pretending to scan her memory. "Don't you have a younger male relative who everyone trusts?"

Reverting to the family peacemaker would be an act of humility for the woman. She'd get to express her views, but then the family would join forces to reject her bigotry.

It was the best outcome Diane could propose.

Her client seemed defeated but then assumed her brave air. "My granddaughter's uncle could help. I didn't want to bother him, but it appears I now have no choice."

"He could be your ally, then."

"He's the one people seem to trust. I'll approach him."

"I think you're making a good decision."

"Yes, thank you, *habibi*. You're always so wise, especially for someone so young."

The comment reminded Diane that her mid-twenties were roaring by while her life stagnated behind two jobs and a special needs brother. But survival required her focus on her client, and she reminded herself of her inner strength. She always finished her readings convincingly and managed to pay the bills. "Thank you. We have time for one more reading, if you'd like."

"Oh, you've done enough for me already today."

"It's up to you, of course."

"No, that's enough for one day."

The woman lifted her huge purse to her lap and fished for a wallet. Moments later, she pulled out a fifty-dollar bill and unfolded it on the table. Diane grabbed it and tucked it into her jeans while standing. She then walked around the table and led the waddling elder out her apartment door.

Alone, Diane checked her client schedule on her phone. She had three hours before her next performance, and that suited her. Running a business in her living room was illegal, and a constant influx of clients would arouse suspicions from her apartment's management. Plus, she needed a nap.

During days off from her department store job, she made extra money with her fortune telling, or she did homework for the university degree she was earning between her income efforts. And she also took care of an autistic brother. When she found time to sleep, she was smart enough to use it.

She kicked off her tennis shoes and set them by the entry door. In her socks, she started retracing her steps through the living room but tripped. Extending her arm, she broke her fall against a sofa and swore in Aramaic. "*Erub!*"

Overly tall for her slim feet, she accepted her clumsiness, considering it a small price in exchange for height, curves, and good looks that turned enough heads to boost her ego.

After verifying her ankle sprain was minimal, she continued towards the only stereotypical mystical decoration she allowed, the beads hanging in the hall's entryway. The living room held other art pieces suggesting the supernatural, but nothing overt to garner unwanted attention from the apartment's management.

A portrait of Diane, gifted from a failed romance, hung behind the dining table she used for her readings. Her sleek jawline anchored the dimensions of her face, and shades of blue, indigo, and purple gave a surreal edge. Black sunglasses rested on a pointed nose that aimed at pouting lips.

On the opposite wall, a colorful painting of a humanoid cat

dressed in carnival garb holding a golden chalice at a wooden table made a fortune-telling scene. Beside it hung a flat wood carving of a feline's face surrounded by astrological symbols. If questioned, Diane could mention her affinity for felines as the basis for her art.

Cats reminded her of herself. As a species of handsome carnivores, they invoked her Roman namesake, a divine huntress with beauty and swiftness. As survivors graced by hidden charms, they honored her name's Greek origins as the moon goddess. Even the feline temperament mimicked hers–affectionate when appropriate but scrappy when necessary.

She continued to the vertical beads, and then she passed the kitchen. She knocked on the first bedroom's door. "Josh?"

No response.

She clicked open the knob and stuck her head through the opening. "Josh?"

Her younger brother sat at his desk ingesting a book on his tablet. He enjoyed reading and had excellent comprehension, as far as she knew.

When she had time, she'd read some of his books, but he struggled to discuss them. She recalled that talking, engaging in nonverbal communications and processing subtlety, confused him. "I'm going to take a nap. Are you hungry? Do you want me to make you some lunch?"

His back turned to her, he angled his head towards the half-eaten omelet next to his phone, and then he pointed his nose back to his book. The gesture sufficed for his answer.

"You have to tell me now if you want anything hot to eat. If you don't, you can always make a sandwich."

She noticed his slight nod.

"Okay. I'm going to sleep now."

As she started closing the door, he called out with an unemotional tone. "Your tarot cards are no good."

"What do you mean? I just had an accurate reading with Nana Gulla, and I put on a great show, if I don't say so myself."

He grunted, meaning she'd missed an obvious and major

point from his perspective. She didn't care what he meant, but she cared about him, which meant forcing her interest in his words. When he spoke, she needed to encourage it.

"I'm tired, Josh. So, I may not be thinking clearly. Can you explain what you mean?"

His voice became edgy. "Your tarot cards are no good."

She entered his room and sat on his bed beside him. "Do you mean I'm using the wrong deck? I like my Rider-Waite cards, and my clients like them, too."

He slammed the tablet down on the desk. With eye contact being a monumental challenge, he yelled at the wall. "You shouldn't use them."

Flustered, she raised her voice. "What's wrong with you? I need to pay the bills!"

He lowered his head, stared at the electronics, and retreated to the solace of solitude. Diane pursed her lips, chiding herself for her outburst. Autism hampered him, and she provided his only routine human connection.

Her special needs brother had led to their parents' divorce, which had led to unmet needs in both children, feeding a downward spiral of neglect. Diane was his sister, mother, and caretaker.

When her single mother's two jobs had robbed the siblings of their parent's time, Diane had stepped in to care for her toddler brother. Though a child herself, she'd spent countless hours substituting for their weary matriarch in helping him learn eye contact, understanding abstract concepts like pointing a finger, and combining gestures with words.

As alcohol had consumed her mother during her brother's early adult years, Diane had inherited the complete burden of guardianship. She'd struggled with resentment.

But her love overpowered all derogatory sentiments, and she'd sensed from her youth a hidden, universal force that promised to always power her through adversity.

Lowering her voice to a singsong tone, she coaxed him back. "Hey, Josh? May I have your attention please?"

Nothing.

She moved next to him and knelt. "May I have your attention please, Josh?" Patience. Love. Repeat. She had the strength. "May I have your attention please, Josh?"

"No."

"I'm sorry I yelled at you, Josh. That was selfish of me."

"Can't you just work more at the store?" He was back.

"I could, but I make more money per hour with the readings. Why don't you like my cards?"

"They're wrong."

She knew they were accurate within the framework of her interpreting them and crafting stories. She'd mastered the psychology of reading people and telling them what they wanted to hear without violating the truth. The cards were her necessary tool, and history had always validated her past premonitions. "They're always right when I use them."

"Stop using them."

She frowned. He'd never warned her away from them in three years of their use. To keep him talking, she humored his perspective and probed. "You've never asked me to stop before. Did you learn something bad about them?"

He looked away. It was a warning, and she felt it, somewhere, deep inside her, in the murky caverns of her intuition.

Rumors and anecdotes suggested special sensory powers in her family, passed through bloodlines from ancient times in Iraq. She had gifts, and she suspected her brother did, too.

Shying away from the deeper practices, she'd skirted the edge of her abilities and limited her exploration to tarot. But she knew her brother's silent, incessant reading into mysticism and occult practices brought him wisdom pointing down the path she'd avoided for lack of time and energy, despite her growing interest. In her hectic reality, the obligations of rent, utilities, and tuition separated her pursuit of deep truths while in his quiet world, he devoured knowledge.

She swallowed, and her hoarse voice carried fear. "Josh, what did you learn about my cards?"

"Nothing. Go away."

"Josh, please."

He lifted his tablet to read it, but she intercepted it and put it behind her back.

He screamed. "That's mine! Give it to me!"

She kept her eyes locked on his as he turned and tried to reach around her. Knowing her acts were harsh for his condition, she continued in desperation. She had to learn his insights. "Not until you tell me what you learned about my cards."

He howled, and she cringed. "Give me my book!"

Defeated, she stood and placed it on his desk. Taunting him had been wrong. "Here. I'm sorry. I just wanted to know what you learned."

He lifted his book and started reading. Having killed the conversation, she retreated and started closing the door behind her.

Before it clicked shut, he spoke in an even tone. "The cards will stop you if you keep using them."

She turned and stuck her head through the door. "Stop me?"

"Yes, but don't worry."

"Don't worry? How can you scare me like that and tell me not to worry?"

He remained silent.

"I mean, do you have any advice for me, Josh?"

Nothing.

"Josh, do you have any advice for me? Please? I'd like to know what's on your mind."

"You don't need the cards. They're a distraction. Your powers are too strong for them."

CHAPTER 3

Liam steadied his rifle scope's optics, holding the crosshair on the target. He squeezed the trigger, and the round's crack surprised him.

Standing beside him with binoculars, his father, Connor, announced the accuracy. "Not bad. You hit the outer ring."

Prone, with his nose inches above frozen earth, Liam lowered his face into the homemade shooting range's ground. He'd hoped for better.

Connor rescued him from self-criticism. "Go easy on yourself, lad. I wasn't much better my first day with a sniper rifle."

"I bet you put the bloody bullets in a tighter grouping."

"I did, but I wasn't facing half this crosswind."

"I should've compensated more from watching the grass."

"You're still excellent with assault weapons at closer ranges."

The young man pushed his knee under his body and then sprang to his feet. While brushing hard dirt from his jacket, he protested. "What's the chance that I'll ever need a sniper rifle?"

"Greater than zero, which is why you'll become proficient."

"Don't get me wrong, since I think all this military and hunting training is awesome, but what's the chance I'll ever get to use it?"

County Cork's January bite made mist from his father's response. "Greater than zero. Therefore, you shall be prepared."

"Yeah? Just like you were prepared forty-nine years ago?"

Expecting yelling in response for his jab, Liam was relieved when his father chose to defuse the escalation. For a man in his mid-seventies, he had an authoritative voice. "My father and I were too late for rifles. Our quarry already had the maiden in the millhouse before we could arrive."

"I'm sorry. I didn't mean to mock you."

"Come on, lad. That's enough for today."

"Really, I didn't mean it, Father."

"Unfortunately, you did. You're frustrated."

Liam scoffed. "Yeah, but I have more class than that."

"We all go through it."

"Go through what? This isn't just frustration. It's been building in me for a long time."

He father gave him a knowing glare. "What has?"

Liam furrowed his brow while seeking the words. "Wondering if I'm ready."

His father grunted. "Come on, lad. Let's get a pint."

The pub was crowded and warm, and Liam hung his coat on a hook by the booth. His father sat opposite him and ordered ales.

Having spent his entire life centered on hunting, Liam felt comfortable talking openly about his true fate. His father assured him eavesdroppers would assume they spoke about nonhuman game.

Often, they did talk about taking down a buck or fowl. Hunting game had provided good practice for their shared higher purpose, killing the human target they addressed as "the wraith".

Letting the room's warmth drive away the winter chill, Liam stayed silent until the beer arrived. He took a gulp and let it loosen his speech. "It's bothering me."

His father sipped his golden fluid and lowered his glass. "What is, specifically?"

"This intense, singular focus on the wraith. I'm dedicating my entire life to hunting a man I may never find."

"Oh, I think many men would trade places with you to have such an obvious and noble purpose."

"What's so noble about it?"

"The chance to save lives."

Liam grunted and reflected upon greater possibilities. Maybe in ancient times his father would be right, but today, he ranked technology ahead of any mystical magic he'd been promised to see. "Really? What if I became an engineer and invented something that saved thousands of lives? I'd rather write software. That's what I did in the robotics club in school. What if that's my true calling?"

"Then I'd be proud of you. You can pursue that life after your next wraith hunt."

"You mean my first wraith hunt. It's your next, and your last."

His father sipped from his glass. "Correct. I don't expect I'll live to be one hundred and twenty-five."

"That's still another year I have to wait to do what I want."

"You'll still be a young man."

"Yeah, but I'm still not allowed to get married." Liam leaned forward and whispered his continued thought across the table. "And I'm not allowed to have sex. Ever?"

"Chastity is a virtue all men should honor. Not just us."

Liam leaned back and chugged half his drink. "That's why normal chaste men get to have wives."

"Not all men are destined to have families. Priests. Monks. Religious hermits. Knights of old."

"Well, I'm no holy man, and I don't feel like a knight."

His father's face wrinkled with a smile, and Liam noted a glint in his eye. "You're not supposed to be either. You're a hunter. You're to find and kill a vile creature, a savage that steals life."

Liam had bagged plenty of challenging animals, and their heads lined the room of his home. Yes, he was a hunter, but so were many people. "So, I'm a hunter. Why can't I have a normal life?"

"Because you know what you're ultimately hunting. Your entire life has been preparation for this one pursuit. It's something wicked and powerful, and it requires a special effort to defeat."

"How do you know? It's been centuries since the last successful hunt, and the only evidence of it ever happening is what's written in an ancient book."

His father pounded a fist into the table, making the glasses jump and reminding Liam that mentioning the book in public was forbidden. "Silence!"

The room's murmur died and then restarted after concerned faces saw no pending brawl.

"I'm sorry."

"You should know better."

"It won't happen again."

"As long as the subject is broached, you may rest assured in the veracity of the victories our heritage has claimed. It's not just written. It's the cornerstone of our oral teachings. It's the first lesson my father taught me, and if you'll be candid with your memories, you'll recall it's the first thing I taught you."

It was true. But the successful hunts had occurred so long ago that Liam considered them misty fables. "I do. But when will we win again?"

His father cast his eyes to his glass. "That answer was lost to us, if it was ever indeed known."

Liam meant the question as a plea, not an accusation. "I know. I didn't mean to complain."

"Bah. Don't let an old man's chagrin dishearten you. You and I may very well break the string of failed hunts."

"Not if my marksmanship today is an indicator." He smiled, trying to lift his spirits and those of his father. The elder man had sacrificed his life to raising his adopted son and to preparing for their ultimate hunt, and Liam realized he needed to minimize his self-pity.

His father returned a half-hearted grin. "It was the same for me and my father fifty years ago. Me, vocally unsure if he'd trained me well enough. Him, quietly unsure if he were too old for his second try. Neither of us mentioning the risk to our lives in pursuing a dangerous prey."

"You think I'm afraid?"

Connor tipped back his glass and emptied its contents. He placed it on the wooden table and responded with the air of authority that gave his son a spark of hope. "I know you're afraid. I trained you. Shame on me if you're not."

"Okay. Maybe a little."

"Good. A little is perfect–for now."

As Liam finished his drink, he expected his father to take him home to read about the latest assault weapons.

But as a waitress cleared the glasses and proposed to fetch more ale, she garnered his father's attention. "A second round and dinner, gentlemen?"

Connor accepted the offer and ordered supper. "Yes. And can we have two house specials, please? To celebrate."

"To celebrate my miserable sniper marksmanship?"

"No, the end of your training."

Liam had much to learn. He considered himself proficient in multiple tracking and assault practices but far from mastery.

While looking through night vision, he could scan his perimeter down a rifle's bore and step without snapping fallen branches or crumpling dried leaves. He could hit the fastest targets out to one hundred meters, but the day's sniper session had proven his doubt at longer ranges. And he questioned his combat skill with a knife.

Not knowing if he'd ever face the monster he sought, he found his life's purpose uncertain and unnerving. He refused to believe he was ready. "How can I be done?"

"Because it's time."

He remembered his father warning of a future hunting window. The revelation of its opening shocked him. "Now?"

"More accurately, it's in several days. But I want you to rest until then to prepare for your destiny."

Liam's lungs froze while he digested the imminence of his fate. His breathing recommenced as he gathered the nerve to make an admission. "Now, I am afraid."

"This is why we traditionally don't reveal timings to our sons, but it's completely predictable."

"And you're only telling me now?"

"It was to protect you. Imagine how I've felt for twenty-four years raising you, knowing the exact date this time would come. Try holding a secret that long."

"Okay, I get it. It's just… wow."

The waitress placed ales and plates of flank steak, potato pie, and sliced carrots onto the table and then departed.

"Are you ready to hear the story behind the timing?"

"Here? In public?"

"I'll refer to events loosely that you should recognize."

"Of course. Tell me everything."

"I will, but first let me tell you the most important thing."

Liam's heart pounded in his chest. "I'm listening."

"He's exposed when he travels, and it's time for him to move."

CHAPTER 4

Forty-nine years had flown by for Jacob, but he'd been wise.

Long ago, he'd decided that each half century required a focus, without which he'd decay into a sloth unworthy of his Master spirit's continued support. Since ingesting a virgin's life in a millhouse's basement in Southern France, he'd concentrated on languages.

Pressurized airplane cabins had become ubiquitous, bullet trains had reached across nations, and a globalized economy had emerged. Long-distance travel had evolved from a luxury to an expectation, and he expected his quirky lording entity to force him across continents for his next sacrifice. He wanted to speak the language wherever his Master would send him.

Adding to his base linguistic knowledge of Western European countries and nations surrounding the Mediterranean Sea, he'd learned Mandarin, Russian, Hindi, Urdu, and Japanese. Forty-nine years provided ample time to add these tongues to his skillset, leaving him fluent in twenty languages.

He'd also kept his survival skills fresh, as always, keeping himself proficient on the latest defenses.

Firearms were no more accurate than during his last dose of immortality, but cameras allowed shooting around blind corners, and bullets could explode within the proximity of targets. Sensors had become powerful and their circuitry tiny with flexible software control, allowing for automated monitoring of the next property he would use in the ritual.

And remembering how close the hunters had come in Anduze, he'd forced himself to master hand-to-hand combat. Long ago, swords and arrows sufficed, but he needed to know he'd win if technology failed and left him face-to-face with his pursuers.

To distract himself from the forty-ninth anniversary of his prior dose of life, he sparred with the karate sensei and skilled partners he paid handsome sums for private lessons. Though he refused formal rank, preferring secrecy over public recognition, his instructor assured him he had the self-control and the fighting prowess of a sixth-degree black belt.

Though exhausted from the prior hour of training, he controlled his breathing and channeled his energy into his awareness, balance, and movement until his teacher gestured for him to stop. Since his instructor and partners spoke Japanese, Jacob's language lessons found immediate use. "What's next, sensei? We're almost out of time."

The smaller, older man adjusted his gi. "Tactical retreat, three against one. Protect yourself, slow your attackers, and work your way out of danger."

"Yes, sensei."

"Begin." The little man zipped across the carpet into striking range, and a sparring partner attacked from either side. In a daze of parrying, Jacob deflected and dodged six hands, six feet, and six elbows. After ten meters of fighting and withdrawing, exhaustion turned his world red, and he called upon rehearsed reactions to protect himself.

The teacher raised his palms. "Enough." After bows, he dismissed the sparring partners and addressed his student. "You did well. Someday, I hope you will tell me who trained you before I met you. You have the self-control of one who has trained for a lifetime."

Between heaving breaths, Jacob lied. "I may tell you, teacher. Someday."

Before showering, he called his chef and ordered filet mignon. The mansion's stone walls, coupled with the custom radio-opaque privacy glass he'd installed, prevented electronic eavesdropping and also prevented connections to local cell towers. But he'd had repeaters deployed throughout the estate, allowing his call to his kitchen.

After showering, he changed into his evening leisurewear and powered through his steak dinner. As his waiter cleared his table, his first pang of anxiety about his wavering life formed in his stomach. Forty-nine years ended tonight.

He needed a distraction, and he sought his manservant, the head of staff. Every ten years, he found new people, and this butler had been loyal for nine. After tapping the screen, he lifted his phone to his cheek.

"Yes, sir?"

Jacob kept a small harem. As a gift through the ages, his Master had directed him to the women he found most satiating, and at the first touch of a sexual servant candidate's skin, he'd know if she was his. His dominating spirit always brought him new talent to keep his influx fresh. Without such sport, he doubted he'd want to keep living. He needed the control and the ego stroking. "I need my top two ladies tonight."

"Of course, sir. When would you like them to be ready?"

"Thirty minutes. In my chambers."

"I'll see to it, sir."

Careful to avoid exposure to his hunters, he minimized his time outside his Bavarian mansion's walls. Although he'd evaded his pursuers after his prior sacrifice, he'd grown paranoid about their tracking capability as improving technology complicated his hiding.

So, he strolled inside, through the sprawling structure's long hallways. Southern Germany's winter bite seeped into the unmoving air, making him shiver as his wonder turned to worry about the next sacrifice he'd make to his Master. When he was ready to be warmed and distracted from anxious thoughts, he walked to his chambers and saw two women waiting on his bed.

With centuries of practice, he knew how to manipulate women into ecstasy. Controlling them fed his ego, and he set his mind to the two toys lying before him. After he gratified himself, he dismissed his employees.

Fatigued from his martial arts workout and sexual escapades, he overcame his rising anxiety and fell into a profound sleep.

He awoke to a vision but then realized he still slept, trapped within a subconscious haze. The waking dream presented him the location of his next ritual, a waterfront cottage constructed of wood and glass. The quaint home was a vacation house situated on a gentle stream, secluded–as always–from civilization.

As his Master unfurled the vision, the modifications required for the ritual appeared. The extra concrete in the basement, the dimensions of the crucifix, and the radius of the candlelit circle materialized in his mind. Paralyzed in his lucid prophecy, he watched a faceless woman–a desirable shapely virgin lacking identifying features–bleed, burn with the crucifix, and then become a heap of ashes.

The final dose of information came without sight or sound. It came telepathically, as the lording spirit habitually sent it.

The generalized location.

Michigan. United States.

He awoke, sat upright, and sniffed his sweaty stench. Panting, he looked at his watch.

Three o'clock in the morning.

His Master always sent him the killing season's invitational vision at that time, the demonic hour, diametrically opposed to Christ's mid-afternoon death on a crucifix.

He reached for his phone and called the leader of his servant team.

His butler answered. "Yes, sir?"

"It's time. I'm leaving." He'd warned his chief servant the departure would be abrupt.

The manservant knew what questions to ask and which to avoid. "Now, sir, or later today?"

"Now."

"Shall I ready a vehicle?"

"No. Call a taxi. Don't mention a destination, but prepare the driver for a long drive and a generous gratuity."

"Of course, sir."

"And contact the realtor to sell the estate. The realtor knows what to do and where to deposit the funds."

"I shall see to it, sir."

Since his Master had rewarded his loyalty throughout the centuries, Jacob emulated him for fear of offending his lording spirit. "Bid farewell to the staff for me. You've all been loyal to me and my need for privacy, and you shall be rewarded. Bonuses will be distributed from the proceeds of the estate sale."

"Thank you, sir. We appreciate your generosity."

Having seen everyone in his life die, he avoided saying goodbye. He hung up the phone and turned his attention to the one item he needed to bring with him to the United States.

He rolled out of bed and knelt by his safe. He wheeled the tumbler through its combination and swung open the heavy door, exposing a locked Polyethylene weapons case. He dialed the combination and pushed open the lid to reveal the dagger.

After closing and locking the lid, he tucked his artifact's case under his arm and marched to his bathroom to prepare for his journey to the United States.

CHAPTER 5

Diane revealed the final tarot card on the tablecloth.

The World.

Completion. Integration. Accomplishment.

Across the covered second-hand table, her friend smiled. "Is that good?"

"Are you kidding? It's perfect. I'm so jealous, you dork."

Her friend, Mary, giggled. "What's it mean?"

"It means your stupid career's going to be perfect. So, you can stop pretending to worry about it."

Mary expanded her smile, blushed, and feigned a modest clap. "Yay, me."

Like all Diane's friends, the young accountant seated across the table was launching a professional career with a university degree, including an additional masters for her present client, while something unseen drew Diane towards an unconventional calling. "Your life's so predictable."

"Come on. Don't be jealous."

"Why would I be jealous? You're practically engaged to a super guy, you've got a master's degree, and you're starting a great job. Nothing any girl wants."

"Stop it. You're embarrassing me."

Diane agreed she'd sounded judgmental. With her friends seeming to outgrow her, she noticed herself pushing them away. "I didn't mean it."

"It's okay. Thanks for the reading. Is it fifty dollars?"

The tarot reader needed the money but also needed her dignity. "You don't have to pay me."

"Don't be silly. You did this for free for all your friends for years. I don't think any of us expect handouts anymore from our famous local mystic."

As Mary withdrew cash from her purse, Diane was envious. She wondered how little fifty dollars was to her friend, and if she'd notice its absence, whereas the paltry amount equated to a significant portion of her rent.

Diane reached for the cash, tucked it into her jeans pocket, and chided herself as she noticed self-pitying thoughts of her struggling finances. "Thank you."

"No problem. Do you want to get some lunch?"

Dining out was a luxury Diane avoided. "Um."

Mary had money. "I'll buy."

Charity was another luxury Diane wanted to avoid, and she had her techniques. Today, she'd offer home cooking. She sniffed the scent of allspice, garlic, and tomato paste from the pot of beef-and-rice-stuffed grape leaves she had simmering in the kitchen. "What about trying my *dolma*?"

"Oh my god, is it ready yet?"

"Probably another thirty minutes."

"Sure. I'll wait."

"Cool. We need to talk about your bridesmaids' dresses."

Mary's face flushed. "Come on. He hasn't even proposed yet."

"But it's a foregone conclusion. You don't want to be caught off guard, do you?"

"Should I just make you my wedding coordinator?"

"I'd better be in the wedding, instead."

"Of course, you are, you dork."

"Well, when's he going to propose?"

"I haven't decided yet. I want to start my new job first and then get engaged."

"It's funny how we just assumed it'll happen when you want, like he's going to follow your orders."

Mary was Diane's smallest friend in stature but the most confident and driven, the kind of person who drew up a life plan in kindergarten and saw it through. "Well, if he wants to be married to me, he needs to know who's in charge."

"Does he know what he's getting into?"

"You tell me. You know me better than he does."

"Does he know you're a raging hormonal bitch?"

Mary's laugh included a snort. "I think I just peed myself."

Diane's giggling squeezed a tear from her eye. "I think I broke a rib." As her chuckling subsided, she heard her brother brushing aside the hallway beads. "Josh, what did I tell you about coming to the living room while I'm with a client?"

He kept his head down. "It's only Mary."

Mary smiled. "Yeah, it's only me. We're finishing up, anyway. Hi, Josh."

"Hi, Mary."

Diane nodded and gestured for her friend, a safe person Josh had known growing up, to approach him.

Mary stood and extended her arms. "Can I have a hug?"

"Yes."

After a hasty embrace, Mary returned to her chair.

Diane disliked her brother's interruption. "What can we do for you, Josh? Did you come out here for a reason?"

"I want to watch a reading."

"Sorry, Josh. We just finished."

Mary flicked her wrist. "No, it's okay. I'm willing to stick around for another one. We can do it while we wait for the *dolma*."

"I want Diane to do a reading for herself."

The tarot reader was taken aback. "You know I don't like doing readings on myself."

Josh walked across the room to the sofa and sat. He lifted his tablet from under his arm and began reading an electronic book.

Assuming the interruption complete, Mary sought a practical line of conversation. "Did you want to talk about dresses, or..."

Diane didn't blame her friend for wanting to ignore her brother. Nobody but a committed caretaker like herself could be expected to show the patience. "No. Hold on."

As a family friend, Mary respected the extra attention Josh

needed, remaining quiet while lifting her phone to her face.

As Diane stood and walked around the table, she appreciated Mary's turning her attention elsewhere while she dealt with her brother. She reached him and sat at the far end of the sofa. "I'll do a reading on myself if you want, Josh."

No response.

After waiting a few seconds, she tried again. "Would you like me to do a reading on myself?"

"Yes."

"Okay. Do you want me to ask a specific question?"

Nothing.

She rephrased her inquiry. "Do you have a specific question for me to ask?"

"Who's coming for you?"

Her brother could be foreboding with his cryptic communication, but this demand seemed intentional in raising her anxiety. "Do you want me to ask who's coming for me?"

"Yes."

"Like a bad person?"

He growled in frustration, the meaning obvious in his mind. "I don't know. You figure it out."

"Do you want me to ask if a bad person is coming for me?"

His face reddened, he raised his voice. "Just ask who's coming for you."

Flustered, she appreciated Mary's intervention. "He's obviously talking about your next boyfriend."

Diane's sensory powers cried for caution, but her friend's assurance nudged her onward. She took the bait and decided on a three-card spread. "Okay, I will."

Taking renewed interest, Mary lowered her phone. "Come on. It'll be fun."

Diane returned to her seat and thought about her love life while shuffling the deck. There was little to ponder, other than dashed dreams and far-fetched fantasies. Her perfect model-like height and slender and shapely physique attracted plenty of men, but not the right one. Not yet.

She tried to picture herself smiling in a wedding dress, standing at the altar with her soulmate. Envisioning a knight with the maturity, confidence, and compassion to marry a woman anchored by an autistic brother proved difficult, but she conjured images from her imagination and then slapped three cards face down onto the table.

Before she could flip the first, her friend stopped her. "Wait. Before you show them, tell me what each card's supposed to mean."

"Why? So, you know that I'm not cheating?"

"Damned right, girl."

"Fine. The first is about me. The middle is about my partner. The third is about the relationship."

"Okay. Just making sure."

Diane flipped the first card.

Two of swords.

A blindfolded woman, seated with two blades crossed over her bosom. In the image's background, a sea filled with rocks and crags presented obstacles to ships which might seek clear passage.

She drew her conclusion. "Perfect. That's me. A balanced and stable mind but no clue what my problem is or what to do about it."

"Well, that's true, except the part about your stable mind."

"Funny. Also, it means I need to address my problem using logic and intellect."

"That's not very romantic."

"Neither is my love life. Vacuums in space aren't very romantic, are they?"

"Enough self-pity. *Yulla*, next card."

Diane held her breath as she revealed it.

The Hierophant.

Exhaling, she found relief in its meaning. "Religion. Tradition. Beliefs."

"Oh cool. That means you'll meet a good Catholic Iraqi

Chaldean man. That's perfect."

Unsure, Diane went with it. "I guess so. Let's see what's going to define our relationship."

"I can't believe how accurate this is so far."

Diane flipped the final card.

Three of pentacles.

Again, a relief of sorts. "Not bad. It means teamwork, collaboration, and initial fulfillment."

"Initial fulfillment? Not forever fulfillment?"

"It doesn't predict beyond that. Can't you just let me enjoy my good reading?"

"Sorry. I'm sure this means you'll meet someone nice."

Diane needed better than nice. She needed a special man who could handle a strong survivor with fortune-telling powers and a special needs brother.

Last week, Josh had ordered her abandonment of the cards. Now, he demanded her self-reading. She needed to understand why.

As she wondered about his peculiar behavior, he stood and disappeared through the beads.

In a moment of clarity, she reinterpreted her cards.

Stalemate. Blocked emotions. Conformity. Collaboration.

She wondered what sort of person she'd meet who'd be bound to conformity, in a relationship governed by collaboration, while she fought within herself to an emotional stalemate.

CHAPTER 6

Jacob completed his interview at Detroit Metro Airport's immigration counter, and then he found his weapons case in the baggage claim. At customs, his journey slowed upon review of his carried item. He offered a story of being a student of archeology, concentrating on ancient artifacts, to explain the dagger, and the officer waived him through.

Thankful his fake passport had allowed his entry, he trusted that his lording spirit had assured his success. He also knew he'd be able to stay a year in the United States unmolested by immigration authorities with his counterfeit graduate student visa. He'd selected skillful forgers in Germany to create his false identity, and he enjoyed the insurance of his supernatural advantage.

A brisk walk brought him to the airport hotel. After checking in, he went to his room and used his phone to shop online for his immediate necessities.

He needed an upper middle-class property, a place that could impress young ladies, and he scoured suburban rental house listings. Several candidates emerged. Then, sorting through transportation options, he found the American fascination with sport utility vehicles practical for his needs. Weapons would come later, as would his wardrobe, and the transfer of Euros to an American bank.

Though comfortable by traveler's standards, his room was strange to him. It was empty and lonely, like his extended existence. As he lay in bed, he closed his eyes and sensed the distractions—the treasures of female playthings—his Master had waiting for him in America.

But a cruel fact gnawed at him—the woman he'd desire most

to ravage, the fairest, would remain a virgin to death, a death at his hands, so that she'd remain unspoiled for fueling his ongoing life. Though it pricked his pride and ate him from inside, he accepted the rule as law.

A week later, he still lacked additional insight into the identity of his sacrifice. But that was predictable. During past centuries, the lording spirit had taken weeks or even months to bring her to him. The clues would come.

And he was situated, driving a Chevy Tahoe and moving into a furnished two-story, four-bedroom house, rented to him by an automotive industry executive on a one-year assignment overseas. Michigan's Bloomfield Township provided the upscale neighborhood he wanted for impressing women.

He parked in the driveway and brought the weapons case and a Subway sandwich into the house's entryway.

After placing his vital artifact on a coffee table, he walked through the spacious kitchen and unwrapped his food. Before he swallowed the third mouthful of ham, his doorbell rang.

He stepped to the entryway and greeted two burly men wearing overalls and winter coats. "Gentlemen."

"Got a delivery of a safe here."

"Excellent. Take it to the master bedroom."

He led the men to his chamber and pointed to the open space on the carpet where he wanted his new gun vault. He stepped aside and let them muscle the eight-hundred-pound monster from their truck to his bedside.

With spare cash remaining from his latest currency exchange, he tipped the men and bid them farewell. He locked the encased dagger in the safe and set the vault's new combination.

Then, without warning, he received a burst of ecstasy.

He dropped to his knees under a stream of dizzying euphoria, which he accepted from his Master as confirmation of the living sacrifice's proximity.

The sensation served as a tactical necessity in tracking

down his prey, and it also rewarded him for recognizing his dominating spirit's desires and obeying them.

As he recovered from his rush, he sensed his next gift. His lording spirit had left him with the promise of a plaything.

A sexual conquest awaited him. "Thank you, Master."

Taking the hint, he prepared to leave the house.

He walked to a full-length mirror in the entryway and checked his appearance. He stood tall, slightly over six feet. Dark eyes stared back at him, and flawless olive skin covered chiseled features with a squared jaw. A blue Van Heusen shirt conformed to the bumps of his lean but defined muscles, and sleek raven hair touched his collar.

Jumping into the Chevy, he went for a drive, letting his overseeing spirit guide him. He was unsure where to go as he drove south on the town's main multi-lane thoroughfare, Telegraph Road.

When he saw a coffee shop, his craving arose for caffeine and sugar. He turned into the corner lot and parked next to a plowed pile of snow that had been graying from a week-old storm. With his overcoat protecting him from the sub-freezing air, he walked into the store and stood in line.

He scanned patrons for a possible sex toy, but thick clothing complicated his search. As his turn to order approached, he shifted his attention to choosing a drink.

A young man with a beard and a pony tail greeted him. "What can I get for you?"

"Caramel macchiato. Medium." Careful to avoid traceable transactions through credit cards, he paid in cash. He then moved to the receiving stand to await his drink and scour the patrons again from his new vantage point.

Across the store, a seated woman caught his eye, and he began to mentally translate her clothing's contours into her underlying physique.

As he calculated his target's allure, he marveled at the immense satisfaction each new conquest could bring. Even with a supernatural edge, the thrill of controlling another desirable sex puppet accelerated his heart.

The woman looked out the window, revealing her profile. She was older, with the onset of crow's-feet, and Jacob paused his mental hunt. His Master had sent him prizes covering multiple demographics, and mature toys brought certain advantages.

He angled his head, contemplating the possibilities as a female voice called out his completed beverage. He mindlessly reached for his drink, and his fingers touched those of his barista.

An electrical impulse tingled his nerves, and he snapped his jaw towards her. Glaring at her face, he saw her irises as pools of fiery lust, illuminated by the supernatural glow his dominating spirit used to mark his gifts.

Finally, after seven days, he'd touched his first local conquest.

The artificial fire fell from her eyes, leaving irises of green. Her expression suggested she was smitten and liked it. "For... Jacob, right?"

He lowered his gaze, checked her nametag, and then inspected his new property.

Buxom and curvaceous, the barista wore sandy blonde hair to her high cheeks. Measured against his high standards of fitness and height, she was short and plump. But she was sexy with an attractive smile and an air of perkiness.

"Yes... Kim. Thank you."

"My pleasure."

Her word choice enthralled him, and he visualized tactics and techniques by which he would give her pleasure as he lifted the beverage and tipped back a sip. "It's delicious. You have skill."

"Thanks. That accent. Where's it from?"

"Me? I'm from all over."

"So, you're new to town?"

Kim's coworker shoved two empty cups beside her.

"Indeed, I am, but I can see that you're busy. Perhaps during your next break, I can tell you more."

"Sure. I'd like that."

He lifted the caramel macchiato towards her as a salute and then sat in a chair from which he could watch her work.

Uncaring that his leering bordered upon creepy for a normal man's enjoyment, he exploited his paranormal advantage and watched her every move. His lust rose, and he sensed her reciprocation, her feeding upon his desire, wanting him and wanting to be wanted by him. The salacious cycle lasted hours, deepening his hunger as he prepared to take her home.

CHAPTER 7

Liam leered at his kneeling father. "Well? Anything?"

"If you'd give me some peace, lad, I might get somewhere with this."

The inactivity of meditation agitated Liam. He'd learned the practice's supposed advantages, such as immunity to extreme temperatures, self-healing, and even levitation, but none of them equated in his understanding to tracking and killing a murderer.

That's why the elder hunter made the quiet introspective effort with his son as the apprentice. In the supernatural arts, wisdom trumped vitality.

"I'm sorry, Father. Should I leave you to it?"

"No. I want you to observe."

"But you've said it yourself. This takes years to master. You can't make me an expert overnight, and I'm only distracting you."

"You wouldn't be distracting me if you'd shut the hell up."

Liam frowned and glanced around the pews. He and Connor were alone in the small Catholic church, but he felt compelled to remind his father of reverence. "That's harsh language, given where we are."

His father surprised him with a chuckle. "Go back and read the Bible again. There's much harsher cursing and damning in it than you seem to remember."

"But seriously, why do I have to be here? I'm not helping a damned... I mean I'm not helping at all."

"This can take hours and days. It's good for you to witness the required commitment."

"Really? Why?"

His father frowned. "I don't know that I have a good reason other than my father made me do it."

"And his father made him watch his father meditate, and so on and so forth, ad nauseum?"

"I can only assume so."

Liam wanted to discard the old ways and use modern techniques to catch their wraith. Hoping for supernatural help was folly, but he didn't dare verbalize his doubts. He just wanted to escape his father's side during his extended meditation. "But why in a church? Doesn't that look like praying?"

"Exactly. What better way to blend in and not draw attention to my efforts?"

"Then I may as well just pray, shouldn't I? I sure won't be able to help you meditate your way to finding our wraith."

"Fine. Pray. Just do it quietly."

An hour later, Liam checked his phone for the time and suppressed a groan. Then, his father opened his eyes and pushed his buttocks onto the seat.

"Did you receive a vision?"

"No. My legs started cramping. So, I'm declaring today's session complete."

Disappointed, Liam risked a challenge. "Why are you putting so much time into meditation now?"

"Because it's within the year of the sacrifice."

"You're sure it's next January?"

"It's always on the full moon in January, every fifty years."

"What if there are two full moons in January?"

"There aren't next year. It's only on January twenty-first."

"But some Januarys have had two full moons."

"Then you'd choose the blood moon."

Unable to recall if the lunar eclipse qualifier resolved all ambiguity throughout history since the dawn of the hunt, Liam shifted the subject of his challenge. "Why can't we commission a team to help us search?"

"You know why. This task was given to our lineage and to

our lineage alone."

"That's antiquated thinking. Are we supposed to forego firearms because someone else invented them? Are we supposed to walk instead of drive because we didn't invent horseless carriages?"

"Shall I insult your intelligence by responding?" His father's glare answered the question.

Liam needed to accept the hunt as a destiny shared with his father and nobody else. The elder hunter had explained the rules during the young man's formative training, and the sudden nearness of the challenge changed nothing except for heightening Liam's eager impatience. "No, I remember the rules, but you can't blame me for challenging them."

"Apply that enthusiasm towards your continued aptitude in modern technology, and it will serve you. But you know that you can't request the help of others in our hunt."

"I understand."

"Good. Now help me up. I wasn't kidding when I said my legs were cramping."

The next morning, after joining his father in another long and draining meditation session, Liam sought the solitude of his basement–his arsenal of weapons, tools, and knowledge. Unsure which weapons and gadgets would serve him, if any, he flipped the switch to illuminate the bright subterranean lighting as he stepped down dusty wooden stairs.

His boots creaked over the dry hardwood floor as he set foot into the narrow, hallway-like cellar. Thick walls of gray and reddish rocks and mortar enclosed the space.

The closest lockers, one on either side, contained firearms. One set of transparent doors revealed a twelve-gauge shotgun and two nine-millimeter pistols purchased and grandfathered prior to the Irish firearms prohibition, while the other paned Plexiglass sealed a hunting rifle's weapon case.

Deeper into the cellar, he saw his surveillance equipment. His sound amplifier, allowing eavesdropping to three hundred meters, hung on a wall next to his tripod-mounted laser microphone which could capture conversations beyond half a kilometer via voices vibrating against windows. On the wall opposite the listening devices, hooks held a cellular jammer, a cellular activity monitor, and his magnetic-mountable GPS tracking device.

At the end of the room, he approached his workbench, upon which lay his newest toys. Small quadcopter drone cameras, less than two inches square, were parked next to their controllers. Envisioning multiple scenarios in which such spy equipment might help him, he'd learned the basics of their maneuvering. With a little practice, it was easy.

He saw the area rug under a workbench. Remembering that the carpet concealed removable planks which gave access to a hidden vault, he ducked, rolled back the strands and exposed the old, underlying wood.

He lifted a patch of floorboards that served as a hatchway to his family's vault.

Digging through the cache, he pushed aside night vision goggles, tactical vest body armor suits, German Heckler and Koch 416 rifles–the kind his father preferred after Navy SEALs had used the model to kill Osama Bin Laden–suppressors, concussion grenades, riot guns, and teargas. There were even lethal fragmentation grenades intended for use when nobody remained alive to rescue.

Heavy boxes of bullets resisted him as he shoved them aside. Below them, he found an oak box and lifted it to his knees. Opening it, he beheld his family's leather-bound book, the tome describing everything his ancestors knew about their calling as hunters of a savage. Its cover contained only the title, written in an ancient language he'd studied but seldom used.

Aramaic.

He recognized the title's loose translation as *Wraith Hunters*, which pertained to the virgin sacrifice that ended in burnt offerings. Recalling the book's contents were encrypted to dissuade prying eyes, he considered opening it to see if he should attempt decrypting and studying the text.

But he thought better of it.

With his father's tutoring, he'd learned its contents verbally, and he expected only frustration if he tried to read its pages. If his father withheld any secrets hidden within the manuscript, he would reveal the truth when ready.

His father's voice boomed from the top of the stairs. "Liam!"

"Down here, Father."

"Come here, lad. There's something you need to see."

After climbing the stairs, he followed the elder hunter through a living room with a high ceiling and a stone fireplace while the lifeless eyes of wall-mounted animal heads stared at him. Square windows gave a view to a snow-covered slope leading to the rocky Cork coastline.

Connor's strides were long, like a younger man hastening towards a destiny, and Liam trotted to catch him. He held his breath when his father accelerated towards the observatory and pushed open its heavy oaken door.

The stone cylindrical silo struck him as being incongruent with the name his ancestors had given the room. The only visible fixtures in the windowless alcove were four perfect vertical lines of whitish mortar marking the cardinal directions and a waist-high circular limestone table rising from the cobblestone floor.

Installed in ancient recesses that once held torches, electric diodes could illuminate the space, but Connor kept the room dark as he closed the door behind his son.

In the blackness, Liam's heart pounded as he waited for his pupils to adjust. He reached for his pocket to withdraw his phone and create artificial light, but he realized his father invoked darkness for a reason.

"Give your eyes a minute."

"Yes, Father." Toying with the young hunter's optic nerves, a feeble bronze elongated triangle cut the blackness of the table's flat surface. Undecided if the tannish, coppery light rose from nothingness or if his pupils were dilating and capturing existing radiation, he stared agape.

"Do you see it yet?"

The dagger his lineage had cherished for centuries rested atop the limestone cylinder. During Liam's entire lifetime, the blade had pointed at the location of its twin's last taking of life, Anduze, France, eight hundred and sixteen miles away.

His entire life, he'd been forbidden from entering the observatory without his father, and he'd sworn to never disturb the knife. He'd considered its orientation towards the French Millhouse symbolic, until now. "I do. It's glowing, very weakly, isn't it?"

"Indeed, it is. Like the bronze has come to life"

"Why?"

"It's bound to the wraith's weapon."

Liam had thought it impossible, but a simple glimmer painted a lifetime of learned legends as possible truths. "Bound. Like magic?"

"I don't like that term."

"Well, what would you call it?"

His father shrugged. "Magic is fine."

"The direction? It's the same? Pointing towards Anduze?"

"Unchanged. But rest assured, it'll change when the time's right. The glow means the wraith's dagger has moved with him towards the site of the next virgin sacrifice."

"Our dagger can tell?"

"Yes. It doesn't know where his dagger is moving yet, but it will. It needs to draw blood first before we get that clue."

"Blood?"

"Unfortunately."

"Will that happen before..."

"Yes."

Liam realized the enormity of vital information his father withheld. If he was going to commit another year of his life, and possibly the rest of it like his father, to a chaste and chivalrous manhunt, he deserved a full explanation of the rules. "I don't mean to be flippant, but what if you die before you reveal all these little details I need?"

"Our lineage has its own Rosetta Stone, safely tucked away. Plus, if you just tried to crack the code in the book, you'd find it rather simple. It's not designed for security. It's designed to keep nosy sons focused on their training until they're ready to read it."

"What the hell's up with all these secrets?"

"Watch your tone."

"I mean no disrespect, but I thought we were a team. Now I'm learning you've got secrets that I don't know about."

"I assure you that the selection of information I share or withhold from you is a proven sequence which has successfully formed young hunters for centuries. And should I die prematurely, my written will contains all the necessary instructions for the remainder of your formation."

Overwhelmed with an influx of information, Liam wondered if his father's slow reveal of knowledge was wiser than he thought. "I understand. I remain your student." He stopped short of sharing his afterthought of disliking the secretive veil.

"I know you do. And yes, lad. To completely address your concern, he will kill before he attempts the ritual sacrifice. He always has, and he must again. We will see an actionable clue before he attacks the virgin."

CHAPTER 8

Jacob accepted his violent task as a necessity. The dagger demanded life in preparation for the next year's virgin sacrifice, and he would feed it.

He rolled from the bed, disturbing the barista, who groaned her protest. "What are you doing?"

"I must leave."

"I'll miss you. Can't you stay longer?"

He found Kim's perkiness amusing and had kept her as his toy all month. He thought he would tire of her soon, but she'd earned the privilege of his continued audience with her spunkiness and the one trait he considered vital—gratitude.

He insisted upon it. Without it, he'd cast off a plaything and replace her with one who'd give thanks for his attention. He liked that she'd expressed her appreciation of the expensive presents, such as diamond earrings and jet-black Prada stiletto heels, that helped keep her repressed under his seductive dominance—aided by his Master's influence. "I want to get on the road right after rush hour."

"Where you are going, again?"

He lied. "I'm visiting clients."

"Is this the business trip you mentioned?"

"Yes. I must be going."

He switched on a lamp and then dialed the combination to his gun vault. The heavy but balanced door swung open. Before withdrawing the encased dagger, he reached for the plastic shell containing his nine-millimeter pistol and the one containing his Taser, and then he lowered the weapons to the carpet.

Lacking American citizenship and unwilling to bother with

the bureaucracy of importing weapons, he'd made Kim buy the pistol in her name.

"How long will you be gone?"

Living his charade as an artifact importer, he lied again. "It depends on the interest of my clients. If they want a lot of merchandise, it could be overnight."

She cleared her throat, and her voice became less raspy. "What's in the safe?"

"Samples."

Her curiosity piqued, she propped her torso on her elbows. "Can I see?"

"You may." He expected the knife's power and his connection to it to remain a secret to her, regardless of his candor about its material history. He flung the case onto the bed and opened it. Half the straight blade reflected the white light, while the other half showed its coppery color. A crossguard protected the user's fingers on the handle, which was cast with grooves to tighten the grip. Engraving in an ancient language labeled the dagger.

"Is that a real knife?"

"Indeed, it is. It's a bronze dagger, from Mesopotamia, dated to the eighth century, BC."

"Wow. That's old."

"And valuable."

"Can I hold it?"

He pushed away her reaching wrist. "No. It's quite susceptible to human oils."

"Sorry."

"It's a common mistake. Everyone wants to touch exotic and beautiful things."

"What else you got there?"

Another lie. "Just more of the same, but not as impressive."

"Okay. Don't forget the new coat I bought for you."

He'd sent her on an errand to purchase the concealing piece of clothing. "I've already packed it in the car. Go back to sleep, and I'll get ready quietly."

Thirty minutes later, he finished showering, dressing, and packing, and he slinked by the sleeping barista on his way out of the bedroom. Stopping in the kitchen, he grabbed a handful of fiber and protein bars and a bottle of water.

Like most late January Michigan mornings, the air was glacial. With rush hour traffic subsiding, he aimed the Chevy southward down Telegraph Road, but to his chagrin, he met traffic at the onramp to the interstate.

Checking the Tahoe's radio, he marked the time as nine-thirty in the morning.

He wondered how normal people coped with their misery, spending their lives swarming to office buildings to slave for the profit and empowerment of others. Mercurial human lifespans spent meeting base necessities were unbearable thoughts, and he shielded his soul from them with a simple reminder.

He'd taken the dagger, the risk he'd faced in acquiring it justified his reward, and he deserved his long life of luxury and leisure.

But he was mortal–probably.

Lacking evidence to his indestructability, he presumed himself vulnerable to a fatal injury or illness, although he'd managed to avoid testing the theory. As an oversized GMC Sierra whizzed by him on the onramp, he swerved to prevent a collision and continue his successful streak of escaping death by impact.

As he reached the highway, he gunned the Chevy to merge with traffic, and the vehicle darted with smooth acceleration. Watching his speed to avoid police attention, he put distance between his Michigan home base and the first preparatory tribute his Master required.

He braced to travel an uncertain duration as his lording spirit unfolded the plan, and he drove south towards the Ohio border and Toledo. When he crossed the state line, his tires' background noise receded on the smoother, quieter pavement. He slowed at the city's outskirts, honoring the lower posted limits.

Sensing his Master guiding him, he veered around Toledo and continued towards Cleveland. An hour driving into the morning sun brought him to a truck stop, where he parked by a gas pump.

Leaving his new overcoat in its garment bag, draped over his encased weapons, he stepped from the vehicle and closed his black Timberland jacket tight over his chest. He lowered his head against a gentle but cold breeze while walking towards the store. Around him, a fresh coating of white snow covered the untouched sections of pavement and the plowed piles.

Inside, the heat warmed him. He found the restroom and freshened up. Then, with cash, he bought a sixteen-ounce cup of coffee, a prepaid phone, and forty dollars of gasoline. He refueled and rebegan his easterly trek through Northern Ohio.

The next hour drifted by as the haziness forming in his head became highway hypnosis. To revitalize himself, he diverted the Chevy into a service plaza. Seeking coffee and hot food, he parked within view of the dining area seats.

With his tablet bag under his arm, he strolled into the center. He stood in line with an early lunch crowd and then ordered a Philly cheesesteak sandwich and coffee. He found a table near a window that gave him a view of the Tahoe and its lethal cargo.

He bit into his sandwich and washed the mouthful down with coffee. Hoping for inspiration, a sign, he reached for his computer bag and withdrew his tablet. Fiddling with daily news posts, he sensed a need to use the Internet to serve his Master.

While chewing his second bite, he tapped search criteria into his browser and then scanned a filtered list of Cleveland's independent escorts. A stream of endless potential victims, their provocative pictures at his fingertips, enthralled him.

During several minutes of intense viewing, he ate half his sandwich and found himself choosing among the expensive prostitutes. They appeared classy and confident. One of them would surely please his Master.

A brunette caught his eye.

Young thirties, dark hair to her shoulders, sharp cheekbones, and large brown eyes that saw the world and suggested a knowing command of it. She wore all black, including her leather collar, her lace teddy, and her thigh-high boots.

A predator conditioned by centuries of hunting, he studied her body, its shape, its contours, and its language. The message rattling around his twisted mind was balance. Nothing stood out suggesting disproportion. Nothing seemed artificial or unnaturally endowed. She was a cut above average and pleasing to his eye, but within herself, consistent.

The aura he sensed was a powerful equilibrium between good and evil. To him, she represented a feminine force that could make a man risk himself for others or kill for sport, depending on her whims.

She was perfect as today's sacrifice.

He lifted his prepaid phone and called her. Her voice was seductive and businesslike. "This is Angela. How may I serve your needs?"

Hearing her speak her name captivated him. "I'm in town today, and I'm interested in your services."

"I have one-hour openings at three o'clock, six, and eight."

His mind shut off, and he observed himself responding by instinct, convinced his overseeing spirit directed him. "I'll take three o'clock."

"I'm staying in room two-zero-nine at the Hyatt Regency Cleveland at the Arcade. I recommend that you bring seven hundred dollars cash, since the city can become expensive, depending on your tastes."

The money was irrelevant, but her control of the conversation unbalanced him. "Um..."

"If you're looking for something more economical, I can refer you to some of my colleagues."

"No, I'll be there. Three o'clock. Hyatt Regency, room two-zero-nine."

"Confirmed."

With hours to wait, he lingered at the service center. Satisfied he'd found his victim, he visualized the attack.

He would enter her room and place his case wherever she'd tell him to. Then she'd lead him through her routine, and when she was within reach, he'd grab her windpipe with the leather gloves he'd claim to need as a fetish. Then, overpowering her, he'd bring her to the Taser, and once she was helpless, the dagger.

Experience had taught him to avoid strangling his victims into submission. Excessive force would bring premature death with an unbloodied dagger, and insufficient incapacitation would allow the tribute to scream.

After downing the sandwich, he threw out the wrapper and got a second cup of coffee. To distract himself from overthinking his day's tactics, he studied the latest types of surveillance equipment he could employ in his ultimate sacrifice of the virgin, a year away.

When the time came to depart, he walked to the Chevy. He tapped the hotel's address into his navigation system and then followed its guidance towards the waiting prostitute.

After an uneventful drive east, he turned north towards the city. Ninety-degree turns brought him between downtown buildings, and then he parked in a garage a mile from the hotel.

He pulled a wool hat over his head and slid sunglasses over the bridge of his nose. He jammed his fingers into leather gloves, and then he grabbed the overcoat from the back seat. After stepping from the vehicle, he ran his arms through the coat's sleeves and then opened the back door to access his weapons.

Quick shuffling brought the dagger into the same case as the Taser, which he tucked under his arm as he walked away.

Assured security cameras would capture an unidentifiable man, he walked through a rotating door into an ornate lobby of chandeliers, crown molding, and mirrors that reflected walls of red maple. He remembered to appear calm while he strode towards the stairs, which he preferred over the elevator and the possibility of being forced into a confined conversation with a hotel patron.

On the second floor, he followed signs to his target's room and knocked on the door. While he waited, the door to the suite behind him clicked open.

A mountain of muscle appeared in a tailored suit and examined him. "Good afternoon. I'm Miss Angela's assistant. May I hold your belongings?"

Shocked, Jacob felt his plans unraveling. He tapped the case. "This is a rare artifact I carry as part of my job. I wouldn't dare leave it unattended in my car, and I don't want to part with it now."

"Miss Angela demands discretion as a matter of professionalism. I will respect the privacy of your possessions and guard them during your stay."

Stupefied with his failure, Jacob extended the case to the man.

The mountain accepted it. "As a matter of security, I'll need your overcoat, as well, and I'll need to check you for weapons."

Thankful he'd locked the Taser and dagger within their casing, he complied and followed the mountain into his room. With his case, sunglasses, wool cap, and coat on the bed, he assumed a passive stance while thick, meaty fingers frisked him.

"You're clean."

"Now may I…"

"Yes, of course. She's expecting you."

The mountain lumbered through his room's doorway and lifted a key from his slacks. He clicked open the courtesan's door and waved Jacob in.

The door closed behind him, leaving him with her.

He stood in mesmerized captivity of the woman's dark eyes. Her attire matched that of her advertisement, a dizzying array of seductive blackness. When she spoke, her sultry tone carried veiled commands. "What should I call you?"

Racking his mind for a perfect lie, he found only the truth. "Jacob."

"Well, Jacob, do you know what you want, or shall I give the commands?"

"I... want you to lead."

For an hour, she toyed with him. She knew where to touch him and when. She knew the exact pressures to apply, the balance between gentleness and force. She knew what he wanted, and she commanded him. He was her puppet and under her dominion.

After paying and collecting his belongings from the mountain, he darted out the hotel and marched to his car.

As he drove around the town, the setting sun cast long shadows, and his brief joyous awe slid into an abyss of powerlessness and emasculation. He wondered why he'd been led into a trap. "Why Master?"

No response. Signs were rare, and he expected the answer to come from within.

He collected himself.

Perhaps his overseeing spirit wanted him humbled? But wasn't he already humble enough in servitude of his Master? No, that couldn't be it.

Perhaps it was a warning. But he was always careful with his planning and diligent in his actions.

What, then, could his dominating spirit mean by sending him a strong woman to dominate him?

Anger.

Yes, that was it. Anger is strength, and she'd fed him the dose he needed. The escort had no right to overpower him, and he concluded his ideal response was rage.

His lording spirit was invigorating him. "I understand now, Master. Thank you."

As the city darkened, he saw a gathering of women at a corner and suspected they were street whores. At a stoplight, he reached into the back seat for cases and brought the pistol and the Taser into a small cubby in the driver's side door.

His heart racing with anxiety and anger, he followed city blocks to circle back to the gaggle of hookers. Slowing, he examined them, and them him.

One stuck out, blonde hair and blue eyes, early twenties. Her overdone makeup hid unimpressive facial features, but Jacob spied the red fiery glint in her eye that marked her as his spirit's target.

He stopped, and he held eye contact with her as her irises transformed from supernatural red back to blue.

She sounded playful. "You partying tonight?"

"How much?"

"Two hundred."

He'd played in the gutters of Europe, and he expected haggling was a universal street-whoring norm. "One hundred."

"One fifty."

"Get in."

She slid into the passenger seat, examined him, and smiled. "You're cute. Where's that accent from?"

"I've lived all over. Where do we go?"

"I have a room, or I know a place we can park your car. You've got enough room in the back if you fold the seats."

"Yes, the car. Tell me where to go."

"Show me the cash first."

He reached into his shirt pocket and withdrew a wad of hundreds.

"I don't have change."

"If you give an inspired performance, you'll earn a tip."

She led him to a quiet parking lot near the Cleveland Metroparks Lakefront.

Passing through a busted gate of a chain link fence, he brought the Chevy to an unused lot of cracked concrete, covered in light snow. Keeping the engine running for heat, he scanned the surroundings. "Are you sure we're alone?"

"This place is safe. Cops never come here. Let's get the seats folded."

"I'll take care of it."

They stepped out, and he grabbed the Taser while she looked away. After stuffing the weapon in his coat pocket, he opened the back door and folded the seats. He crawled over the flattened makeshift bed and opened the far door for her.

She opened her coat and ducked into the vehicle.

Seeing her exposed flesh under her collarbones, he grabbed his Taser and jammed it into her chest. She contorted in electric shock and then lay motionless. He pulled her clothes apart and then reached for the dagger's case as he crawled out the door.

Quick steps brought him around the Chevy's side panel, and he popped open the hatchback while lowering the case to the ground. He dragged the writhing woman to the thin layer of snow.

Exposing the knife, he lifted it, counted down her ribs, and pushed it into her heart. He let his furious hunger drive the thrust, and anger flowed down his arm and into his victim.

Like forty-nine years ago, the dagger glowed sanguine.

He interpreted the reddish glow as a proper tribute to his lording deity, and confirming the success, his Master gave him a mental image.

The address of the cottage for the ritualistic stabbing of the virgin flashed in his mind. Trusting that tonight's sacrifice had kicked off a year of killing that would culminate in renewed life, he sidestepped responsibility for the prostitute's fate.

His Master had selected her to die, and arguing with a godlike entity was pointless. Judging her existence miserable by observation, he considered himself an assassin of mercy. And declaring himself merciful fed his ego. As an agent of a deity, he himself was a demigod, called to dominate another human.

And he had dominated her.

The world's order had been restored.

As she died, he wiped his dagger on his overcoat, adding blood to the unknown amount spattered against its fibers. He reached into a cooler in the back of the Chevy, opened it, and lifted a can of gasoline and a pack of matches. He poured a hasty half gallon over his victim. After final wipes with his sleeve to clean the blade, he shirked off the overcoat and draped it over her.

With a flick of a match, he set her on fire.

As the blaze grew behind him, he drove away slowly to minimize attention, and then he aimed the Chevy out of the city.

From the corner of his eye, he saw a spectral vision appear in the passenger seat wearing a milky white gown. The young woman whose body burned behind his vehicle had become a ghost, clothed and whole in the afterlife.

Her voice carried deep, haunting tones that chilled him. "Why did you kill me?"

"I had to. He demands it."

"You betrayed me. I will be avenged." Like her predecessors, she disappeared after her warning.

At the first interstate highway service area, he parked in a far corner for privacy. He stepped from the door and skirted the side panels to the rear, where he opened the hatchback. From the cooler, he withdrew a bottle of diluted vinegar and a rag. He reached into the Chevy, pulled his dagger case to him, and opened it.

While dousing the rag in water and vinegar, he glanced around the parking lot to verify that nobody saw him. Having tucked the wetted weapon inside plastic bags to prevent staining the case, he slid it out and exposed the bloodied bronze. He wrapped the rag around the blade to absorb trace evidence of blood, and then he lowered the knife and stained bags into the cooler.

He closed the door, jumped back into the vehicle, and accelerated onto the highway.

When he'd committed the evening's crime, his Master had burned the address of the cabin for next January's ritual into his memory. He lifted his phone and wiggled his thumb over the screen. Finding the listing, he sighed in relief when he noticed it was for rent.

Of course, it was for rent, he realized. His lording spirit had gifted him the address.

He called the realtor and set up a viewing.

With his future taking shape, he lowered the phone, placed both hands on the wheel, and drove the Chevy farther from the killing year's first tribute.

CHAPTER 9

Liam dreamt of a young woman burning on a cross, blood pouring from her heart's puncture wound. In the surreal scene, sickness ate him for his failure to save a life and stop a monster.

Waking to the musty scent of ancient walls, he looked across the stone table at his father, seated opposite him. With the observatory's dimmer switch at its minimal setting, he saw the weak lighting paste a ghastly image over the elder hunter's wrinkled face.

"Whoa."

"What's wrong?"

"I fell asleep."

"I hardly noticed. This is tedious, isn't it?"

Before Liam could respond, the dagger's feeble bronze glow shifted to a darker reddish hue. He sprang to his feet and glared downward. "Father?"

"Don't move. Don't do anything hasty."

Having dedicated the entire day with his father to the observatory, assuring the knife's constant watching, Liam wondered why the dagger waited until the late hour to shine.

January thirty-first, the year's first full moon, had less than an hour remaining in Ireland. His father had assured him the killer would strike this day, beginning a year of tributes leading to the virgin sacrifice. The dagger had to glow red with the blood of the wraith's weapon.

And it would have to move, pointing to its supernaturally bound twin, wielded by the predator.

"Run, lad. Get the compass."

Withholding his cascade of forming questions, Liam exited

the circular space and darted through the living room. A turn brought him to the cellar.

Inside the basement doorway, he turned on the lights and descended the steps to the bottom. He saw the armaments and equipment lining the hallway-like space, but instead of continuing towards the cache, he turned and ducked under the stairs where piles of dust-covered heirlooms rested.

Brushing aside cobwebs, he moved deeper into the darkness. He lifted his phone in flashlight mode to illuminate his search, and atop a pile of books lay a metal annulus. He hoisted it to his waist and then tucked it under his arm.

Retracing his steps, he returned to his father and handed him the metal ring. "Now what?"

"We wait. It shouldn't be long now."

Liam labored through shallow breaths and glared at the sanguine dagger, daring it to move. Then, with imperceptible grace, the knife that had pointed towards Anduze, France his entire life started its rotation. It accelerated to a snail's pace, declaring its deserved reverence with its elegant slowness. The young hunter admired the living bronze. "It really does move."

"It's been forty-nine years since I've seen this."

"It's shifting towards Spain now."

"Indeed. But don't rule out Northern Africa. It's showing us a direction, but it can't give us distance, unfortunately."

As the reality sank into Liam's thoughts, he shared his gloomy observation. "This means he's drawn blood."

"Yes, sadly. More specifically, it means he's killed with the knife to a woman's heart. This begins the year of killing leading to the ritualistic sacrifice."

Remembering insights his father had shared during their day awaiting the knife's animation, Liam articulated the details, the atrocities of which both sickened him and inspired him towards his inherited destiny. "He just killed a woman by stabbing her heart with the dagger. She didn't have to be a virgin, she didn't have to be of the proper age, and she didn't have to be of the proper bloodline."

"Correct. She was an unfortunate victim of convenience he had to sacrifice to the spirit that controls him. It gained him nothing but the right to do it again at the next full moon, which will be a repeat of tonight's crime and so on and so forth until the ritual at next January's full moon."

"We now have less than a year to stop him. Three hundred and fifty-five days, to be exact. This semicentennial cycle ends January twenty-first."

"You've done your research. Good."

As the dagger showed no signs of relenting, Liam cocked his head and estimated its direction. "It's pointing to Portugal, now."

"No need to keep guessing. Let's put some measurement to it." Connor stepped around the room's central stone cylinder and raised the annular heirloom over it. Lowering it, he spoke. "It's important to not disturb the dagger while doing this. It's tempting to hurry, but don't."

The ring of metal appeared made of bronze and designed as a perfect fit over the table. Four small grooves in the flat surface matched with notches in the annulus, setting its orientation. As his father slid the metal over the stone, Liam noticed engraved ticks on the bronze, marking it as a compass.

"Run to my study and grab a straightedge."

"Yes, father." Liam trotted to the office, grasped a meter-long ruler, and returned. He handed it to the elder hunter.

Connor balanced it on the compass edges in alignment over the dagger. "It's pointing to bearing one-seven-two."

"I think that's Portugal. I'll verify." Liam stepped out of the observatory to capture a cellular signal, and he navigated to a page showing bearings from his home in Glengarriff. After tapping in the direction, he pulled the screen to his face, examined the map, and returned to his father. "Portugal, Morocco, all of Western Africa."

"It's still moving. He's traveled by sea or air this time."

While the knife mimicked a slow compass needle rotating across the Atlantic Ocean and South America, Liam's mind shifted to hyperdrive with questions. "What if he's already moved from the scene of the crime?"

"I'm sure he has. He's not stupid enough to become an easy catch for the local authorities. He's mastered the art of murder."

"What if he's planning to travel the globe all year during his killings to throw us off? He didn't have that ability throughout his history."

"He had access to airplanes in nineteen-sixty-eight."

"Well? Did he use them?"

"No. The locus of deaths was around Anduze. It's always been that way."

Answers begat questions. "Why?"

"He's drawn to the location of the sacrifice. The ground upon which it will happen is significant. It's usually an ancient burial site or a site of one or more wrongful deaths. He won't be able to venture more than a few hundred miles from it for the next twelve months."

The dagger continued its slow swing through the Yucatán Peninsula, prodding Liam's thoughts of Mayan sacrifices. "Why's it moving so slowly?"

"That's a mystery to our lineage. I don't have all the answers. But I encourage your questions."

"In the ancient times, did word ever spread of a madman stabbing women in their hearts?"

The elder man nodded. "Yes, but communications were slow and thin compared to today. By the time our forefathers learned of a killing, the subsequent attack had already taken place. Most killings became isolated stories that eventually devolved into legends and myths."

"I can't imagine that our forefathers ever caught a wraith."

"He certainly has the advantage, and he always has. But some wraiths have made mistakes, and we've capitalized upon them."

Liam pondered a successful hunt. "Wouldn't the rituals have stopped when our forefathers captured the killer?"

"They did temporarily, but mistakes were made on our side. We had both daggers in our possession after the last successful hunt, but members of our lineage failed in their duty to guard them. The one we now track, was stolen."

"Stolen by the savage we now hunt?"

"Correct."

"And today's killing? With modern communications we should be able to know everything about the crime, but we're not going to see a story about a woman stabbed in the heart, are we?"

"It's unfortunate for us, but it's understandable that law enforcement agencies would keep such details private, at least until next of kin are informed. That may take days, depending on the victim."

The answer frustrated Liam. "But the information's right there to be had. If we could access it now, this would be so much quicker."

"We can't solicit direct help."

"Well, I can join G2, or whatever it takes to get access to intelligence when this happens fifty years from now."

"You wanted to be an engineer the last time we spoke of a supplemental career."

"I didn't know all the details of the hunt back then. You raised me as a hunter, and you told me I'd be seeking an evil man. You never mentioned these predictable semicentennial details."

"Alright. Fair enough. Yes, you can join an intelligence agency, if one will have you. But don't join just because you lack patience. We'll probably know the location of tonight's murder within days, when the authorities release it."

"If they release it, you mean."

"Have faith, lad."

Liam nodded his affirmation and looked back down to the rotating knife. "If it keeps going, it might point towards an area where it's still daylight. Is that possible?"

"No, it must stop before then. The moon must be risen

during the killing." As if the older hunter had willed it, the blade came to rest. He shifted his straightedge over the settled knife and read its final bearing. "That's it, then. The dagger points to bearing two-eight-eight. It's never pointed that way in our history. It's always been within the lands of the ancient empires."

Liam tried to impress his father. "After you told me that he strikes every fifty years, I did some research. This is the first time, as far back in history as I can tell, with blood moons in successive Januaries. His first and last kill in this cycle will be under lunar eclipses. Perhaps there will be several firsts in this hunt, based upon the unusual astronomy."

"You may have a point. There's nothing in our deposit of knowledge addressing this, but the connection with the moon is undeniable. I will need to speak with the head of our order."

Liam inhaled and then released an extended sigh. "We're part of an order?"

"I'll tell you more about it, in due time."

"Well, while you're thinking about that, I'm going to put some technology to use."

"That's perfectly acceptable. We'll need every advantage we can get."

Liam stepped outside the stone silo with his phone extended to get an update with the final bearing. He pulled the screen back to his face and watched the curvilinear bearing traverse Eastern Quebec, cut through Ohio, shoot between Dallas and Houston, and continue through Mexico. Beyond land, the line covered a long stretch of emptiness in the Pacific Ocean. He closed the heavy oak door behind him and shared the news. "It's pointing towards North America. Here. Take a look at the possibilities." He extended the phone over the table to his father, who accepted it and squinted at the small screen.

"I see. Is there a way to make this easier to read?"

"You mean to get better resolution? To make it bigger?"

"Yes."

"We'd be better off with a larger screen."

"Well, the dagger's done its duty for the night. Let's lock up here and retire to my study."

Shelved books covered the office's walls. Preferring the convenience of electronic books, Liam considered the collection archaic, but he also knew some old volumes carried valuable secrets, like the one under the workbench in the cellar with its encrypted notes. But resolving that riddle would have to wait.

Behind a huge oak desk, his father sat in front of a keyboard and monitor, but then he stood. "Why don't you handle this?"

Liam moved into the armchair, looked into the screen, and grabbed the mouse. He started typing and found the website he sought for his geographical help.

Tapping in the two-eight-eight bearing with their home as the starting point, he followed the line in greater resolution than his phone had allowed.

"The next full moon's due to rise March second, is it not?"

"That's right, Father."

"Given the population centers near this line, if we gain no more clues, I'd set up our base of operations in Memphis, Tennessee."

Liam studied the map and agreed. Memphis was central to the possible areas where the killer had just struck. Though he wished he could prevent the next attack, he accepted the reality of operating a step behind his quarry. "We have to know the murder site soon."

"We will, lad. Diligence and discipline will serve us."

"We need to move out, Father. Let's gather our equipment and chase down this monster."

CHAPTER 10

Diane dreamt of a young woman burning on a cross, blood pouring from her heart's puncture wound.

Time stopped, accelerated, and slowed again as the surreal nightmarish scene unfolded. The victim seemed distant, and then Diane was the victim. One moment, she was a sacrifice, then the next she was the savior. An unseen battle for good and evil raged in her subconscious mind.

Then a vision appeared in which an unseen wind flapped a milky gown over a female frame. The young woman, exposed and pierced during her death but now clothed in dignity and unblemished in the afterlife, called out in French. "Avenge me."

Diane understood her words and replied. "Who are you?"

"We descend from the same line."

"What line?"

"They called our ancestors witches."

"I'm not a witch."

Rejecting the phantom's comment begat overwhelming terror in Diane's dream state. A gash ripped open the woman's chest, and red fluid stained her dress. The ghost's irises became red, and then her eyes became pools of black. She screamed. "Avenge me!"

Staring at ceiling lights, Diane woke up in the men's shoes section of her department store. Her supervisor and two paramedics stooped over her.

"What happened to me?"

The paramedic was in his mid-fifties. "You grabbed for your chest and passed out. Your coworkers were afraid that you were having a heart attack, but all your vital signs are fine."

She felt a blanket covering her. "My chest hurt."

"You mean, it still hurts?"

She inhaled and felt dizzy and weak, but she remembered a pain that had vanished. "No, I'm fine. I think I remember my chest hurting, but I don't feel any pain now."

With her helpers' assistance, she recovered to her feet and walked to the breakroom. She sat and gathered her thoughts. "How long was I out?"

"You've been unconscious for half an hour."

"Really?"

"It's like you were sleeping, or in a trance. I've seen this with heavy sedation before, but you couldn't have been working if you had that quantity of sedatives in your system. I really can't explain it. I recommend hospitalization."

"But you said everything's normal."

"Your vital signs, yes. But not what happened to you."

She considered herself too strong to quit. "It's just a fainting spell. No big deal."

"I advise against it."

The supervisor, a quiet and pudgy man Diane considered unfit to manage, interjected. "It's not a good idea."

"You're understaffed today already, and I'm fine. If it happens again, which it won't, I'll head to the hospital. But I want to get back to work."

Her will overpowered that of her supervisor, and she got her way.

Young and fit, she rejected the idea of a chronic health issue. She spent five hard hours a week at her apartment's gym, and she trusted her heart's strength. Writing off the episode to stress, she returned to the floor and approached the nearest customer to turn her charm and fashion savvy into income.

After closing the deal for a pair of Kenneth Cole loafers matched with the same designer's jacket, she achieved two days' worth commissions with three hours remaining in her shift.

When she clocked out, she mentally tallied her day's income at more than twice her norm. While she walked to her car, her fainting spell drifted into her distant memory.

Driving home her fifteen-year-old beater-mobile, she placed speakers into her ear and called her brother.

"Hello, Diane."

"Hello, Josh. I'm coming home now. Do you know what you want for dinner?"

"Spaghetti."

She loved how simple and cheap he was. "Okay. I'll make spaghetti. Can you set the table for us?"

Silence.

"Josh, can you set the table please?"

"I already set it."

Since he was rarely proactive, she appreciated the initiative. "I'll be home in twenty minutes."

Twenty minutes later, she entered her apartment, and Josh was curled on the sofa reading his tablet. Seeing plastic plates and cups filled with water next to folded napkins and utensils on her dinner table, she felt a strong loving bond for her brother.

Although she'd resented him as he'd become her burden, she'd corrected herself. She resented his problem–not him. Then, as she'd evolved into his caretaker, the bitterness had begun to erode, leaving her with a cherished companion. And she knew she needed him. "Thank you for setting the table, Josh."

"You're welcome."

She passed through the hanging beads and turned into the kitchen, where she set a pot of water to boil. While waiting, she propped her elbows on the counter and lowered her chin to her palms. Watching her brother, she thought he seemed perturbed. "Are you okay, Josh?"

"I don't know."

The answer was a warning. She probed carefully to prevent him from shutting down. "Oh, that's interesting. Did anything unusual happen today?"

"Maybe."

His face remained in the tablet, but she sensed he wanted to share something. "You can tell me, if you want."

"Okay."

The interrogation would require patient coaxing, and to slow the conversation, she glanced over her shoulder at the pot. Steam rose, and she walked to the stove. She grabbed a carton of pasta, dumped its contents into the water, and returned to the counter to query her brother, using misdirection. "Are you hungry?"

He nodded.

"Dinner's going to be ready in about ten minutes. That gives us a little time for a story before dinner."

"Okay."

"Would you like to tell me a story?"

He shook his head.

She volunteered a tale. "That's okay. I can tell you a story. Would you like that?"

He nodded.

"I sold a beautiful pair of black shoes today with a matching jacket that was very expensive. The commission was nice."

"Okay."

She embellished with believable fiction, having sold a lot of clothing to local celebrities and visiting athletes. "What if I told you I sold them to a Detroit Pistons player?"

"Which one?"

She groped for an answer. "Um, Lebron James."

"He doesn't play for the Pistons."

"I was just trying to liven up my story."

"You had a boring day."

She recalled her episode. "Well, I didn't want you to worry, but I actually had a dizzy spell and passed out."

Still facing his tablet, he scowled. "That's bad."

"Yeah, my chest started hurting, and everything went black. Then I woke up on the floor."

He lifted his eyes and scanned the room, indicating his deepest thinking towards his secret conclusions. His gaze settled back on the tablet. "Me too."

"You too, what?"

"My chest hurt, too, and I woke up on the floor."

As she feared he was regressing into mimicking her speech, she stepped away and ran the noodles through a colander. She then dumped the spaghetti into a bowl and opened a can of pasta sauce. Carrying the food to the table, she called to him. "Come on, Josh. Time for dinner."

Keeping his eyes on his reader, he walked to the table and sat.

After dishing out noodles onto the plates, she poured sauce from the can onto their meals. "Enjoy."

"Thank you for dinner."

"You're welcome, Josh."

She slurped the first bite, chewed, and swallowed. Watching him for the right moment, she waited and then engaged him. "What are you reading?"

"It's a book about extrasensory perception."

"I thought you were reading a book about tarot cards."

"I finished that one."

"Oh, you do read fast."

"You have extrasensory perception."

"Yeah, I know. I get real lucky with the cards, don't I?"

"You should stop."

"You told me to stop, but then you told me to do a reading on myself."

"I wanted you to do a reading so it would scare you and make you stop."

She tried wrapping noodles around her fork to see how much she could hold, and then she stuck the spaghetti into her mouth, chewed, and swallowed before risking deeper probing. "But my reading was positive."

He frowned. "You're wrong. It was bad. I told you to stop."

She wanted to ask what he suggested doing to replace her card-reading income, but the question would've sent him into a forest of abstract thoughts. Remembering who he was, she kept it simple and candid. "I can't make any promises, but I'll review our finances to see what stopping would do to us."

"Thank you."

"You're welcome, Josh."

"You don't believe me."

"About stopping tarot?"

"You don't believe me about my chest hurting today."

Her pulse accelerated as she choked down a mouthful. "I wasn't sure you wanted to talk about it."

"It happened in my room. When I woke up, it was ten minutes past six."

A pit formed in her stomach, and she reached into her pocket. She withdrew the paramedics' report and unfolded it. It said her episode had coincided with her brother's. She hoped he was joking. "Did someone from work call you?"

"No."

He was right. Her absent alcoholic mother remained as her employer's emergency contact. She made a mental note to change that. "So, you didn't know about my fainting until I told you before dinner?"

"No."

"I fainted at work at the same time, Josh."

He lifted his eyes and processed something he seemed to find intriguing. Then he returned to reading and talking between bites of spaghetti. "This makes sense. You're connected."

"What do you mean?"

He frowned as she yet again missed an obvious fact. "I said you're connected."

She digested the insights and wondered if they entailed a significance greater than anecdotes and fainting spells. "I understand that I'm connected. That makes sense. We're all connected in some way."

"No!"

"It's true!"

"Not this way."

Conceding, she assumed him right, though her definition of

"this way" had to morph moment to moment to keep pace with him. "Okay, okay. You're right. Not this way. Do you know who I'm connected with this way?"

"It's not just me. You're strong. There are others."

Her calmness surprised her as she realized the sane person's response would be panicking. "Do you know anything about them? Maybe what they look like? Boys or girls? Old or young? Anything you know or can remember would be great, Josh."

"You're so stupid!"

After years of practice, she responded to the insult with a level voice. "Josh, that's not nice."

"I told you everything."

She ruminated over his salient points. She had evidence for a newly discovered empathetic connection with her brother. Josh had claimed the connection reached beyond themselves to the others. Both their hearts had hurt before they'd passed out. Was she missing something?

When Josh became frustrated, it usually meant his vision was simpler than the complex answer her mind sought. He'd told her everything, in simple terms.

"People with... pain in their hearts?"

"Maybe."

"Broken hearts?"

"I don't know what a broken heart is."

"It means someone's very sad."

"No!"

She sought a darker definition. "People with bad hearts? People having heart attacks?"

"People with dying hearts."

"That's the same thing as bad hearts!"

"No! Bleeding. Dead."

Having evoked the macabre definition, she lowered her fork and pondered her new world, but it was overwhelming. "That's a lot to think about. I don't know what to do."

"You need to learn about your powers."

"Okay, I get it. I'll get advice from Nana. She knows a lot

about this sort of stuff."

His conclusion unsettled her and committed her to visiting her grandmother. "You should talk to Nana because your powers are stronger than you know."

CHAPTER 11

Jacob awoke beside his concubine. Careful to prevent Kim from waking and launching annoying questions, he slid from the bed and crept to the bathroom.

The memory of last night's kill enthralled and haunted him.

Some profound part of him retained a soul, and a distant echo of humanity reverberated inside him. But he'd evolved into a monster that craved immortality, and he rationalized murder as necessary for his survival.

By accepting homicide as a necessity, he could ignore moral self-examination and allow the thrill. Although his Master had humbled him with the hotel prostitute, it was a justifiable means to the proper end. The humiliation had fueled him, rekindling his zeal for extending his life by dominating others. And dominating the street whore had fed a hunger and had satiated an addiction.

His renewed vigor compelled his day's early start. That, and the address of next January's sacrifice his Master had emblazoned in his memory during the prior evening's kill.

After his morning preparations, he walked across the room to his closet and dressed. Jeans and a polo shirt sufficed, but he wanted extra clothes in case the Northern Michigan cottage enticed a longer stay. He folded extra articles into a duffel bag, slung it over his shoulder, and headed for the bedroom door.

Kim's groggy voice stopped him. "Are you leaving again?"

He looked over his shoulder at her disheveled sandy blonde hair poking from the blanket. "Yes."

"You just got back. I hardly saw you."

He continued his charade. "I had a fruitful trip and was referred to new possible clients I must visit today."

"When will you be back?"

Unable to find the right words to manipulate her continued service, he trusted his Master's supernatural intervention to drive her continued loyalty. "I'll return when I return."

He clicked the door closed and darted for the Chevy. With his dagger and other weapons locked in his vault, he began his day's unarmed journey of discovery.

Early rush hour traffic was annoying during his northbound trek until he passed Auburn Hills and broke free of suburban Detroit. The Tahoe carried him past Flint, which had survived as a city despite a toxic water crisis, and then it took him into the sparse and vast lands of Northern Michigan.

His navigation system guided him straight up the interstate, towards the Mackinaw Bridge that joined the state's upper and lower peninsulas. A quick stop for coffee, energy bars, and a filled gas tank marked his drive's midpoint.

An hour later, near Grayling, he exited the interstate and drove west towards Traverse City. Accumulated snow struck him as plentiful compared to the southern side of Michigan, and he saw snowmobile paths paralleling the road. He passed a single helmeted rider who sent his red machine airborne over a white mound.

Following the stark blackness of concrete against the blanched hills of pine trees, he approached the outskirts of the city. When his navigation system placed him a couple of miles from his destination, he noted he was early. He turned back and headed for a small diner he'd seen minutes ago.

He stopped for lunch, ordering a roast beef sandwich and coffee. As his appointment approached, he paid, departed, and drove to the property.

The driveway held a Cadillac Escalade, signaling a successful realtor, one he hoped could simplify the transaction and remove obstacles to accelerate his access to the house.

He parked beside her, stepped from his vehicle, and waved. To masquerade as a mid-winter renter of a summer property, he tried to hide his excitement. But fifty years between rites left him with a jumpy eagerness. He spoke with enthusiasm. "Good morning."

As she stepped from the vehicle, he studied her. Sunglasses covered her eyes above high, wide cheekbones. Her smile revealed perfect teeth, and gentle lines around her mouth suggested a woman in her late forties. Black hair fell straight to her coat's collar. With a leather binder under her arm, she extended a black glove. "Good morning. It's still morning, isn't it?"

Glove to glove, he shook her hand. A distant warning suggested he needed to touch her flesh, to get a read on who she was, but he'd wait until an appropriate opportunity. "Barely. It's almost noon. I hope you don't mind that I'm a bit early."

"No, not at all. How was your drive?"

"Splendid. I've never been in the area, but it's highly recommended by my colleagues."

She angled her head. "May I ask what you do, if you don't mind?"

He launched his façade. "I'm a writer."

"Oh, how nice. Anything I might've read?"

"It's mainly articles about ancient cultures." He smiled but glared, warning her to stop probing. He had a prepared lie about publishing to academia through subscription-only sites if she wanted to look for works of his she'd never find.

"Great. Let's get out of the cold."

He followed her to the door and expected her to fumble with the lockbox. But she reached into the purse draped over her shoulder and pulled out keys. As she stepped into the foyer, he questioned the abnormality. "You didn't use the lockbox."

She looked over her shoulder and smiled. "I'm not just the realtor. I own this house."

He wanted to avoid needless banter, but he found her enticing. Through her winter jacket, she appeared curvaceous. She could be a new, mature toy, a gift from his Master, but he set aside lewd thoughts to advance his purpose. "Then let's see your house."

"Let's start with the kitchen."

For a cottage, the square footage for food preparation was generous, and the view over the dining area through a wall of windows showed a small backyard descending to a gentle, frozen river. A spacious living room held sofas and lounge chairs positioned for conversations or enjoying the waterfront view, and a far hallway led to the bedrooms.

The windows had curtains for the required privacy, but he needed to see his future work site–the basement.

He labored to feign interest as she walked him around the ground floor and called out highlights, including three modest bedrooms, and the impressive property sold itself.

She stopped and faced him. "Would you like to see the basement?"

"Yes, please."

"The stairs are just before the kitchen. The house used to end there, but the kitchen and garage were added by the prior owner."

At the top of the stairs, the musty odor of cheap carpet and dirt embedded into wooden walls assaulted his nose. The steps creaked on the way down, and as he set foot on the floor's thin fibers, he saw what he wanted.

The rectangular floorplan held a wall of windows and a walkout door along one long edge. Like the upstairs, curtains offered the privacy he'd need, and couches, a wet bar, and a half bathroom covered an area of adequate size for his ritual.

He envisioned the circle of candles in the center and the bolstered crucifix by the nearest wall, giving him an easy exit to the backyard. When he would finish the ritual, the cleansing fire would spread throughout the house and leave the crime's evidence in ashes.

Diverting suspicion of his motives, he voiced requisite criticism. "It's a bit, how to phrase it, stuffy down here."

The shrewd professional countered. "All waterfront properties around here with walkout basements have the same issue. The soil is moist, and renters go in and out all the time."

"I see. You seem to know what you're doing."

"Real estate is my livelihood."

"What was the rent, again?"

"For a full year, it's nine hundred dollars a month, plus you'll have to pay for utilities."

Again, he feigned protestations. "Is there any room for negotiation? I'm not quite as prolific in my writing as I would hope."

"If you're handy with repairs and don't call me to fix anything less than a catastrophe, I can do eight-fifty."

He found the suggestion perfect, giving him an opportunity to customize the basement for his ritual. "I'm quite handy, and I'm interested. In fact, I find the property an excellent environment for my writing. What's the process for me to become your tenant?"

"I'll need to do a background check, but that's rather simple. Assuming that works out and you can make a two-month deposit, you can move in soon. When might that be?"

"As soon as possible. Today, if it's feasible. It is the first of the month, after all, and very convenient to start a lease."

She reached for her sunglasses, and as she removed them, he hoped for the red irises that would mark her as a present from his Master. But instead of red, her natural sparkling green eyes ate into him, and he thought her smirk suggested defiance.

He wondered if his wanton lewdness had tricked him into mistaking her for a toy, or had his Master teased him.

"Today may be difficult to get a lease signed, but I'll see what I can do."

That afternoon, after the agent had leased him the cottage, he parked the Tahoe in the two-car garage and procured an Uber driver to take him to an automobile dealer.

The sky became black after a satisfied salesman accepted his check and handed him keys, and Jacob drove his new GMC Acadia SUV to a Costco for rapid stocking of basic food, toiletries, and spare clothing. A safe also caught his eye, and he purchased it for next-day delivery.

He then returned to his leased house where he parked his new vehicle beside the Chevy Tahoe he intended to keep hidden in case a group of street prostitutes in Cleveland had reported it as evidence to a murder.

The next morning, he awoke in the master bedroom of his furnished cabin. Unlike his mini-mansion in Bloomfield, which served for his recreation, the Traverse City property was a grave matter. His Master had selected it for him, and during the next year's first full moon, an eclipsed blood moon, he would claim his next fifty years of life in its basement.

But history proved the tenacity of his enemies, and his success in the ritual and his self-preservation called for preparing the cottage to defend itself.

After showering and dressing in jeans and a maize and blue University of Michigan sweatshirt, he looked out the living room's windows and saw the day's first vendor arriving in a delivery truck. Swinging the door open to the winter's cold, he met a quiet man who appeared too skinny to lift a feather but too young to notice his size disadvantage.

His partner, a portly older man, did the talking. "Morning, sir. I'm delivering a safe you ordered yesterday."

"Yes, that's correct. In the master bedroom."

He led the men through the living room, down the hallway of bedrooms, and to his chamber. Stepping aside, he let them muscle the eight-hundred-pound replica of his weapons vault in Bloomfield to his bedside.

After the delivery truck departed, he waited less than an hour for his next supplier, a home security system provider.

Through the living room window, the truck appeared small compared to the prior delivery vehicle. One man, a handsome thirty-something dressed in slacks, approached the door. A hasty greeting commenced the evaluation, and Jacob led the consultant around the structure's interior.

"You want cameras in addition to the motion sensors?"

"Yes. I want every type of sensor you can offer."

"It's good to meet someone who appreciates the need for home security."

The upsell affirmation tactic irked Jacob, but he concentrated on his tactical needs. "I want cameras outside, too. All angles, all approaches."

The salesman glanced through the wall of glass showing the stream abutting the small backyard. "Of course. Would that be just on the home itself, or would you like cameras installed across the property's perimeter?"

"The perimeter."

"I have to warn you, that can be expensive to install. We'll need to run power from the house."

"Money's no object."

The man nodded in apparent satisfaction of his rising commission. "I assume you want a monitoring package, too. We've got the highest consumer ratings in monitoring service quality."

"No monitoring."

"It's free for six months."

"I said no monitoring. Let's go outside."

As the consultant led him around the yard, the biting cold reminded Jacob how far north he was. The frozen stream, the crunching snow, the petrified blades of dormant grass snapping under his boots.

After setting up a scheme to blanket his ritual site with the latest surveillance technology, he wrote a check, dismissed the consultant, and wondered what sort of countermeasures to his modern technology the hunters were preparing.

CHAPTER 12

Liam was disgusted. He didn't know how else to feel.

His phone showed the newspaper article of a street prostitute stabbed to death two days earlier. Standing beside his father, he reached out, grabbed the yellow crime scene tape, and looked at the cracked concrete of the parking lot. "This is the murder site?"

Wearing a saddle brown field coat, his father nodded. "You were expecting something more grandiose?"

"It's just so… pathetic, as a place to die."

"It's isolated and convenient for the unfortunate victim's livelihood. I can't imagine what sort of horrible conditions forced her into making a living like this."

Liam had memorized the public report on the flight across the Atlantic Ocean, trying to conceive a way he could have prevented the attack. Though no answer had come, he considered the young woman's death his failure. "She was young. No mention of any family. No comments from anyone, other than the victim's colleagues seeing her leave with a single man in a dark SUV and the police report confirming the stabbing and burning."

"The wraith's work, obviously."

"Unless there's a similar murder being kept private by authorities elsewhere, this was his work. No other stabbing murders showed up on the dagger's line of bearing from our home."

His father lifted his eyes to the distant lakeshore. "It's sad isn't it?"

"Obviously."

"There's endless wrongful and needless death in this world,

but when you're connected to it, it stings. This brings back memories of a half century earlier. Excuse me."

As Connor wiped moisture from his eyes, Liam understood the value of family teamwork. "It's okay, Father. We're in this together."

The elder man forced a smile. "Come, lad. We've seen all we can see here."

Liam stepped into the rented Jeep Grand Cherokee's passenger seat and navigated while his father drove. He reached for his phone to tap in a location, but he released it to instead aim his eyes at the sidewalks. "I'm not entirely sure how to find street prostitutes."

"I'm no expert, either, but I'm sure we'll figure it out. We can assume he picked her up nearby." The Jeep rolled forward, and Connor turned it from the lake, towards the city.

Dipping below the horizon, the winter sun receded behind the rising buildings as Liam studied the cold, barren streets. When he started seeing people walking the sidewalks for early dinners or late commutes home, he figured his father had taken him beyond the outskirts they sought. "Turn right. We need to double back to the west."

His father brought the vehicle to the inner city's fringe.

Liam saw a group of women in the shadows between two brick buildings. "Slow down, Father. Let's see if they come."

"You seem too well rehearsed in this."

"This is designed to ensnare men who are using the mini-brain between their legs. It can't be that difficult."

"Well, apparently, it's not. Here they come."

Liam watched three women break from the larger group and approach his window. He rolled it down and smiled. "Good evening, ladies."

The tallest and oldest one, who appeared to be in her mid-thirties, responded while stooping to see the Jeep's occupants. "Two of you, huh? You got a cute accent. Where you from?"

"Ireland. Can't you tell?"

"Well, look at you, all high and mighty. I didn't know I was talking to royalty."

Liam cleared his throat and took on a serious tone. "You're not. You're talking to a friend who's trying to figure out who killed your colleague two nights ago."

"My colleague?"

"The stabbing victim."

Her black curls swung as she shook her head. "Wrong corner, sweetie."

"Won't you help me help her?"

"You want to play hero? You can't bring her back to life."

He snorted. "No, but I can bring her justice the police can't."

She pursed her lips and studied him. "You a bounty hunter or something?"

"Yes. I'm a bounty hunter, or something."

"Well, we don't need Johns stabbing us. I know who you're talking about. She worked on Eighty-Fifth Street. It's that way, two blocks, turn right."

The first stranger's face he'd seen supporting his effort filled him with a strange peace. Though shallow and brief, the exchange brought human reality to his cause. "Thank you for your time."

"You just get that son of a bitch."

He tapped his father's knee, motivating him to drive away. An awkward silence weighed as the elder hunter started the vehicle forward, and Liam expected him to question his newfound comfort in talking to prostitutes.

Instead, his father took the congratulatory route. "That was skillful. When did you conceive the idea of introducing yourself as a friend?"

"I don't know the victim, but I feel a kinship while I'm trying to avenge her."

"That may be a stretch, but I won't say that you're wrong."

"I need to believe I'm right. It has to be personal. She needs to mean something to me, as do all those I'm protecting."

He heard himself mentally appending "and avenging" to his statement, but he had to believe he could save those the monster had yet to seek.

"You have the right attitude."

"Turn here."

"Oh, yes." His father rotated the wheel, and as promised, another group of women came into view. The Jeep stopped curbside, and two girls stepped forward and pressed their palms into its door.

Liam lowered his window and inspected his audience.

The elder appeared twenty-five, and he guessed the other was legally a minor. Based upon success with his prior discussion, he launched straight into his agenda. "Ladies, I'm a friend of your former colleague, and I want to find who killed her."

Smiles evaporated, and the younger alleged prostitute trotted away. But the elder one held her ground. "You don't look like a cop. You sure don't sound like one."

"I didn't say I was."

"You don't sound like anyone's friend. At least not from around here."

"I've traveled a long way, but I assure you, my purpose is to bring the savage who did this to justice."

She moved closer and stared at him with light blue eyes. Under her teased strawberry blonde hair and overdone makeup, he thought she otherwise resembled many of the girls who attended secondary school with him back home in County Cork. "You've got an honest face."

He snorted. "So do you."

She looked beyond him at the driver. "Who's that?"

"My partner."

Connor smiled and nodded. "Good evening, young lady."

"Hi there, old-timer. What's on your mind?"

His father had taught the young hunter basic interrogation techniques, and he intercepted her question. "What can you remember about the man who picked her up?"

She looked away to tap her memory and then turned her head back to Liam. "I didn't see much."

"But you saw something. His face. His hair. His gloves or bare hands."

"He was a white guy with a tan, or maybe Hispanic."

"Black hair?"

"Yeah, straight and long, almost touching his shoulders."

"Could you hear his voice?"

"Yeah, I didn't hear what he said, but he had an accent–not a cute one like yours. It was sort of ugly and heavy."

Expecting Hebrew or an Arabic dialect as the wraith's maternal tongue, Liam found her assessment accurate. "What about his vehicle? The newspaper said it was an SUV."

She nodded. "It was a Chevy."

"Was it big, small, in between?"

"I'd say it was average size. It was dark, too, probably black, but I looked at it pretty quick."

He expected the wraith to have rented a vehicle under a fake identity, but if he'd been sloppy, the SUV could be traceable. Since the woman displayed a willingness to help, he continued. "Did you see the license plate, perhaps remember the state?"

"No, sorry. I only saw it from the side."

The woman's younger companion who'd fled his initial questions hovered on the edge of a small huddled group.

From the corner of his eye, Liam saw her teased blonde strands roll across her back as she shot a glance at him. He raised his voice and expanded his question. "Is it possible that anyone else here might have seen the license plate?"

The woman at Liam's door turned her head and yelled. "Did anyone see the license plate of Jasmine's John?"

Jasmine. She had a name, or at least a professional alias. The young colleague with teased hair took a half step towards the car but stopped.

Liam looked at the blonde. "I think she did."

The nearer prostitute protested. "Don't push it. Talking only gets us in trouble."

"Sure."

"We look out for each other. Nobody else does."

"I understand. I appreciate your help. If there's anything else you can tell me…"

Surprising Liam, teased blonde strands appeared by the window, and the younger woman spoke with a soft voice. "It was a Chevy Tahoe. Michigan plate."

Liam aimed his nose to her. "You're certain?"

"Yeah. I was moving in on him, but she beat me to it. It could've been me, you know." Hardened by the streets, she appeared ready to cry but unwilling to display weakness.

"Okay, then. If you're certain, that's good enough for me. We'll look for a Chevy Tahoe from Michigan."

"Tell the cops, if you think it'll help. I didn't talk to them."

Liam nodded his agreement. "By the way, what was her real name, if you know it?"

The elder woman shrugged. "No idea."

Water formed in the eyes of the younger woman. "I know it. She was nice. She didn't deserve this."

Liam sensed her genuine sadness. "I'm sorry."

"It's not your fault, but if you can help catch the guy… I don't know. Do what you can for her. Her name was Kaitlin."

CHAPTER 13

Two weeks later, Diane watched her grandmother sip tea and then lower the cup.

Unlike her tarot clients, her mother's mother used little makeup and wore a minimal covering of gaudy jewelry. One oversized ring of garnet, one of opal, and a necklace of pearls stood out, but Diane considered the rest of her appearance subdued compared to her cultural contemporaries.

The elder woman's voice was deep and strong and carried a heavy Middle Eastern accent. "You both felt it at the same time?"

Diane looked at her brother, seated beside her on the old, ornate oaken couch. "Yes, Nana."

Nana tightened her wrinkled face. "A pain in your chest, like a heart attack?"

"I don't know what a heart attack feels like, and I don't want to find out. But I imagine so."

"Then you both passed out?"

"Both of us, at the same time, but in different places."

Nana nodded knowingly.

Diane noticed that whether she understood something or not, Nana always nodded knowingly. The habit annoyed her.

"My grandmother, back in Mosul, she always said she could feel the pain of any family member. And it was true. So many of our uncles and cousins told me stories to prove it."

Diane knew her matriarchal lineage had sixth senses of varied strengths. She'd always suspected she'd inherited more than the tarot reading skill, but it didn't account for her and Josh feeling pain from an unknown source. "That doesn't explain why we both felt chest pains while neither of us had a medical problem."

"Maybe someone else in the family had a heart attack. Maybe a relative you don't even know."

"Can you find out?"

The old woman gave her annoying knowing nod. "It may take time because our family is so big, but I'll make the calls and find out."

Diane recognized the understatement. Her extended family was enormous, averaging five children per marriage per her reconstruction of her ancestry. If a distant relative had suffered a heart problem, her grandmother faced long odds learning of it.

But she'd learned to respect the power of gossip among her elders. Each time she'd underestimated the reach and efficacy of the informational network at her grandmother's lips, she'd been surprised by the speed with which her family's matriarchs shared news.

And she respected her grandmother for more than her role as a major hub in a web of words.

With her mother sidelined by addiction, she turned to Nana as her mentor. The elder woman had urged her to finish her college degree, keep her job, and add tarot readings to her income. Now she needed her grandmother to tell her who she was. "Thanks, Nana."

"It's no problem. You want to come help me with the cooking?"

Taking the hint, she followed her grandmother across the open living room and climbed the step into the adjacent kitchen. An avid cook, Nana needed a huge stage upon which to prepare food.

After traversing the cool linoleum to the stove, Diane stood beside the elder woman and watched her stir a huge pot of reddish-orange sauce. Shells of ground rice and minced beef, suspended in tomato sauce and lemon juice, held stuffing rolled together from allspice, ground beef, and onions. "The *Kubba Hamuth* smells great."

"Of course, it does. I used fresh lemons, like always."

The mix of citrus sourness and tomato sweetness enticed Diane's nose. "You're amazing, Nana. You always get it right."

"How's your dating life? Do you have a good man yet?"

Valentine's Day was yesterday, reminding her that her romantic knight had yet to arrive. "I don't have time to date players and boys. I'm holding out for a real man who can handle me and my responsibilities." She cast a glance at her brother. Though she understood he was a logistical burden, she doubted she could live without him. He was her definition of family.

"I know. Come, we talk over here." Nana placed the lid on the pot and cornered the kitchen's back exit.

Diane followed her through a formal dining area into a sitting room that abutted the house's front wall. Joining her grandmother on a couch, she sensed an educational lecture.

The elder woman became a guru. "I didn't want Josh to hear. I have much to tell you."

"Okay."

"I always knew you had special powers, but after what you and Josh just told me, I think you're much stronger than you know."

The revelation echoed that of her brother. "You advised me to do tarot, but you think I can do more?"

The elder woman flicked her wrist. "You can do much more than tarot."

"Now you sound like Josh."

"Josh said that?"

Unwilling to spoil her grandmother's independent thoughts, she withheld her brother's deepest insights. "Yeah, more or less."

"I see. That's interesting, but we talk about you now. You need to know what powers you have."

Supernatural powers sounded fantastic, but Diane realized they'd come with responsibilities–and with risks beyond her understanding. She hid her excitement with an understatement. "That would be nice."

"You know about predicting the future?"

"The tarot cards, sure."

"No, I mean just knowing. Sometimes, I can tell when someone's in danger. Sometimes, I even see the danger ahead of time and can warn someone."

Diane remembered a doomed tourist bus her wealthy grand-uncle had been scheduled to take with his family during one of his vacations to Southeast Asia. With her Nana's impassioned plea, her traveling relatives had forgone the ride, sparing them when the vehicle's brakes had failed, launching it into a roadside valley. "Like your brother?"

"Exactly. And did I tell you about when I told my sister to break her engagement to that *daywanna* from Erbil? I had visions of him hitting her."

"No, I don't think so."

"I told her bad things about him. I even lied about seeing him kissing another woman."

Sarcastic observations about her grandmother's habitual truth-bending swam through Diane's head. Knowing love was the motivation, she snuffed her assessment and even chided herself for being judgmental. But she sensed her grandmother wanting to justify herself, and she offered the opening. "Nana! You lied to your sister!"

"I had to save her. Later, she thanked me when that jackass beat the woman he married. I saw it coming."

Diane added clairvoyance to her inventory of possible skills. "That's cool. At least she appreciated it."

"I have many more stories about me and my grandmother. She said women in our family have been able to do this forever."

"Does this make us witches?"

The elder woman shrugged. "Maybe. I don't know anything about magic potions or spells. But who cares what you call us?"

"Sorry, I didn't mean to cut you off."

"Sometimes, I see things far away."

Diane wondered how her grandmother discerned a real-time vision from a premonition. "While they're happening?"

"Yes, of course. How do you think I knew your other grand uncle's wife was cheating on him?"

"Yuck! You saw it in your head?"

"Yes."

"I thought it was some evidence you found."

Nana shrugged. "How do you think I always know where to look for things? I see half the problems while they happen, then I go look for evidence so people believe me."

"How can you tell if it's happening now or possibly in the future, like a warning?"

"I just know."

Remote viewing–another ability Diane tagged for exploration as a power she possessed. "If I have that ability, will I know, too?"

"Of course, but you have to learn the difference. It took me years, but I had to learn alone because my mother and her mother had to learn by themselves. So, they made me learn alone. But you can learn a lot faster since I tell you."

Diane let her grandmother continue with educational anecdotes about reading people's thoughts and emotions and sharing information with others via paranormal means. She added empathic mind-reading and telepathy to her mental list of traits to watch for.

Before she could ask Nana how to determine which powers she had, the elder woman stood. "You stay here. I'll be back."

Diane heard the elder woman's footsteps descend the basement stairs, her rapid rummaging through a container, and then her slow, echoing ascent.

When she returned, Nana carried a large wooden box, which she lowered to the coffee table while sitting on the couch. "Go ahead and open it."

Diane flipped back the lid and beheld unmatched pieces of jewelry resting beside a leather-bound book, which held her attention. Its cover contained only the title, written in an ancient language. She withdrew the tome, and when she held it, a rush of conflicting emotions flooded her.

Her pulse accelerated, and her breathing became shallow. An omen within her heart made her suspect she should fear its contents, but a quiet confidence trumped her trepidation.

The book became a curiosity in her hands, inviting her reading, but she sensed its knowledge was overwhelming, and she placed it on the table. "What's this say?"

"The title? It's about knowing what we know."

Diane flipped over the cover and examined the front matter. "It's all in Aramaic, right?"

"Yes."

"Can you read it?"

"Nobody can anymore. I tried to translate it, but none of it makes sense. It's a bunch of gibberish."

"Gibberish? Like a code?"

"Maybe. We keep it in our family, and now I give it to you, but you have to protect it."

Diane inspected the book. Its edges looked old and worn, yellowed by decades of exposure–but not centuries. "How old's this?"

"Oh, hundreds of years."

"Nana? Come on, it doesn't look that old."

"Oh yes, I remember now. This one's a copy. The real one's with family back in Mosul."

Unsure how to regard the gift, Diane frowned. "Thanks, I guess. What should I do with it?"

"My grandmother said when the time is right, one of our daughters will use this. Whatever's in here, it's very important, she promised me."

Diane closed the volume and pushed it aside. Spying a pendant with a red ruby affixed to the center of circular silver, she lifted it and felt horrible. As she sensed its power to inflict addictions, sickness, misfortune, heartache, and financial problems, she dropped it. "Yuck."

"Try another one."

Diane sampled two more broaches with gemstones, one of amber and one of sapphire, receiving insignificant impulses.

Then she grabbed the last one, a disk of silver holding a milky iridescent ovular moonstone, which lacey, gothic metal twists surrounded with a sharp point at the bottom. Examining the silvery structure, she thought the stone's setting suggested a dagger underneath a full moon. A strong chain of white gold served as the pendant's necklace.

An initial rush of excitement ran over her, raising the hair on her arms, but then came an enduring calmness.

Clutching it for comfort, she adored it. "What's this one?"

"It's perfect for you. The first one you held was cursed. I'm so happy you tossed it. The others were nothing. This one is blessed. It will protect you from evil spirits."

Using the universe's unseen powers to discern the outcome of a decision with tarot cards was one thing. Belief in evil spirits was another, although Diane suspected their existence. "I've never seen this before. Why don't you ever wear it?

"Because I don't need it. But with your power and the trouble you'll get into, you do. The more you use your powers for good, the more you'll attract evil."

Diane was uncertain if her grandmother was helping with her self-awareness, trying to scare her into respecting her abilities, or both. "So, which powers do I have? You never told me."

"I don't know. You have to figure it out. You have to receive them all and stop fighting them. No more being afraid."

"Would it help if I told you I had a nightmare? I dreamt of a young woman on a cross bleeding from her heart."

Nana gasped. "That's awful."

"How awful? Does that mean anything to you?"

"That depends if it was seeing something happening now or if it's a vision of the future."

"I have no idea."

Startling her, her brother appeared in the dining room, staring at her with burning brown eyes. "I know what powers you have."

"Shit, Josh. You scared me."

"You have them all." His creepiness required challenging, and for this conversation, she overlooked his autism.

"How do you know? You keep saying that, but you're not giving me any reasons or telling me what to do about it. You have to tell me what you mean."

He became silent in an apparent overload of abstract thoughts and an infinite combination of concepts buzzing through his brain. Finding his salient point, he trembled with frustration but voiced it. "Do what Nana says."

"Nana told me a lot today. What do you mean?"

"You need protection. Wear the necklace."

CHAPTER 14

Liam's shoulder fatigued, but he held the German Heckler and Koch 416 steady. Through his scope, the human silhouette showed a respectable grouping of two dozen rounds centered on the chest, but he sensed his father behind him.

The elder hunter demanded continued accuracy. "That's good so far. Relax, and hold the barrel steady."

Liam exhaled and curled his index finger. The rifle kicked, and the hole pattern remained unchanged.

"Excellent. Right through the center of your grouping. Now try five headshots."

Withholding a grunt of frustration, Liam elevated the barrel and focused on the target's head. He squeezed the trigger, and a point of light appeared in the target's nose.

"Perfect."

Tiring, Liam hurried through the final four shots, each round walking down and outward from the nose to outside the neckline.

"No, you rushed."

Liam lowered the rifle and welcomed the relief in his aching muscles. "I've never seen you empty ten thirty-round magazines in semi-auto."

"It's the duty of the son to handle the physically taxing work. I trained this way for my father long ago."

Ignoring his soreness, he agreed with the importance of holding a steady weapon. "I understand, Father."

"Keep the rifle on the counter, and use your pistol."

Liam inhaled and gathered himself. He judged his father's request logical, simulating the shift from rifle distance to room-to-room combat. Reaching to his right hip, he grabbed the holstered Heckler & Koch HK45. Extending the weapon towards the target, he found its weight light compared to that of the rifle.

"Wait." His father reached beside him and pressed a switch. A motor hummed and rolled the pulley that brought the target within realistic pistol range.

"Thank you."

"Go ahead."

Liam ripped off ten rounds, and then the bolt locked back. The smell of gunpowder wafted over his nose, and he reached into his jacket pocket for a replacement magazine. He reloaded and prepared to fire again.

"Stop. Ten kill shots out of ten. That's good enough for today. Let's clean these weapons and return them to the armory."

That evening, Liam sat in a pub sipping a Great Lakes Brewery Irish Ale. He picked at his planked salmon while working his fingers over his laptop's mousepad.

"What's so interesting in that machine?"

"I'm looking for him."

"You've been looking for weeks. There's a reason why fate assigned this task to us and not to some random do-gooder with a computer."

Liam turned to his plate and lifted a forkful of fish to his mouth. The pink meat tasted zesty and lemony with a slight saltiness, and the moist flakes melted over his tongue. He turned back to his screen and started a new search for crimes involving a black Chevy Tahoe from Michigan. Nothing. "You've got a point. It looks like I'll have to trust our traditional tactics."

That night, Liam sat in his bed in the extended stay suite, turning the pages he'd photographed and printed from his father's leather-bound book. Leaving the original vellum version in their home's cellar for preservation, he flipped through the printouts. Beside his hip lay papers with penciled encryption schemes for the ciphered characters.

The simple homophonic substitution scheme for the Aramaic passage he translated used multiple symbols for each of the common letters, complicating a frequency-based hacking. But with only one potential hacker every fifty years, Liam's lineage had developed a simple enough scheme for a fledging cryptologist to decrypt with diligence.

He'd already read the volume's vellum pages, and he embedded its knowledge into his long-term memory while typing its contents into a text document.

Reading the page about rules governing the wraith, he typed and digested a passage stating that during the fiftieth year, their prey was bound to three days' traveling distance on horseback from the site of the sacrifice. Liam's forefathers had estimated the savage's range at three hundred miles from the site of the virgin sacrifice.

Then the handwriting changed, taking a backwards slant and shrinking to fit within the extra space at the page's bottom. The new author, who Liam imagined had inscribed his observations at least five centuries ago, said the distance would tighten as the ritual approached and drew the wraith to the sacrifice site.

With this cycle's first crime taking place east of Cleveland's center, Liam doubled the wraith's three-hundred-mile limit to define the maximum distance to the savage's next strike. If the wraith had used his full distance, venturing three hundred miles from the ritual site to Cleveland, the next kill could happen out to six hundred miles from the lakeside murder site.

Beginning with new handwriting, the next page mentioned an ancient evil spell placed upon the dagger which allowed it to steal life. Halfway down the paper, a new writer updated the warning by mentioning the second dagger, the one in Liam's possession, which his forefathers had commissioned as a replica of the cursed knife.

Having a spell cast to bound the second bronze blade to the first, the hunters had gained a way to track their enemy's ritualistic weapon. As he kept reading, he digested the passage highlighting his only supernatural power.

During the fiftieth year, a hunter's observation of the dagger imbued its bronze with a glow while a victim's blood covered its twin cursed dagger. Recalling his first encounter with the supernatural illumination in his home's observatory, Liam thought that any onlooker would mistake the subtle glimmer for the reflection of ambient light. But when it glowed, he knew it meant his weapon was awake, serving as a beacon to a recent murder.

And it was a beacon only in a hunter's sight, turning red and rotating towards the site of the wraith's latest attack. When outside his observation or that of his father, the dagger lost its magic.

He flipped to the next page to read about the questions the overview of the daggers' pairing raised.

Hunters in his line had cornered and killed a wraith one thousand years ago. That's when they had cast their weapon and bound it to the savage's. A raid on a hunter's home had then allowed the evil dagger's escape, and the presumed will of its demonic master spirit had delivered it to the next wraith.

Two hundred years later, hunters had killed their second monster and had taken his dagger back into their custody. Then, five hundred years ago, a strange phenomenon had occurred. Raiders of the wraith's lineage had sought their cursed weapon again, calling Liam's forefathers to their purpose of protecting their vault. But the younger hunter, the son of the pair, had violated the rules of the book.

Realizing he was outnumbered, he'd sought support from the local townsfolk, but the direct request for help had invoked a supernatural backlash. His house had burst into flames, burning down its walls, disintegrating the door to the vault, and killing the elder hunter. The younger hunter had lost the dagger to a new wraith, the one who since then had lived half a millennium.

The one who eluded Liam.

A week later, the second day of March arrived, bringing Liam heartache. A month had passed in the United States without a sign of the wraith.

He sat at the extended stay suite's breakfast table and glanced at the bronze blade. He verified the position of the camera on its tripod over the blade and its connection to a laptop. Balanced on its crossguard, the knife pointed towards the prior kill. "The day's shadows are growing. He must be moving towards his kill."

At the kitchenette's counter, Connor raised his head from the sandwich he was preparing. "Of course, he is. It's the full moon."

"He's going to kill someone we're supposed to protect, and we don't even have our bloody weapons yet."

"I share your frustration. Our forefathers never faced such a problem. Staying armed was easier when everyone carried their swords and bows across whatever borders they wished."

Liam wondered why the Bureau of Alcohol, Tobacco, Firearms and Explosives needed two months to approve the importing of their weapons from Ireland. He also lamented that the nation that loved handguns forbade nonresidents from buying them. "The Renaissance era history lesson isn't helping."

Connor carried his simple dinner to a dining table and reached for a wooden chair. "Patience, lad."

"No, not there."

The elder hunter looked at the dagger and realized his mistake in risking perturbation of the dining table tonight. He responded while moving back to the counter. "My mistake. I'm an old creature of habit."

"I suppose the dagger would give us the proper direction anyway, whether you bothered it or not."

"It should, but there's no need to test it."

Liam walked across the kitchen and into the den. He sat on the couch and lowered his eyes to one of his computers with a cornered window showing the camera's overhead view of the knife. It maintained its cast copper hue and its motionlessness. "Someone's dying tonight, and we're just sitting here waiting for a dagger to move."

"We can't save everyone. We've never caught a wraith during his year of tribute killing. There's just never been enough information about his whereabouts early enough to allow it."

The delay in receiving his weapons irritated him, but the elusiveness of his unidentified prey hurt him worse. "You don't even seem to be trying."

"What would you have me do?"

Liam glanced at his laptop's screen showing the feed from hundreds of first responder circuits. Most sensitive encrypted information from police scanners was firewalled beyond his reach, but he monitored EMS and fire radios covering his watch area. "You can help me listen for radio traffic of a stab wound."

"Surely, you jest? Do you mean in every city, country, and town within six hundred miles?"

"Six hundred miles covers a lot of municipalities, I admit, but the technology allows it. I'm watching the circuits now."

"How can you watch someone's voice?"

Liam's computer savviness seemed instinctual. If fate hadn't forced him into hunting, he'd seek a life as an engineer. Machines made sense to him. Perhaps, someday, he'd enjoy a normal career, although he admitted he sensed a growing equity in his purpose in stopping the wraith. "I'm watching the number of listeners. Each time something interesting happens, amateurs flock to the channel with the most chatter. I've been mapping the channels within six hundred miles. I'm not even close to having all of them, but I am watching the biggest ones."

"Impressive. So, that's what you've been doing with your face in those machines all month?"

"I can't practice marksmanship all the time."

Connor finished chewing a bite of his sandwich and then swallowed and winked. "You're getting better at shooting–

almost as good as your old man."

"You've been a great teacher my entire life. Perhaps it's time I teach you something."

"Your technical gadgets? I think not."

"Using the computer's easy. I'm already listening to the hundred largest population centers within our radius, and I'm building the list day by day. I can only automate and examine so much, though. A second person would help."

The elder hunter washed down a bite with a sip of water. "If those machines can help tonight, I'll consider it."

"They'll help. Maybe."

"Whether they do or not, you can try again next time with a smaller search radius."

"Don't say that. You make tonight sound like a foregone failure."

"It's true. There's no use fighting it."

Liam hated conceding it, but scanning emergency channels would at best accelerate their learning of the next murder after it happened. Preventing the crime was impossible. Three laptops and a mobile hotspot spread on the coffee table before him, he toggled windows on the rightmost machine and called up the city in his radius with the earliest sunset–Portland, Maine. "The sun's setting in Portland."

"Very well, lad. Let's get the compass running."

Liam rose from the couch and strode into his bedroom. Rummaging through his backpack, he brushed aside the copies of his father's leather-bound book and fished under a spare mobile hotspot for a dual-antenna GPS receiver. He grabbed it, carried it to the kitchen, and turned it on.

"It'll get a fix soon and show us true north."

Returning to his seat, Liam watched the unmoving knife and sought municipal emergency channels with abnormal listening audiences. For thirty minutes, the followership remained small, but then an EMS channel in Providence rose to the top of the list. Two hundred and ten people listened, and he inserted speakers in his ears to join them. "I got something in

Rhode Island."

Standing at the counter, the elder hunter looked up while chewing.

Liam listened to the distant paramedic team reporting the treatment of a crime victim. His adrenaline rose and fell again when he learned the nature of the attack. "Never mind. It's a gunshot wound."

His father nodded and returned to his eating and reading of a local newspaper.

Liam removed the earbuds and leaned back into the couch. Fifteen minutes later, he saw listeners jump on a Montreal channel and placed the buds in his ears. His upbringing had required language skills, and he understood the French basics. A paramedic mentioned a *pistolet*, tagging the injury as a gunshot wound. As night crept over the American Midwest, he watched for murders for another hour but saw nothing. Then Southeast Michigan provided his first stabbing. "A knife wound!"

"Where?"

Shame snuck up on him as he repressed his excitement for a stranger's suffering. "Detroit. It's a knife wound to the belly."

"That's not him."

Liam tossed the earbuds to the coffee table and reclined on the couch. Wondering if his attempt to fuse technical monitoring with the dagger's ancient power would yield disappointment, he tracked the sun's setting across the western limit of the wraith's reach. "The sun just set in Des Moines."

"Understood. Now, no matter where he is, he's racing against the rising sun."

During another hour, a gunshot wound in Louisville earned his attention, followed by one in St. Louis. Then, as fatigue and futility began creeping up his spine, the window with the dagger showed a reddish glow. Liam aimed his nose at the table. "Father!"

Connor was hovering over the weapon, watching it. "I see it, too. Good eyes, lad."

Liam moved to his side. "He's done it again. Bloody hell. We failed again." The thought sickened him.

"We must look at it as another death we can avenge."

From its westerly orientation towards the prior death in the lakeside parking lot, the dagger started its slow rotation. Unlike the prior killing, the knife settled quickly. Liam slid the compass beside the steadied, glowing blade and eyeballed the direction. "Bearing two-seven-six."

This time, when he returned to the couch to face his computers, his father followed and watched him type the bearing into an online calculator.

With Liam's prodding, a map appeared showing Toledo, Chicago, and Cedar Rapids and possibilities on the great circle arc. "What if he's attacked in Cleveland again?"

"He always spreads his early attacks to avoid tipping his ritual site's location."

The younger hunter nodded, mentally filed away the knowledge, and glued his eyes to a computer screen. "Something has to show up."

"Perhaps."

An hour passed, and nothing appeared on the dagger's line of bearing. Liam found his mind wandering and his will weakening. "We could give up and just wait for the newspapers to catch up with his attack."

"Why don't you take a break, and I'll watch for a while."

"Would you know what to do if a channel gets hot?"

"Getting hot means acquiring a lot of listeners?"

"Yes. It will rise to the top automatically."

"Of course. I'll call you over here should it happen. Get some dinner."

Liam walked to the kitchenette and made a hasty sandwich of ham and cheese. As he washed down his third bite with a diet cola, he looked across the room.

His father pointed to the screen. "I think there's something here. It says it's a Chicago EMS channel."

Liam hurried to his father's side, slipped on his earbuds, and listened. His eyes grew wide as he digested the report. Female. Late twenties. Found dead with a knife wound to the chest lying on a bed in a hotel room. "That's got to be him, Father."

"If it's a hotel room, we'll never see the crime scene."

Subsequent emergency reports stated that the victim had been burned postmortem and that the hotel's sprinkler system had been activated. "Bloody hell. He may be escaping during the pandemonium of the fire. Acting like a hotel guest evacuating for his life."

"Such behavior fits his mindset, but given the time delay between the dagger and the emergency reports, I'd assume instead that he's using a time-delay device to start the fire."

Liam chided himself for missing the time-delay device. "Yeah, you're right. Regardless, it's him. I've heard all I need to hear."

"Very well, then. Let's assume you've heard all we need. Draw the second data point on our map."

The intersection of three-hundred-mile circles from Chicago and Cleveland carved a vertical eye between the Great Lakes. Though saddened he'd lost the night's battle to the wraith's successful kill, Liam consoled himself knowing he'd gained ground in the war to tighten the noose around his enemy.

CHAPTER 15

In Diane's dream, a woman lay on a hotel bed with a bronze dagger lodged in her chest. Blood flowed, and her eyes were black.

The ghost whispered. "Avenge me."

Diane awoke to a stabbing agony in her heart.

She writhed in her bed until the pain subsided, and then she caught her breath. The recurring nightmarish theme of knives to women's hearts struck her as an omen, and she feared its possible connection to reality.

Rolling to her feet, she grabbed her phone from the nightstand and noticed the time being after eleven o'clock. She darted to her brother's bedroom door, knocked, and entered. "Josh? Are you awake?"

"Yeah, my chest was hurting."

The chance of coincidence dwindled, and she wondered what dark forces tormented them. She shot across the room, sat on his bed, and hugged him. "Are you okay now?"

"Yeah."

As his big sister, she held herself responsible for protecting him, but she was lost. "What's going on? What's happening to us?"

"I don't know."

"I'm sorry, Josh."

"I want Nana's book."

His proposed solution sounded to her like a special child's desperate attempt to hide in his world of distractions. She loosened her hug. "What for? Can you even read Aramaic?"

His frame became tense. "I want Nana's book."

"Okay, I'll get it for you tomorrow. I promise."

"When?"

"I said tomorrow."

He squirmed away from her. "I want it now."

"Nana's asleep now. I'll get it from her tomorrow and bring it home from work. Is that okay, Josh?"

In the dim light the hallway sent into the room, his ghastly face tightened in frustration. "I want Nana's book."

"I'll get it tomorrow and bring it to you."

Knowing she'd hit a barrier, she left him and returned to her room. Thoughts tormented her as she lay in bed, and she wrestled with the hardest question for hours before fatigue and futility released her to sleep.

Who was she in this incongruent mess of nightmares, chest pains, and supernatural phenomena?

The next evening, she visited her grandmother after a shift of subpar commissions selling menswear. Blood throbbed through her arches as she pried off her shoes and sank into the elder woman's couch. "It happened again to me and Josh last night."

"What did? The chest pain?"

"Yeah. Right after eleven o'clock. We were both asleep, but it woke us up."

"This is not supposed to happen to the men in our family. Josh, he's special."

"Nana, you have to tell me what's going on."

The elder woman lowered her teacup to her coffee table. "I checked with the family everywhere. I checked in Michigan. I checked in California. I checked in Mosul. Nobody had a heart attack last time you hurt."

"That doesn't clear up anything."

The elder woman's knowing nod annoyed Diane. "You have to learn to use your senses."

"I don't know how to do that!"

"Have you tried?"

"I wouldn't know how to begin other than tarot readings."

"Try to communicate with someone far away."

She found the suggestion an odd starting point. Frustrated, she lifted her phone and wiggled it. "That's what this is for."

"You take this seriously or spend the rest of your life scared and not understanding."

"Fine. Who should I contact?"

"Try Josh."

Diane rolled her eyes. "He's hard enough to talk to when he's sitting right next to me. You think I'm going have a nice telepathic chat with him?"

"You try."

"How?"

"Just think of him and repeat a message in your head. I leave you alone to think."

As the elder woman stood and walked towards the kitchen to refresh her tea, Diane sighed and made the attempt. Picturing her brother reading her grandmother's book, she let the idea circle her mind that he was wasting his time. The leather-bound manuscript would resist his effort to learn anything useful from it.

She questioned her brother repeatedly on his plans to learn from the book. What did he hope to find within its pages?

After a minute, she gave up. "It's not working."

With steam rising from the cup in her hand, her grandmother returned to her seat. "How do you know?"

"He didn't answer."

"Did you ask him to answer?"

"I didn't know I was supposed to."

"I don't know if you are. I don't have the same power. Sometimes, I see the future, but I can't talk to anyone far away."

Diane restrained a cynical smile.

Nana's most pragmatic supernatural skill was defeating the slots at the MotorCity Casino. Since retiring from selling dresses for forty years in a bridal business she'd built from nothing, the elder woman generated disposable income once a week by outmaneuvering gambling algorithms.

"So, I'm on my own? Nobody to prove I have powers. Nobody to teach me. All I have is you telling me I supposedly have gifts I need to figure out."

"You have to trust me."

"Fine. I'll keep working on it."

The elder woman stared at Diane's chest and scrunched her wrinkled face. "Why you're not wearing your necklace?"

Diane disliked jewelry, preferring subtlety in her fashion. Finding her grandmother's moonstone-in-dagger pendant gaudy, she lied to protect Nana's feelings. "It's too nice to wear. I'm afraid to lose it."

Again, the elder woman gave her knowing nod. "But you say you feel its protection."

"Yeah, I did when I picked it up last time."

"You wear the pendant."

Until last night's dream, Diane had considered protection unnecessary, but her recent episode of chest pain opened her to suggestions. "Okay. I'll put it on when I get home."

"When you do, you try communicating with someone."

"Yes, Nana. Can I see your old book again?"

"You want the old book?"

"Well, Josh does."

Another annoying nod, followed by a waggling finger. "That boy, he's smart. He might be able to read it. I give it to you. You take it to him."

In her apartment, Diane held the leather-bound manuscript in both hands as she shouldered through her hanging beads. At her brother's ajar bedroom door, she hailed him with a singsong voice. "Hey, Josh. I have a present for you. Can I come in?"

"Yeah."

Barefooted, she strolled across the thin second-rate carpet to the desk where he sat reading his tablet. When she reached him, she extended the volume. "I've got Nana's book."

"Put it on my desk."

His cold reception tested her patience. "I had to make an extra trip to Nana's for this. Aren't you at least going to thank me?"

"Why don't you think I can learn from this?"

"Excuse me? I never said that."

"You asked me an hour ago."

Diane remembered her attempt at telepathic contact, sitting on her grandmother's couch. Suspecting the elder woman's trickery, she questioned her brother. "Did Nana put you up to this?"

"No."

"Why do you say that I don't think you can learn from this?"

"Because I heard your thoughts when you said that you don't believe in me."

CHAPTER 16

Jacob inhaled the pungent sickly-sweet taste of marijuana, adding to his mellow buzz. He returned the joint to an ash tray and picked up the joystick to continue the first-person shooter game he played on the theater system in his living-room-mancave.

Beside him on the couch in his Bloomfield house of leisure, his concubine snuggled up to him and pressed her lips to his neck. "I want you now."

He was growing tired of her. "I'm in the middle of a game. Get us some food."

"I'm not hungry, not for food anyway."

As she nipped his ear, he felt a rush of lust. But he sensed the target of his desires being someone else, distant. He sensed that a new sexual conquest awaited, and he needed to seek her. His lording spirit compelled him to head to a restaurant. "Thank you, Master."

"What?"

"Nothing. Get dressed. We're going to dinner."

"Take me to bed first."

Finding her company increasingly predictable, he acquiesced. It would be less draining to please her than to argue. "Very well, then. Have it your way."

Two hours later, he parked his GMC Acadia in the Red Lobster parking lot. He escorted Kim into the restaurant, greeted a smiling welcoming party, and then followed his concubine past the hostess stand. The young lady leading them to their table wore all black, accentuating her thinness. She was skinny for his tastes, and he made no attempt to touch the hostess.

As his play toy scanned her menu across the booth, he surveyed the other customers for his new toy, and a table of young women attracted his attention. Studying them, he noted multiple objects of his desire. "I'm heading to the restroom. Order me the surf and turf, rare."

Kim nodded her agreement.

He followed a path by the women, seeking eye contact. A young lady with an ovular face looked away and smiled, kindling his lecherous thoughts. He continued to the restroom, relieved himself, and washed his hands while undressing the mental image of his new potential concubine. As he headed back towards his table, he rounded a corner at the hostess stand and collided with another restaurant patron.

She wore a bright blue blouse, and the color remained in his mind as he closed his eyes in defense of the collision. The edges of her hands, which held her phone, pressed his chest to absorb the impact. As she recoiled, he examined her.

Blue eyes, matching her blouse. Slim, with modest curves. Average height. Dark brown hair running behind her back. Ovular face.

He'd wanted to touch her since seeing her seated with the others. "Excuse me."

"Oh my god, I'm sorry."

"Are you okay? I didn't hurt you, did I?"

"I'm fine. Thanks."

Sensing she was the gift from his dominating spirit, he extended his hand. "Well, let's agree to never do that again."

In silent obedience, she moved like a marionette, hesitant but unable to help herself.

As they shook, an electrical impulse tingled him, and he stared at her inviting smile. Her irises became red rings of lust with his dominating spirit's mark. Satisfied with his Master's offering, he released her hand, and the artificial fire fell, leaving irises of radiant blue.

She seemed hypnotized, in his power. "I agree. We'll never do that again. But what should we do next instead?"

"Tell me your name, give me your phone, and call me exactly at midnight tonight."

She handed him her phone. "I'm Jessica. I'll call you at midnight. What's your name?"

"Jacob." He punched his number into her phone and dialed it. When he heard the ringer in his pocket, he hung up and handed the device back to her. "I suggest you save me as one of your favorites, and I also suggest that you make yourself ready to visit Bloomfield tonight."

"I will. Of course."

As she stood under an evil spell, he brushed by her and returned to his booth.

In quiet obedience, Kim awaited. "Where were you?"

He flashed a fake smile. "Just chatting with a random stranger."

"I ordered dinner for you."

"Good. Also, you have an early shift tomorrow. It's best that you spend the night at your apartment."

She pouted. "But my apartment's so boring and lonely."

"I need my privacy tonight. I wasn't asking."

The next morning, he awoke to a new scent lying beside him.

Jessica.

Desiring solitude, he nudged his newest plaything and launched his lies. "Wake up, Jessica. You must leave."

"What?"

"I'm sorry, but I'm late for an appointment."

"What time is it?"

"Almost nine. You were up late entertaining me."

"It was all a blur. Was I drinking?"

"Not at all."

"No, I guess not. I don't feel hungover."

"I need to be across town in an hour to meet a client."

She rolled off the bed and started dressing. "I understand. I'll leave so you can have your privacy. I can't wait until I see you again."

"You will. I promise."

Seeking activity beyond the exploitation of supernaturally enslaved women, Jacob decided to spend the morning maintaining his martial arts skills. He practiced his techniques in the basement, building up a sweat with kicks, punches, knees, and elbows against a kicking bag, and then he returned upstairs to shower.

Having worked up a hunger, he cooked an omelet and washed it down with coffee. He sought his next distraction in a life centered around power and leisure, grabbed a bottle of Canadian Mist whiskey, and measured a shot into his coffee.

With the boost of caffeine and the deceptive fleeting kick of the alcohol, he sought a balance with the mellowness of a cannabis buzz. He lit his joint and inhaled, and then he moved into the mancave to enjoy his day of playing.

As morning became the afternoon and then slipped into a cold March evening, he gained levels in his game and ingested his mood-altering substances at a determined rate.

His mind wandered, but he retained enough sensibility to recognize his overseeing spirit's call. He paused his game to listen. "Master?"

The wordless message entered his head with clear meaning.

Tomorrow, he would meet the virgin.

Every killing cycle, the dominating spirit introduced him to the source of his renewed life at varied times. The first week of March was earlier than the average, but he'd met past sacrifices in January and February. "Where should I go, Master? When shall I begin my search?"

The address flashed in his mind, and he needed to be there tomorrow morning. "Of course, I'll be there. Thank you, Master."

The sun floated low in the bleak morning sky, and Jacob

arrived at the day's opening of the Somerset Collection, an upscale mall located in Troy, Michigan.

Three floors covering a full city block presented a difficult search, and while he walked the stores, he noticed a bridge reaching over six lanes of traffic to the collection's second site. With such an imposing amount of square feet to cover, he would need days or even weeks to investigate every employee and shopper until he encountered his sacrifice.

The vastness of the search and the energy he'd need to devote to it were tests of commitment that amused his lording spirit.

In past centuries, the spirit had sent him to villages and had forced him to search entire communities for weeks for his virgin. To his Master, he was a puppet, and to keep the flow of supernatural gifts, he accepted the mischievousness. He had to let himself be a plaything for the capricious spirit in order to enjoy his enduring life.

He stuffed the shame inside him and churned it into an anger to be meted out as fuel for his killing drive.

To set up his search pattern, he studied the mall's map at a kiosk and committed the walking paths to memory. The bridge would serve as his starting point, and he marched to it.

Starting at the exit of the main three-story shopping area, he stepped onto the walkway and studied the faces of every woman who appeared to be in her mid-twenties.

Struggling to separate late teens and youthful thirty-somethings from his target audience, he counted dozens of women before entering Saks Fifth Avenue, the first department store on his route. Wandering section to section of the large retail area became tedious, and he realized the daunting enormity of his task.

After Saks, he tried each smaller shop on the first floor as he walked towards Neiman Marcus. In a Swarovski crystal shop, a sandy blonde saleswoman greeted him, and she kindled his desire. Her voice was soothing and pert. "Are you looking for anything particular?"

He lied. "Yes. A cross pendant."

"We have them over here."

Following her to a showcase, he ogled her body and liked what he saw. "Price is no object. Let's look at your best."

As she unlocked the case, withdrew a top-shelf crucifix of silver laden with white crystal, and extended it, he feigned eager clumsiness by brushing his fingers against hers while reaching for the jewelry box.

When their flesh touched, he looked to her eyes in hopes of red fire, but her face scrunched and then recovered with a rehearsed but strained smile.

She was nothing to him.

He had to retreat and continue his search. Glancing at the cross and frowning, he uttered an excuse. "Is this the best you have? I was looking for something better. Here." He shoved the box into her hands and marched out the store's exit.

In the mall's hallway, he passed shops with rapid steps, shooting glances at clientele and workers. The embarrassment of failure with the Swarovski woman weighed on him, getting heavier as he questioned why he'd considered her his property.

Had he misinterpreted his Master's subtle clues, or was his puppet master toying with him for sport? Neither case pleased him.

Nothing in the shops caught his eye, and he continued his journey into Neiman Marcus.

In the menswear department, a tall, thin woman with long dark hair attracted him. She reminded him of a model, but she had respectable real-world curves. Her heart-shaped face showed swarthy skin, signaling the lineage he sought tying her to ancient Nineveh, outside modern Mosul, Iraq.

Part of his mind warned him that many such women made Southeast Michigan their home and that the bloodline had been diluted over enough generations to reside within platinum blondes and fair-skinned redheads.

But this lady looked perfect, and when she greeted him with a warm smile, he ignored his inner warnings and hoped she was his sacrifice. "Hi, can I help you find something?"

"Yes, perhaps a blazer."

"Of course. Is it something to go with what you're wearing, or is it for another outfit?"

He checked himself. Dressing well came with his five-hundred years of savings and investing. Today's wardrobe was a Ralph Lauren theme, with black loafers, beige slacks, and a black button-down shirt. "Matching this outfit would be fine."

"Let's start with something beige to match your pants. I'd guess you're about a forty-two-inch chest."

"Exactly. You're good."

He followed her to a coatrack, and as she reached for a blazer, his sought her bare flesh.

Shooting his hand upwards behind hers, he hit the back of her hand, creating skin-to-skin contact. When she looked at him, he checked her eyes but saw dark brown irises.

Enraged, he sought his retreat. "I just remembered I need to be somewhere."

He marched towards the mall and returned to its grand hallway. Shooting rapid glares at the people within the shops, the only red he saw was his own rage. Angry with his overseeing spirit, he mumbled while scanning for his sacrifice. "You're not going to make me labor months for this, are you, Master? Scouring these halls ad nauseum?"

Outside Louis Vuitton, a searing agony cut through his heart, and he fell to the ground clutching his chest. Immobile, he lay on the tile in pain, laboring for air with shallow breaths.

He heard the clopping footsteps of sales representatives trotting from the store. As two concerned faces appeared over him, the lips of an older man with a pudgy, round face moved, but his words were inaudible.

As the pain receded, Jacob rolled to his knees. He wobbled to his feet and took staggered steps towards the nearest exit. As he regained his awareness and understood the reason he suffered his quick and intense anguish, he whispered his apology. "I'm sorry, Master. I was wrong to question you. I'm sorry."

Remembering his subservience, he vowed to search the mall for days, weeks, or even months as his lording spirit required.

Continuing his long life was worth the humiliating frustration.

But the anger would build, and the tributes would pay.

CHAPTER 17

Liam appreciated the year's first warm day, a Thursday in mid-March. Having showered and put on his underwear, he sat in bed checking his computer for the local weather. It was a good day to be outside. He called to his father, who cleaned the remnants of their breakfast in the kitchenette. "I want to practice with the drones today."

"I'm not entirely convinced those toys will be useful."

"Maybe if I showed you."

To Liam's relief, his father consented. "Well, I suppose it would do us both good to be outside. What did you have in mind?"

"Since he has a history of operating near rivers and streams, I thought I'd practice in an environment that might simulate his."

"That's logical."

"There's a place called Lawton Park that looks perfect."

With the wraith's second killing in Chicago, Liam and his father had relocated closer to the geographic center of their updated mapping of the savage's potential territory.

As hunters, they tracked the beast towards the ground zero the evil spirit had selected for his sacrifice. The intersection of three-hundred-mile arcs from their first two clues, murders in Cleveland and Chicago, had drawn a vertical eye between the Great Lakes.

Their home, pending the full moon on the month's final day, was an extended stay suite in the southern half of the map's iris, located on the northern side of Fort Wayne, Indiana.

"So be it. Let me shower, and then we'll go to the park."

Liam invoked his computerized notes and then reached to

the ground for his backpack and the copies of his father's leather-bound book. He pulled the papers up and compared them to the electronic text document. Each time he read, a new fact solidified in his mind, or he found a possible loophole in his father's prescribed hunting routine. As he watched his father walking towards his bedroom in full-length gray pajamas, he called out. "Why not involve the police?"

Connor stopped, looked through Liam's bedroom doorway, and scowled. "You know why. You've read the book enough times."

Liam rolled his eyes. "Yes, of course. Direct help creates supernatural disturbances that ruin everything."

"Don't be so hasty with your sarcasm. The last raid on a hunter's household returned the cursed dagger to the wraith and nearly left our bloodline in ashes."

"What I meant was, why not help the police help themselves? There's no rule against them doing their jobs and stopping a homicidal maniac for us."

The elder hunter raised an eyebrow. "Would you like to call the Chicago police and tell them you have an enchanted dagger that proves the connections between the murders?"

"I don't mean the magic."

Connor frowned again. "I dislike when you call it that. It trivializes our purpose."

The conversation was déjà vu. "What would you have me call it, then?"

"Bah. Magic is fine."

"What about the police?"

"They'll see the pattern soon enough, I imagine. There's bound to be a database connecting the stabbings of our victims, once enough murders take place to reveal the pattern."

Liam wondered if he'd ever be able to speak with detached inevitability about his failure to protect homicide victims. "Why not help them with an anonymous tip?"

"Because your anonymous tip would be their first lead, putting us in the trail of evidence."

He sensed a flaw in his father's argument. "You know I could find a way around that."

"Perhaps. Perhaps, I'm underestimating your skill with all this technology that honestly confuses me."

"I could find an untraceable way to tell them what we know."

Connor faced his son and folded his arms. "Alright, then. Let's say you can. What of it? Two prostitutes killed in two states a month apart with knife wounds to the chest. I think you'd garner no interest."

"Wounds to the heart. Left ventricle, specifically, and on the full moon."

"Even if that caught someone's attention, it would require a federal investigator, and very few of them are twiddling their thumbs awaiting cases."

The argument upset Liam. He found his life hunting a prey across vast territories with minimal trackable evidence frustrating. "It just seems wrong."

"Of course, it's wrong, but think of how many other women are victims of violent crimes. Chasing one lunatic across state lines is a poor use of time for detectives who have enough violence in their own jurisdictions."

"So, we spend our days training, looking for a Chevy Tahoe that may lead us to nothing, and waiting for March thirty-first to arrive so we can fail again."

His father's tone became consoling. "We know he gets sloppier during the year."

Liam lowered his gaze to the computer screen in his lap and scrolled to the passage concurring with the elder man's words. "Our forefathers described him as becoming 'desperate'. I believe that's the best translation."

"My father told me that he's in complete control of his faculties for forty-nine years, but in the fiftieth year, he becomes an animal with a growing hunger for eternal life. Each kill serves his demon spirit as tribute but does nothing for him personally except for heightening his hunger."

Liam realized the wraith's existence must be hellish, reduced to survival with nothing but hedonistic distractions from his lot as a lonely tool of a demon. He continued reading, and the written wisdom confirmed the beast's decreasing freedom to travel as the night of the sacrifice approached. "How fast does his radius shrink?"

"That's an unfortunate unknown in the first few months of the year, but it becomes very tight by November."

"I know the book says he's been seen no further than a day's travel by November. But I want him dead long before then."

The elder man pursed his lips. "There's no problem in setting lofty goals, but remember that our definition of resounding success is sparing the virgin in January."

Liam recalled the scorecard in the book.

A thousand years ago, outside the walls of Jerusalem, the hunters had killed the savage before the sacrifice. During the subsequent successful hunt two hundred years later, the murderous ritual had been completed before the hunters had caught the rejuvenated wraith as he'd attempted to escape to the Nile River.

Then, for three hundred years, his lineage had served as guards of the dagger until its theft five hundred years ago. Since that loss, his ancestors had suffered abject failure, including his father's prior hunt. "But we haven't succeeded in five hundred years."

"That's only nine previous hunts. The odds are against us, but our bloodline perseveres in our duty. Victory will come again, and if we keep our wits about us, it may come for us."

"I apologize for expressing such doubt."

"Better to talk about it than to let your doubts fester."

"Did you protest as much to your father?"

Connor chuckled. "That's a matter of opinion, I'm sure. If he were still alive, I imagine it would be a split decision. May I shower now so that we may head outside for the day?"

Two hours later, Liam watched his large drone sitting in an open field. Sunlight reflected off the black plastic.

He grabbed a tablet and repeatedly hit an up arrow until reaching the number thirty, representing the altitude in feet. He then pressed an icon to commit the command to the aircraft. The tablet's instructions imparted a constant rate of rise to the hovercraft, which rose above the tree line and stopped in midair at its prescribed altitude limit.

Sitting beside him on the park bench, his father adjusted his cap while watching the drone's four rotors hold it steady. "Wow. That looked easy."

"It's designed for ease of use."

"What am I looking at?"

Liam glanced at the second tablet in front of his father, which contained the camera controls and views. "That's an infrared view of the park from the drone."

The elder man pointed at bright pixels. "I suppose that's us?"

"Yes, sir. Wave at the camera." Pixels of bluish hues became yellow-whitish waves.

"Can this see through walls?"

"Not quite. It's designed to let firefighters find people in blinding smoke."

Once resistant to the technology, his father showed a surprising enthusiasm. "Can I move the camera around?"

"Sure. You have three-sixty rotation horizontally and almost a full one-hundred-eighty degrees vertically. Go ahead and play with it."

His father fiddled with icons on the screen, aiming the camera around the park. A pickup soccer game showed the participants as whitish running forms.

"Now try the visible light camera."

"How do I do that?"

"Tap that icon."

The elder man obliged, and the pixelated hues became a high-resolution rendering of reality. "This is truly amazing. It was unthinkable when I was your age. This contraption may prove useful."

Liam thumbed his controller and landed the drone. "This

one's got all the latest controls. I can give it flight limits with a ceiling, floor, and a radius. It's got GPS, too, to send it to coordinates we can enter through the tablet."

"Can you set it to overfly the river on a preset pattern?"

"I'll do that next, but first, I want to try the harder one." He lowered the big drone's controller and picked up the console for the smaller model. Resting on the table in front of his father, the mini quadcopter appeared small enough to eat. The tiny craft rose five meters into the sky, and Liam brought it back towards his father, who watched the grainy video on his tablet. "Stick out your hand."

"Whatever for?"

"I'm going to land it in your palm, using the video feed."

"Then maybe you ought to turn your back and use just the video so that you don't cheat."

Liam followed the advice and knelt with the controller on his knee and the tablet in the grass. He set the camera looking straight ahead as the mini-drone flew while he nudged the joysticks. His father's hand grew large in his tablet, but then he bounced the quadcopter off the elder hunter's forearm.

"I think you need a little more practice."

"Persistence wins this hunt, and I believe that's in our bloodline. Stick out your hand and I'll try it again until I get it right."

CHAPTER 18

Sitting on her living room couch, Diane slipped her grandmother's moonstone pendant over her neck, claiming it as her own.

The moment it settled over the collar of her tee shirt, she sensed its calming protectiveness.

Following her grandmother's advice, she closed her eyes and tried to communicate with Josh. She tested her power and thought of him making her a sandwich. Her hunger helped, and when he walked through the beads, her heart jumped into her throat. "Did you come here to make me a sandwich?"

"No."

She moaned and lifted the necklace over her hair. "Ugh. This isn't working."

"No, you have to keep it on."

"It's useless."

"It's protecting you."

"I doubt it. Why can't you hear my thoughts?"

"I don't know. What were you thinking?"

"I was asking you to make me a sandwich."

"Well, okay, I'll make you one, I guess." His minimal culinary skills included pressing meat, cheese, and vegetables between two pieces of bread, and she often let him contribute to light lunches.

"No, that's not what I meant. I mean, yeah, go ahead. Make us both sandwiches. But if you can't hear my thoughts, who can?"

"Sandwiches aren't very interesting."

"Huh?"

"Using telepathy to ask for a sandwich is dumb."

She found his assessment sound, but she needed to address

125

the social miscue. "Josh, what have I told you about using mean words?"

He looked away.

"Josh, is it mean to call something dumb?"

"Yes. I'm sorry."

"I agree that ordering a sandwich is a bad use of telepathy. Can you think of a good use of telepathy?"

"You need to say something important."

"How do you know that?"

"That's what the book says." He turned around and walked into the kitchen.

Curious about his new knowledge, she stood and moved across the carpet towards the counter. In her haste, she missed a step, rolled onto her undersized foot, and fell sideways.

Bracing herself against the back of a chair, she recovered and was grateful her ankle had survived her clumsiness. Through the half wall, she saw Josh focusing on the food, minimizing her embarrassment.

She sat on a stool by the counter and let her eyes follow him, appreciating how he did what he could to contribute to their lives together. Knowing better than to fluster him while he performed a task, she watched him combine cold cuts, romaine lettuce leaves, and whole grain bread on two plates.

She exercised the patience she'd spent her lifetime honing on him, letting him prepare the food at his comfortable pace. When he finished the sandwiches, he followed his habit of carrying the plates to the dinner table. She darted behind him into the kitchen, filled glasses of water, and joined him at the table. "I brought the water, Josh."

"Thank you."

"You're welcome. And thank you for making our lunch."

"You're welcome."

"So, you were reading Nana's book?"

"Yes."

"What did the book say?"

"It says you need to wear the moonstone pendant."

"Wait. I thought the book was written in code."

He swallowed his mouthful of meat and bread. "It is."

She surprised herself with her constant patience as she worked to extract information. "Did you figure out how to break the code?"

"Yes."

She bit into her sandwich and savored the ham. "How did you do that?"

"It's a simple encryption."

"Can you explain the encryption, Josh?"

"There's a lot of code characters in the book that get used for common letters in real Aramaic. Then there's some letters in real Aramaic that get only one code character in the book."

"But you don't even know how to read Aramaic, do you?"

"I found a site that lists the most common words.

"Huh. That's clever, Josh. You're really smart."

"It wasn't hard. It's just an alphabet."

Wanting to ask about the significance of his statement, she withheld her question while swallowing another mouthful. Letting his words linger, she tried to infer his meaning.

An alphabet. A set of characters. Symbols representing sounds. The way his mind worked, ignoring the innuendos and subtleties that weighed down words with layers of multiple meanings, he would see the text as a puzzle like an eager child learning a language's basics.

"When did you learn how to break codes?"

"I started reading about it when Nana told you about the book."

Diane flagged his success as another piece of evidence for an above average intellect hiding behind the walls of his social ineffectiveness. "What kind of code was it?"

"It's homophonic substitution."

She wondered if Josh had demonstrated his genius or if the text had been designed for easy access to anyone willing to look. Certain that deeper questioning about the encryption would frustrate him and confuse her, she moved onward. "And you've translated it into English?"

"Almost. I'm not done yet."

"Can I see your translation?"

"No."

His resistance reminded her he hated to share his work before he considered it complete. "Can you at least tell me why I have to wear the pendant?"

"It protects you from evil spirits."

"What does that mean? What evil spirits?"

He became quiet and continued eating.

She let him become calm while she kept pace with her sandwich, and then she pried from a different direction. "Josh, did the book give any examples about how the pendant can protect me from evil spirits?"

"It will protect you. That's all."

"Oh, I understand." She didn't, but her ploy to claim comprehension enticed him to volunteer more.

"Your visions will be better."

"Well, that's good news."

"The book said you have empathic powers."

"Can you explain what that means?"

"I'm still translating it."

She knew to slow her inquiry. "I understand. Have you learned anything else yet that you can share with me, Josh?"

"You'll be able to talk to people telepathically."

"Have you learned of any other powers yet?"

"No."

"Telepathy is interesting. That's what I want to do, but it's not working."

"The book didn't say anything about how to use it."

The unexpected answer irked her, but she knew to release her brother from questioning until he could delve deeper into the text. "Thanks, Josh. I really appreciate your help."

Two weeks later, Diane dreamt of a young woman burning on a cross, blood pouring from her heart's puncture wound.

Time stopped, accelerated, and slowed again as the surreal nightmare ambushed her. The victim seemed distant, and then Diane was the victim, seeing a fire burn around her as she bled on a cross.

She called out in her dream. "The pendant is supposed to protect me."

Then the familiar woman from the prior vision that left her unconscious on a department store floor appeared, an unseen wind flapping her milky white gown. She spoke in French words Diane understood. "It is protecting you, and so am I."

The fires subsided, the wounds healed, and Diane stood on soft, cool earth. "Who are you?"

"We descend from the same line."

"What line?"

"The line of Nineveh."

"What's Nineveh got to do with anything?"

"They called us witches, but they were wrong. We are empaths."

"What do you mean empaths? I can barely read tarot cards."

The phantom looked away as an inaudible sound seemed to startle her. "I must go."

"What do you mean?"

"Avenge me." The ghost disappeared.

Diane's world became black nothingness.

Then she gained new vision, seeing the world through a stranger's eyes. In her remote viewing of reality through another woman's senses, she experienced someone else's reality. Unmoving on her back in a bed, she heard a man's heavy breathing as he hovered over the body she shared with a pending victim of violence.

Paralysis. Stark terror.

The helpless woman issued her silent scream, which lodged in her choking throat but landed in Diane's hearing. "Protect me!"

"Who are you? What can I do?"

The hovering man moved closer, revealing a demonic face of

inhuman horror. Hollow sockets of black glared at the Diane-stranger tandem, and a forked reptilian tongue slithered through fangs as the entity spoke with a bellowing, haunting voice. "You are tribute."

Diane protested. "No, I'm not. We are not."

The beast drove a bronze dagger into the woman's chest, and Diane awoke expecting the stabbing agony in her heart. But this time, her return to reality was painless. She clutched her pendant and whispered to herself. "You were right, Josh."

After rolling to her feet, she trotted to her brother's door, forgot her normal concern for his privacy, and barged into the room. "Josh!"

The shadowy lump under the covers remained stationary.

She said his name softly. "Josh?"

He was sleeping.

She backpedaled into the hallway and reached for the door, but his groaned greeting stopped her.

"Diane?"

Excited, she needed to talk, and she flew to his side as he propped himself against his headboard. "I'm sorry I woke you up, but I just had a dream. I mean a nightmare."

"You mean a vision?"

"Yeah. Did you have it, too?"

"No."

She looked away. "You didn't? Are you sure?"

"I'm sure. I didn't have a vision, but I know you had one."

Her first instinct was to control her frustration with his terse communications, but then her yearning to explore his message focused her on the new wrinkle. "How?"

"I sensed you having your vision while you were sleeping."

"But you were asleep, too."

"Yes."

"How's that possible?"

"I don't know."

"You don't know how it happens? Do you know anything about how you can be asleep and watch me?"

Consumed in thought, he looked at the shadows cast by the hallway lights. "No. I only know it works."

CHAPTER 19

The last day of March brought a full moon, and Liam watched the dagger turn red and rotate on the breakfast table. Counting another life taken, he called out to the elder hunter. "Father!"

"I see it. It's turning north, as we might expect."

Liam stood from the couch and walked into the kitchenette. "Because of the Michigan plates?"

"It's a clue we cannot ignore. His first kill was sloppier than expected for a new cycle. I believe the Tahoe was his."

"Wouldn't he have gotten rid of it by now? I've stopped looking for it online."

"Probably, but the damage was already done in our favor when that young lady saw his license plate."

The dagger stopped, and Liam slid the compass beside it to eyeball its new direction.

Bearing three-one-three.

He returned to his makeshift command center, his collection of laptops on a coffee table. He sat on the couch and watched emergency channels, but municipalities on the new line of bearing remained quiet. "Bloody hell."

"Nothing yet?"

"I'm looking. It's all quiet. There aren't that many large cities in that direction."

"It may be a late night. I'll make us some tea."

An hour later, Liam sipped his third cup and welcomed his father's help in watching the channels spanning northwest from the upper side of Fort Wayne–Elkhart, South Bend, and, across Lake Michigan to Milwaukee. He concentrated on the largest population center. "Does his three-hundred-mile limit include travel over water?"

"He's spread his kills over the Mediterranean Sea before."

"Then Milwaukee's in play." As activity on an EMS channel spiked, Liam dialed it in, and a few minutes of chatter confirmed another hotel room murder. Then came the fire and the hotel's sprinkler system, confirming their prey's calling card. Becoming hardened to the trail of death, he placed a pixeled pin on his computerized map over southeast Milwaukee, marking the wraith's third kill.

"It's an uncertain science with much of our knowledge lost to the ages, but yes, I would think so."

"This biases our search northward a bit. Maybe there's something to the Michigan license plate, after all."

"He's still human and capable of mistakes. Killing outdoors in Cleveland and showing his Tahoe to witnesses was a mistake."

"The next full moon's in thirty days. I want to get ahead of him and start predicting where he'll strike."

"Based upon the stories my father told me, he'll feel a tighter pull towards the ritual site before the end of April."

Liam zoomed in on his map and drew three-hundred-mile radii around the kill sites. The addition of Milwaukee to the geography skewed and shrunk the eye-shaped area of the savage's potential sacrifice site. The pull towards Milwaukee pushed Columbus, Cincinnati, and Cleveland outside the boundary of possibility while the original Cleveland murder, in turn, ruled Milwaukee out as the site of the sacrifice. Indianapolis, Toledo, Chicago, and most of Michigan remained. "That didn't help much."

"It will get better over time."

"How much tighter will his distance limit be next time? We need to get ahead of him."

"Two hundred and fifty miles, perhaps. It's a guess."

"Bloody hell, I hate this uncertainty."

"Patience."

Liam glared at the screen and voiced his assumptions. "He's slowly becoming more restricted to the ritual site."

"Yes. By the first snowfall, we'll be dealing with tens of miles."

"He also gets hungrier and sloppier over time."

"Yes. His first kill in Cleveland was a sloppy aberration I cannot explain, but Chicago and tonight were well executed as I'd expect. Escort women in hotel rooms provide him with privacy and a head start to escape with no vehicle to be seen. As long as he's in a disguise, video surveillance will give police forces no leads."

Liam wished he could see the surveillance video, but he remembered the supernatural consequences of asking for help and the impossibility of being believed if he explained his need to see it. "He'll stay in metropolitan areas where his crimes get lost in the noise of frequent murders, right?"

"He will, until he loses his full faculties and feels the ritual site pulling him in."

"Then, while he's still thinking clearly, he'd be a fool to skip Detroit."

"I agree."

"Then that's where we should move. Tomorrow."

"I can't argue. At this point, our wits and intuition are as useful as anything. He has money and favors luxury hotels. We'll make reservations at a centrally located one."

"Maybe." Liam reached for his mouse, called up a browser, and started typing his search criteria.

"What are you looking for?"

"Detroit escorts who work in luxury hotels."

"That's logical, but do they advertise their hotels?"

Liam scanned the filtered results and saw plenty of service offerings but no signs of chosen worksites. "Apparently not." He grabbed a notepad and scribbled the numbers of the top service providers on his screen. Then he stood and walked towards the door.

"Where are you going?"

"To buy a burner phone. I need to call some independent escorts and find out where they work."

His new phone in hand, Liam pushed open the jingling convenience store door. Streetlights lit the sidewalk, and the full moon brightened the sky. He wondered how the simple lack of a shadow over the earth's natural satellite caused the heavens to regulate the madness of serial killer.

Checking the clock on his prepaid device, he realized night had become morning, and March had become April. Time passed like lightning in his helplessness to stop the butchering, and unless he broke the pattern, the next victim would die in thirty days.

So, he did something.

He reached into the pocket of his windbreaker and pulled out his notes. Lifting his phone, he dialed the first number and heard a voicemail greeting.

After hanging up, he tried the second number and heard a businesslike feminine voice. "You're talking to Amber, honey. What's on your mind?"

Her seductive voice unnerved him, and he hung up. "Damn it, I'm a coward." Steeling his nerves, he tried again.

The woman's greeting was harsher and more rushed. "It's Amber. What's on your mind?"

"Sorry. I think we got disconnected."

Her enticing tones returned. "That's okay, sweetie. Tell me what you need, and Amber will take care of you."

"I'll be in town at the end of the month, and I'm interested in seeing you."

"I like a man who plans ahead. When are you coming?"

"April thirtieth."

"Let me see... I'm free all night except between six thirty and eight." Her professional tone made him forget he was scheduling an illicit sexual encounter.

"That should work. How long are your... appointments?"

"Usually half an hour, but take all the time you need."

Wanting to avoid confronting her, he picked the time least likely to place him near her. He selected a time by which he hoped to have already killed the wraith and left town. "Can I take half an hour starting at eleven thirty?"

"You sure can."

To sound authentic, he asked about the price. "Should I bring a gift of some value?"

"How sweet of you to ask. I like your cute little accent. Five hundred dollars is good."

"Um. Okay. That's fine."

"I'll see you April thirtieth, at eleven thirty."

"Where should I meet you?"

"I'll text you my room two hours before your appointment."

"Can't you at least tell me what hotel, so I can plan ahead?" He held his breath hoping for an answer, and her delay made him wonder if he'd asked a taboo question.

"Since I like that little accent of yours, I'll let you know. It's the MGM Grand. Everyone knows all girls work there."

CHAPTER 20

Jacob patrolled the halls of the Somerset Collection. Six weeks of seeking had brought him nothing, but he walked the mall daily per his overseeing spirit's urging.

He hated the tedium, but his Master demanded the homage.

Allowing himself a daily indulgence, he purchased a cappuccino at Starbucks as part of his routine. He grabbed the hot cup from the counter and headed into the mall's ground floor arcade.

By a fountain, three apparitions blocked his path, and he stopped. Wearing milky white gowns, his latest murder victims–Cleveland, Chicago, Milwaukee–floated in front of him. In unison, their deep, haunting voices taunted him. "Why did you kill us?"

He responded in his native Arabic. "Damn you all. You're just tribute. He demands it."

An elderly woman wearing a hijab glared at him and frowned, reminding him that his native tongue was the primary language for many in Southeast Michigan.

Hoping the passerby heard a minority of his response, he looked back at the ghosts, but they faded away, leaving him with their audible warning. "You betrayed us. We will be avenged."

For centuries, tributes had threatened vengeance, but the threats had been idle for five hundred years. He ignored their worthless warnings and accelerated his search pattern, glancing in stores for his sacrifice as he stormed through the mall.

He feared another day of his lording spirit's teasing as he dutifully followed his habitual path. At the western end of his trek, he entered Nordstrom. The high-end retail space's eye-pleasing entryway was a familiar hypnotic blur. He entered the premises and marched the store's floors.

As he saw the men's shoes department, an employee caught his eye.

He'd seen her before, or so he thought.

She'd been nothing to him until today, as she stood out with special interest. Taking a seat at the fringe of her workspace, he lifted a phone to his face and pretended to read, but he ogled her while she tended to customers.

When she turned in his direction, her long straight black hair bounced. He noticed her pleasing face, with expressive thoughtful bright eyes, and sharp and long nose. He liked her defined lips, long neck, and her soft, smooth skin.

He thought she was Chaldean, a pure descendent of his sacrifice's line. Enticing her customer, she flashed a sweet smile but composed herself with authority.

Taking payment at her register, she finished with her customer and then flowed to the next source of her commissions. As she greeted the middle-aged man, Jacob felt a rush of energy flooding his body, and he saw a red aura rise around her. The sanguine light blossomed in his vision, and the woman and her life force became his complete world.

His Master was painting her as the next sacrifice.

The red illumination receded, returning the normal view of the visual spectrum. The middle-aged man shook his head and departed the saleswoman's presence, and then Jacob moved to her.

He needed to touch her, seduce her with his supernatural support, and enslave her.

She was his sacrifice, the source of his next fifty years.

As he approached, she looked to him and smiled.

Instead of waiting for an opportunity to brush her skin at a coat rack, he extended his hand to shake hers upon introduction. Though awkward for a customer's greeting, he needed to touch her.

Before she could reach out in response, a thin man darted across the carpet and stood in front of her, blocking his path. As the new arrival lifted something towards the young lady's face, he mumbled an inaudible order, and then she answered.

"What are you doing here, Josh?"

"You forgot this."

"I can't wear it today."

"You have to."

"It's not right for my outfit."

"You have to."

She sighed, shifted her weight, and grabbed a necklace, which she slipped over her head. "Fine. Are you happy now?"

"Yes."

"Go wait in the breakroom. I'll deal with you later."

The young man shot a chilling, knowing glance over his shoulder as he walked away.

Shaking off the interruption, Jacob stepped to her.

She showed straight, white teeth as she smiled. "I'm sorry about that. That was my brother with a hyperactive imagination."

"I heard. It's no problem. Let's start over."

"Thanks. I appreciate your understanding."

He stuck out his hand, and she accepted.

When their flesh met, his body turned cold, and he recoiled. She also snapped her arm to her side, and her smile became a blank stare. Something was wrong.

Nothing had ever gone wrong in attracting his sacrifice. Confused and afraid, he retreated. "I'm sorry. I mistook you for someone else." He shot glances at her while he walked away.

She appeared dazed. "Yeah, bye."

Needing to digest the horror of his sacrifice resisting his supernatural charms, he marched through the mall's halls in a panicked rush. She was supposed to show him the red irises. She was supposed to obey him. She was supposed to become his property to prepare for the sacrifice.

He questioned his dominating spirit. "Have I done

something wrong, Master?"

As usual, his lord responded with silence.

To remind himself he deserved enduring life, he recalled how his Master had chosen him, five hundred years ago.

In his memory, history played like today's reality as he relived his glory.

Hiding behind a berm in a small town outside Jerusalem five centuries ago, he aimed an iron dagger at the gate of an estate's high wall. A half dozen of his young kinsmen huddled around him. The eldest of his cousins moved close to him. "What do you see, Jacob?"

"No guards, but the gate looks strong. We'll have to go over the wall."

His cousin, wearing a short but thick beard, reached into a satchel and withdrew a grapnel tied to the end of a rope. "Then we go over the wall."

"This house is well guarded."

"Only by two men, and one is long in the tooth."

Jacob glared at his cousin. "But they have a strong god, and they fight with unmatched zeal."

"You would deny me this treasure out of cowardice?"

Moving with lightning instinct, Jacob pressed his iron blade beside his cousin's neck. "I am no coward, and never accuse me of it again."

"Watch yourself, cousin."

Jacob looked down at the retaliatory knife pressed against his loins and lowered his weapon. "You speak of a treasure within those walls, but you haven't described it. Why should I risk my life for it?"

"It's a magical treasure that rightly belongs to our forefathers."

"What magic?"

"A dagger of mystical power."

Jacob scoffed. "From the looks of this place, there's enough gold inside to merit our raid, but don't insult me with hopes in a faded legend."

"Suit yourself, cousin, but my father will reward us all handsomely if we return it to him."

Booty and the promise of a reward offered enough allure for Jacob's greed. "I am committed. We take the house and kill the owners."

"Yes!" His cousin raised his blade and compelled the surrounding kinsmen to do the same.

Jacob raised his iron to his lips. "Quiet. Let's move." He trotted to the wall and threw the grapnel to its summit. The metal caught, and the rope became taut. As he climbed, a yellow arc of light rose in the sky. His hands gripped the gritty mortar, and he pulled himself to the edifice's summit.

Fire was consuming the targeted house, and he looked down to his elder cousin for guidance. "What do we do?"

"Keep going!"

"Into the fire?"

"Quick, before it consumes everything. Get the dagger."

Jacob's boots hit the earth, and he sprinted to the house. Kicking in the door, he darted into its foyer, and bursts of heat wafted over him. He extended his iron knife forward in defense and angled through hallways seeking his spoils.

Cornering an intersection, he saw a central room. He ran to the door and kicked it, and it flew open. In the center of the space, a coppery knife shimmered with the background light from the flames that tickled the hallway's ceiling. He marched to the dagger and clutched it.

When his fingers grasped its handle, he felt an urgent rush of power. His god's will seemed infused in the weapon, and by holding it, Jacob had become his chosen human.

He sensed the full force of Ashima, the god of his Hamathite people, living within the dagger.

His elder cousin appeared at the room's door. "You found the treasure! Now, give me the dagger, and I'll assure my father rewards you well."

The knife's invaluable power resonated within Jacob's bones, and he needed it. "Of course." He stepped towards his kinsman and thrust the blade into his belly. Slicing upward into vital organs, he assured his cousin's demise. The body dropped, the killer stepped over it, and then he trotted towards the nearest exit.

He scurried into the hillside, carrying his new prize and turning his back on his family and his people.

His vision returned to the Somerset Collection.

Interpreting Diane's resistance as an obstacle his Master had either allowed or created to challenge him, he redoubled his resolve to extend his life with the ritualistic sacrifice.

If she remained beyond his supernatural control, he'd find other means to regain his glory as his god's chosen man.

CHAPTER 21

During her break, Diane retreated into the room tucked beside the pathway to the inventory of shoes. Within the breakroom, her brother sat on a sofa reading his tablet.

"Josh?"

"Yeah."

"How'd you get here?"

"Uber."

She knew the cost and wished she could return the twenty dollars to her checking account. "Didn't I tell you to use Uber only for emergencies?"

"Yes."

"Well, what was the emergency?"

"You forgot your pendant."

"I'm safe at work. Why could I possibly need it?"

"Ask Nana."

Diane bit her lip to restrain her frustration. "Did she put you up to this?"

"Yes."

"Oh, really?"

She stopped and collected her thoughts. "Wait. How did Nana know I didn't have my pendant?"

"I told her."

"You called Nana to tell her?"

"Yeah."

"Why in the world did you to that?"

He withdrew within himself, and she shifted into caretaker mode, sitting beside him. "I'm sorry I raised my voice, Josh."

He squirmed.

"Can you forgive me, Josh?"

He remained unresponsive, aiming his eyes at his tablet.

"Please, Josh. I feel terrible."

From the edge of the breakroom, Nana's guttural voice startled her. "Maybe I can help."

"Nana!" Diane sprang from the sofa and hugged the older woman. "What are you doing here?"

"I'm taking Josh to dinner. Then I take him home for you."

"Why are you giving him so much attention all of a sudden?"

"When he called me, he was scared for you. He knows he needs to protect you. So, I told him to bring you your pendant. It's yours now. You wear it always. Too much danger around you."

Recalling the odd handshake with her lost customer, the one with shoulder-length raven hair, she lamented the forfeited commission. The man dressed like he wanted to buy expensive shoes, and she knew how to upsell prospects like him to shirts, slacks, and jackets. But she recalled the handshake's icy chill. For a moment, he'd revolted her, and she wondered if the cold blast had been a warning. "Okay, I promise I'll wear it from now on."

"Josh knows you're in trouble. I don't know what he knows, but he's special."

"I just upset him. So, I'm not sure if he'll go with you."

"Josh, are you ready for dinner?"

"Yes, Nana." Reading while moving, he stood and walked to the older woman's side.

Though she knew her brother best, his quirkiness sometimes stymied her. "Just like that?"

Her grandmother gave her annoying knowing nod. "Come on, Josh. I take you to dinner."

Without a word, her brother followed her grandmother out of the room.

Three hours later, Diane stood with two coworkers on an otherwise unpopulated carpet.

One coworker played a game on his phone. "Slow, huh?"

The other coworker read a social media post. "Like a graveyard."

Diane checked the time. "At least my shift's over in ten minutes." Considering it homework, she read fashion articles on her phone while waiting for her shift to end. At nine o'clock, she punched out, slipped on her jacket, and hurried to the exit.

With her department abutting the exterior doors, she was outside in seconds, and a cool April breeze chilled her. Serving as a funnel, the covered parking worsened the wind.

She lowered her head and squinted.

Hearing footsteps behind her, she turned but saw nobody.

She forged ahead, looked up, and saw the dented bumper of her beater-mobile jutting from its parking space. As she reached for her keys, her world turned white, and her muscles writhed with random impulses.

Paralyzed, with her mind receptive to pain but helpless to govern her shocked body, she fell. As her convulsions subsided, she stared at the concrete ceiling while strong arms slid her backwards to the door of a black SUV. Her constricted muscles relaxed, but then an arm reached over her and jammed a Taser into her chest.

The sensation made her think of a cattle prod, and pain shot through her body. While she writhed in stunned agony, her abductor opened the door and tossed her into the back seat. Two hands smashed duct tape over her mouth and then wrapped lengths around her wrists.

Her kidnapper spoke with an accent like she'd heard in her family's older generations, but it carried a more distant, older feel. "I won't hurt you if you do what I say."

She doubted the offer's veracity, and her skin hurt where the electrodes had struck.

"Stay out of sight while I'm driving, or I'll hit you again with the Taser. Nod if you understand." From the driver's seat, he looked over his shoulder. Dark eyes stared at her, and flawless olive skin covered chiseled features with a squared jaw.

She recognized him as the man with the icy handshake.

Though terrified, she nodded.

He drove out of the parking lot and into suburban traffic, glancing at her when he could. "You're doing very well. Don't let yourself be seen."

Merging onto the nearby interstate, the vehicle rolled her against the seat with its acceleration. She hoped they were heading south and into civilization, but she feared they aimed north towards sparse lands with fewer potential witnesses to her plight.

But when she closed her eyes and called upon her inner vision, the message was clear. No witnesses would help her, and her captor intended to kill her. She thought about the countless lakes, streams, and ponds in the state's northern climes and envisioned herself tied to cinderblocks underwater. She then saw herself being buried in the wilderness, her body lost to history. A final mental torment placed her in a woodchipper. She shuddered.

She feared breaking down into tears but felt better when her inner voice whispered a final reprieve. The danger she faced would be delayed. In the immediate future, she was safe and had time to observe, think, plan, and act.

As she heard cars overtaking them on the left, she realized her abductor drove in the slow lane to avoid police intervention. After the drive endured her best guess of two hours, she tried to get comfortable, but the pressure on her bladder became undeniable. She moaned, and as he looked at her, she moaned louder.

"Be quiet."

She frowned, looked at her bladder, and shifted the tone of her moan to a gravelly statement.

"Do you need to urinate?

She nodded emphatically.

"Go in your pants."

Behind the tape, she howled.

"Very well, then." In a dark stretch of road, he stopped on the shoulder. She heard him exit and walk to the door near her feet. He opened it. "I'm going to tape your ankles together so you don't run."

She slid her feet back and wailed into the tape.

"Would you rather urinate in your pants?"

Sighing, she acquiesced and extended her feet. He pulled off her shoes, bound her ankles, and closed the door. After walking around the SUV to its other side, he opened the door by her head and reached under her shoulders. Strong, he held her torso while she dug her heels into the seat. With a lurch, he lifted her, pulled her outside, and stabilized her on the roadside. He stepped around the open door as a gesture of privacy and then glanced over his shoulder. "Well?"

She raised her eyebrows and whined.

"Squat here and urinate. There's nobody coming, and nobody could see you anyway."

Desperate, she opened her belt and unbuttoned her pants. Straining and wiggling, she lowered her underwear and jeans, squatted, and emptied her bladder. Urine flowed towards the dirt.

Relieved, she stood and yanked lace and denim up her legs, but her clothing proved tight for bound hands. She wanted to cry but forced a firm grunt.

"Aren't you done yet?"

She looked to her pants.

"I see. Allow me. I'll watch where I put my hands."

She shook her head violently.

"Okay, but I see headlights. You have thirty seconds."

Abandoning hope for her jeans, she worked her underwear up her buttocks and front and then presented herself for help.

He stepped to her and clutched her jeans and belt. He then stopped, withdrew her phone from her pocket, and tossed it into the weeds. "I should have dealt with that earlier. Now, let's get you dressed."

Forceful, he lifted, and she slid into her pants. But as his knuckles brushed her bare buttocks, she felt the same icy chill of his handshake, and she noticed he recoiled. Wondering if something in the spirit world protected her from his touch, she hoped he'd ignore her moonstone pendant. She began to believe in it as an amulet, a ward against his touch.

"Hurry. Get in and stay down."

She obeyed as he returned to the driver's seat.

To assure her compliance as the approaching headlights passed, he reached into the back seat and held the Taser over her stomach. The car passed, and he placed the painful shocking weapon into the console. Surprising her, he extended headphones between the seats and dropped them onto her stomach. "Put them on."

She grunted her protest.

"Don't pretend that you can't. You can do it with your wrists bound. Make sure you cover both ears."

She nodded.

"From now on, unless I tell you otherwise, keep those over your head and lay down so that you can't see where we're going. You're also going to wear my jacket over your head. If I see you looking, I will Tase you. Do you understand?"

Again, she agreed.

"Good. You've been well behaved. When I get you home, I may even let you have reading material tonight. Now put your headphones on."

The concept of their destination being a home terrified her with the fear of a long stay, but then she recalled her spiritual hope. A long stay meant she had time to observe, think, plan, and act.

And with time in her favor, she'd be damned if she'd let him win whatever game he was playing.

Fumbling with the headset, she worked it into her fingers and slid the plastic arc over her hair. She mashed one foamy cover over an ear, and half her head registered an eerie silence. Then she covered her other ear.

Noise canceling headphones. She wondered what sounds he wanted to hide.

He tossed his jacket over her face, and her world became

muted darkness.

CHAPTER 22

Jacob drove the Acadia into his garage and parked it next to his Tahoe.

He reached for the remote controller to the overhead motor but reminded himself to minimize the clues he would reveal to his captive about her whereabouts. Though her headphones silenced her world, he doubted their perfect efficacy, and he saw no need to reveal the presence of a garage.

He stepped from the vehicle and, with delicate force, detached the chain mechanism from the motor. Exhaling, he estimated the click had been inaudible to his prisoner, and he stepped to the massive door. To his relief, it rolled down tranquilly, and the enclosed space became a private, quiet workspace.

He opened the SUV's back door, revealing his prisoner lying backwards with his jacket over her head. Pulling a leather muff from one of her ears, he spoke. "I must prepare you to walk to your room."

After returning her to silence, he stepped to the hatchback and raised it. In the trunk, he found several lengths of chain and padlocks he'd purchased from a Home Depot. Unable to find better restraints during the short duration between meeting his sacrifice and kidnapping her, he intended to improvise until he could acquire leg irons.

He stuffed one padlock in his pocket, grabbed another, and flopped a length of chain over his shoulder. After closing the hatchback, he returned to his prisoner and removed a muff. "This may be uncomfortable, but you'll get used to it."

She groaned.

He slid the chain behind her hair, which felt like cold strands of ice against his hands. Remembering that her touch caused him an otherworldly freezing shock, he lowered his items to the ground and put on his gloves. Again, he freed one of her ears to hear. "Lift your head."

Her face under his jacket, she moaned.

"Would you prefer that I shock you again?"

Her nose was a moving bump on his jacket as she rolled her chin to her chest.

He lay a length of chain under her hair, and then he pushed her head down. Under his jacket, he unfolded the chain over her throat. Pulling it tight, he joined two links with the padlock, and then he ran his gloved finger between her skin and the steel to assure a tight fit without choking her.

Looking to his workbench against the garage's far wall, he saw spare cloths. He stepped to the bench, grabbed a few rags, and tied them together.

He circled the vehicle to the other side, opened the door, and unraveled the tape from her ankles. Then he returned to the door by her head, reached under his jacket, and transformed the rags into a blindfold.

Keeping the jacket blanketed over her for assurance of her blindness, he lifted her out of the SUV and balanced her on her feet. He grabbed her shoulders and guided her forward. She seemed to trust his restrained strength, and she stepped forward in her deaf darkness. Reaching ahead of her, he twisted the knob giving access to the kitchen. He nudged her through and then closed the door behind them.

With an inherent bias towards permanent privacy, he kept the curtains and blinds closed behind every window in his cottage, allowing him to manhandle her in secrecy inside his rented Traverse City home. A quick check of the windows within view verified their concealment, and a few paces brought them to the basement stairwell.

He cupped her deltoids, slowed her, and aimed her towards the stairs. Then he stopped her and lifted a muff to warn her. "First step down."

Blind, she probed the air below her toe. He nudged her, and she resisted, and then he half-lifted and pushed. Acquiescing, she lowered her weight. As the ball of her foot hit the tread, she curled her leg until her heel hit the riser, showing her ability to adapt to her darkness.

He pushed her into her next step, and she moved with surprising certainty, in confident acceptance of her fate. Her poise under the pressure of captivity bothered him. He'd expected more timidity.

Sliding her foot until her heel hit the riser, she lowered her weight onto the tread and then sent her next foot downward.

At the bottom, he twisted her torso sharp left. He checked the glassy exterior wall for full curtain coverage and then walked her through the finished basement. After guiding her by the stools and the wet bar, he halted her by the bathroom door. A longing look at the spot where he intended to mount the sacrificial crucifix immobilized him.

He lamented the eight and a half months separating him from the night of the ritual, but he hoped a lording spirit fickle enough to disallow paranormal enslavement of his sacrifice might allow an early implementation of this semicentennial ceremony.

His knowledge of lunar time played in his head, and he hoped the blood moon in July might provide him an accelerated awarding of his renewed life. Somehow, his Master would reward him for his diligence and courage. The fear of abandonment was insufferable, and he forced himself to believe.

Having reached her dungeon, he removed her headset and tossed it onto the ground behind him. "Turn left."

As he followed her through the doorframe into the bathroom, he closed the door and lifted his jacket and blindfold from her. He spoke as he extended the free link to her bound wrists. "Tie the other end of the chain under the toilet, tightly."

Moaning, she raised her hands and shrugged.

"I didn't say it would be easy. Just do it."

Kneeling, she pushed the chain under the tank and then pushed herself back to her buttocks. To complete the wrapping, she leaned to the far side of the porcelain but strained while reaching. She braced herself on the toilet, backed up on her haunches, and shook her head.

He withdrew the Taser from his pocket. "I suggest you try harder."

Accepting her lot, she repeated her effort but rolled onto the tile to extend her joined hands closer to the wall. Grabbing the chain, she wiggled backwards.

He stooped and extended the lock under the seat. "Here. Lock it tight."

She fiddled with the padlock to work it through adjoining rungs, and then she snapped it shut.

"Very good. Now follow me and see how far you can go."

He backed into the living space, and she took two steps outside the bathroom before the chain caught her neck.

"That's good for now. Go back in and sit."

Backtracking, she entered the bathroom and lowered herself to the toilet lid.

He ransacked the cabinets, shower, and drawers to examine the toiletries he'd inherited. Checking for anything usable as a weapon or a tool, he sought aerosol cans, flame sources, and metal objects. Making a pile in the living room beyond her reach, he tossed a pair of scissors, dental floss, hairspray, matches, razor blades, spray bottles of perfume, and rubbing alcohol. As the mound became massy, he reversed his approach and removed everything first, and then returned to her benign objects of necessity.

As she sat mesmerized watching him fiddle with a heap of consumer products, he set aside liquid soap, a towel, toilet paper, a toothbrush, and toothpaste.

"That's all you need."

She shook her head and grunted.

"What?"

She looked at her crotch.

"I don't understand."

She rolled her eyes, sighed, and let out a demeaning grumble.

"I see. What brand?"

Her head fell forward in futility, and he realized he'd asked a foolish question of a woman who couldn't talk. His prisoner, his sacrifice, his right to life, had embarrassed him.

The humility enraged him and he stepped forward to slap her, but an invisible force stayed his hand. Balling his shaking fist, he lowered it to her mouth, and, obeying an unseen power, he extended his fingertips to the tape and ripped it from her skin.

"Ouch!"

"What brand?"

"Tampax Ultra."

"I'll buy you Tampax Ultra and some clothes."

Her tone started civil but ramped up to display her overpowering vocal chords. "Thanks. Wait. Screw that. What the hell's going on?"

"Watch your volume with me!"

"The hell, I will! You just kidnapped me. Who the hell are you? Who the hell do you think you are?"

He powered the duct tape back over her mouth, accepted the chill as his fingers hit her flesh, and glared into her eyes. But he had to release her and look away to lie. "I kidnapped you and am holding you against your will. Accept that, and let's move on. I have my reasons, and I may explain why later. You're a smart girl. So, I'm sure you've realized that if I had the intent to harm you, I would have done so already."

As he hoped she believed his lie, her shoulders slumped, and she relaxed. Discerning that she'd let down her guard against her emotions, he watched water form in her eyes.

"No crying. I hate crying women."

Her body became rigid.

"That is, you may cry, but not in front of me. Understood?"

She nodded.

He recalled the mental checklist of rules he'd drafted during the day. "There's also no yelling, ever. No banging, ever. No making any loud noises, ever. No tampering with the toilet or your chain, ever. You keep this bathroom clean, always. The Taser is your punishment for breaking a rule. Understood?"

She nodded again.

"Very good. In exchange for good behavior, I will feed you, I will give you a bed, and I will provide you reading material. I will also extend your chain's length and move you from the padlocked collar to leg irons, provided you behave." He reached for her mouth, pinched the corner of the tape between two fingernails, and yanked.

"Ouch!"

"Repeat my rules."

"No crying in front of you. No yelling, ever. No banging, ever. No loud noises, ever. No tampering with the toilet or my chain, ever. Keep the bathroom clean, always."

"Very good. Also note that my security cameras will see your every move outside the bathroom." He pointed at cameras mounted on opposite corners. Two additional cameras poked through the opposite edges of the curtains covering the glass wall to the backyard, but they were incapable of turning towards his prisoner.

Her eyes flitted over the spying mechanical eyes.

On his phone, he called up the home security application and tapped his way to the two interior lenses. He saw himself standing next to her, and then he extended the phone to her face. "I can watch you all the time from anywhere."

"Are you going to watch me shower, too?"

"Did you see a camera in the bathroom?"

She lowered her gaze, and he enjoyed the shame he inflicted with a simple belittling question.

"No."

"Very well. I will go shopping now for your needs."

As he turned and walked away, she called out. "What should

I call you?"

Having forgotten to predict the question, he sensed divine inspiration guiding his answer. "If you ever need to address me, call me 'Master'."

CHAPTER 23

Diane dreamt of a woman on a cross, blood pouring from her wound. Time stopped, twisted, and turned, leaving the dreamer as the burning, bleeding victim. She called out in her dream. "The pendant is supposed to protect me."

The familiar francophone woman from prior visions appeared floating above the fire, an unseen wind flapping her milky white gown. Diane considered her part ghost, part angel. "It is protecting you, and so am I."

The fires subsided, the wounds healed, and Diane stood on her feet. "How are you protecting me?"

"I am always watching. I am always here."

"Who are you?"

"We are empaths from the line of Nineveh."

"What does that mean?"

"You are never alone. You are always connected."

The answer confused her. "What does that mean?"

"People in need seek you. Let them find you."

In her dream, Diane found the advice overwhelming in its expectations and ineffective in its vagueness. "How?"

"I must go."

"Don't leave me. I'm trapped!"

"Avenge me." The ghost disappeared.

Diane's world became black nothingness. She awoke in the middle of the night, rolled on her back, and let her eyes adjust to the darkness. Her breathing echoed in her confines, and she realized she was sleeping in a small bathroom.

Hopes of connecting with a protective angelic ghost faded, and the weight of a horrible reality grew.

The abduction, the long drive, and the imprisonment in

a basement had happened. To confirm her predicament, she reached for her neck and ran her fingers over the metal rings. The air mattress and pajamas her captor had purchased allowed her to rest, but she was a shackled prisoner.

Seeking her phone, she ran her hand towards her hips, but instead of feeling the denim of her jeans, she touched cotton bottoms. Her abductor had insisted upon the pajamas, which lacked pockets for hiding tools or weapons.

Light from a lamp in the living room issued under the closed door, providing illumination to discern shapes within her confines. She curled her torso and sat, locking her arms and propping herself on her palms.

Her first clear thought was her brother's safety.

He'd be terrified by now, wondering where she was. He'd be alone and confused. She prayed he'd call Nana for guidance.

Hearing decluttering sounds outside the door, she braced for her jailor's invasion of her privacy, but he surprised her by knocking.

"I'm awake."

"May I enter?"

His courtesy backfired, aggravating her. "You kidnapped me, and now you're pretending that I get a say in what happens?"

"I must respect your privacy."

Anticipating no advantage by aggravating him, she toned down her venom. "You can come in, but I need to move the mattress, first."

"Very well."

She put her bare feet on the tiled floor and flipped the mattress and blankets against the cabinet. "Okay."

The latch clicked, and the door swung open. In the same clothes he'd worn during the abduction, he appeared tired from a long night. His frame blocked half the light coming from the living room.

Unwilling to show him weakness, she stood with her arms folded and watched him.

He nodded at the living space behind him. "I've cleaned the

area for you."

She raised a hand to her collar. "Does that mean you're taking this off?"

"Not yet, but I have ordered shackles for your ankles."

"Then why'd you bother to clean an area for me?"

He lifted new lengths of chain. "So that you can be more comfortable. You'll be able to reach almost half the living room."

"Okay, how do we do this?"

"You lay down, and I tape your ankles. Then I tape your wrists. It's only temporary, I assure you."

Obeying, she reclined on the cool tile and waited while she heard him reach for a roll of duct tape and unfurl it around her ankles.

When he finished, he crawled closer and bound her wrists. "Roll onto your stomach."

She complied.

"I need to kneel over you. It's only a matter of security, I assure you."

With his knees on the floor, he straddled her lower back and worked a key into the padlock at her neck. He snapped an additional length into the tether with a twist and a click, and then he added a third span-and-lock combination. His final adjustment brought cool links across her throat and a tight fit around her neck. "Let's get you to your feet and test it."

In a smooth motion, he dismounted her, clasped her underarms, and hoisted her to her knees. With bound ankles, she needed help to her feet, and his strength in lifting her defied his leanness.

As he yanked the chain with violent bursts, it held. "I'll untie your ankles now." From behind her, he unwrapped the tape.

Her feet's freedom felt good.

"See how far you can walk." He strode ahead and turned to examine her movements.

As she stepped into the rectangular basement, she saw dim yellow lighting and a room of brown. Worn walls of wooden panels, dark tannish cloth upholstery over aging furniture, a fading hardwood floor, and tables and bookcases of faux grain laminates. Brown everywhere.

"Come to me."

She stepped towards him and stopped when the chain tightened around her neck.

"Further."

"You want me to choke?"

"Pick it up. I need to see your limits."

She elevated the links and gained a half step. He walked around a musty couch and waved her the other way. Keeping the chain high, she walked to him.

"Can you reach the books?"

She aimed her bound arms at a shelf. "It would be easier if my hands were free."

He grabbed the tape and unraveled it.

She placed one hand against the wall for balance while fingering through the spines of paperbacks. "I can reach."

"Good. Now try the couch."

She stepped back to elevate her tether and lifted the links over the furnishing's back. "I can't walk around the couch."

"Roll over the back."

"I don't want to."

"You should sleep there."

Admitting his suggestion's appeal, she conceded. "Okay." She pressed her stomach against the backing and then reached a free hand into a soft cushion. Confident she could land without snapping her neck, she rolled onto her back and landed in softness. After hours in the back of an SUV and atop an air mattress over linoleum, she sank into the cushions.

"Now make sure you can get back to the bathroom without my assistance."

Finding the energy, she twisted towards the backing and pulled her torso up. Then she elevated her knee and thigh atop the couch for leverage. A combination of pushing and pulling brought success, and she dangled a foot towards the floor behind the couch. She stood, adjusted her collar, and faced him. "Now what?"

Frowning, he sounded irked by the question. "Now you sleep."

"That's it? I sleep? Did you kidnap me to watch me sleep?"

Appearing agitated, he lowered his head and ignored her while he walked across the room.

She considered yelling her question again as he rounded an end table.

But he slowed as he approached the staircase, placed his foot on the first step, and stopped. "I'll tell you whatever I wish to tell you, when I wish to tell you."

"After all you've done to me, can't you tell me why I'm here? You owe me at least that."

He turned and faced her to render his answer before continuing up the creaking stairs. "I owe you very little. I will provide you with clothing, food, a bathroom, and reading material."

She wanted to withhold the dozens of questions whipping around her head to appear strong. She wanted to take the advantage in whatever game he played by convincing him she withheld secret advantages. She wanted to convince herself she would find supernatural ways to overcome her captor. But her tired and hazy mind betrayed her, and a fearful plea slipped from her lips. "Why can't you at least tell me why I'm here?"

"I'm in charge. I don't have to tell you anything."

"Come on! You have to tell me!"

He aimed his head up the stairs and responded as he lifted his leg to the next step. "No, I don't."

His smugness enraged her, and she turned towards the toilet to attack her tether. Wrapping the links around her wrists, she took the tightest hold her skin would allow without tearing. For leverage, she stood on the seat and arched backwards.

She muffled her scream into a lengthy hiss while pushing with her legs and straining her back. The chain defied her, and her exertion left her with chafed hands and sore bones.

Defeated, she gave up, sat on the floor, and fought back tears.

CHAPTER 24

The last day of April arrived, and Liam expected the wraith to kill under the coming full moon. But this time, he gave himself a chance to intercept the savage.

The ornate lobby of the MGM Grand Hotel fused luxury appeal with the glitz of its attached casino. Chandeliers twinkled, and plentiful mirrors reflected colorful lighting.

As a month-long hotel guest, he was a fixture in the lobby, and he'd even gambled several days a week to appease any discerning onlookers. More importantly, he'd identified four women he thought worked as independent escorts within the upstairs rooms.

He sank into a leather armchair and watched the revolving doors. With the sun still lighting the sidewalk, he saw the first of the working women stride into the lobby. As she approached the reservation counter, he reached for the shotgun microphone in the backpack at his feet and slipped it under the jacket resting on his thigh.

After he aimed it at her, he sent his free hand across his body and tapped the mousepad on the laptop on his other leg. He dialed up the volume, and from the earbuds dangling down his chin, the sweet sounds of the escort's voice reverberated in his head.

At the counter, she gave the clerk her advertised name, took her key, and then walked away with her luggage. Liam assumed the rolling bag served the charade of her being a traveler while in reality containing the wardrobe and tools of her trade. During her exchange with the hotel employee, he'd heard the numbers he sought.

Seven one nine. Her room number.

He slipped the shotgun microphone into the backpack and then called his father.

Connor answered with an eager voice. "Yes, hello?"

"Bambi just showed up and will be working in room seven one nine tonight."

"Who's Bambi?"

"One of the escorts who works in our hotel."

"You're sure of all this?"

Liam rolled his eyes. "I just heard her entire conversation at the registration desk."

"I hope you weren't obvious about it?"

The younger hunter pursed his lips and considered explaining the modern snooping device.

The elongated microphone heard sounds from multiple angles throughout the room but used its orientation to filter out unwanted input, lowering the noise floor of the signal received from the subjects' voices. It also used reflections of the desired voices arriving at odd angles to reconstruct and boost their speech.

Though he found the concept simple, he thought better of distracting the elder hunter with technobabble. "The microphone allowed me to listen from a distance."

"So, it really works."

His father's doubts in technology frustrated him. "Yes. I've been testing it in the lobby all month." When dealing with spy gadgets, he noticed his father's hesitancy to lead. High-tech activities lifted the younger hunter to the primary hunter role.

"Right. Shall I deploy a camera outside her room?"

Liam planned on his father mounting fake smoke alarms outside the escorts' rooms to see the wraith. Motion sensors would trigger the hidden cameras to alert him and see their prey. "Not yet. Wait until sundown. I don't want an observant hotel employee to stumble upon it before we need it."

"Understood."

Half an hour later, another escort entered the lobby, and Liam eavesdropped on her conversation with the registration clerk.

Room eleven zero five.

He stood and piled his possessions on his seat. Extending his fingertips towards the ceiling, he flushed blood through his muscles, and he looked through the glass of the hotel's front where darkness was replacing the sun's fading light.

Walking to stretch his legs, he thought a caffeine boost might help his alertness. He stopped at a self-service stand and ripped open a packet of black tea. After pouring a cup, he tasted the fluid's bitter warmth and returned to his seat.

Sinking into the leather, he prepared for an evening watching for the remaining escorts and the man he hoped to stop from murdering one of them. He called his father.

"Yes, lad?"

"The moon's out. Please deploy the cameras on the seventh and eleventh floors."

"I shall handle it."

Ten minutes later, his father called, sounding giddy with the enjoyment of his clandestine work. "The cameras are deployed. They look just like real smoke detectors."

"Good job. Did you test the video feed to your phone?"

"Oh, damn. I knew I'd forgotten something. I will right now. And... something's wrong. I, uh... I don't see anything."

"Did you open the app?"

"Oh, yes. Sorry. There we go. I can see the one on the seventh floor."

"Try the eleventh."

"No. Something's wrong."

"You're too far away. You need to head upstairs. See if you can monitor both of them from the ninth floor."

"Will do."

"Call me back."

Five minutes later, his phone vibrated, and Connor sounded giddy. "Amazing, this technology. I can see from either camera."

Giving his seventy-four-year-old father orders felt weird,

but the protocol worked for them when playing with gadgets. "Keep walking the floors. See where you get good signals and where you don't."

An hour passed, and doubts about the final two ladies arriving entered Liam's mind. Mondays were average nights for the women he watched, slowed by a lack of local clients who preferred weekends but boosted by travelers arriving for new weeks of remote work.

But then the third escort walked into the lobby, animating him into action with his microphone. He listened, learning of her assignment on the tenth floor.

As he sought his phone to call his father, he saw a man enter through the revolving door.

He was tall, reaching over six feet, and made of lean muscle. Olive skin covered chiseled features with a squared jaw. Sleek raven hair touched the collar of his overcoat.

An uneasiness made Liam fidget, and he sensed he might need to make quick moves. He slid his laptop into the backpack.

The man looked at him, and Liam saw pools of black instead of irises and pupils. Recalling the leather-bound tome's wisdom and his father's lessons, he knew the wraith would appear inhuman to his eyes.

Slowly, as the man kept his gaze upon him, the human form slipped into something supernaturally sinister.

The ancient warnings paled compared to the reality.

Morphing in Liam's eyes into a disgusting demon, the man's true self was revealed. His face became a twisted aberration of sagging and torn skins. Fangs protruded from the slimy mouth, and the long, crooked nose hinted of a devil. The beast, its inner essence exposed in nakedness, had a body of scarred and blighted leather, and at its extreme ends, horns, a pointed tail, and cloven hooves.

The wraith.

In a flash, Liam reached for the pistol in his backpack, surprising himself with his decisiveness to kill on sight.

But the beast seemed imbued with a reciprocal awareness of the hunter, and he ran back the way he'd entered the hotel.

As Liam realized he was the first hunter in a millennium of pursuit to ambush a wraith, he wondered if he could kill in cold blood. He had to find out.

He grabbed his backpack, slung it over his shoulders, and sprinted after the animal.

Years of conditioning paid off as he accelerated to his top speed. His lungs heaved as his cardiovascular system fed his body fuel. Seeing the wraith holding a pace ahead of him, he realized the chase would endure beyond his maximum sprinting range, and he slowed his cadence.

With his bag bouncing off his back, he turned the corner onto the next city block, and he saw the savage crossing a street. Keeping his constant velocity, Liam thought he was gaining on his prey, who burned energy while fleeing terrified at his top speed.

The wraith turned into a building under a parking sign, and the young hunter pursued him up the ramp. Gaining ground, Liam dared to hope he would fulfill his life's purpose within seconds.

But as he cornered a parked Honda Odyssey minivan and looked up the next ramp, his intentions changed from hunting to survival. Instead of seeing the exposed fugitive, he saw the grill of a dark SUV pulling out of a parking space.

Tires squealed, and the SUV angled towards him. The beast's face appeared ghastly behind the windshield as the vehicle accelerated downhill.

Liam stepped between parked cars and dropped his backpack. As he reached within it, he made the split decision.

Instead of wasting bullets to cut meaningless holes in moving steel, he reached for a magnetic GPS tracker. As the SUV shot by in a flash of black, he slapped the magnet against the quarter panel.

He grabbed his pistol and loaded it, and then he hoisted his backpack over his shoulders and sprinted down the pedestrian stairway. On the sidewalk, he spied the garage's exit, and he ran towards it. As the SUV broke through the gate and turned away, he leveled the pistol.

Overcoming his fear of attracting unwanted attention, he squeezed off rounds until the bolt slid back. Aiming for a rear tire with a pistol had been futile, and the rounds had bounced off the pavement, but he assured himself that he'd needed to try.

The vehicle sped out of sight.

With gunpowder's scent caressing his nose, he returned his weapon to his backpack. Huddled pedestrians glanced at him, and he jogged in the opposite direction of the hotel.

Planning to double back after distancing himself from his gunshots, he lifted his phone and opened his tracking application.

The GPS device held to the SUV, and Liam watched the wraith's path as he drove through the city.

CHAPTER 25

Diane swallowed a mouthful of Kung Pao chicken and fried rice. Her captor's disinterest in cooking benefited her with a decent variety of quality take-out food as her main staple.

When he'd chained her to the toilet ten days ago, she'd expected to go mad, but the soothing assurance of a supernatural sensation comforted her with knowledge of her short-term safety. An unidentified spirit guide made her feel protected, and her abductor's behavior had been more pleasant than she could have hoped.

Something otherworldly forced him to treat her humanitarianly.

Joined together by steel chains, the humane-restraint padded leather leg irons around her ankles reminded her of the removed annoyance of a collar, and the tripled lengths of links shackling her to the bathroom allowed her to climb over the back of the basement's nearest couch.

As she lay against propped pillows, she read a paperback version of a romance novel. Though outside her preferred genre, the book, one of three dozen in the cabin's makeshift hand-me-down library, distracted her from her imprisonment.

Resting her eyes, she craned her neck to see the far corner of the room. Slow blinking released the tension in her head, and she scanned the room's familiar surroundings.

Thick drapes covered the wall leading to the outside and her potential freedom. During the day, cracks of sunlight would slip through the outer boarders near the room's corners, but in this evening darkness, she saw no sign of a world beyond the drapes and glass.

On the shorter wall of the room, a television was a silent and dark rectangle. Though she had its remote within reach, it lacked batteries.

The room's far corner had the staircase which she'd descended into the basement, and the closer long wall contained a wet bar with stools. The empty shelves behind the counter framed a dusty central mirror.

Behind her couch, the chain ran into the bathroom, and the room's back wall held a large but unimpressive painting of deer running through a forest. Below the painting, an old wooden bookcase held the makeshift library.

She returned to her reading and powered through another sappy scene. After finishing a chapter, she closed the pages and shut her eyes. A minute later, she forced herself to scan the final passages and reach the expected ending. Rolling from the couch, she lifted her chain, walked to the bookshelf, and plunked her predictable but heartwarming novel to the bottom shelf.

The escape from reality had been welcomed but fleeting.

Missing her phone, she guessed the time. With Michigan's late sunsets in the upper latitudes at the western edge of the Eastern Time Zone, she estimated an hour and change since she'd seen the last light, and she placed the evening at ten o'clock.

A voracious reader, she hungered for an engaging book and scanned the spines. A detective novel caught her attention, and she lifted it to her face. The futuristic cover and the title, *Dome City Blues*, hinted at a deep web of intrigue, and she turned back towards her couch.

Her undersized feet betrayed her, and she rolled her ankle. Falling forward, she braced her landing against a sofa cushion and the wooden coffee table, but the novel slid under an armchair. "Damn it."

She stood, and in a motioned she'd perfected, she narrowed her shackled steps while walking between the coffee table and the couch. When the links reached the sofa's far side, she crouched and then crawled along the dusty wooden planks. Careful to avoid exacerbating her problem, she extended her arm under the chair and caressed the book towards her.

With the novel safe in her hand, she carried it to her couch.

As the vibrant first-person narrative engrossed her, flashes of white overcame her, and her world became a lucid life in another person's body. Like her prior nightmare, she was inside the unmoving body of a young woman.

Thoughts became images, images became words, words became thoughts. Intellects merged in shared meaning, and Diane lost the distinction between her mind and the other's.

Immobilized on her back in the rear of an SUV, she heard a man's heavy breathing as he hovered over the body she shared with a pending victim of violence.

As with her prior vision, she succumbed to stark terror.

The helpless woman issued her silent scream in their shared thoughts. "Protect me!"

"I'm a prisoner. How can I help you?"

The man moved to the victim's face, revealing a demonic image of inhuman horror. Hollow dark sockets glared at the Diane-stranger tandem, and a reptilian tongue slithered through fangs as the man-beast tore open the woman's shirt.

The animal reversed direction and disappeared. Then Diane felt him grab her ankles and drag her outside the vehicle, under the full moon. Her head cracked concrete, and the jolt turned her world white. When she saw the starry sky again, the evil monster appeared over her. "You are tribute."

Diane protested. "No, I'm not. We are not."

While the woman regained use of her arms, she pushed against the assailant's face, but he brushed aside her hands. Furious with fear, the young victim fought back harder, this time punching her attacker's ribs without effect. "Help me!"

"Why's this happening? How can I help?"

The man-beast slid a bronze dagger down the shared symbiotic Diane-stranger body.

Fearing another fatal chest stabbing, Diane offered insider

advice. "Cover your heart!"

Obeying, the woman shielded her chest from the knife.

The killer overpowered her and pinned her wrists to the concrete, but the hold occupied his arms and trapped him in a stalemate. "Damn you."

Diane shared her idea. "Head butt!"

The young woman swung her forehead upward into the beast's nose, stunning him, but his weight remained on her.

"Bitch!" He released a hand and punched her jaw repeatedly until she became dizzy with blurred vision. The women's shared arms fell to the cool pavement.

Enraged, the animal pricked the exposed skin covering his victim's beating heart, and he grasped the knife's handle with both hands. White knuckles squeezed the weapon, and the man lifted his torso behind the blade to drive it downward.

The Diane-stranger tandem shed tears as they accepted their pending death.

A supersonic chirp whizzed overhead, followed by a rifle shot's cracking echo. The beast snapped his jaw in frantic directions, and then a second chirp and echoing shot sounded.

The animal yelped his shocked reaction and rolled off his victim. Covering his left side, he looked at the source of the gunfire as he screamed and sprang behind his vehicle. "Bastards!"

Accepting they may live, the women lay motionless in disbelief of their last-minute savior. Tires squealed, the SUV sped away, and the sounds of the revving engine faded into the distance.

"You saved me."

"You saved yourself."

"Who are you?"

"I was going to ask you the same question."

"I'm Judith."

"I'm Diane."

"Why can we hear each other's thoughts?"

"It's me. I've got special powers."

"Why'd this happen? Who attacked me?"

"He's a serial killer. He's obsessed with sticking knives into young women's hearts." She heard trotting footsteps, and two faces appeared above Judith.

A handsome man in his mid-twenties leaned over her and spoke with an Irish accent that Diane thought enhanced the rough charm of his strong facial features. "Are you okay?"

For a few seconds, Diane succumbed to the weakness of Judith's victimhood. Feeling safe, her adrenaline subsided, and she released her fear through sobbing. "He tried to kill me."

"You're okay now."

With impressive speed, Judith regained her composure. "I am okay. Help me up."

The man and his older partner assisted her to her feet. "We'll drop you off somewhere safe."

"No, I'm coming with you."

"Excuse me?"

"If you're going after him, I'm going with you."

"You're in no condition. You're not trained."

"What's your name?"

"Liam."

Diane felt the young woman's strength. "Liam, have you ever been so close to death that you thought you were already dead?"

Her rescuer shook his head.

"Well, I have. I want to stop him from doing it again."

The young man exchanged a look with the elder, who shrugged and nodded. "Right, then. You're coming with us, but we need to hurry. Our car's over there."

As the would-be victim became an agent of vengeance, she broke into a trot towards the men's vehicle.

The young man called out while she ran. "What's your name?"

Over her shoulder, she yelled as the men jogged to catch her. And as the escaped tribute's own strength absolved her of her need for supernatural support, Diane drifted from their tandem connection.

The last words she heard before her awareness returned to her basement jail cell were spoken with a young woman's renewed strength.

"My name's Judith. Let's get this son of a bitch."

CHAPTER 26

Liam sat in the passenger seat as his father drove the Jeep Grand Cherokee. The GPS tracking map on his phone showed the wraith with a four-mile head start driving up Southeast Michigan's main interstate artery. "He's on seventy-five heading north."

The elder hunter's eyes seemed to challenge him as he scrunched his body towards the windshield. "I don't see any entrance ramps."

The younger hunter offered assistance. "Hold on. I'll open my navigation app."

The voice in the back seat was deep and strong for a person spared from death by milliseconds. "I know where to go. Head straight two blocks, then right."

"You heard her."

"I'm too old to argue with a young lady." His father pressed the accelerator and aimed the Jeep per her instructions.

"What's going on? Why'd he try to kill me, and who are you guys?"

Unsure how much to share of his divine purpose, Liam measured his words. "He's a serial killer, and we're bounty hunters."

"Really? What's the bounty?"

He sought an honest answer that protected her from the burden of the truth. The only booty would be the cursed dagger, and he couldn't claim a compelling market value for a small mass of bronze. So, he generalized. "Not enough. With this guy, it's more personal for us."

"Why?"

With his lineage of hunters working against the lineage

of wraiths descended from the Syrian Hamathites, he gave a compelling and truthful answer. "He's attacked members of our family."

"Oh, I see." She sounded unconvinced but accepting.

"If you don't mind, I need to ask you a few questions."

"Yes."

"How'd he grab you?"

She sounded ashamed. "He asked me for directions. I was stupid."

"Don't beat yourself up. He's charming and dangerous."

"When I got near his car, he jumped out and chased me down. Then he jabbed a Taser into me. I should've known better."

"Don't blame yourself. He's a master at appearing normal and friendly." Liam glanced at his GPS, verified that the savage stayed on the highway, and checked his father's speed. They were keeping pace with their prey.

"I know better than to walk alone at night."

He wanted her mind off any mistake she thought she'd made. "Where were you going?"

"I was trying to clear my head by walking by the river."

"He attacked you by the river? That's open to witnesses."

"I don't know if anyone saw. It's open, but it's quiet. That's why I was there, to be alone. He stopped by the roadside and asked for directions to Chelios, and he looked harmless. I was stupid."

Liam tried harder to elevate her thoughts from her victimhood. "What was on your mind?"

"Schoolwork. I let it overwhelm me. I put too much pressure on myself, but I should know better."

"What are you studying?"

"Nursing at Wayne State. I graduate this year."

"Awesome. By the way, your accent. What is it?"

"Haitian. I'm on a student visa."

Having studied French at his father's demand, he switched to her native language. "That's great. I speak French. So, does my father."

She responded in a French that was more relaxed than the Parisian version he'd learned. "Connor's your father? I don't see a resemblance."

"He's adopted."

"You speak French, too?"

"It's been a long time, but yes, I remember much of it."

Thinking in a foreign language slowed Liam's mind, and he reverted to English. "It's better to talk in English so I can concentrate. This guy's smart and desperate."

"Why desperate? Doesn't he think he's gotten away?"

"He's driven to kill during the full moon. He's still looking for someone to kill tonight."

"That's horrible. Why's he doing this?"

Liam sidestepped a lie with a platitude. "Who knows what drives any madman?"

As she seemed to accept the answer, her tone became conciliatory. "I can't thank you enough. You saved my life."

"You were putting up a good fight. I couldn't have saved you without your help. It took me half a minute to line up the shot."

"Can't you just accept my appreciation?"

"Yes, I'm sorry. I do. It's just… I'm angry with myself. If I had better marksmanship, he'd be dead already."

Connor was conciliatory. "Don't be so harsh on yourself. It was a long-range shot, even for a sniper rifle. You did well to graze him with two tries. I could have done no better, even at your age."

He heard Judith stirring in the back seat. With all his weapons encased except for the sniper rifle, he twisted to watch her. "I don't suppose you can handle a weapon?"

"Not really. But I can handle this." She lifted a first aid kit and slid it to the seat beside her.

"Where are my manners? I should've thought of that."

Opening the lid, she angled her head to examine the contents. After withdrawing a bottle of isopropyl alcohol and a box of cotton swabs, she poured the liquid onto a white fuzzy ball and then dabbed it against the abraded skin of her jaw. "Don't worry about me. Follow him."

Liam looked to his tracker and saw the savage approaching the major exchange with Interstate 696. As the GPS signal showed him continuing north on Interstate 75, he noticed the wraith slowing. "He's down to seventy now. He's got no idea that we're following him."

"So, if you guys are bounty hunters, what are you going to do if we catch up to him?"

Remembering the moonset time for Detroit being at a quarter to eight in the morning, Liam realized the killer had plenty of time to find another victim. But the wraith would be anxious, especially after two thwarted attempts to claim a tribute. He'd strike at his first opportunity. "I was thinking a shotgun to the face."

"I'm okay with that since he tried to kill me, but it's not me who'd go to jail for murder. Vigilante justice isn't a legal defense."

The absurdity of criminal law protecting a monster frustrated Liam, but he accepted the facts. He needed to risk himself to stop the savage, and if it meant a lifetime in prison, so be it. "I'll take that risk. Drive faster, Father. We can catch him."

"Eighty?"

"That's good. Police around here seem to be okay with that."

The elder hunter accelerated the vehicle. "Nature may take care of this for us. Are you sure you missed him completely?"

"I winged him at best. Seven-point-six-two-millimeter rounds from a high-powered rifle... if I'd hit him, I think we'd know it. I'm afraid I hit his overcoat and little more.

"He moved pretty fast when he jumped from me."

To bolster his commitment, Liam restated his resolve. "I'm ready to kill him."

Connor kept his eyes on the road. "So am I."

"So am I."

Liam shot her a questioning stare.

"Or not. I can leave the killing to you guys."

The drive continued in silence while Liam watched his tracking application. After forty-five minutes of uneventful pursuit, the wraith turned right onto an auxiliary interstate spur. "He's heading towards Flint."

"Do you guys know anything about the area?"

Liam shook his head. "Not really. We're from Ireland."

"That explains your accents."

"What's wrong with Flint?"

"Other than toxic water? It has worse areas than Detroit."

"Worse?"

"If he's looking for a place to get away with murder."

Following their prey, the driver turned the Jeep right onto Interstate 475 while Liam verified their pursuit coordinates. "We're gaining, but we're still a mile and a half behind."

He kept his eyes on the tracking application and saw the wraith's vehicle stop. "He just pulled over! It's a corner. A fast food place, a convenience store, a gas station. He parked on the side of the road. Bloody hell."

Judith sounded frightened. "Why 'bloody hell'?"

"He's parked out of sight of security cameras. Hurry, Father."

A red light stopped them three cars from the intersection. "I'm rather stuck."

"Go around."

"I'll do my best." His father accelerated into oncoming traffic and forced a honking car to shift lanes. Slowing to see crossing vehicles, Connor pushed through the intersection and gunned the engine.

Seeking a visual on the dark SUV, Liam shifted his gaze between his application and the road, but the dark mile between the Jeep's windshield and the wraith hid his prey. Then one mile became half a mile, and street lights illuminated the approaching intersection. "He should be in sight." Then a quarter mile. "Where the hell is he?" Perplexed, he grew anxious. "Judith, there's a case back there. A small black one."

"There's a few black ones."

"Hand me the top one. Quick!" Liam turned towards the back seat as she lifted the plastic enclosure. He grabbed it and opened it on his lap, hunching over it to hide it from his passenger. The dagger glowed red and maintained an orientation pointing towards the GPS fix of the wraith.

"What's in the case?"

Liam snapped. "I'll explain later." As his father pulled towards the intersection, the dagger twisted to the right. The young hunter looked towards the sidewalk and saw dancing arcs of yellow and orange rising behind ruffled bushes. "Stop!"

His father obeyed, and the car screeched to a standstill.

Liam trotted across the sidewalk to the unkempt hedges bordering the parking lot of an abandoned restaurant. He leapt over the bushes, and on the other side of the greenery, a pair of lifeless eyes belonging to a homeless woman looked at the full moon.

Fire consumed her tattered coat and baggy pants while working its way into the flesh surrounding her chest wound. A newer vestment, the overcoat he'd seen covering the wraith in the hotel lobby, burned as well.

Sickened and angered, Liam retraced his steps to the Grand Cherokee and saw the magnetic GPS device in the grass. He stooped, picked it up, and returned to the passenger seat. "He killed a homeless woman, probably in her forties."

"That's older than usual, but it apparently satiated his needs. Let's move on and continue our chase." Connor moved the Jeep forward again.

"Do you guys know where to go?"

Liam lifted the tracker. "He saw this on his quarter panel when he came back to his car. Now he's back on the road, but he knows we were tracking him. So, he'll speed up and take a deceptive route, which means we have to guess now."

As the old hunter took the Jeep around Flint's northern edge, the wraith's SUV eluded Liam's eyes, and he heard the sadness in the voice coming from the back seat.

"That could have been me. Someone else died because I didn't."

The young hunter needed to prevent her survivor's guilt, and he also needed someone to support to avoid wallowing in his own defeatism. "You were random. She was random. The only difference is that you fought back. If she'd fought back like you, I'd have stopped him again. You're alive because you fought. Never forget that."

"Thank you, but shouldn't we call the police?"

"I'd like to, but it's too risky to call attention to ourselves."

"So now what?"

"He didn't know we were tracking him until he reached Flint. That means the route from Detroit to Flint marks the way to his lair. It gives us a direction to his base of operations somewhere north or east of here, and while he's driving scared, we'll risk my father getting a speeding ticket to try to catch him tonight."

CHAPTER 27

Jacob swore in his native Arabic. "Damn them to hell!"

His true irritation, however, was aimed inward.

Had he let the hunter's ambush blind him with rage and deafen him with fear? Is that why he'd failed to notice the tracker clicking against his Acadia in the parking garage?

Shame. Anger. Doubt.

Was his lording spirit dismissing him? Had he already been abandoned?

No, his Master had presented the homeless woman on the sidewalk as a gift. The god of his dagger remained with him. The hunter's luck in predicting his location was a test of Jacob's wits and determination, and he'd survived. The red glow of his blade in the homeless woman's heart had signified the acceptance of tribute.

After pulling into a rest stop in Saginaw, he stopped the SUV at a gas pump and hurried through its menu. He squeezed the handle and looked at the store. Through its front window, he saw a rack of ballcaps and considered altering his appearance, but against the hunters, a disguise was useless.

The young enemy had appeared like a ghost to his eyes, and with the rapid response the hunter had displayed, Jacob knew his pursuer had seen a paranormal perspective of him.

He remembered the image of the hunter, the snapshot vivid in his mind as if still threatening him.

The azure humanoid figure and its backlit sky-blue aura mocked him with its angelic hues. Eyes of pure white stared at him with feigned peaceful acceptance, but the hunter's hate and drive for Jacob's demise were palpable.

Though he despised the hunter's heavenly appearance, he

appreciated the revelation of seeing his enemy's exposed essence. The recognition inside the hotel lobby had given him the warning that had allowed him to flee.

The blood trickling from the burning flesh on the back of his upper arm had dried, and the bullet's grazing suggested he'd been lucky. He humbled himself and verbalized his appreciation to his demonic god. "Thank you, Master."

As the nozzle clicked, he withdrew it and jammed it into its cradle. With haste, he jumped into the driver's seat and sped away to the east, avoiding Interstate 75 in case his pursuers sought him.

Following state routes, he drove an hour due west and then turned north to parallel the Huron-Manistee National Forest. Another forty-five minutes brought him to Cadillac, and then he turned west, then north again, pointing him towards the cottage in Traverse City.

While he relaxed in the freedom from his pursuers, a spectral vision materialized in the passenger seat wearing a milky white gown. The homeless woman whose body burned many towns away leered at him with spheres of black onyx masquerading as eyes. Her voice carried haunting, chilling notes. "Why did you kill me?"

"Stop asking me! All of you! You know he demands it."

"You betrayed me. I will be avenged." Like her predecessors, she disappeared.

He slapped his arm against the passenger seat to verify her departure, and then he let the highway hypnotize him.

During the drive, his anxiety fell, and the view of his approaching cottage soothed him. The artificial but undeniable gravitational pull towards the sacrifice site was growing, and, as he parked in the garage, he suspected he would expend an increasing amount of energy to travel from the property.

Certain he'd escaped his pursuers, he exhaled and enjoyed a moment of calmness. He reran his mental checklist of activities to set his world right. He had much to do.

The one fact he needed to verify before retiring was the safety of his life source. He checked his phone and saw Diane sleeping in his basement.

Carrying his weapons cases, he entered the kitchen. Before forgetting, he prepared a solution of water and vinegar in a crockpot, opened the dagger's case, and removed the bronze blade from its bloodied plastic bags. He slipped the knife into the fluid and let it sanitize the metal.

He turned to the basement door and unlocked it. He opened the door, turned on the lights, and tiptoed down the steps.

Diane's deep, soft breathing confirmed her slumber, and he continued his soft steps behind her as she slept on the couch.

In the bathroom, he closed the door over the chain, turned on the lights, and inspected the links one by one. None of them appeared damaged. He crouched and looked at the bolts around the toilet, finding them in place.

To verify his second line of defense against her escape, he walked to the far wall of glass and checked the bars blocking the movement of the sliding doors. They were locked, and the security film he'd laid over the glass was an added deterrent.

But it wasn't good enough, and neither was the lock at the top of the stairs. He made a mental note to reconsider the prison's barriers with a fresh mind after sleeping, yielded to his exhaustion, and walked towards the stairs.

Casting a furtive glance at his sleeping possession, he climbed the first steps, seeking his bathroom. After a quick walk through the living room, he entered the hallway to the bedrooms, found his personal space, and stopped in the master bathroom. There, he found his first aid kit and applied gauze and antiseptic to his arm.

Then he crawled under the sheets and fell asleep.

The next morning, he awoke late and frustrated, and he called his first concubine, Kim.

"Hey, stranger. Where've you been?"

"Busy. Come to Traverse City today."

"I have to work. Why can't you come here? I haven't seen you in over a week."

The question dug a pit in his stomach. He was becoming increasingly bound to the ritual site. His play palace in Bloomfield was now a memory. "I can't go back. You must come here."

"I get off work late, and I have to work tomorrow."

"Call in sick tomorrow. I need you here."

The supernatural force his Master lent him overpowered her resistance. "Okay."

"Good. Stop by my house after work and get all my weapons and as many of my clothes as you can carry."

"Okay. Where should I meet you?"

"We'll meet at a hotel. I'll text you the address."

"Okay. See you tonight."

He called his second concubine, Jessica.

"Good morning, Jacob. Where are you?"

"Far away. Where are you?"

"I'm at work, like everyone else on a Tuesday morning."

"I want you to meet me in Traverse City this weekend."

"Meet you? You don't want to drive up together?"

"I'm already traveling. You'll arrive Friday night. I'll text you the hotel address."

Again, his Master's divine will worked in his favor. "Okay. Sounds great. I can't wait to see you."

After hanging up, he conducted his morning routine and changed into clean clothes. It was a day of errands and labor, and jeans and a tee shirt sufficed.

He walked into the kitchen and grabbed breakfast bars. Then he unlocked the basement door and found his way to his inmate.

Illuminated by dim lamps and the cracks of sunlight shining around the sides of the curtains, she sat on the couch reading a book.

"I have your breakfast."

"Breakfast bars again?"

"Would you prefer that I starve you?"

Instead of answering, she looked away and then replied. "Can I have some clean pajamas and underwear? I'm tired of washing my underwear in the sink every day. That's embarrassing and uncomfortable."

"Yes. I'll wash them today, all your clothes."

She rolled her eyes. "What am I supposed to wear while you wash them?"

Somehow, she weakened his mind when in his presence, and the humiliation ate his innards. "I will buy you replacements this morning, and then I will launder the ones you're wearing."

"Can you get me some real food, too?"

"I bring you back an excellent variety of dinner every evening, and still you complain?"

"I mean for lunch and breakfast. Bars and leftovers are getting boring."

He bit back his venom, reminding himself that placating her minimized the chances of her resistance and staved off his lording spirit's spite. "What would you like?"

"I want something hot from the kitchen."

"Do I look like I intend to cook for you?"

"I see your point. Okay, granola, oat meal, raisins, prunes, dates, brown sugar, milk."

He frowned. "Isn't that what's essentially in the breakfast bars?"

"Ugh! I need the dried fruits for fiber, unless you want to take me to the hospital with constipation."

He withdrew his phone from his jeans and tapped in her shopping list. "Very well. I'll get them. What else?"

"Whole grain bread, lettuce, and sandwich meat."

"Anything else? I don't plan on doting over you."

"I could use some new books. I've read all your good ones."

"Very well, then. What titles do you want?"

"How should I know? I have no idea what's been published because I'm trapped in your basement."

"I can't just buy the top twenty books from a grocery store without attracting attention."

"Well, give me a Kindle reader."

He glared at her. "You would have me leave you with an electronic communications device and a wireless connection to the Internet?"

"Fine. Can you get me the top four hardcover fiction books on the New York Times best seller list and then order me the top twenty paperbacks from the Amazon Metaphysical genre?"

"I'll do what I can to make you stop complaining. Now, is that all?"

"Yeah, I guess."

"Very well. I need to inspect your chain."

Familiar with the routine, she raised her legs to the back of the couch.

He viewed and tugged the leg irons and the padlock connecting them to the chains. He then followed the links to the toilet, doublechecking the two additional padlocks holding the lengths together. Finally, he verified the toilet free of tampering.

He grabbed her garbage bag from the bathroom and, as he carried it to the stairway, he silently thanked his lording spirit that she let him leave without an additional demand.

In the kitchen, he grabbed a couple of energy bars and chewed one while he sought the keys for his Acadia.

He intended to buy the prisoner's requested food, but he discerned a need for something more. He remembered his concern the prior evening about his captive's pen.

Despite his surveillance technology, the basement prison seemed lacking in security, and he intended to boost his defenses against her escape.

And he smirked, thinking of the simplicity of the ancient method that would serve the need.

CHAPTER 28

Liam dreamt of a young woman burning on a cross, blood pouring from her heart's puncture wound. The prior night's murder haunted him, transforming the maiden into the homeless woman he'd discovered burning in a parking lot.

When he awoke, he shook off the nightmare and powered through his morning routine. He met his companions for breakfast in the hotel's dining area and gobbled his first plate.

Having earned a healthy appetite from last evening's chase, he returned to the brunch buffet line. A few sausage links and scrambled eggs landed on his plate, and he returned to the table with his father and the young student he'd saved last night.

Fishing for a response, he sat and tossed out a controversial comment. "We should talk about taking Judith home."

"Why should I go back? What's there for me?"

"School. A career in nursing."

"It can wait. I'm close enough to graduating. I can always finish next semester if I have to, but I can't always stop a killer."

"This hunt may take us weeks or months."

The gravity of the commitment pushed her into deep brooding, and she lowered her fork of salmon. "But I want to help."

"I appreciate that, but eleven hours ago, you were walking alone by the Detroit River stressing out over your homework."

"But then ten hours and fifty minutes hours ago, I was lying on my back saying my prayers. It changes your perspective."

His face hidden behind a bagel with cream cheese and lox, Connor added his thoughts. "She has a point."

"I understand, Father, but what of the practicality? We can't ask her to help us, can we?" He gave his father a harsh look and awaited his insights on the paranormal law against seeking direct help from others.

"We didn't ask her. She volunteered."

Wondering how the elder hunter could be nonchalant about skirting ironclad supernatural rules, Liam squirmed, and his throat tightened as he talked. "We can't let our little team grow unconstrained, can we?"

"Perhaps after brunch we can have a more private chat in our room, lad. Now, I think I'll also have some seconds."

In his hotel room, Liam challenged his father. "Rules are rules. Accepting direct help is a whisker's difference from asking for it."

"But it's not the same. If she wants to help, let her try. If she has something to offer, we'll figure out what it is. If not, she'll bore of us faster then we'll bore of her, and she'll find her way home."

"What about the dagger?

"It's twenty-eight days away from being useful again."

There had to be a flaw in the logic. "What if she runs off scared and asks for help? Wouldn't that bring divine wrath upon us?"

"It most certainly would, but we would implement safeguards."

Liam accelerated his pacing across the floor. "What sort of safeguards?"

"I haven't thought that far, but if she were to run for help, I'm sure we could avoid her and her would-be assistants. And I know we're allowed to accept volunteers as divine gifts. Remember, we have until the twenty-ninth to sort this out. Until then, we're just regular bounty hunters to her."

"Bounty hunters from Ireland, working in the United States, chasing a guy with an ancient Arabic accent who speaks British English, and we're doing this because the American police forces can't catch their own serial killer. What could possibly make her suspect something abnormal?"

Sitting on the extended stay suite's sofa, his father gave a paternal smile. "We don't know if there's a domestic search for him yet. There are enough murders now for lawmakers to draw a pattern, but they don't always publicize their searches."

"Understood."

"Just let her draw her own conclusions. We could use the company. Frankly, I think you could use someone your age to talk to once in a while."

"So, what's that mean? We set up our base here and continue our training and hunting while she, what? She ignores her schooling? Does her homework in the suite next door? Has friends and family worried about her spending time with strange men?"

"I'd say she'd be able to enjoy an adventure of a lifetime."

"Yeah, maybe in twenty-eight days. She can join us then, but not before then."

"You'd risk hunting with a stranger? You should get to know her before the next full moon, and it wouldn't hurt you to practice your combat first aid with her."

Liam ceased pacing. "This isn't a debate. You're telling me the plan because you're the man in charge, aren't you?"

"We're not particularly endowed with any spiritual powers or magic, but we must trust our intuition. Mine says she's valuable, and that's my final stance."

"We'll do it your way, Father, but what does that mean?"

"We invite her to live in the suite next door for the month. In exchange, we interview her for everything she saw and noticed about him and his possessions. Now that we've had a good night's sleep, we can recommence our detective work."

Liam started walking and turned towards the door. "Shouldn't we both visit her and tell her the news?"

"No, invite her here and make sure we always respect the privacy of her room."

"I'll get her." Liam stepped onto the second-floor walkway, continued to the adjacent room, and knocked. When she answered, wearing the same clothes from the prior evening, he forced a smile. "Can you join us in our room, please?"

"Yes."

She followed him to his father, who gestured to the empty chairs around the coffee table. "Please, sit. Both of you."

When all three were seated, Liam spoke. "My father and I have reached a conclusion."

"Yes, we'd like you to stay with us as long as you'd like. We can't promise you a better outcome than what you've already experienced. But you're welcome to stay in this hotel as our guest and join us in pursuing the man who attacked you."

Tears welled in her eyes. "I want to tell you something, but you'll think I'm crazy. I think I'm crazy."

"We chase a madman as our daily occupation, young lady. I can't see you saying much that would shock us."

"When I thought I was going to die, there was a stranger in my head who could hear my thoughts. And I could hear her thoughts. It was like we were sharing our spirits."

Liam remained silent while his father shared his wisdom and guidance.

"That is shocking. But by no means does it mean you're crazy. Under such duress, the human mind can play tricks."

Tears trickled down her face. "It didn't feel like a trick. It was a real conversation, and it ended when I knew I was safe."

"I'm sure this is all sane behavior. Please don't burden yourself with defeatist thoughts."

"I'll try not to."

"Liam, get her some tissues."

The young hunter marched into his bedroom, turned into the bathroom, and grabbed a handful from a dispenser. As he walked, he overheard her next claim.

"She's the one who told me to guard my heart. She saved me. It was like she was sent to protect me, but she said she was a prisoner. It's all too bizarre."

Liam returned to the living room and handed her the tissues. Since his father seemed drained of advice, he took over

191

the conversation. "We know he targets the heart. It's crazy that a woman none of us has met would know to warn you."

"I've learned enough of my mother's voodoo to know about lingering human souls and communicating with spirits."

"But you don't believe in it, do you?"

She shot him a wounded stare. "Why? Because it's witchcraft?"

"No, because you're studying western medicine."

She lowered her defenses and offered personal insight. "I believe what I experience. I've been sensitive to people's thoughts and emotions my entire life. My mother always said I was born to care for people. That's why I'm going to be a nurse. But there's no amount of medical training that can take away the importance of understanding people's nonverbal cues."

"Nonverbal, to include paranormal."

"If the evidence supports it, yes. And it just happened to me. So, make what you want of it."

Liam turned his back and paced towards the kitchenette. "I'd just like to understand it better. If this woman's real and she contacted you, she could be a clue. She could be an ally."

"She already is an ally to me. Her name's Diane. She told me."

Liam stopped at the breakfast table where pistol parts were laid bare on a towel for cleaning. He kept his back to her. "Understandable. But she's of no further use unless you can communicate with her again."

Conner reentered the conversation. "It's possible that strong emotion is the bridge. Extreme fear, but possibly extreme love, compassion... or even envy may drive such connections."

Liam placed pieces of the weapon together, assembling it with minimal noise. "That sounds reasonable, Father, but is there any evidence for such a thing?"

The questions probing into their ancestral secrets created an uncertainty in the elder hunter's voice. "Not that I've seen, at least not recently. I'm an old man, and anything I may remember from my youth is hazy."

Liam detected the half-lie as the elder hunter's attempt to

conceal the truth. Legends from their lineage recounted the survivor of a failed sacrifice one thousand years ago having been able to communicate telepathically with the ghosts of past victims. The survivor's testimony had given rise to the hunting sect that sought wraiths, and it confirmed the importance of extreme emotions. They were the bridge to telepathy. "You're sure you don't remember anything, Father?"

The elder hunter grunted. "No. Let's move on."

To allow himself the time to finish assembling the weapon, the younger hunter asked an open-ended question. "Is there anything else you remember about this woman, Diane, who helped you? Her voice? Her age? Her whereabouts? Was she alone? Could you hear or see her surroundings?"

"Take your time, young lady. He's being overzealous."

Liam moved the pistol's slide into place with a gentle click and then buried the barrel in the small of his back as he turned. He walked to the kitchen counter, opened a browser on his phone, and searched for a woman in Michigan named Diane who was abducted. The results confirmed she was still missing. "Sorry. I didn't mean to push."

"No, it's okay. She… Diane… had a voice that was strong but sweet. She seemed compassionate and concerned for me. She must be very empathetic. She said she was a prisoner, but she didn't say where or who held her, and I couldn't hear or see anything on her end. She did say she had special powers to allow our connection, though."

Convinced he needed to take decisive action, Liam finished typing notes into a text message, turned his phone sideways, and maximized the font size for ease of reading.

Sliding the phone in his pocket, he reached to his back for his sidearm, aimed it at Judith's face, and marched towards her. "I've heard enough of this shit! I know you're working with him. I know a setup when I see one. I don't know what you're after with your bloody lies, but you're not getting it. You've seen too much, and now you die."

His father stood and yelled. "Liam!"

"She's seen too much, Father. Way too much."

He pulled the trigger.

The weapon dry fired, and the bolt locked back, exposing the empty chamber.

Judith screamed and then curled forward in hysterical tears.

Liam withdrew the phone and placed it under her nose. "Focus, Judith! Focus, Diane! Read this, now!"

The text showed Diane's full name, the names of the hunters, a request for Diane to tell Judith everything she could about her imprisonment, and a commitment that the three pursuers would stop at nothing to rescue her.

Between tears and gasps, Judith spoke. "She sees it."

"Let her talk, Judith. Make her talk. Father, take notes."

"Right!"

Liam knelt in front of her to give the distant Diane a face to concentrate upon, and he pushed the pistol into the nursing student's temple. "Judith, stay scared. I'm crazy. I could kill you at any moment. Stay with Diane. Be afraid!"

"Okay! Okay!"

"Diane, stay with Judith as long as you can. I can only play this trick once, and this may be the last time we can connect with you. Tell her everything."

CHAPTER 29

The link was holding, and Diane shared her memories with Judith. Focusing on the face of her abductor, she willed his image into their shared mind. "Can you see his face from my memory?"

The would-be victim's voice was clear in Diane's mind. "Yes. That's the man who tried to kill me."

The successful identification encouraged her, but the recognition of her jailor as a killer scared her. "Is he going to kill me?"

"He kills only during full moons, and he always burns his victims. That's what Liam and Connor told me."

"That makes sense. I feel horrible stabbing chest pains when he kills. I just felt one last night, and I remember looking at the full moon while we... I mean, she was dying."

"He killed a homeless woman in Flint."

She thought of her brother, hurrying as Judith's fear ebbed. "Please tell my brother Josh what's going on. He must be terrified. He's autistic and will panic without me. I hope he's with Nana."

"Who's Nana?"

"My grandmother. She lives in Sterling Heights, Two-One-Eight Dover Street."

"I will visit her and find Josh."

She remembered she'd taught Josh to avoid strangers, unless they could prove they were her friend. Feeling the pressure of time, she mentally blurted her first idea. "To earn their trust, tell Josh that I started tarot readings because Nana told me to, and that I stopped tarot readings because he told me to."

"I will. Tell me more about where you are. Did you see

anything about the building?"

"I was blindfolded and wearing noise-canceling headphones when he moved me. I'm stuck in a basement, chained to a sink." She explained the floorplan as a series of memories, and Judith ingested the information like lightning.

"Tell me more. Can you hear anything?"

"I never hear people, but sometimes I hear splashing, like a fish in a pond or river."

"Got it."

The young man, Liam, faced her and interjected. "Can I ask a question?"

Rapid experimenting had revealed limits communicating outwardly to the Irishman. Judith had to remain silent to retain the focus on Diane, but she could nod or shake her head.

Diane compelled Judith to nod.

"Can you see any sunlight or shadows?"

Another nod.

"Good. Were you looking at the sunlight or shadows before you slipped into Judith's mind?"

Another nod.

"Share that memory with Judith. She'll draw it later. The angles of the sunlight or shadows can help us find you."

Diane recalled her last glance at the rays that had cracked through the curtains' edges. One of them had cut a line over the area rug, and she prayed the hunters could benefit from the image.

Judith digested the memory. "Good. I've got it. I'll draw it."

"Can you ask Liam what I should do?"

"Not now. I would lose you. I'm afraid I already..."

"What?"

"I'm losing..."

The connection died, returning Diane to the confining, brown basement.

Alone, she let herself cry to process the rush of emotions that were a blend of her own and those she'd inherited from Judith. The tears expunged toxic chemicals and bad thoughts, and when she was done sobbing, she worked her leg irons over the couch.

When she reached the bathroom, she wiped her eyes and blew her nose. The persistent, pestering thought was the identity of her captor as a murderer.

She could have deduced his killing capacity as a logical conclusion of her abduction, but the finality of the shared insight with Judith consumed her with a tingling chill.

The chill worsened when she heard a door opening upstairs. To eliminate any chance of her captor suspecting her telepathy, she returned to the couch and opened a book. She frowned at herself when she realized her paranoia–telepathy left no clues, but appearing on the couch where he expected her was wise.

Through the locked door atop the staircase and through the walls and floorboards, she heard him stepping about the kitchen. He opened the refrigerator, cupboards, and cellophane wrappers.

The door clicked open, the staircase light came on, and his footsteps creaked.

He appeared at the bottom of the stairs with a plate of food balanced on four books. "A sandwich of low-fat turkey, low-fat ham, lettuce, and wholegrain bread."

She sensed he appreciated, or at least expected, cordiality. "Thank you."

"I'll leave it on the bar for you. And I have your books." With four hardcovers under the plate, he moved his fingers aside, lowered the books to the bar, and balanced the food on them. "I'll be back with your new clothes."

She recalled that serial killers could display excessive charisma, but this one seemed undecided between charming her and torturing her to death.

If he wanted her as his next victim, she wondered why he was waiting. From her fusion with Judith, she'd picked up on the lunar timing, but he'd taken her prior to yesterday's full moon.

Why had he killed a homeless woman when he had an easy victim available in his basement? Could she be an insurance policy against a failed night of killing, like reserve sustenance in a predator's lair?

Worried she may become food, she stared at her lunch.

"Well, if you don't eat it, I won't bother making you sandwiches again."

In the unfolding game of innuendoes and charades, she thought appeasement offered her the best advantage. "I'm sorry. I'm sure it's great."

He grunted, turned, and answered over his shoulder. "I'll bring your new clothes."

Hungry, she performed her couch-acrobatics to reach the sandwich, and she grabbed a cup of water from an end table to wash down bites. She powered through half her lunch, scanning the titles he'd left her–Grisham, Childs, Brown, and Patterson. She expected at least one of them to hold her interest.

Carrying clothing bags, the murderer returned and heaped new underwear and pajamas onto the couch. "I got different colors so that you can tell them apart."

"Thank you."

Again, he seemed unsure how to behave. Something about her, the house, or perhaps her unseen powers, unnerved him. "You'll need a laundry basket."

"I'll use these shopping bags for now."

"Very well. Do you need anything else?"

She wanted him gone, and she dismissed him. "I'm fine."

He departed up the stairs.

Sinking into her couch, she processed the information surrounding her predicament. The freshest knowledge from Judith weighed heavily atop the shreds she'd been gathering since her ordeal had begun.

But before she could make headway, she heard the electronic beeping of a large truck moving in reverse.

Unwilling to torment herself with the false hope of a

rescuer, she listened and evaluated.

For minutes, nothing happened. But then she heard renewed beeping coupled with hydraulic hisses followed by a loud rumble. Then again, silence.

Trying to calm herself before sorting her thoughts, she grabbed a hardbound book and propped it open on her lap. After reading two chapters, she heard a commotion in the back yard.

A squeaky wheel and the echoing thud of hard cement against metal grew louder. Against her will, her hopes rose of rescue, but then she saw her captor pushing a wheelbarrow full of cinderblocks.

He left the construction material in place and departed. Moments later, he came down the stairs and rushed to the wall.

She studied him with curiosity, but while watching him, she let her thoughts wander back to herself.

Strengthened by her telepathic union with Judith, Diane's confidence in her empathic powers soared. Tarot cards had been fuzzy feelings, stabbing victims had been painful pleas, but Judith was her first repeated connection, both symbiotic and effective with its clarity.

Through Judith and by accident, she'd learned to fuse two minds, reaping the benefits of both intellects while overcoming the spiritual and emotional baggage of either.

Success brought her to a new plateau of self-understanding and a tendency to trust herself more.

As she watched her jailer tend to his task, he seemed distant from a desire to kill. She judged him as hyper-arrogant but selective in his violence based upon her read of his comportment, and she recognized his internal struggle.

He fought against himself to respect her.

She realized that she meant something to him beyond tallying another kill. He needed her for something, and it hurt his ego to know it.

Exploiting a possible vulnerability, she tested her intuition against his actions. "What are you doing?"

"You'll see." He stepped behind the curtain, unlocked the bar blocking one of the two sliding doors, and wrestled the glass aside.

Pondering what he might be building, he dashed her expectations of an exterior facade when he reversed the wheelbarrow into the basement and dumped blocks onto the worn area rug.

As she watched in puzzled curiosity while he muscled a dozen loads into the room, she realized he intended to build a wall inside the basement.

But her astonishment faded when she grasped that his behavior suggested his need for her. The barrier would serve as a failsafe against her possible luck in overcoming her chains, and its construction signaled her importance to him.

And being important implied leverage.

With leverage and growing empathic powers, she allowed herself to fantasize for a moment about her evasion. She thought of hugging Josh and promising to care for him forever, and she knew she'd fight with every resource she had, material or ethereal, to protect him.

Her jailor started the bottom row of blocks running along the wall closest to her. As he turned to parallel the exterior wall of glass, she realized the perpendicular foundation would buttress the final impasse of her escape route to the outside. Then he completed the bottom row by extending another perpendicular foundation at the far wall by the unused television.

He darted up the stairs, and she heard running water and a gravely sound like sand being poured. She then heard heavy steps descending the stairs, and he reappeared, muscling a five-gallon bucket. Walking around his piled inventory, he reached his line of foundational blocks and lowered the plastic tub to the faded rug.

He lifted a trowel from the wheelbarrow, jammed it into the bucket, and withdrew gray mortar. Spreading it over adjoining halves of two blocks, he seemed uncaring about the mess he made while dripping gray drops of goo.

He rested the trammel on the growing wall, reached for a block, and lowered it onto the mortar. With the tool, he shaved off the excess gray matter and deposited it onto the next set of blocks.

She blurted her question. "Why are you doing this?"

"Don't be dull-witted. It's a wall to keep you in."

"You've kept me in with chains."

His response sounded cynical. "I've been having a run of bad luck recently."

"I can't break out of all this metal!"

"You're smart enough to find a way if given enough time. Maybe you're lucky enough, too. Stop talking."

Her interest became passing glances during the hours he moved with methodic discipline. At the curtains' corners, she saw the sun's light fading to orange as the checkered wall reached his chest. His economization of material caught her attention when she noticed he'd spaced the blocks apart to save material and weight.

The wall was becoming a barrier, but she'd be able to see through its gaps–if she ever broke her chains and could rip down the curtain.

He continued for another hour, and then he ran out of bricks two feet below the ceiling. Instead of revealing frustration, he seemed pleased with his perfection.

Analyzing his architecture, she realized he was leaving a way out over the top–for himself. It was an elevated exit for someone with the athleticism to climb, unencumbered by leg irons, and the strength to break the glass wall despite poor leverage.

She speculated why he'd leave himself an escape route, but definitive answers eluded her.

He grabbed the bucket and headed towards the stairs. "I'll also be installing a deadbolt at the top of the stairs. I don't want you thinking you can escape, not by any route at all."

CHAPTER 30

Earlier that morning, Liam stooped over the recovering nursing student, extending a cup of tea. She'd just lost the link with Diane, and watching his new partner's suffering hurt. "I'm sorry."

She wrapped her hands around the steaming beverage. "You scared the hell out of me."

"I thought it would help, but I am really sorry."

"Yeah, it helped, but you didn't even give me a chance to try it another way. Maybe we can communicate in our sleep."

"You slept last night and didn't mention anything about it."

"So what? That was cruel!"

"I said I was sorry."

Healing from his handgun act, she sipped her tea. "What's done is done. Give me some paper."

Liam darted to a desk and grabbed a hotel-branded scratch pad and a pen. As she set her teacup on the coffee table, he placed the pad on her lap, and she drew.

The crude scribbling showed a dark curtain covering a wall of glass with a streak of sunlight reaching out over a hardwood floor but falling short of an area rug. She ripped off the paper and handed it to him.

As she started an overhead rendition of Diane's basement, Liam stepped into his bedroom and grabbed his compass. He reversed direction, darting outside the suite to check the angle of the shadows.

He aligned the streak in Judith's drawing with the shadows, and then he balanced the compass on a flat handrail. When the numbers settled, he had a sense of the orientation of the structure surrounding the captive.

Lacking an angle of declination to the sun feeding the rays into Diane's basement, he gave up hope of establishing her latitude, but knowledge of the geography of the prison's glass wall had become a clue.

He returned to the room to share his analysis with his father and Judith. "The back wall runs on the line of bearing between three-zero-five and one-two-five, plus or minus twenty degrees, I'd say."

"She's drawn the basement floorplan, too."

"Good. That'll help. Now comes the hard part of putting it all together."

Recovered from her scare, Judith sank into her chair with her tea. "We need to hurry. The guy who's holding her is the man who tried to kill me."

"You're sure?"

Her response was defiant. "Of course, I'm sure."

"I had to ask. That's good news, actually. It means we're chasing only one guy for two reasons–to stop him from killing a tribute in twenty-eight days and to rescue Diane."

"She says she can hear splashes in some nearby water once in a while, like jumping fish, but no nearby people."

"That's useful. She's near water in a secluded area."

"You guys know that describes half of the houses up north in Michigan, don't you?"

"Then that's half we don't have to look at." Liam grabbed a laptop from the kitchen and brought it to the living room. He lowered it into his lap as he sat on the couch. Hoping for assistance and confirmation from his partners, he voiced the parameters he considered for his search criteria. "I don't think he'd buy a house. I'm looking primarily for rentals."

Finished with her notes, Judith leaned sideways in her chair. "Why wouldn't he buy?"

"It's harder to fake his identity for a real estate purchase, and the movement of that much money from outside the country might grab federal attention. It's possible that he bought, but I'd rather start with rentals."

"Every house in Michigan has a basement. That's still a lot of real estate to look for."

Liam reflected upon the wraith's timeline. The soonest he would have known about the ritual site's location was December.

Connor added his knowledge. "But we also know he wasn't looking before December, and since he took Diane on the tenth, that narrows our timing."

"How can you guys be sure about December?"

The young hunter shrugged. "We just know."

She pursed her lips but left the evasive answer unchallenged. "That's the off-season. Hardly anyone goes up north in the winter."

Her comment stimulated Liam's idea for a shortcut. "He's methodical, not one to leave something to chance. He probably rented the place before April. And it was a long-term rental, too. It would more appropriately be a lease. He'd probably take it for a year."

"What good is all this? It's still a big search."

"If my logic's correct, his house is no longer on the market. If we can find all the houses that were listed in Northern Michigan between December and early April, we'll have the house where he's keeping her."

"And then you filter out the ones that are still available for seasonal rental, or still for sale, to be complete?"

He sensed the possibility of attacking the savage in his own lair, saving not just the virgin sacrifice but months of tributes. "Correct. It's still a lot of properties, but most of it can be done with hard work and automation. There may be several dozen rental and purchase sites, but I can create some bots to crawl them, scrape their screens, and download the data for comparison."

"I don't follow."

"I'll buy access to some archives, take weekly snapshots of listings from December through March, and then I'll set up a program to peel off and download the addresses. That's all it takes for establishing the possible universe of houses."

"Then you'll filter out what's still available."

"Right. I'll also filter where possible by houses that don't have basements. Not all search sites have filters. I'll have to use keywords in some searches."

His father offered a valuable filter. "And single-family properties. He wouldn't risk a shared property for the type of things he does."

"Good point, Father."

Connor perked up as he contributed. "Oh, and I can get you the same access to listings as real estate professionals."

"Multiple Listing Service? How?"

"Through the order, of course."

Liam glared at the elder hunter with an inquiry about the order at his lips, but his father shook his head to preempt the question. Connor's tight eyes told the younger hunter he'd learn about the order when the secret decided to share itself.

Judith leaned forward and glanced at her scratchpad of notes, as if her handwriting validated her memory. "I remember her saying she couldn't hear people but sometimes hears splashing fish from a pond or stream."

"The isolation is consistent with his mode of operation. I might be able to prioritize houses that are listed as waterfront, but I wouldn't rely on it as filter. Maybe as a sorting function based upon keywords. This will get tricky."

The older hunter leaned forward in his chair. "You can also limit your geography. Since he came from the southeast and was driving north through Flint before discovering he was being followed, you can rule out anything south and east of Flint."

The student nodded her agreement. "More or less. He was on the major highway heading north. He might have veered a bit to the northeast of Flint, though."

Then his father added a final, revealing constraint. "Remember the three-hundred-mile arc from Cleveland, too. That will clip off portions of your search."

Judith probed. "What's up with Cleveland and three hundred miles?"

Liam realized his newest partner was unwilling to accept a fact without its historical context. "It's weird, but you'll have to believe us. He never travels more than three hundred miles from his... home, at least his temporary home. He moves every so often, sets up a new home, and does his killing within a three-hundred-mile radius."

A frown darkened her face. "How can you know that, and the police don't?"

"The police don't want him as badly as we do."

"How long have you been chasing him?"

Flustered, Liam ran lies through his mind to explain how his seventy-four-year-old father had spent his entire life hunting a man who looked thirty-three.

But his father's choice of words provided a truthful response. "I reckon time differently than you younger people. I hardly remember a time when I wasn't hunting him. For Liam, it's been since his childhood."

"He must've done something awful to someone in your family?"

"We'd prefer not to talk about it. In fact, I've asked Liam to consider it a sort of family secret. Perhaps we'll share more after we have our revenge."

Grateful his father deflected Judith's curiosity, Liam looked to his computer to identify real estate listing sites for his archive retrieval. "I'm going to start our online search. Once I get my automations going, I'll see how many properties we need to look at. It's going to be a lot, probably several thousand. Then we'll have to look at maps, floorplans, satellite images... whatever it takes to narrow it down one by one."

"This might work. We've got twenty-eight days, at least."

Liam shot an angry stare at his father. "We've got twenty-eight days, period."

The elder hunter nodded, and Liam questioned their agreement on the urgency. Before he could voice a penetrating question, Judith lifted her phone towards her ear. "I know some people at school who'd be willing to help. I'll call them now."

Liam cried out. "No!"

"Why not? I'm sure they'd want to help."

"That's not the problem."

"What's the problem, then?"

Liam sought a truth that skimmed the surface. "That link you had with Diane... we know that if you ask for help and share your experience in this hunt, bad things will happen. Your link may become weaker. You may lose it completely."

She stood and glared at him. "You both saved my life and have been perfect gentlemen, but I think that's crazy. It's time you start including me in your secret club."

Liam sighed in defeat and looked to his father. "Well?"

"I think we owe the young lady some answers."

"Good. I deserve some answers. We can talk in the car. I just remembered that Diane wants me to contact her brother. She thinks he's worried about her."

Liam saw a flaw in her plan. "What would we tell him? You've established a telepathic link with his sister, but it only works when you're terrified, and we don't know where she is?"

"She said he's autistic. I don't know how he'll respond. But she wanted me to contact him. Since she didn't leave a phone number, I suggest you both pack a bag and prepare for an overnight visit."

"This is dangerous."

His father added his wisdom. "But he might know something useful to our efforts."

"What could an autistic kid know that could help us?"

"We don't know until we ask him."

"Connor's right. I sensed a special connection between them. I think he'll be receptive and helpful."

The young hunter found the data influx bordering on overwhelming. "Fine, then. We'll take our chances seeking out her brother, but I want to know more before we go."

"I feel like I need to talk to him as soon as possible. Why should we wait?"

"Let me scour the Internet for a few hours first. I want to understand how complex the online search will be. If I'm going to give this young man any hope, I want an estimate of how many houses we need to check to find her."

CHAPTER 31

That night, Jacob rolled from the mattress to his feet. His back and arms were sore from constructing the cinderblock wall and from the evening gratifying himself with his servant, Kim, the barista. "You stay here. I need to leave."

"Where are you going?"

He turned to the bed and grabbed her arm. Glaring at her and feeling his hunger for power, he strengthened the red ring rising around her pupils. "You will never again ask me where I'm going."

Trapped in his domineering spirit-god's spell, she succumbed to his command. He noted a hint of sadness, as if part of her lamented her otherworldly servitude. "I won't ask again."

He released her. "Good. You'll stay here through Thursday midnight. Until then, don't travel more than five miles away. I want you ready for my call."

"I'll be here."

He raced into his clothes and grabbed two weapons cases from the floor, equipping him with the M-16 assault rifle and the twelve-gauge shotgun she'd registered in her name and had carried to Traverse City.

Carrying a case in each hand out of the hotel, he hurried to his Acadia and placed the weapons on the back seat. Lifting his phone, he checked his basement cameras to verify his prisoner's compliance.

As he expected, she lay sleeping on the couch.

He accelerated the vehicle into the dark street, and he drove a memorized path to his cabin. The short trip passed in a blur, and he reached the driveway, where he slowed the vehicle and reached for his garage door opener.

A barrier of white materialized ahead of the SUV's grill, and he stepped on the brake.

Standing, a legion of countless ghosts blocked his way. Each female apparition wore the milky white, flowing dresses of their afterlives, and each one stared at him with black, lifeless orbs.

Led by the French maiden he'd bound to a cross and murdered in a millhouse half a century ago, the nine sacrifices of the past five hundred years formed a phalanx in front of the horde. Behind those from whom he'd stolen life, countless tributes stood in a rectangular formation, becoming a ghastly blur boring through the cabin and into the woods beyond.

He'd never seen them all at once, and they terrified him.

The French maiden's colorless lips moved. "Why did you kill me?"

Refusing to answer, he sought the accelerator to drive through them and transform them into mist.

But his leg rejected his brain's command.

He remained paralyzed, staring at the horde.

Floating, the maiden moved towards him, slipped through the Acadia's engine compartment, and lowered her head through the windshield. "Why did you kill me?"

Trembling, he watched her, and she leaned her translucent face an inch from his nose. Her voice boomed with glacial frigidity and then rocketed to a torrid shriek. "You betrayed me. I will be avenged!"

She passed through him, chilling his internal organs, and the next ghost appeared, howling in his face. "You betrayed me. I will be avenged!"

One by one, all the victims of his dagger shot through him, pelting him with their wailed warning. "You betrayed me. I will be avenged!"

Hyperventilating as the train of the final phantom's dress whipped through his face, he spent helpless minutes recovering from shock. As his breathing slowed and his thoughts cleared, he shook with rage and pounded his fist into the dashboard. "Damn them!"

He drove the vehicle into the garage and parked. He clicked the motor into motion, concealing his two SUVs. Trembling in anger, he barged into the house and hurried down the stairs to his inmate.

The pending sacrifice lay sleeping. He glared at her and kicked the couch. "Wake up!"

Startled, she cringed and opened her eyes. "What?"

"Make them stop!"

"Make who stop?"

Her ignorance of the ethereal attack infuriated him. He would have preferred defiance, which he could have addressed with cruelty. But she appeared unaware of the phantoms' tormenting. "You don't know what I'm talking about?"

"I have no idea."

"Damn you!" He trotted up the stairs.

Aftershocks of the fear his victims' ghosts had inflicted upon him flooded him with adrenaline and drove him to desperation. He staggered into the living room and dropped to his knees. "Master, I beg you. What must I do?"

The response burrowed into his head with non-sensory but tangible meaning. His lording spirit wanted him to offer Diane, his intended sacrifice, as tribute under the next full moon.

A drastic change.

The revelation of transforming a sacrifice into a tribute frightened him, until he reflected upon it.

Diane had been troublesome since the beginning. The cold shocks when he touched her skin were a warning that someone or something protected her. She was dangerous, and his domineering spirit's command to convert her from a sacrifice to a tribute was logical.

She was an aberration requiring removal.

Falling forward to the carpet, he thanked his demonic lord for his guidance. After a minute of silent homage, he rose to his feet, and he let a question pass through him.

Would his Master provide him a substitute sacrifice before the January full moon?

Convincing himself of an answer, he paced.

Of course, his Master would. He had to. He'd demanded tribute, tribute implied followership, and followership implied reward.

Growing calmer, Jacob walked to his bedroom, continued over the worn carpet to his bed, and knelt before the monstrous safe. He pinched the mechanical tumbler and twisted it back and forth to his memorized code. Opening the massy door, he saw his weapon case. He grabbed it and marched towards his prisoner.

At the bottom of the stairs, he turned on the overhead lights, illuminating the dark room. Admiring his day's work, he noticed the grayish cinderblock barrier providing the basement an unfinished air, but it reflected the lighting better than the brown curtains.

Under the lighting, his prisoner moaned as she awoke. "Why'd you wake me up again?"

"Stand up."

"Why?"

With her shortened sentence, he hoped his lording spirit would allow a lessening of his politeness. "I said stand up!"

She pushed her blankets aside and heaved her leggings to the floor. The chain tethering her to the toilet tightened over the couch's back as she balanced herself on her feet. "What's in your hand?"

He lifted the weapon case. "Oh, you like this?"

"I just asked what it was."

"I'm glad you asked. I'll show you." Kneeling, he placed the case on the hardwood and opened it. The bronze dagger shone with the lighting's reflection as he stood and aimed it towards her.

As her eyes focused on it, her features froze in fear, and the reaction surprised him.

"You've seen this before?"

"No. It just looks… special."

He pinched the blade between his thumb and fingers and extended the handle over the coffee table that separated them.

She hesitated to accept his offer.

"Hold it."

"No."

"Hold it!"

She reached up with her right hand, and as her fingers met the handle, the familiar icy chill of her skin worked its way through the bronze and to his flesh.

Recoiling, he dropped the knife, and it clanged against the table.

She outpaced him in reacting, and her grip found the dagger before his. She lifted the weapon between them.

"You're not threatening me with my own knife, are you?"

"What if I was? Would you Tase me again?"

For her insolence, he wanted to threaten her with a pistol to her kneecaps, but he sensed his Master preventing it. Instead, he spoke the truth. "Yes, I would Tase you again."

Reversing the dagger's direction, she cradled the blade in her palm and offered him the handle.

"No, put it down."

She placed it on the table.

"Step aside three paces."

Rolling her eyes, she obeyed, and her shackles clinked as she shimmied. Though she appeared lean, he respected the possibility of her hidden strength and wanted her out of punching range.

When she'd moved beyond his estimate of her reach, he stooped, grabbed the blade, and lowered it to his hip. "Now come back."

She stood before him, staring at him with defiant eyes.

"You've been trouble since I met you."

"I could say the same about you."

"You're lucky that I have patience for your impertinence."

"Well, your knife is lovely. Did you wake me up again just to show it to me?"

Hoping to see a sign of the force that protected her, he looked for an aura he'd missed or something off kilter with her energy. She seemed normal, but he sensed the icy barrier, even from a distance. "Something's wrong."

"Yeah, you kidnapped me."

"Something's... standing between us."

"There's nothing between us."

He inspected her.

She wore blue and black checkered pajamas, panties, and a tank top, all of which he'd purchased. Her personal possessions included two rings, a bracelet, and a necklace.

He'd considered the jewelry innocuous. But after his demon spirit's latest guidance, he felt leeway in challenging them as her protective source. "Take off your rings."

She yanked off a silver ring with a cast shape of a tree and ring with stones of Pearl and Tourmaline.

"Place them on the table and stick out your hand."

She obeyed.

With her fingers dangling over the coffee table, he tapped her knuckles, which felt icy. "Now remove the bracelet."

She unclipped the sterling silver chains and dropped the piece to the table.

He glared at it and noticed the carved tarot shapes of a wand, a pentacle, a sword, and a cup. "Your hand."

Again, she obeyed.

He tried the touch test again, but the icy chill endured. "Now the necklace."

"It's a gift from my grandmother."

"I don't care."

"I promised her I'd never take it off. You seem to be a man of your word. Certainly, you respect promises."

"I didn't make the promise. Don't move." He lifted the bronze blade to her collarbone and inserted it under her necklace. Jerking the knife's edge upward, he severed two links, and the moonstone with its silver-shaped dagger backing hit the floor.

She stooped to retrieve it.

He extended his free hand and seized her wrist. Her skin's warmth excited him. Separated from the moonstone amulet, she was touchable, and during a moment of discovery, he locked eyes with her. The red aura he'd seen when his Master had originally revealed her as his sacrifice had faded to a distant memory. The red irises he expected in his servant playthings were also absent. She remained flesh and blood with her native brown eyes, reducing her to a tribute. "Step away."

As she backed up, he released her.

Unwilling to touch the pendant, he grabbed a book off the table and used it to swat the fallen jewelry beyond her reach. He glared at her.

She seemed defeated and weak, unworthy of providing his source of continued life.

And that suited him. In twenty-eight days, she'd join ranks with his victims.

CHAPTER 32

After breakfast, Liam checked the final run of his automated filters. They listed six thousand and eighteen possible houses in which the killer could be imprisoning Diane.

He computed the effort, allotting ten minutes to each property, resulting in more than one thousand hours of work. Although he hoped to work faster, he accounted for inefficiencies, breaks, and distractions in the redundant and mind-numbing task.

Three people working ten hours a day would need thirty-four days to whittle the list to a subset of structures for spying upon with the drone.

Assuming one in twenty properties would be worthy of the hovercraft's inspection, he counted six hundred short-list candidates. Allotting half an hour for each aerial operation and ten hours per day of spying, he added another thirty days to the task.

Sixty-four days of work.

With the law of averages, he expected to lose one tribute at the end of the month. If bad luck trumped his efforts, another might die under June's full moon.

He tried to concentrate on the positives, the lives he would save, including Diane's.

Carrying an overnight bag, his father emerged from his bedroom. "Are you ready?"

"No. Sorry, I've been busy. It won't take me long to pack."

"How many houses did you find?"

"A lot. The more interesting question is how many did I reduce it to. Just over six thousand."

"What does that mean for our search?"

"About thirty-four days of full-time work for all three of us to look at each listing online. Then we'll rule out the ones that don't match what we know about the physical description and investigate them. That's another thirty days."

"That sounds like a lot of work."

"It's tedious, but it's far better than waiting."

"I'll have to trust you."

"I'll start looking in the Jeep, if you'll drive."

His father's eyes were soft and inquisitive. "You know, you've failed to mention one important clue in your search criteria."

Liam anticipated the elder hunter's meaning. "Do you mean the requirement that the ritual site is located on desecrated land, connected to violent deaths?"

"Yes. Precisely."

Liam tried to minimize his cynicism. "Real estate search engines don't normally track that."

"But there must be other sources."

"Of course, there are. Sites of famous killings, haunted sites, locations of old battles. We may never know, but my guess given Michigan's history is that we'll find the wraith's lair on a Native American burial mound."

"But such knowledge can't help you find him?"

"Unfortunately not, but we'll use the knowledge I have." Liam dashed into his bedroom and packed clothes for an overnight trip to Southeast Michigan. Thinking ahead to possibilities, he grabbed his large drone, in case a spying opportunity arose.

A quick detour into the mid-morning sunlight and to the adjacent room found Judith prepared to leave, and the trio climbed into the Jeep with Liam setting up a mobile office in the back seat.

Judith navigated as his father drove, and the young hunter's laptop consumed his interest. Sorting by city, he started close to Flint and moved west and north. With his bots having created a list of single-family units that had been available during the off-season but were now off the market, he'd generated an Excel spreadsheet with his six thousand and eighteen candidates.

He opened a browser and typed in the first rental's address. Though he thought the wraith's lair would be a vacation rental farther north, diligence demanded his inspection of residential properties, and Flint contributed hundreds to the list. When the first address appeared on a map, land surrounded it.

Without a nearby body of water, he switched to his spreadsheet and updated the house as an exclusion. The next seven properties lacked adjacent water, but he judged the ninth within earshot of the Flint River.

He clicked a dot on the map, bringing up pictures of the structure, a ranch resting on a slab foundation. Lacking a basement, the home fell from his list.

The tenth candidate had a basement, but its rectangular shape ran north and south, diverging from the angle of the sun Judith had seen through Diane's eyes in her prison cell.

He grunted.

Judith took pity on him. "How's it going back there?"

"Ten down, only six thousand and eight to go."

"Can I help?"

Expecting the nursing student to be adept with information technology, he reached into his backpack and withdrew a second laptop. "Sure. I'll forward you a subset of the list to search. We'll combine results later."

An hour later, Liam noted the Jeep was within twenty miles of the houses he searched. Inspecting the twenty-first property on his list, he found a structure oriented the correct way, near water, and with a basement. "Here's one."

"Where?"

"About seventeen miles away, in Flint."

"There's no hurry to visit Diane's grandmother."

"Let's do it. There's a park nearby called Mott Park. Let's go, and I'll launch the drone from there."

After grabbing the latitude and longitude of an advantageous vantage point in the property's backyard, he reached over the seat into the trunk for the hovercraft's controller. He typed in the coordinates, the desired hovering altitude above ground, and the direction for the camera's pointing. He waited for his father to exit Interstate 75 and navigate to the park before unpacking the aircraft.

When the Jeep stopped in the concrete lot, Liam stepped out and opened the hatchback. As part of his daily routine, he verified the secure location of the dagger's case, and without opening it, he knew the weapon inside was safely stowed.

He withdrew the aircraft from the trunk and placed it on the Grand Cherokee's roof. As his curious partners joined him, he tapped the controller's touchscreen, placing it in automatic mode. "It's going to fly to the location by itself."

He invoked a final command, and the drone whipped its four rotors to life and ascended. Glancing at the tablet resting in the trunk, he watched the drone's visual view of the park from the sky.

Judith grabbed the tablet and stared at it, mesmerized. "That's all it takes?"

"That's it. Cool technology." Liam realized she lacked the disposable income or leisure time to enjoy such a toy.

She pointed to the screen. "There. I think I already see the house."

Liam stooped beside her and watched the aerial perspective overfly a small subdivision. Indicating the drone's descent, the targeted house grew larger, and the Flint River passed underneath. With graceful ease, the camera stopped, pointed to the back of the house, and hovered.

The basement was a walkout, but instead of a glass wall, it had several windows cut into a façade of vinyl siding. Through the panes, Liam saw movement by a lamp. "Let's try something, just to be sure." He tapped an icon on the tablet to switch to the infrared camera, and he saw the outlines of three warm bodies in the basement sitting around a table in a

219

reading position.

"They're probably Kettering students studying."

"I'll scratch this one off this list and bring back the drone." With one touch, he commanded the hovercraft into its return flight to the Jeep. In under two minutes, it landed atop the SUV, and Liam packed it in the trunk.

As the drive continued, Liam and Judith reviewed more than fifty properties, citing two additional candidates worthy of hovercraft review, but future inspections would wait until after the attempt to meet Diane's family.

When Connor pulled the car into the Sterling Heights subdivision of Diane's grandmother, Judith voiced an objection. "I should do this alone."

Liam took offense. "I thought we were a team."

"It's just a sense I got from Diane. Too many people will scare her brother."

"Okay, do you want us to park out of sight?"

His father corrected him. "You're thinking like a hunter. Think instead like a gentleman. It would be wrong to make a lady walk the distance, and it would appear odd if she showed up unannounced without a vehicle. Let's find a coffee shop where you can show me how to search for houses, and we'll let Judith take the car."

Fifteen minutes later, Liam sipped a green tea latte while his father tipped back his brewed coffee. Through the shop's window, he watched Judith merge the SUV into traffic, and an odd thought entered his mind. "How stupid would you feel if we never saw her again?"

"That would be quite a turn of events. What would make you think of such a thing?"

"Part of me says, if I were her, I'd keep on driving back to Detroit, finish my degree, and get a job as far away from here as possible."

"Oh, I think you're overreacting."

"Think of what she's been through in just three days. Someone came within milliseconds of ramming a dagger through her heart, yesterday I dry-fired a pistol into her face, and then she had a telepathic link with an imprisoned stranger begging her for help."

His father lowered his cup. "Let's trust divine providence a little more than that, shall we? She seems genuinely engaged in joining us. And whether she comes back or not, you still need to teach me how to look at houses on the computer. So, let's not bother with such defeatist thoughts."

Liam slid closer to his father, focused the elder hunter on the laptop resting open on the table, and braced himself to invoke infinite patience as a teacher.

Thirty minutes into the lesson, Liam thought his father was reaching self-sufficiency in searching.

His phone chimed, and he lifted it to his ear. "Hello, Judith?"

"I'm with Diane's brother and grandmother. You wouldn't believe what I've learned already. You'll be glad we came."

CHAPTER 33

Diane paced behind the couch, her leg irons jingling with each step. Weeks of bondage compounded the aggravation of her imprisonment, and she wanted to kick her legs to enjoy the freedom of flexibility.

Sustained walking provided modest movement and an outlet for processing her feelings. The loss of her amulet the prior evening weighed upon her, and she tried to walk off her nervous energy and avoid falling into despair.

Recalling that losing her protective pendant had given the killer access to her skin, she feared he'd exploit the newfound liberty with physical abuse. As she tried to walk her mind into calmness, her imagination tormented her with unmentionable scenarios.

She wanted to scream and cry, but she swallowed back her emotions. Hearing footsteps in the room above, she was aware of her captor's presence, and no matter what happened, she would deny him any sadistic satisfaction in her suffering.

She paced faster.

Without her amulet, she questioned if her murderer could wield power over her to block her telepathy. Though she hoped Judith's silence since the blade had severed the necklace was a coincidence, she sensed a growing danger. Fueled by paranoia, supernatural insight, or a blend of each, her intuition braced her to expect increasing evil.

She paced faster.

Mulling over the madman's behaviors, she noticed stymying inconsistencies. At first, he'd wrestled with an internal conflict to treat her with dignity. As his need to keep her had overpowered his ego, he'd provided for her comfort, and she interpreted yesterday's cinderblock construction as validation of her value.

She paced faster.

But when he'd shaken her awake to brandish his dagger and to scan her for a protective artifact, her fate had shifted. His demeanor had become harsher, and she sensed her value falling. Whatever comfort she'd drawn from believing in the temporal distance to her pending danger had diminished, and time had become her enemy overnight.

She stopped pacing.

A tingle crept up her spine, and she spun around.

The apparition facing her had appeared from nowhere.

She wore the milky white, flowing dress of her afterlife and stared with black, lifeless orbs. Speaking French but with clear meaning, she greeted Diane with a peaceful tone. "I have been allowed to help you."

Diane reached for her, and her hand passed through the intangible mist of the ghost's frame, chilling her skin. "How do I know you're real?"

"You are an empath. You know."

"I'm an empath from the line of Nineveh. I remember that from my dreams, but I'm not dreaming now, am I?"

"You are an empath. You know."

Accepting the terse reply, Diane agreed she was awake and the ethereal maiden was real, but she found her vexing with her vagueness. "I got that, but who are you?"

"I am the one who was sacrificed before you."

The implication stung. "I'm going to be sacrificed?

"You were destined for it, but now you are destined to be offered as tribute, unless you heed me."

"Heed you?"

"I have three insights."

Diane found the ghost's offer lacking substance. "Insights? I'm trapped down here waiting to be raped, tortured, and killed–who knows what that freak's going to do to me–and you're going to give me advice?"

The maiden continued, undeterred. "First, you must escape by the next full moon, or you will die. You have twenty-seven days."

Her heart racing, Diane panicked. She'd suspected the pending doom, but hearing it as a prophecy pained her. "Is that news supposed to help me?"

The ghost kept her unearthly composure while leaving the question unanswered. "Second, selflessness is the key to your power."

Digesting the knowledge, Diane began to doubt the apparition's value. "So, I'm supposed to be selfless while I get killed?"

"Remove the distractions of selfishness. Care not for your needs but for the welfare of others, and your clear and caring mind will invoke your powers. You will see truths, view remote visions, communicate over distance, and sense people's emotions."

"How does any of that get me out of here?"

"You have allies, the tribute you saved and those who hunt the one who threatens you. Seek them."

"The Irish men? Liam's the name of one of them?"

"Yes."

Diane's breathing slowed as she grasped her first tangible option to save herself. If the apparition told the truth, tapping into Judith's mind again could lead to her escape. But she wondered how to accomplish the feat. "I lost my amulet, and now I'm afraid he's got some power over me. He can touch me now, and I can't sense anyone outside these walls."

"You never needed the amulet to harness your powers. You never needed the tarot cards. You never needed a book. You need only your selflessness, compassion, and love, which you have demonstrated. This is where many before you failed. This is where I failed."

The advice sounded like an undeserved compliment. "How have I demonstrated all that?"

"Your dedication to your brother."

Caring for him had been automatic, and she'd never considered it special.

"Focus your thoughts on others, abolish selfish distractions, and realize your empathic power."

Unsure how the advice would play out in reality, Diane wanted to delve deeper into the concept.

But the ghost continued. "Third, our line is meant to hold the dagger. You are meant to hold the dagger."

"How? He uses it to murder women."

"No, those that hunt him carry the antithesis to the cursed weapon, a blessed dagger. The weapons are cast in identical bronze, but their powers are opposing."

"Why don't the hunters just use it themselves?"

"They see it as a tool. They can't see it for what it really is."

"What's that?"

The apparition cocked her head. "It's a weapon, of course."

Wondering if ghosts had senses of humor, Diane tempered her cynical reaction. "It's just an old knife. How can it help me?"

"When you grasp it, you will know. In your hands, it will channel extreme power. Bring the hunters. Bring the blessed weapon. Free yourself."

"You want me to kill the murderer, with the dagger the hunters need to bring to me?"

"Yes."

Remembering her past dreams of the maiden, Diane dared to hope she might escape, and she anticipated the spirit's final command. "I'm not sure exactly how to do all this, but I'll do everything I can to get out of here. And I assume that means I'll avenge you?"

The soft corners of the ghost's mouth turned upward. "I believe in your abilities and trust that you shall avenge me. But more importantly, I pray that you will redeem me."

CHAPTER 34

Watching the gemstones in the old Chaldean woman's rings move as she talked, Liam sipped the strongest tea he'd ever tasted.

Nana frowned. "I file a missing person's report, and the police tell me there's nothing they can do."

Liam was apprehensive about asking a probing question as he scanned the room's other occupants. Seated on old cherry wood sofas with embroidered cushions, his father, the thin young man who kept his face in a tablet, and Judith remained quiet. So, he had to probe. "Did they check the department store's surveillance video for suspicious people? Or perhaps the parking lot video?"

"Of course, they checked. But they see nothing. They don't know who took her. She's been gone for three weeks, and the police, they can do nothing."

"I'm sorry. We'll do what we can to help."

"Why you want to help?"

Unwilling to blurt out his life's purpose to a stranger, he glanced at Judith, who rescued him. "We believe the man who tried to kill me is the same man who took your granddaughter."

"Because Diane, she talks to you in your mind?"

"Yes. It's happened twice already."

The older woman nodded and pursed her lips. Although Liam found the gesture annoying in its smugness, it signaled her openness to the concept of telepathy. "Diane, she's special. Josh, he's special, too. Sometimes, I know when something bad happens before it happens. Our family, we all have this. I'm not surprised she can talk to you."

Judith nodded. "Then you know I share a special connection with her. I want to help her. I believe I can help her."

Liam offered the grandmother hope. "All three of us can help."

"Who are you again?"

Suspecting he should let his father answer, he looked to Connor.

Taking the hint, the elder hunter lowered his teacup to a coffee table. "We're bounty hunters. The man who has your granddaughter is our bounty."

"Bounty?"

The elder hunter demonstrated more patience for the grandmother's language barrier than Liam could. "A reward for capturing him, or even killing him. He's committed crimes, and it's our job to bring him to justice."

"So, you're the police?"

"Sort of. We work for a reward, but we have no legal authority."

"I don't understand."

Keeping his gaze on his tablet, the young man sitting at the end of a couch blurted a response. "They kill for money, Nana."

Her eyes grew big with surprise, and then she gave another annoying, knowing nod. "I hope you kill him for what he does."

Liam interjected. "Maybe you can help us. Or perhaps Josh can."

The younger man squirmed and frowned. "Diane felt it when the women were stabbed in the heart. I felt it, too."

Judith showed an empathy that eluded the hunters. "That must have been horrible for you."

"I felt them because of Diane. I'm connected to her. She felt them because the book says she can communicate telepathically."

Liam's chest tightened with anticipation, and then he snapped. "What book?"

Josh ignored him, earning him Judith's scolding. "You need to be nicer."

"Sorry."

"Josh, Liam didn't mean to raise his voice. He's just excited that you have a book."

The grandmother interjected. "It's been in my family for generations. It tells about how we have our special powers. It's in Aramaic."

Nana's clarification increased Liam's hunger to read it. "Can I see the book?"

Carrying his tablet in front of his nose, Josh stood and walked out of the room.

The young hunter looked to Judith, who seemed to understand the quirky man's ways. "Does that mean he agrees?"

"Give him a moment."

"He's hard to read."

The nursing student frowned. "You don't have to read everyone. Just let him do what he's doing. What's your hurry?"

"We have a few weeks until the full moon, but we have a lot of work to do."

Josh returned reading his tablet with one hand and carrying a leather-bound book under his other arm. The tome's paper edges looked worn and yellowed by decades of exposure, and the faded animal hide cover held a title in large letters, which Liam recognized as Aramaic. The young man found his place on the sofa, sat, and looked at one of the living room's ceiling corners. "This is Nana's book. Do you have one like it?"

Questions buzzed in Liam's mind about a peculiar young man questioning the secret volume of his lineage. "Me? Are you asking me if I have one like it?"

The elder hunter spoke in a coddling tone. "Why, yes, Josh. Liam does have one much like it, don't you, Liam?"

"Well, yeah. I do. But it's far away."

Connor continued his coddling. "That may be true, but I'm sure you have a copy, don't you, Liam?"

"Yes, that's right. I can share a copy. I typed up notes of the decrypted translations."

"No, I want to see the original words."

The younger hunter cleared his throat. "It's encrypted in Aramaic characters. Are you sure you want that, Josh?"

"Yes."

The request irritated Liam, but he sensed everyone wanted him to cater to his new quirky acquaintance. "Aramaic encrypted, it is. I have it scanned electronically. I'll make my cloud storage folder public and send you the address so you can download it."

"Okay."

"Can I have your email address?"

Josh mentioned his email, and Liam sent the younger man the address for sharing the file. In silence, Diane's brother tapped his tablet and retreated into the information flowing through his private world.

"Did you get the file with my book, yet?"

"Yes."

Losing patience, Liam hungered for more knowledge about Diane's family's text. "What does your book say, Josh?"

"It says Diane inherited empathic powers and an amulet of protection from Nana's ancestors."

Doubting he'd learn more until reading the book himself, he left Josh to his reading and then welcomed the old woman's breaking of the silence. "What's your plan to get back my granddaughter?"

The picture of Diane on an end table beside Nana showed a beautiful young woman. Her features became emblazoned in his memory, striking him with an allure so profound that he knew he'd recognize her when needed. "We tracked him to Northern Michigan and know enough about the house he's living in to find it in a couple of months."

"A couple of months? She could be dead by then!"

Allowing wisdom to speak, Liam deferred to his father. "We're quite certain your granddaughter's kidnapper resorts to violence rarely, and only under a full moon. The soonest we'd expect any danger would be at the end of the month.

Diane should be safe until we can reach her."

"He says a couple of months to find her. You say the end of the month she could die. That sounds too close."

The young hunter needed to share his concern. "I'm sorry, ma'am. You're right. My father's being too optimistic. The truth is, the timing is dangerous. I assure you we're doing everything we can, though."

"You say it's dangerous. Why not go faster?"

Believing a random innocent woman would die if the search continued beyond the twenty-ninth, Liam acknowledged the need to accelerate. "We'll just have to work hard and put in the extra hours."

The thin man stirred in his seat. "I'll help."

Liam scowled but then relaxed his face as he remembered to be gentle. "Thank you, Josh. How do you think you can help?"

"I can look online. I like computers."

Setting aside concerns of the young man's reliability, the young hunter accepted the offer. "That's great. I'll show you our search parameters when you're done decrypting my book."

"I'm done."

Unable to help himself, Liam stood and shot to the man's side.

Josh cringed and looked away, and, overcome with anticipation, the hunter had to remind himself to control his vocal volume.

"I didn't mean to scare you, Josh. I'm... just so impressed with how fast you did that."

Silence.

Judith stood, moved to Josh, and spoke sweetly. "We're all very impressed, Josh. Can you show me what you did?"

The younger man looked at the floor. "It was easy. It's the same type of encryption as Nana's book, but it uses a different combination of characters."

Fearing his anticipation would give him an aneurism if he endured another minute without digesting Nana's tome, the young hunter bit his lip to restrain himself. Instead of ripping the manuscript from its steward, he let Judith pose the next question.

"So, you can read Liam's book, Josh?"

"Yeah. It looks pretty cool."

"What did you find that's so cool?"

"I didn't translate all of it yet. I need more time."

"But, have you noticed anything?"

"Yeah."

His patience exhausted, Liam shrugged and looked to the nursing student, who rescued the inquiry. "Can you tell me what you noticed, Josh?"

"The first chapter in each book has three hundred and forty-three characters. They're written in the same shape. They both make crosses on the page."

Judith looked to the young hunter for guidance.

He knew of the crucifix shape of his book's first chapter, and he'd played with the numbers to realize that seven to the third power, a mix of mystical numbers, resulted in three hundred and forty-three characters, but he'd considered it mere artistic symbolism. Clueless of any meaningful conclusion, he shrugged but urged her next question with a wave of his fingers.

Judith continued. "Did you learn something from the first chapter of Liam's book?"

"Yeah."

"Can you tell me what you learned, Josh?"

"If I use the decryption of Liam's book on the first chapter of Nana's book, it makes a whole new chapter."

"I don't understand."

Liam interjected, disbelieving his theory as he verbalized it. "He used the encryption scheme of one book on the other. That means the books were intended to be read together when they were originally written. Isn't that right, Josh?"

"Yeah."

Having solicited the terse response, the young hunter risked the subsequent question. "Can you tell me what's in the new chapter?"

"I need to ask Nana."

The elder woman angled her head towards her grandson. "I'm listening. Go ahead. Josh."

"What is *Skeena* in Aramaic?"

"*Skeena*? That's a sword or knife."

Words leapt from Liam's mouth. "A dagger? Do you mean a dagger?"

As she gave her knowing nod, which he found increasingly annoying, Liam clenched his fists to slow himself and let the nursing student continue the patient inquiry.

"What does it say about the dagger, Josh?"

"It says the hunter needs to give his dagger to the virgin."

Liam had avoided questioning Diane's sex life, but he appreciated her virginity rising as a topic to clarify her role as the monster's sacrifice.

The nursing student pushed for the conclusion. "Why, Josh? Why does the hunter need to give his dagger to the virgin?"

"It becomes a powerful weapon in her hands. She can free herself and the souls of the innocent victims."

CHAPTER 35

Anxiety had plagued Diane since her afternoon discourse with the ghost. Though the murdered maiden had rendered actionable advice, her warnings were frightening, and she'd given no assurances of survival.

Fighting the fear required constant diligence. One minute, she resolved to implement the apparition's divine guidance, but as the next moment of doubt besieged her with futility, she resigned herself to dying.

The oscillations between instinctive despair and willed determination etched a battle in her heart. She paced behind the couch, jingling her shackles in a rhythm that concentrated her thoughts.

To strengthen her commitment, she vocalized her intent. "I'm going to see Josh again."

While walking, she watched the shrinking blooms of fading sunlight that cracked through the curtains and reflected off the wall behind the cinderblock edifice. Night was falling, and she expected the calming twilight to help her follow the apparition's advice.

As she replayed the insights in her mind, she remembered to prioritize other people. Selfishness erected a barrier. Selflessness constructed a bridge.

She rolled over the back of the couch, sat on a cushion, and prepared herself to reach out. "I'm an empath. I know."

Trying to remove distractions, fear, and discomfort, she closed her eyes and sought distant emotions. "But what do I know?"

Silently, she answered her own question. She knew how to touch other people's feelings. So, she scanned her mental inventory of connections to her strongest relations.

Judith had been a connection, but the survivor had gone dark since the scare with Liam's pistol. Nana would be suffering the loss of her granddaughter, but the Chaldean woman had hardened under a lifetime of stresses, blunting the edges of any emotions that would make her telepathically detectable. Her friend, Mary, would be saddened by Diane's disappearance, but she'd already turned away from their friendship in favor of a future fiancé and a career.

The obvious solution rose above the others, and she targeted her brother. Tapping her own emotions, she paralleled those she expected were flowing within him.

Sadness. Fear. Loneliness. Anger.

He needed comfort, and she offered it.

Siblings united by subconscious wavelengths, they touched across space and beyond matter. She detected a bridge, a reflection of her feelings roaring back to her, amplified, aimed at her, concerned about her, stamped with her brother's quirky edges and peculiar frequencies.

Her lips unmoving, she invoked her caregiving and patient voice in her mind. "Josh?"

"Diane?"

"Josh! Can you hear me?"

"Yeah. Where are you?"

"I'm being held prisoner."

"I know. Judith told me. She's with me."

"That's great. I told her to find you."

"We're with Liam and Connor, too. We're looking for you."

She dared to expect liberation. "Do you know where I am?"

"No."

The rapid dashing of her hope jolted her handle on her emotions, and Josh slipped away. Opening her eyes, she returned to her seated body and uttered the quandary to tune her attention upon it. "They don't know where I am. Nobody knows."

Dragging her tethering links over the back of the couch, she took rhythmic strides across her chained limits over the floor. The walking calmed her and enabled her rational thoughts.

Of course, her location remained unknown to her rescuers. Otherwise, they'd be breaking down the doors. She had to accept the challenge and reengage her allies.

Returning to her sitting meditation, she explored her own emotions. She ignored the great distance to her brother. She forgot the cramped confines of her dungeon. She blocked out the dangers of her deranged jailor.

She channeled her energy towards her brother. "Josh?"

"Diane."

"I'm back."

"Where'd you go?"

"I lost our link. I'm still figuring out how to do this. I got too scared, I think."

"We're looking for you. The hunters are friendly and know what they're doing. They want to help."

"Tell them to hurry. I only have until the next full moon. A ghost appeared to me and told me I'm his next victim."

His thoughts stopped, and his rising fear jolted the connection. She lost him, but instead of backing away, she stayed in her trance and waited for his panic to subside. "Josh? Josh?"

Nothing.

"Josh!"

"Diane?"

"Yes, I'm still here. I almost lost you."

"I'm scared for you. The full moon's coming."

"Stay with me, Josh. Please don't get scared again."

"I'll try."

"Please tell the others about the timing of the full moon."

"Okay."

"Will you remember to later tonight?"

"Okay."

"Also tell them there are cameras looking at me. I think the killer has cameras all over the house and the property."

"Okay. I'll tell them. But don't leave yet. I like this. I like that I can hear you like you're in my mind."

"I like it, too, Josh. But why can't I see through your eyes? I can't hear or sense anything you're experiencing."

"I don't know."

To probe the question herself, she silenced her selfish concerns about escaping and surviving. She quieted the litany of self-serving ideas and words circling her head, and the simple answer revealed itself.

He was blocking her.

"I think you're not letting me. Can you let me see through your eyes, Josh? Just for a moment, to see if I can?"

"I guess so."

For several seconds, she saw a blurry rendition of the tablet in his lap. As she grasped from his coldness that he disliked the phenomenon, she relinquished the visual link, and her world became sterile darkness. "Thank you, Josh. That was enough."

"Okay. Are you still safe?"

"I think so, but I don't like what's going on. He built a cinderblock wall in front of the glass wall to make sure I don't get out, and then he started acting suspicious of me. He took my amulet."

"The amulet was supposed to protect you."

"It did, but then yesterday he took all my jewelry."

"Is he hurting you?"

"No, not yet, but I'm scared."

"I want to find you. I want to help get you back."

Having spent a month without companionship other than her jailor, she found the familial connection soothing. "I know you do."

"You have to help us find you."

"I don't know how."

He paused his communicative signals and masked his mind. Even in a telepathic link, Diane recognized the need to allow his uniqueness. Then he reopened his consciousness to her. "You need to see where you are."

"I can't see anything except this basement."

"You need to see through his eyes."

She considered his meaning. "You mean the guy who wants to kill me?"

"Yes. See what he sees."

"I can't connect with him. He's not human."

"He's still human. Every human is capable of every emotion."

"I can't. I hate him."

"You're supposed to love everyone, even your enemy."

Every cell within her resisted the concept, but inwardly, she conceded. "You're right, but I don't know if I can."

"Please, Diane. Try for me. I need you."

"Can't you just hurry up and find me?"

"We're looking as fast as we can, but there are so many houses. Liam says we need more than two months to check them all."

The timing explained why he'd panicked with her revelation of the full-moon deadline. Giving herself fifty percent odds of surviving, barring divine intervention, she wrestled with her fright. She pushed him away. "I think I'm losing you, Josh. I'm scared now."

"That's okay. Let me go now."

Predicting she needed a telepathic bridge with a serial killer, she wanted to stay with her comforting brother. She realized that melding with a madman would be risky as she recalled the sicknesses she'd suffered after tarot readings with the lying, cheating, and stealing ex-clients she'd seen as her reputation had grown. "Wait! I need to know everything I can about him."

"He's bad. He kills people when it's a full moon."

"I know that. I need to know more, everything you can learn. Please ask the hunters. If I'm going to make a telepathic link with him, I can't be surprised when I'm connecting with him."

"Okay. I'll ask. Connect with me later, and I'll tell you everything I learn."

"Thank you, Josh."

"You can always connect with me because I love you. You're my sister."

"I love you, too, brother."

CHAPTER 36

Jacob aimed the Acadia towards the hotel where his barista concubine and a night of sport awaited.

In an instant, his plans changed.

His domineering demon issued him a command, a beacon flickering throughout his entire body, and he stopped the car. Obeying the immediate and unspoken order, he screeched tires as he turned the SUV back towards his cabin.

Frustrated, he grunted while obeying his lording spirit and accepting the abrupt change of plans. Instead of sport, he faced work.

Dangerous work.

Setting deadly traps.

His historical routine called for waiting until January for establishing his cruel defensive scheme of explosives and tripwires. Delaying to the final moon cycle minimized the chances of the collateral damage and attention that could jeopardize his ritual.

But today his ethereal superior demanded a different schedule. He'd warned him that the hunters sought to save the sacrifice-turned-tribute, Diane, forcing an acceleration of the cabin's defenses.

The hunters were coming.

Zealous to serve the source of his power, Jacob offered homage. "If they find me, I will break the line of hunters once and for all, Master. They have mocked you long enough. They have tormented me long enough."

The voiceless response conveyed supernatural approval.

While driving home, Jacob ran through his checklist of locations across the property to place his incendiary bombs and ways to poise them for burning trespassers.

As he brought the vehicle into the cabin's driveway, he braced himself for ghostly harassment, but the misty legion of ladies in white stayed away.

He parked in the garage, and the overhead motor clicked into motion to conceal his movements within the space. After stepping from the SUV, he turned his back to the entryway into the cabin and walked towards gray cabinets covering the distant wall.

Recalling the combination, he twirled the lock and slid a door open. Capped with crown stoppers, several dozen half-pint glass bottles lined the shelves.

He glanced at his collection of self-igniting phosphorus grenades. The upper section of each container showed a clear air pocket, below which a volume of tannish gasoline rested on a layer of water, which was suspended atop a yellowing base of phosphorus. Within each weapon, a black strip of raw rubber cut arcs between the incendiary fuels, serving as a thickening agent.

Confident in his creation of each device, he expected each explosive to combust in fierce fire upon the shattering of its casing. But having used his last explosive a half century ago, he committed the evening to a functional trial.

With foresight, he'd prepared for it, having set aside a test unit when filling the bottles. He grabbed the unique grenade that held a small fraction of the fluid, and, with both hands, he slowly set it to the cement floor.

He locked the shelves, lifted his test grenade, and clasped it in his hands. He walked to a tool bench and lowered the bottle near the back of the wooden surface to avoid any chance of knocking it over.

Scanning his inventory, he glanced at spools of fishing wire, lengths of plywood, handsaws, wooden dowels, a hammer, a vice, hinges, pulleys, a hand drill, and a box of nails. He satisfied himself with his tools and supplies.

He put his hands to work.

After making quick cuts of plywood, he connected two pieces with a hinge. Another flat slab of wood provided the backing for the connected parts. The laborious effort of drilling a hole in the front of a square base consumed his time and energy, as did driving a smaller hole through a length of a dowel.

His shoulders and wrists sore from the manual labor, he moved to the delicate work. Threading fishing wire through the last hole, he tied the line to the wooden rod. A final task, twisting a pulley into a separate plank, finished his crafting.

He grabbed his wheelbarrow, and after piling everything into it except the explosives, he wiped sweat from his brow.

He trotted to the wall-mounted switch and opened the garage. He grabbed the handles of the wheelbarrow and pushed his supplies into the gentle spring evening. The yard's soft grass and the tree stand's pine needle floor slowed the solitary wheel, but he muscled his supplies to his destination.

Reaching a strong oak, he stopped and parked his gear in the grass.

He stuck long nails between his lips, tasted stale metal, and slid his hammer into a belt loop. He reached into his wheelbarrow, found his crafted wooden cradle, and lifted it to his shoulder. Seeing an eight-foot-high crook, he extended his woodwork and placed it upon the tree. Climbing, he grasped bark and pulled himself to squat with his feet balanced at the central union between three major branches.

One branch paralleled the property, and looking through the dense foliage separating the distant road from his yard, he considered his location appealing to assailants for spying upon him and for providing an approach to assault the cottage.

He pushed his weight onto his knee as he leaned forward and pressed the cradle against the branch. Palming plywood against bark, he pinched a nail over the flat surface and reached to his hip. He grabbed the hammer and tapped the nail.

Several nails later, he'd secured his small platform to the branch. Reminiscent of a birdhouse, his creation had a hinged door that swung open with gravity. He descended the tree's trunk, retrieved the dowel and its tethered fishing line, and then returned to the elevated crook.

He closed the hinged door, slid the dowel into the larger hole he'd drilled, and wedged the door shut. After experimenting with friction and forces, he found the right exposed extrusion distance allowing the wooden rod to block the door.

Back on the ground, he stepped over pine needles and stood before his remaining supplies. Directly below the platform, he pressed the plank into the earth, and then he threaded the fishing line through its pulley. Continuing to a nearby pine tree, he wrapped the wire around its trunk tightly.

As his final preparatory step, he walked through the darkness seeking a flat rock. Within ten paces, he found one the size of a cinderblock and lifted it from the ground. He carried it back to the plank and repositioned it under the bomb cradle he'd nailed to the branch above.

He trotted to the garage, grabbed the test grenade, and marched back to the trap. After a careful climb, he lay the bottle onto his elevated platform and descended the tree's trunk.

Backing the wheelbarrow, he withdrew his supplies from the booby trap and looked forward to proving his effort's efficacy.

As he delved deeper into the stand of trees, he placed himself on a potential intruder's side of the rigged oak. Scanning the moonlit ground for fallen branches, he found a natural ten-foot pole, lifted it, and pressed it into his invisible ground wire. When he saw the fishing line's reflection of moonlight, he inhaled and prepared to test his deathtrap.

He stopped and dropped the branch as he sensed a foreign entity entering his mind.

Accustomed to his lording spirit's unannounced issuing of inaudible instructions, he knew his Master's style.

This was different.

It was an invasion.

Wondering if a past victim had found an otherworldly means to torment him, he closed his eyes and sought to drive out the intruder.

His scorning hatred of their ilk fueled his attack, and he aimed telepathic barbs at his ethereal assailant.

No effect.

He redoubled his efforts, and then he sensed resistance. With the resistance came friction, and with the friction, freedom.

The invader was gone. The attack on his mind had passed, but it triggered anxiety, as he thought the women he'd killed refused to stay dead.

Squatting on his haunches, he took several breaths to calm himself, and the sounds of the night became clear. He heard crickets, the trickling stream shaping the backyard's boundary, and the gentle whoosh of a breeze in the leaves.

Assuring himself the telepathic attack had been an aberration, he returned to his task. He pushed the branch two inches forward to simulate a man's foot against the wire, and then he darted behind a pine tree.

He heard the tinkle of breaking glass and the incendiary combustion of phosphorus and gasoline. Orange light illuminated the stand and then returned the foliage to the evening's darkness. A burst of heat shot over him, singeing his forearm hairs.

Success.

Mashing pine needles, he walked to the shattered glass and examined the aftermath. It was perfect, and he knew he could replicate the trap with his full inventory of explosives around the property, slowing or even killing those who would come for him.

But the nagging concern of hostile entities invading his mind bothered him, and a blasphemous thought ran through him.

He questioned his Master's commitment to protect him.

CHAPTER 37

Liam sipped strong tea with cardamom, and the smooth caffeine influx kept him alert during the late evening. The small team huddled in the living room with Diane's grandmother, watching Josh.

The young man opened his eyes. "She got into his head."

Unable to withhold his enthusiasm about the brother's connection with his sister, Liam wanted to lead the interviews about his discoveries. But he accepted Judith's recommendation to sit on the opposite side of the coffee table.

Her voice was placating. "Diane got into the killer's head?"

"Yeah. She said she could see through his eyes."

Seeking clues, Liam leaned forward but pursed his lips to remain silent. He listened to Judith's peaceful tone. "Did she say if she saw something interesting?"

"She saw him working in the woods."

"What was he working on?"

"A wire on the ground that makes a bomb fall from a tree."

Liam thought he understood the meaning but looked to his father for confirmation.

"He's used incendiary devices before. They're like Molotov cocktails, but instead of throwing them, he sets them up in gravity-driven traps. They'll trip by kicking wires on the ground or by merely brushing aside branches. They're quite simple but quite dangerous."

The nursing student continued her interrogation. "What else did she see?"

Josh squirmed and looked away.

"It's okay, Josh. You can tell me when you're ready."

Unable to make himself hold it in, Liam released his critical concern. "Did she see the house? Ask him if she saw the house."

His interjection earned Judith's glare. "Can't you see that he's already overwhelmed? You need to calm down."

"It's hard to keep track of when he's connected to her, but I'm certain he said a break or two ago that she somehow knew she was targeted to be the tribute on the next full moon."

She scowled. "Your point?"

"We need to hurry, for Diane's sake."

"We all got that part. Pressuring Josh won't help."

Setting his tea to the coffee table, Liam conceded. "Okay. I'm sorry again."

Josh shook his head. "No."

Judith waited a beat before responding. "What are you saying no to, Josh?"

"She didn't see the house."

"Did she see anything else?"

"No. She's tired. She said the link with the bad man was tiring. She went to bed."

"Are you okay, Josh?" The concept of asking about the young man's state hadn't crossed Liam's mind, but Judith's concern proved insightful.

"I'm tired. Very tired."

"This must be exhausting for you, Josh. Maybe we should all get some rest. It's getting late, and we have a lot of work to do tomorrow."

With the day's discoveries replaying in his mind, the young hunter disagreed with Judith's suggestion. He wanted to tame his thoughts before sleeping. "I still need to look at Nana's book."

She gave him another glare. "Tonight?"

"Yes. It can't wait." He feared he'd blurt out curses if she challenged him.

Instead, she displayed her understanding by turning to Josh. "Can Liam have Nana's book?"

"I'm not done reading."

Recognizing defeat, Liam waived his hands. "Never mind. I'll wait until the morning."

That night, Liam dreamt of a young woman burning on a cross, blood pouring from her heart's puncture wound. His fear for Diane placed her into the lead role, and her deathly face became visible as that of the sacrifice.

The nightmare convinced him that letting Diane die would bring his own demise.

The next morning, he awoke in the old Chaldean woman's guest room. While hurrying through his bathroom routine, he processed the prior day's learning.

The full-moon deadline had shifted from a random stranger to Diane. Though he'd yet to meet her, he knew her through her family and her connection to Judith. He judged fate's subjective reckoning of time peculiar as he realized his decades of training yielded only days to familiarize himself with his allies.

Quirky allies.

A high-functioning autistic young man, a nursing student who'd escaped death with telepathic help, a grandmother of pure Ninevite lineage who'd passed down an amulet and a secret companion manuscript to his hunting family's own tome, and the sacrifice herself who'd claimed through supernatural intervention to have been transformed into the next tribute.

As he descended the carpeted stairs, his head spun with conjecture, but every idea he could invoke to explain the abnormalities led to a succinct conclusion.

He needed to accelerate his search.

As the scents of breakfast enhanced his appetite, he hoped a good meal might boost his mental acumen. In the kitchen, he found the home's owner grilling potatoes, eggs, and meats. "Good morning, Nana."

"Good morning."

"You're up early."

"I make breakfast for everyone. Sit. You eat."

He sat on a stool at the kitchen island, and she placed a plate of eggs, sausage, and potatoes in front of him. Pitchers of water and juice were within reach, as were utensils and napkins.

"Thank you."

"You want coffee or tea?"

"Tea, please."

As she poured steaming water into a cup, he heard footsteps in the stairwell. She placed his beverage before him, and he sipped its hot bitterness.

Connor arrived and sat beside him. "Good morning, all."

After salutations, a meal appeared in front of the elder hunter, and Liam tested assumptions against his father. "We can let Josh help, us, right? Because he offered, just like Judith did?"

"That's correct. My father taught me that volunteered support is a divine gift we can accept if we so choose."

In that moment, Liam accepted a dose of wisdom. He realized no amount of reading, listening, or training could prepare him for living. His father had needed to learn while doing when he'd hunted the wraith fifty years ago, and this hunt was his turn.

How many more rules remained unknown until he asked about them or stumbled upon them? How many more surprises awaited? "We can take him with us and set up a four-person online search team."

"That might work, if it's okay with Josh and his grandmother."

The old woman gave her annoying nod of approval. "Anything to help Diane. I come with you, too."

Examining her, Liam considered her assets and liabilities. She seemed tough, but if the hour grew late to save her granddaughter, he feared she'd suffer a nervous breakdown. Then again, he could address that later and remove her if needed. In the meantime, she could cook, do laundry, and handle the tasks that chewed time. "Thank you, Nana. Are you and Josh able to join us up north for a few weeks?"

"Whatever it takes."

"That would be great. I'm still making a lot of assumptions, but that could reduce our search time to six weeks."

The dismayed grandmother protested. "She could be dead by then. We have to go faster."

The young hunter hoped he could improve the search speed with the growing team. "I know. We'll just have to work harder."

Creaking floorboards announced the waking of the house's final two occupants. Barring brilliant ideas from Josh or Judith, Liam expected a difficult race against time.

His father had other plans. "We can economize our search if we set up a mobile base."

Liam missed the point. "Huh?"

The elder hunter wiped yolk from his lips. "A recreational vehicle."

"I'm still not following. How does that help?"

"We can work in parallel. While the online search team searches, we can drive the vehicle along our search pattern. As we uncover candidate properties, we can launch the hovercraft from the RV and investigate them in near real time."

Liam saw a gaping flaw. "But you've just consumed a person in driving, and then you'd have to take someone off the search team to run the hovercraft."

With a glint in his eye, the older hunter looked to the Chaldean women. "Nana, I noticed a car in your garage. Can you drive?"

"Of course, I can drive. You want me to drive an RV, though? You kidding? I can't do it, and it's too expensive."

"I wouldn't worry about that. I can get support from an order back home to overcome financial obstacles."

Liam bit his lip to refrain from asking about the fabled order his father had yet to explain.

"I cannot drive it. An RV's too big."

"For Diane, I urge you to reconsider."

The annoying nod came. "Okay. I do it for Diane."

"Great. You won't have to be our only driver. We'll take turns to make sure you're not overwhelmed. Such vehicles are designed to be driven by mature people like us."

Having accepted the challenge, Nana seemed defiant. "That's good, but you let me drive while you look for Diane."

"I don't suppose you also have a knack for playing with electronics? We could use your help in operating our hovercraft."

With his tablet near his face and Nana's book under his arm, Josh appeared.

Like a guardian angel, the nursing student trailed two steps behind him. "It's a new day. Josh, are you ready in case Diane contacts you?"

"Yeah. I guess. I miss her."

The team sat together on the island eating breakfast. Josh placed the grandmother's leather-bound copy of the family's text next to Liam, who uttered an awkward response. "Thanks?"

He flipped through his new source of knowledge and scoped the workload in digesting it. He'd need hours to transcribe the translation scheme and make sense of it.

When he looked up from the book, Judith was giving him a harsh stare. He realized the nursing student had seen something amiss in his treatment of the younger man, and, as a dense male of the species per her reckoning, he'd been ignorant of his insensitivity.

He was relieved when she released him from her gaze and looked to Josh. "I'm sure you do miss her. Do you know what to ask her if she contacts you?"

"No."

Across the island, the nursing student winked, convincing Liam she'd struck the balance between pampering and pushing Josh. "May I suggest that you ask her to get inside the bad man's head whenever she hears him around the house?"

"Okay."

"Around the house, Josh. We want her to see what she can through his eyes while he's in the house or right outside it."

"Okay."

Judith verified his understanding. "Can you repeat that, Josh?"

"In the house or right outside it."

"Good, Josh. I think we can trust you. You're ready."

Liam ran through his mental checklist of activities for the day. Rent an RV, gather the hunters' belongings from their extended stay suite, pack everyone's items into their new mobile home, and recommence the intensive search for Diane.

Favoring the younger teammates for the online search, he envisioned a splitting of duties. "Father, can you and Nana get the RV today while the rest of us search through properties?"

"Oh, I think we can manage."

"Get one with a big television so that we can all look at properties together."

"Consider it done, lad."

"And get one with its own mobile hotspot and the fastest data plan you can purchase. I want multiple mobile networks."

The elder hunter gave a look suggesting everything would be okay, despite the doubts nagging Liam. "I shall spare no expense to get us every possible advantage."

CHAPTER 38

With a growing hunger and a lingering fatigue, Diane awoke on the couch.

To orient herself, she looked towards the basement's back wall. Through gaps in the curtains and the cinderblock barrier, blooms of crepuscular orange signaled dusk's arrival.

She'd slept half the day, her slumber consuming valuable time she needed to apply towards escaping her dungeon.

And although she'd succeeded in tapping her enemy's mind the prior evening, she questioned the invasion's value against its cost. She'd exhausted her energy and had forced herself into a long recovering slumber, advancing three-quarters of a day closer to her full-moon murder, in exchange for watching her killer play with fire in the woods.

She crawled over the back of the couch and lumbered into the bathroom. Clanking her chain, she turned on the steaming water and stepped into the shower.

The comforting hot water relaxed her and released muscular tension. While lathering herself clean, she questioned what her telepathic intrusion into her killer's mind had gained. From her first retrospective impression, it had been an exhausting waste, but after toweling herself dry and putting on clean pajamas, she hoped the hunters could share evidence of having profited from her reconnoitering.

Seeking their feedback, she climbed back over the couch, sat, and thought about who to contact.

She wondered if Nana would be receptive, or if the new friend she had yet to meet in person, the nursing student, would respond to her call.

But with Josh being near them and serving as her ideal

supernatural receiver, she delayed experimenting until she had more energy.

She hailed her brother.

Anxiety. Love. Anger. "Josh?"

In their shared spirit, his voice warmed her. "Diane?"

"I'm here. Can you hear me?"

"Yeah."

"What day is it?"

"May third."

She knew the answer to her next question but wanted to hear it from him. "Remind me. When's the next full moon?"

"May twenty-ninth."

Twenty-six days to death. "Do you know where I am yet?"

"No, but I'm going to help them look. We're using computers to search for you."

"Oh, I bet you're good at that."

"Liam gave me a list of houses, and I just have to look at them. I'm looking for houses with water near them and a basement like yours."

She trusted him to manage his share of the task since it allowed him to concentrate without the distracting complexities of human interaction. But she also knew time worked against him. It worked against her. "Can you get more help to look for me?"

"Connor said it's not allowed."

"Did he say why?"

"Ancient rules."

She knew better than questioning her brother beyond his understanding, and she also accepted she was playing in a supernatural game with murky rubrics. As she explored her abilities and learned her limits, she sensed that breaking the rules would either be impossible or bring horrible repercussions. If her rescuers claimed a size limitation to their team, she had to accept it, and that meant she needed to help them help her. "Did you learn anything about the bad man?"

"Liam said he thinks you know everything about him

already. He kills women with his special bronze dagger, but he only kills when the full moon's out."

"Did my vision with the bad man help at all?" Calling him a "bad man" seemed simplistic for her brother's hidden intelligence, but she sensed Josh didn't care.

"Connor said the bad man has used bombs like that before."

The affirmation sounded useless. "Does that help Connor find me?"

"No."

"Did Connor or Liam give you any advice for me?"

"They said to look through the bad man's eyes when he's in the house or right outside it."

It made sense, and she welcomed the affirmation. "I'll try it, but it's so hard. I slept all day already recovering from getting into his head last night."

Her brother's voice was pleading. "You have to try."

"I will."

"Promise?"

"I promise, Josh." Wanting to save her energy for attacking the man who planned to kill her, she let her brother go.

Relinquishing the link, she opened her eyes. She stood and paced in front of the couch, trying to sniff an opportunity to launch her second attack on her jailor.

Nothing evoked her hypersensitive paranormal radar, and she continued her rhythmic clanking walk.

At the end of the couch, she stopped and cycled through deep knee bends to maintain her leg strength. During her third squat, she heard a door closing above her.

Her kidnapper was in the house.

As fast as she could shimmy with leg irons, she bolted to her preferred spot on the cushions and closed her eyes. "Come on, Diane. Relax and focus."

Seeking the killer, she invoked emotions within herself that sought to connect with his.

Lust.

She tried it, but she found faking the vice impossible.

Moving to emotions she could at least fake, she probed.

Anger. Envy. Haughtiness.

The combination had worked last time, and she tried it.

Resistance. Cold resistance and an ancient anger met her. His words were inaudible, but his meaning was obvious.

He wanted her out of his head.

She kept her inner voice silent to avoid revealing a clue about her identity, but with images and urging, she demanded access to his eyes.

Rejection. Anger.

In response to her failure, her ire grew and approached the intensity of his, strengthening the link, but still, she saw nothing.

Then she became arrogant, and the foreign feeling which normally sickened her became pleasurable within her connection.

Her empathic abilities gave her an advantage, and when she merged with him, they made her feel superior.

She played with the emotion and let it grow. Like the first taste of an addiction, the feeling of superiority drew her towards a dangerous path, but it gave her a tighter bond to her enemy.

In a flash, she saw through his eyes.

His hand reached outward to the light switch of a bathroom, and the doorway issued into a bedroom. It was his chambers, a master bedroom, with a large safe on the carpet.

The brief view lasted seconds before he pushed her out.

Her consciousness returned to her body, she slumped sideways, and sleep's grip tightened.

But she vowed to send a message before falling into another recovering nap. She sought her brother again. "Josh?"

"Diane?"

"I saw through him again. The master bedroom has a private bathroom attached to it."

"Okay."

"Did you get that? The house I'm in has a private master

bathroom. Tell your hunter friends. Tell Liam and Connor."

Before she passed out, she heard footsteps in the stairwell, and fear kept her semi-conscious. Her jailor's boots clicked against the hardwood floor with the cinderblock edifice muting the echoes.

When the sound ceased, she sensed him above her. She opened her eyes, and the killer stood over her, glaring. The anger in his dark eyes commanded obedience. "Wake up."

She pushed herself upright.

"I've been having bad luck with people invading my mind. You wouldn't happen to know anything about that, would you?"

Reminding herself she was the empath–not him, she risked the lie and the feigned curiosity. "I don't know what you're talking about. What people?"

"Never mind."

Seeing his unease, she tried a new tactic to worsen his instability. She offered assistance. "Do you want my help or not?"

"I didn't come to you for help."

"Then why'd you wake me up?"

"Shut up. I brought you food. Look." He pointed, and she aimed her nose behind the couch. On the ground by the bathroom door lay a fifty-pound bag of rice and a coffee cup with a spoon. "I suggest you make it last. I don't have plans to bring you anything else. You can forget the past favors I showed you in bringing you meals to suit your pathetic demands."

Defiant, she challenged him. "How long?"

He took the bait. "How long, what?"

"How long do you suggest I make it last?"

"Depending upon your behavior, the rest of your life. And if I catch you lying to me, I'll make you wish for that time to be short."

CHAPTER 39

The next morning, Liam shopped with Josh.

Stopping his cart on the floor at a Best Buy in Flint, he pushed aside two topline hovercraft and lowered spare batteries beside them. Trailing him, Josh walked with his tablet in front of his face.

As he pushed the cart towards the computer section, he noticed his companion's absence. He reversed his steps and wheeled back to him. "Are you okay, Josh?"

His companion's constant attention to his tablet hid his telepathic link to random onlookers.

But the hunter recognized the blank stare as a signal of the supernatural communication conduit. "Take your time, buddy. Get all you can from her."

While waiting for the younger man, Liam lifted his phone and thumbed open photographs of Josh's translations of Nana's book.

The text read like his hunting lineage's tome of ancient knowledge, except it targeted an audience of female empaths. He found it intriguing but useless without Diane, with instructions on establishing telepathic links, advice about sensing the world through another's body, discernment of lies, and refinements of prophecy.

But the new section, the double-encrypted version requiring both books, fascinated him.

Cross-encrypting one book to the other revealed a deep, ancient... what? A conspiracy? An alliance? A covenant?

A prophecy?

Someone, or a group united by a common cause, had foreseen the line of hunters and the line of empaths merging.

Finding the implications overwhelming, Liam set the concept in the back of his mind and thought instead about the new chapter's insight on the dagger.

When he'd discovered the hidden words, Josh had understated the virgin's potential while wielding the dagger. He'd spoken the truth, saying it would become a powerful weapon in her hands, but Liam read words claiming more.

The new chapter said the virgin's hand would imbue the knife with its own divine force and strike terror into the hearts of any enemy who threatened her.

Planning to put a bullet into the wraith, he expected to deny Diane her chance to experiment with the prophesized weapon. Killing the savage was his job.

But as he digested the tome, he reconsidered.

The dagger could also free the souls the wraith had imprisoned, and the guidance left him unsure if that required leaving the savage alive for Diane to deal with.

The autistic man's salutation startled him. "Liam?"

The hunter closed the book, moved closer to his companion, and verified nobody stood within earshot. "Yes."

"Diane saw through his eyes again."

"That's great news, Josh. Did she tell you what she saw?"

"She said it was a private bathroom in the master bedroom."

The knowledge wouldn't feed a filter, but Liam trusted it would somehow help. "Thank you, Josh. We'll have to remember that."

"There's no filter for it."

"I know, but maybe it'll help with some keyword searches."

"Maybe."

"Come on." He pushed the cart towards the computers. "Do you like Apple or Windows?"

"Linux."

"Seriously?"

"Yeah. Low overhead. More flexible."

"I know. I just didn't think you'd be able to use something so... involved. We'll get you a Windows machine and you can download Linux later."

"Remember to buy a bigger hotspot."

"I will."

Twenty minutes later, two new computers and a mobile hotspot for handling more Internet traffic landed in the cart atop the new hovercraft and spare batteries.

Liam checked out, led Josh to the Winnebago, and carried the new drones, hotspot, and batteries through the door. "Josh, can you grab the computers, please?"

The young man frowned and kept his face in whatever book he was reading on his tablet.

"Never mind. Just get into the RV."

Josh lumbered up the steps, and Liam followed, balancing the laptops in his arms. He piled them on the passenger seat and then returned to the parking lot to stow the cart.

When he climbed back into the Winnebago Journey, he marveled at its décor.

Marble flooring with grayish white streaks, gray leather furniture, and cherry wood cabinets with coffee-glazed colored stain created a luxurious feel. His father had wanted an upscale and efficient workspace, and with his secret order paying the bill, Liam accepted the decision.

As he carried the computers into the living room and lowered them to an ottoman, two of which served as coffee tables, Liam hoped the team's performance would prove his father correct in his choice of luxury.

Josh sat in the solitary lounge chair.

Seated between the elder teammates on a long couch, Judith looked up. "How was the shopping?"

Liam was happy to declare success but feared asking how the other three teammates had fared in the computer lesson. His father's hesitance with technology concerned him, and he judged Nana a greater risk. "Great. We found everything we needed. Uh, how's the training going?"

"Well, Nana doesn't like the computer."

The Chaldean woman pursed her lips and waved her hand. "I

don't like them, but I'm good with the drone."

Liam tried to hide his surprise, but it was pointless. He knew his face revealed disbelief.

Nana frowned. "You don't believe me? I show you."

Glancing at the hovercraft sitting on the floor, Liam walked to the couch and sat beside his father. He turned his face towards the Chaldean woman and watched her tap icons on a tablet.

The rotors on the hovercraft whirred to life.

"I send it three feet high." Within seconds, the grandmother had the drone levelled in the middle of the RV's forward compartment.

Judith gave the next request. "Now make it look at Liam."

The Chaldean woman pressed her index finger into the tablet, and the craft rotated in the wrong direction. As Nana showed her abilities and limits, Liam realized she could handle the basics.

"I send it the wrong way."

Rooting for Nana, the nursing student anticipated success. "That's okay. It's a circle. Just let it go."

Patience paid off as the drone twisted by Josh, pointed away from the seated foursome, aimed at the television, monitored the view through the windshield, and then presented Liam its lenses.

Nana tapped her tablet, and the hovercraft stabilized, pointing at the young hunter.

He was impressed. "Not bad. I think you can handle this. Let's see where we stand on our search." Intending to control the summary, he reached towards a laptop.

The nursing student showed her initiative by grabbing the television's controller and illuminating the screen. Columns and rows of Excel appeared. "I'll broadcast from here. I've got the spreadsheet called up with Chromecast."

Liam hoped Judith had made progress in his absence. He considered the student an ally in finding and manipulating useful data. "How many do we have?"

"I need to re-filter. Hold on." The nursing student re-ran a filter on a column tracking houses that team members had already explored in detail, culling the list. "We've got about five thousand, six hundred left to review."

"Then let's start reviewing."

"There's also one we need to investigate with the drone."

"Which one? Let's get that resolved first."

"I'll show you." She called up a browser and showed a listing for a three-bedroom ranch with a basement. The orientation of the back wall ran in the correct direction per Diane's old description of the sun's rays, and a neighboring lot had a pond.

"That's good work, Judith. I also forgot to mention that Diane contacted Josh when we were in the store. She saw through his eyes again. He was in a master bathroom. So, we know the house has a private master bath."

Apparently unwilling to accept the hunter's second-hand account, Judith turned to Josh. "Did your sister tell you anything else?"

The young man shook his head.

"Alright. Let's see." With quick mouse work, she enlarged the property's description.

"It doesn't say anything about a master bath. Try the picture gallery."

Her touchpad manipulations sent photographs of the house's interior whizzing across the screen, but the angles prevented a conclusion. "I can't tell. We'll have to check it out."

"That's why we have the RV. Call up a map, and let's pick a place to park."

She highlighted the address, called up a second browser opened to a map, and pasted the location.

Seeing a street behind the house, Liam stood, walked to the television, and pointed. "Get this spot into our RV's navigation system."

"I'm sending the destination to our vehicle. And... it should be sent."

"Nana, can you check please?"

The older woman looked up at him. "Check what?"

Liam reminded himself this was their first training run. The operation would get smoother as they learned to work together. It had to. "Please go to the driver's seat and see if our next destination is in the head unit's navigation system."

As she stared at him, his father rescued her. "I'll help, Nana. Perhaps we can figure this out together. After you, please."

The older teammates stood and walked towards the windshield. While passing Liam, Connor leaned to him and whispered. "Patience, lad. This technology's difficult for her, but she understands how important it is for Diane. She'll get it."

The older hunter's tone placated him. "Thanks, Father."

"Also, get Josh working. He's in need of guidance."

As his father continued to the passenger seat, Liam looked to Diane's brother. "Josh, can you please get one of the new computers working? You can set it up with Linux if you'd like."

Silently, the young man lowered his tablet, walked to the ottoman, and took a computer box back to his chair.

Liam returned his attention to the television and his one-woman audience. He tapped the screen in the backyard of the house he wanted to see. "Can you get the coordinates of this point?"

Judith moved the cursor, right clicked, and copied the coordinates. "Got them. I'm sending them to the hovercraft controller. Our default altitude is ten feet."

"You've gotten pretty good at this."

"Practice makes it easy. We're a small team, but we're all going to learn our jobs because we want to help her."

From the passenger seat, the elder hunter aimed his voice into the spacious room. "Nana's ready to drive. Mind the slide outs please."

Judith stood and walked to Liam's side. "Okay. We're out of the way."

With Connor's guidance, the grandmother in the driver's seat tapped buttons, and the extended space with the couch slid into the living room. The confines became cramped but cozy with an enthusiastic team as the Chaldean woman drove the vehicle from the parking lot.

Twenty minutes later, Nana parked the RV on the side of a residential road, and Liam raised his voice. "Let's see how fast we can do this. We want to minimize attention to what we're doing so we don't have to explain ourselves to the local police."

"Hopefully, mature people of my generation and Nana's stepping out of an RV won't attract much attention."

"It's the hovercraft I'm worried about. Use the RV as a shield. Launch it from the side with the fewest possible onlookers."

"We're good to launch it from outside the door now. We'll have to remember to park in the proper direction next time. We got lucky this time." Connor reached behind his chair and lifted the hovercraft. "Nana, I believe you're our pilot."

The Chaldean woman stood from the driver's seat, opened the RV's door, and grabbed the drone. As she gingerly descended the steps, Liam darted behind her. "I'll watch over your shoulder this time, Nana."

"Okay, good. Thank you."

He grabbed her tablet from beside her seat and extended it. "Remember your tablet."

"Of course. I forget." She tucked it under her arm while carrying the drone.

"Place the hovercraft on the ground."

"Right here?"

"Sure. The most important thing is to be clear of trees, but it'll fly around most of them anyway."

She bent forward and grounded the hovercraft. "Now?"

"Go ahead."

After she tapped her tablet and the drone ascended, Liam marched back into the Winnebago and looked to the nursing student. "You set up her tablet to cast to the television, didn't you?"

"Ye of little faith. The screen showed the hovercraft's perspective rising over trees and then angling to a lower altitude. As the property's basement came into view, a pool table appeared.

"That's not Diane's prison."

"No, way. No curtains. No cinderblocks."

"Have Nana bring it back."

Connor raised his voice towards the door. "Bring it back, Nana."

Minutes later, the grandmother lumbered into the vehicle with the craft. She placed the drone on the floor as she lowered herself into the driver's seat.

Liam ran numbers through his head. Even if Nana could handle the driving, the navigation, and the drones by herself, the other four searchers raced a cruel clock.

Unless something changed, he feared Diane would die. But he needed to keep everyone's spirits up. "Good job, Nana. Now drive us out of here."

CHAPTER 40

Diane awoke on the couch.

She pushed herself to her feet and noticed orange crescents above both ends of the cinderblock wall. The setting sun signaled dusk's arrival, and a solitary lamp illuminated the dim basement. "Damn it. I slept away another day."

Speaking French words that conveyed clear meaning, the ghost corrected the inmate's assumption with a peaceful tone. "You slept three days."

Leg irons clanked as Diane turned her back to the setting sun's rays and faced the apparition. "Three days! Why?"

Behind the couch, the wraith's prior sacrifice wore the milky white, flowing dress of her afterlife and stared with black, lifeless orbs. "You're an empath. You know."

Diane's acceptance of supernatural interventions had eroded her awe of the apparition, and she yelled her demand for real-world advice. "Stop the cryptic crap! If you're here to help me, help me. I don't have time for games."

Unfazed, the presence remained silent while Diane assumed she tapped into whatever divine lord governed the rules of her corporeal communications. "You drain yourself when you attack with hatred. You risk dying by pushing too hard with anger."

"You mean if I push too hard, I may never wake up again?"

"Correct."

"How else am I supposed to connect with him? I need to match his emotions for my telepathy to work."

"Remove the distractions of selfishness. Care not for your needs but for the welfare of others."

The prisoner found the words familiar. "Didn't you say that

already? Haven't I been caring about Josh when I contact him?"

"Not Josh. Everyone."

"Everyone? Including... him?"

The white form slipped through the couch and stopped with its dress disappearing into a cushion. "His name is Jacob. He is still human. Love him as such."

"Love him? That's disgusting."

"Love is the tool of the empath."

Her breathing shallow, Diane thought she'd hyperventilate. "I can't love a barbarian."

"You must."

"Why can't you just tell me where I am? Why aren't you helping me get out of here?" The words sounded selfish as they circled the inmate's ears, and she grasped the answers as the apparition stared at her with cold judgment.

After an uncomfortable silence, the soft corners of the ghost's mouth turned up in a slight smile, and she confirmed Diane's suspicion. "You're an empath. You know."

"So, I need to find a way to show love to this barbarian."

"Jacob."

"I need to find a way to show love to Jacob." His name tasted bitter.

"To avoid destroying yourself, you must. To learn your location and be rescued, you must. To avenge me, you must."

"You say I need to love him. I can't!"

"Love is acceptance. Love is patience. Love is kindness. Love is empathy. Love is selflessness."

"I'm not sure I can share any of those with him."

"To redeem me, you must." The maiden vanished.

Alone, Diane assessed her updated situation. Glimpses through the monster's eyes–Jacob's eyes–had become bouts of physical exhaustion to the point of threatening her life. With three weeks until the full moon, she needed a faster and safer approach, but the ghost's instructions to show love to her enemy revolted her.

Stressing over the conundrum dizzied her, and she realized

the toll of sleeping three days included hunger. Famished, she climbed over the back of couch but stumbled on her way to the bathroom. Slapping her palm against the doorframe, she caught herself. She curled her leg behind her buttocks and wiggled her foot to verify the function of her ankle.

Thoughts of neglect consumed her as she jabbed her coffee cup into the huge bag of rice. Where had her jailor been for three days? Did he really expect her to survive on rice?

She ran the bathroom's hot tap water until it steamed, and then she filled her cup. While waiting for the rice to absorb the water, she tried to appreciate the food.

Somehow, she realized that gratitude was a springboard to love and its constituent emotions, a necessary step to surviving a telepathic link with the monster.

As the white grains became puffy, she scooped a spoonful and ingested it. Though her food was crunchy and hard, she chewed and swallowed. Hunger took over, and she downed the cup of half-cooked rice and starchy liquid while standing over the sink.

She refilled the cup with rice and hot water and then carried her second serving over the back of the couch. Placing her food on the coffee table, she let it stand as she prepared for a telepathic link. She sat upright on her favorite cushion and closed her eyes.

Before risking a stab at the killer's mind, she checked in with her brother. "Josh?"

"Diane!"

"I'm here."

"Where have you been? It's been forever."

"A ghost appeared to me–the same one as last time, and she said I slept for three days. Is that true? Is it already the eighth?"

"Yeah."

She considered sharing the maiden apparition's deeper insights about love, but she kept her message simple. "I've only got three weeks left."

"I know. We're still looking for you."

"Do you think you'll find me in time?"

"Liam acts like you'll be okay, but I can tell he's not sure."

"Is Liam in charge?"

"Sort of. I don't know. Sometimes it's Judith. Sometimes it's Connor."

Diane sensed the team included one more member. "Where's Nana? Is she with you?"

"Nana's driving the big Winnebago."

"Seriously? What Winnebago?"

"Connor bought one. He's rich, I think."

Her rescue team's commitment encouraged her. "That's good, Josh. Please thank them all for helping me. I appreciate you helping, too."

"Yeah. Okay."

"I'm going to go now, Josh. I'm going to try to enter the bad man's mind. Do you understand?"

"Yeah."

With time slipping away, she verified his comprehension. "What do you understand, Josh?"

"You will enter the bad man's mind."

"If I'm not back for a long time, that may be why. Do you understand that, too?"

"Long time. Yes."

"One more thing. I think I know the bad man's name. The ghost told me it's Jacob."

"The bad man is Jacob. Okay."

"Tell Liam, please. Tell everyone who's with you." She released him and opened her eyes.

The rice had become fluffy, and she downed several bites.

Remembering to somehow generate feelings of love, she closed her eyes and sought the murderer with the emotional combination she'd used to identify him before.

Anger. Envy. Haughtiness.

The proven mix of feelings worked again, and she met cold resistance and an ancient anger. She was in. He sensed her cerebral invasion and wanted her out.

With silent urging, she drove her consciousness towards his eyes, but she sensed an overbearing pride and a scorning lust. He was satiating his yearning to dominate someone.

He was having sexual intercourse.

Expecting any sensual information she might gain would be useless during his rutting, Diane wanted to retreat. But she was inside, and as she'd demanded, she shared his eyes.

Underneath him, a sex partner faced him with a subservient expression. Appalled, Diane scorned the woman but then gleaned a hint of sadness, like an evil spell kept her as the murderer's involuntary plaything.

She wanted to urge the woman to mouth their location, contact Josh, or gouge out the killer's eyes, but the sexual victim was beyond her telepathic reach. Diane could only pity her.

Love for the beast named Jacob was inconceivable.

The link broke, and Diane returned to her seated body on the couch in the dismal dungeon.

Exhausted from battling her host's resistance, she sensed herself falling into another supernaturally induced extended slumber. Facing lost time in recovery, she vowed to limit her assaults on her captor to his presence within the house.

She refused to stumble upon her jailor again while he engaged in debauchery, and she reminded herself to attempt a link of positive emotions to the animal who remained human, the man named Jacob.

CHAPTER 41

Leaving his second slave, vaguely recalling her name as Jessica in his panic, Jacob scurried out the hotel door.

The hauntings in his head were driving him mad, and he drove back to his cabin, seeking his Master's mercy to stop them. While rounding a turn, he lifted his phone to his face and checked the views from his basement's cameras.

His captive lay on the couch, where she spent most of her time. Her sleep seemed a hibernation.

As he brought the Acadia into the driveway, a jolt of fear struck him.

The horde of those he'd killed appeared in milky white dresses, hundreds of black pools of retribution staring through him.

Gasping, he aimed the SUV's grill at the first sacrifice of the phalanx, but the vehicle braked itself. He tried to order the legion away, but his throat tightened, and he struggled for breath.

The maiden of the millhouse slid through the engine compartment and lowered her head through the windshield. "Why did you kill me?"

Paralyzed, he watched her, and she leaned her translucent face into his. Her voice boomed with glacial frigidity and then rocketed to a torrid shriek. "You betrayed me. I will be avenged!"

She passed through him, chilling his organs, and the next ghost appeared, howling in his face. "You betrayed me. I will be avenged!"

Then all his deceased victims followed, taunting him. "You betrayed me. I will be avenged!"

"You betrayed me. I will be avenged!"

"You betrayed me. I will be avenged!"

Frozen as the train of the final phantom's dress whipped through his cold bones, Jacob whimpered. "Stop them, Master. I beg you!"

The Acadia returned to his control and rolled towards the garage. He parked it, regulated his breathing, and darted into the house. Staggering into the living room, he dropped to his knees. "Master, I beg you. What must I do?"

The wordless response burrowed into him with tangible meaning. His lording spirit lacked the power to stop the dead horde that haunted him, but he would address a corporeal threat.

Against the hunters, Jacob would have help.

The godlike spirit strengthened his hold over the concubines, offering them to Jacob as sentinels against his enemies.

After five hundred years of predictable laws, the monster's world turned upside down.

An independent escort had been allowed to humiliate him in Cleveland, a young hunter had ambushed him in Detroit early in the killing year, his virgin sacrifice had been repurposed as his lording spirit's next tribute, a half millennium of victims taunted him from beyond the grave, and now his sex slaves were permitted on the ritual site.

Though scared, he humbled himself and verbalized his appreciation to his demonic god. "Thank you, Master."

He rose to his feet and hurried downstairs where he stood over his captive. Unsure of her role in his recent otherworldly sufferings, he glared at her. Sleeping, she seemed innocent, and his domineering spirit's unwritten edict to leave her unspoiled constrained his actions.

He wondered if he could let his concubines punish the prisoner, but he thought better of challenging fine lines in his Master's orders.

The half-eaten warm cup of rice on the coffee table

suggested she'd been awake recently, and he kicked the couch. "Wake up."

Nothing.

He kicked again. "Wake up!"

She remained in a deep slumber that added to his fear. She seemed beyond his reach in a supernatural sleep, and the unknown forces affecting her compounded his confusion.

He needed help, and, acting upon his new freedom to solicit support, he called the closer concubine.

Jessica answered. "Hello."

"I will text you the address where I'm staying. You will check out of the hotel and come here immediately."

Her voice carried a renewed submissiveness. "Yes, Jacob."

"You will also take a leave of absence from your job, effective immediately."

"How long do you need me, Jacob?"

He counted the days to the full moon. "I need you for at least three weeks. Beyond that, is speculation."

"I will check out and join you immediately. Tomorrow morning, I will call my boss and take a leave of absence. If that's unacceptable to my boss, I will quit my job to serve you."

"Good."

He hung up and called his first concubine, the barista.

Kim answered. "Hello, Jacob."

"I will text you the address where I'm staying. You will drive here immediately."

Though she sounded tired from a long day of serving coffee drinkers, her voice carried the same obedience as Jessica's. "Yes, Jacob."

Silently, he thanked his overseeing spirit for the power boost over his slaves. "You will also take a leave of absence from your job, effective immediately. I need you for three weeks minimum."

"I will drive to you immediately. I will call my boss and take a leave of absence. My duty is to serve you."

Twenty minutes later, Jessica parked her car in the driveway and appeared at his door. Carrying an overnight bag, the slim young woman of average height looked at him with obedient eyes. Dark brown hair ran behind her back and framed her ovular face. Her blue irises had changed to a red so deep that its bloodlike color unsettled him. "I'm here, as you commanded, Jacob."

"Very well. Come in and leave your bag in the entryway. I have something to show you." He led her down the stairs and showed her the sleeping inmate. Kicking the couch, he yelled. "Wake up!"

Diane remained unmoving except for her deep breathing.

"Why does she sleep like that?"

"I don't know, but I don't like it. You will watch over her, and you will have help from my other... sentry. Her name is Kim."

"Yes, Jacob."

"You can see where the cameras are mounted throughout my house and yard. I will be watching you, Kim, and the prisoner. Be sure to obey me always, or I will punish you."

"Yes, Jacob."

Uncertain what signs he sought in the inmate's activities, he gave his new guard vague instructions. "Watch over her for strange behavior."

"Yes, Jacob."

"If she wakes, call me immediately."

He left the women downstairs and retired to his chamber. Sitting on the bed, he lifted his phone and checked the basement cameras.

A sleeping statue, the inmate continued her rest while his concubine-turned-guard sat in a chair facing her. Jessica's seated posture was ramrod perfect, inspired by a supernatural power. In her role of tedious boredom, watching over the unmoving captive, she seemed prepared for keeping an unfailing vigil.

He grabbed a bottle of narcotic painkillers from his bedside table and downed a dose to calm his nerves. Sliding under the sheets, he sought sleep but tossed and fidgeted for thirty minutes. Doubling his dosage, he ingested additional pills and then drifted into a dark dream.

In his nightmare, he lay on his back, frozen in helplessness. An infinite legion of countless ghosts in white dresses floated over him, each one driving a dagger into his heart.

A ringing phone ripped him from his slumber. He awoke with a start and answered. "Yes."

Despite the five-hour drive, the barista's voice carried its usual perkiness. "I'm in your driveway."

"I will meet you at the front door." He walked to the entryway and noticed Jessica's overnight bag where he'd told her to leave it. Opening the door, he saw sanguine irises and waved the short, shapely barista into his house.

"I'm here as you ordered, Jacob. I drove as fast as I could."

"Very well. Follow me downstairs." As he'd done with his other slave, he led Kim to the basement, past the cinderblock fortification, and to the sleeping inmate. Again, knocking the couch with his foot, he yelled. "Wake up!"

Diane remained unmoving.

The new sentry questioned the inmate's state. "Is she drugged?"

The question reminded him to prevent his sentinels from making dangerous inquiries. "Ask me no questions about my prisoner's identity or my intent with her. That applies to both of you. Is that understood?"

The sentinels responded in unison. "Yes, Jacob."

"The wall I built behind you and her chains are to keep her here, in this room. She is never to leave, unless I say otherwise. Is that understood?"

Again, the women answered together. "Yes, Jacob."

"Address me as 'my lord'. I don't want the prisoner knowing my name. Is that understood?"

"Yes, my lord."

"Other than monitoring her, I want you to attend to her basic needs. She has great value to me. I want her kept healthy. Is that understood?"

"Yes, my lord."

"One of you will always be here watching her. The other will be available for errands and any task I demand. You may each choose your bedroom upstairs and sleep when you're not serving me. Is that understood?"

"Yes, my lord."

"Neither of you will talk about your lives outside this house to each other or to the prisoner, and neither of you will contact anyone outside this house without my presence and my permission. Is that understood?"

"Yes, my lord."

Assuming the sentinels would handle their introductions and manage a watch schedule to meet his needs, he headed towards the stairs. But a new thought entered his mind and stopped him. "Tomorrow, Jessica, you will buy two twelve-gauge shotguns in your name and bring them here. Kim has already purchased weapons, and now it's your turn. I'll explain the threat later, but you both need to be ready to shoot buckshot. We have a house to defend."

CHAPTER 42

Diane awoke on the couch and noticed a human form sitting in a chair facing her.

Expecting her jailor, she found the stealthy presence creepy, but when her vision focused on female leather boots, she propped herself up with a start. "Who are you?"

"I am your caretaker."

"What do you mean? Get me out of here."

"I cannot."

Dumbfounded, Diane watched the slim brunette with perfect posture place her phone to her cheek. Something seemed wrong when she recognized the woman as Jacob's sexual partner from her prior invasion of his mind. "She's awake, my lord. No more than half a minute ago. I will ask her."

Aiming irises of disturbing blood-red at Diane, the stranger appeared under a spell. The shotgun beside her thigh confirmed the abnormal threat of the young lady's presence. "He demands to know if you command the army that taunts him."

"I don't know what he's talking about."

"He demands to know if you invade his mind."

Though guilty as accused, she refused to admit her solitary advantage. "Again, I don't know what he's talking about."

"She claims ignorance, my lord."

The basement's new occupant slid her phone into her jeans, and her silence became uncomfortable.

"My name's Diane. What's yours?"

"Jessica."

Surprised she'd answered, Diane realized the dominion of the force ruling the new arrival was imperfect. Despite the odd companion's creepiness, she was an exploitable opportunity. With darkness behind the cinderblock wall, Diane assumed the sun had set. "What time is it?"

Jessica withdrew her phone and glanced at it. "Eleven fifteen in the evening."

"What day?"

"May fifteenth."

"What?"

"May fifteenth."

"How long was I out?"

"You slept for a week."

Diane sprang to her feet and paced. "That's impossible."

"But it happened."

The last invasion of Jacob's mind, the one that had repulsed her while he'd defiled the woman who now sat before her as a deputy guard, had exhausted Diane worse than the other episodes combined. Recalling the ghost maiden's warning, she realized she'd failed to show love to her jailor, and she wondered if her inability to obey the apparition's order had brought her close to death. "Shit. Shit. Shit."

"Worrying won't help."

Diane stopped her pacing and studied her companion. "How did you get here?"

"I cannot answer that."

"Are you here to help me?"

"I may tend to your basic needs. Are you hungry?"

The question brought Diane's hunger to her awareness. "Yeah, I'm starved. All he left me is rice. Can you get me some real food?"

"Yes."

"Great! Can you get me Chinese takeout?"

"I cannot. I may only feed you what's in the house."

The silence above her head suggested Jessica was her only present housemate. She made a wild request. "Can you unshackle me so that I can pick the food?"

"I cannot."

"What can you do to feed me?"

The deputy appeared to ponder how to obey whatever unseen entity ruled her mind. "I will take pictures of our inventory and show them to you."

"Thanks."

As her companion carried her shotgun up the stairs, Diane sat and closed her eyes. "Jessica. You feel betrayed, helpless, angry... maybe ashamed, though it can't be your fault. I bet I can find you." As she sought the young woman, she sensed immediate and strong validation of the emotions she emanated. With ease, she found Jessica and focused her energy on her.

But something blocked her connection.

Instead of pushing, she retreated and repositioned herself at a new angle of attack. Pitying the supernaturally enslaved woman, she radiated compassion and empathy. Within the spiritual realm, Diane offered a safe outlet for Jessica to exorcise her pain. "Jessica?"

The new jailor's unspoken words were tinny as they echoed in Diane's head. "I'm sorry."

"It's not your fault. I can help you."

"There are two of us. Kim and me. We're under his control."

Careful to avoid a possible trap, Diane withheld the secrets she wished to guard. "Work with me. I have empathic powers. If we team up, we can do this. If you or Kim can free me..."

The rejection sounded like an apology. "I cannot."

"Can you tell me where we are? The address? The city?"

"I cannot."

Changing tactics, Diane tried to soothe her companion. "Can you tell me about yourself?"

"I cannot."

"Can you tell me if he's hurting you?"

"I cannot."

"I know I look like the only prisoner, but do you want me to help you to escape?"

Diane sensed agony from her link's partner before the

connection snapped.

She inhaled and sighed, and then she heard the real-world Jessica descending the stairs. In eerie silence, she carried the shotgun to her chair and laid it against the arm. Standing on the opposite side of the coffee table, beyond Diane's reach, she showed the phone. "Can you let me hold that to look at it?"

"I cannot."

Giving up on quick tricks to fool her companion, she tended to her hunger. The phone showed an open refrigerator with cold cuts, sliced cheese, assorted vegetables, and bread. "How about the cupboards?"

Jessica rolled the phone to a second photograph showing noodles, pasta sauce, energy bars, canned goods, and snacks.

"Will you make me a sandwich with ham, cheese, lettuce, and tomatoes please?"

"I will."

Carrying her firearm, the deputy jailor returned up the stairs towards the kitchen.

Diane closed her eyes again and prepared to connect with her brother, but Jessica came back down the stairs and interrupted her.

"Kim will bring you your sandwich."

"Kim? She's home?"

"She's asleep now, but her shift starts at eleven thirty. I must wake her."

Diane saw an opening. "Kim's so quiet when she sleeps. Is she in her bedroom?"

"Yes."

Taking a snarky tone, Diane tried to break through a gray area in the black and white rules governing her companion. "Does she snore like a freight train?"

"I... I don't know."

"Is it weird sharing a bedroom with another woman?"

"I don't know."

Bingo. "I'm sorry to bother you. I'll wait for Kim to bring my sandwich. I look forward to meeting her."

"Goodnight, Diane."

Nobody had showed her kindness in person for weeks, and she sensed the real human hiding under a monster's magic, trying to escape. "Goodnight, Jessica. I'm glad you're here."

The sentinel turned and walked up the stairs.

Carrying an urgent update, Diane felt her heart fluttering. She needed extra minutes to calm herself and create the connection with her brother. "Josh?"

"Diane!"

"Are you okay?"

"I'm worried about you."

"I have news. Please tell Liam. There are two women working with Jacob who are guarding me. They're under some sort of spell. I tried connecting with them, I mean one of them. I haven't met the other one yet. Their names are..."

Her eyes fluttered open, and she realized she'd overwhelmed her brother. "Come on, Diane. Softer."

She recreated the link. "Josh? Josh? I'm sorry, Josh. I'll be more careful."

"Diane? I'm here."

Unsure why her mind, or perhaps her heart, always returned to Liam, she thought she shared an unexplored attraction to the young Irishman. "Can you talk to Liam for me and let me hear him through your ears?"

"I don't know. I'll try."

"I'll talk real slow and use small words."

"Okay. I guess so."

"Talk out loud for me, Josh. Okay?"

"Okay."

"Here we go, Josh. Can anyone hear me? Liam, this is Diane. Can you hear me? Liam, this is Diane. Can you hear me?"

Echoing with garbling reverberation, Liam's voice circled throughout the cavern of the joint Josh-Diane mind. "Diane? This is Liam. Diane?"

"Can you hear me?"

"Yes. I hear Josh's voice, but is that you?"

"It's me. There are two women here under Jacob's spell. Red eyes, like blood."

Though the young hunter tried to sound businesslike, she sensed his underlying selfless concern for her safety. "Two women under his spell. Red eyes. Got it. Go on."

"I've met only one, but she mentioned the other. Jessica and Kim are their names."

"Jessica and Kim. Go on."

"I connected with Jessica telepathically, but there was a shield, like a firewall, blocking most questions."

"You linked to Jessica but were mostly blocked. Go on."

"I think I figured out this house has at least three bedrooms."

With rising excitement, the hunter's reverberating words rose half an octave. "Three bedrooms minimum. Are you sure?"

"Jessica said Kim was sleeping in her bedroom, and I asked her if it was weird sharing a room with another woman. She said she didn't know."

"Well done! That will help immensely."

Diane still sensed her doom. "But does it guarantee you'll find me in time?"

"Guarantee? I need to rerun the filters, but I don't think so. It will turn the odds in our favor, though."

"I need to get back into Jacob's head, but my last attempt cost me a week."

"We know. Josh sensed you were okay, but we were frustrated to say the least. Nana's beside herself with worry."

"My next attempt could be my last, but I know I'm going to die if I don't try."

With her prophecy of doom, she pushed her brother beyond his coping skills, severing the link.

Regaining her local awareness, she saw a new deputy guard carrying a shotgun in one hand and a plated sandwich in her other.

The young curvaceous woman wore sandy blonde hair around her cheeks. Compared to Diane, she was short and buxom, but she carried herself with a charming perkiness.

As she set the food before the captive, the new arrival looked up and exposed white teeth under haunting sanguine irises. "Jessica told me what you wanted."

"Thank you. My name's Diane. What's yours?"

"Kim."

"It's good to meet you, Kim. I look forward to getting to know each other."

"I cannot."

As the new guard sat on the chair with perfect posture facing her prisoner, Diane smiled. "I know. But I've got a feeling we'll manage to get along anyway."

CHAPTER 43

Eleven days later, Liam sensed frustration rising through his exhaustion.

Standing in front of the RV's television, he watched the Excel spreadsheet flicker to its new numbers.

The single cell gathering the Winnebago occupants' attention showed the remaining time to filter the list and examine the houses with a hovercraft.

He counted eight days. "That's better than it was before Diane last contacted us and told us about the three-bedroom minimum."

Judith sounded angry, like the search for Diane represented her revenge. "It's still not good enough. The full moon's in four days. We've been searching for too long for this to fail."

Spying on possible prisons had proven the greatest time challenge in investigating candidate houses. In response, Liam had adjusted the team's schedule to spend more time driving between properties at the expense of searching online.

In his easy chair, Josh continued his online searches with admirable resolve. By Liam's judgment, the young man slept less than six hours a night.

Nana and Connor also maintained a tireless vigil, swapping chauffeuring and hovercraft operation duties, to keep the Journey moving across the state. When free, the older hunter searched for properties on a laptop.

Judith searched online, ran the laundry, cleaned, and made a continual fuss about the messiness of the three men who seemed to fall short of her impeccable standards of cleanliness.

Liam helped Judith, looked for houses, drove, and did whatever else was needed, but most of all, he worried. Though she remained a stranger, Diane struck him as a vital presence for his life's purpose. "It's a coin toss that we get to her on time. Bloody hell. I thought we had this all but locked down when she narrowed this to three or more bedrooms."

With the growing fear of failure, Nana suffered the worst. Age, fatigue, and anxiety were wearing her down. The younger members had rallied to maintain the workload, but the need to jam eight days of combing the remaining houses into the four days before the full moon created a somber mood.

Connor drove, allowing Nana time on the couch. Half asleep with her head propped on her palm, she awoke with a fuss. "Why can't we call the police now? We're out of time."

Liam empathized with her. "I want everyone in the world helping us, Nana, but we just can't. It defies the rules."

The grandmother raised her voice. "What rules? You say you can't get help, but you have all of us helping. You make no sense!"

Careful to filter his rising frustration, the young hunter measured his words. "We can't ask for help. We're quite lucky that you all volunteered."

"Then we go ask for help. Why not?"

"We can't let you do that, either. It amounts to the same thing as us asking."

Overhearing the conversation, Connor pulled the RV to the side of the road and parked. He turned and joined the conversation. "I think it's time Liam and I show you one of the secrets of our lineage."

"Father?"

"Get the dagger."

Obedient, Liam reached into an overhead cabinet and pulled out a case. He lowered it to the floor in front of the ottomans, and everyone except Josh leaned towards him to view the contents. He opened the case, and with his eyes set upon it, the bronze dagger pointed toward the prior killing's location in Flint.

"Now hand the dagger to Nana."

Liam grabbed the handle, kept the blade's orientation steady, and extended the weapon to the old woman.

Having never shared the dagger with anyone, Liam deferred to his father's lead. "Careful, Nana. It'll surprise you with its stubbornness. It won't move in certain directions."

The Chaldean matriarch grasped the handle. "What do I do with it?"

"See if you can point it at Liam."

Her knuckles became pink and then white, but the blade remained pointed towards the side of the Winnebago.

"Try as you may, it will always point towards the site of the last murder, as long as Liam or I are looking at it."

The magic made the grandmother smile and blush, and Liam judged his father's sharing of the secret worth the risk.

Judith reached for the weapon. "Let me try!"

Like a pantomime of zero-gravity clumsiness, Nana shoved the dagger to the nursing student.

Wide eyed, the student struggled against the handle. "Oh my God. I can't twist it at all."

Connor sounded satisfied. "Welcome to our secret club. Josh, would you like to try?"

The young man who had been dutifully investigating properties set his laptop on the seat as he stood, and he walked to Judith. He wielded the dagger, and it obeyed its ancient laws. "Cool."

"Now Liam and I will look away. You can all try moving the dagger around again."

Obeying his father, Liam turned his back and heard his colleagues' gasps as he expected that they regained natural control over an un-enchanted chunk of bronze. Connor told them to return the dagger to its case, and Liam heard Josh conceal the weapon.

"So, you see, we are subject to rules beyond our understanding. I've shared a story with Liam about how our ancestors suffered a horrible loss when they reached out to local townsfolk for help. It's beyond our understanding or our

284

power to change, but we must abide by the rules."

"It's frustrating, but Father's right."

"We must trust Diane to guide us. This may be conjecture on my part, but I have deep knowledge of this subject and believe she's the most powerful empath of her lineage to date."

Rejuvenated, Nana stood, walked towards the driver's seat, and addressed the elder hunter. "How far are we from the next house?"

"About ten miles. It's right outside the city of Grayling, near the interstate."

"I'll drive. You look for Diane."

Connor stood. "Thank you, Nana. So be it. Shall I make us a pot of tea, everyone?"

Judith bolted towards the kitchen. "I'll handle it. You're all too messy. I'd have to clean up after you anyway."

While the nursing student worked in the kitchen, the elder hunter passed her on his way to the bathroom, and Liam returned the encased dagger to its cabinet.

Judith stood by the stove waiting for the water to boil. She looked exhausted but tough, as a nurse would be.

Connor emerged from the bathroom and moved to the couch. Liam joined him, and the elder hunter leaned to his ear, speaking in a low voice. "Our mission isn't saving Diane, nor is it saving the two in his power."

The conversation's premise irritated Liam. "Jessica and Kim, Father. They have names."

For the first time in recent memory, Connor raised his voice and showed his ire. "And so do each of the hundreds of innocents we must protect! Never forget that!" As their colleagues looked at them from three directions, the elder hunter lowered his voice. "Just because three of them are known to you, just because we're teamed with the family of one, doesn't change what we are or what we're tasked to do. Don't sacrifice hundreds of lives trying to save just one."

"You can't ask me to not care."

"Do you care for Diane more than Jessica or Kim?"

"I don't understand. I've never met any of them."

"That's my point. They're all strangers. If you try to save Diane, you'll put Jessica and Kim in the line of fire. He may even use them as human shields. But if we come at this smartly, we can ambush him without jeopardizing them."

During his moments of rest during the past weeks, Liam had been rehearsing visions of assaulting a house. The concept of an ambush outside the house had escaped him. "You believe an ambush is possible? Lure him out of the house?"

"Lure him out? No. There's no bait we have that can lure him. But what you're overlooking is the opportunity to study his living patterns and ambush him when he's unaware."

Liam found the logic sound but unnerving. "Our ancestors have always assaulted him on his ritual site. It's his de facto lair in the year of killing, and we're supposed to challenge him there."

The elder man raised an eyebrow. "You only assumed so because every one of our ancestors had no choice. They never found the lair until the wraith was cooped up inside it preparing for the sacrifice. But with Diane's telepathy and your technical skill, we'll find him before the year of killing is half over. I believe that's an advantage that destines us for great success, but not if we die trying to assault a fortress."

"I hate this. We can't give up on Diane."

"I've never heard of the wraith having help defending the ritual site, but the lives of his two slaves count as much as Diane's."

The young hunter's heart hurt. "Diane's special."

"Of course, she is. But we're not gods who decide whose life is the most valuable. I'm asking you to fulfill your destiny of stopping a monster. He will kill forever unless we stop him."

The realization hit Liam like biting cold. "You want to let Diane die?"

"I do not, but you need to consider the tactical necessity. It will depend on my assessment of the house once we find it. Don't misunderstand that it's my assessment and not yours.

Our historical pairing has always relied upon the wisdom of the elder hunter."

Respecting his father's assertion of his lead role, Liam bit back his frustration. He also applied a little wisdom of his own, knowing to avoid a needless argument.

He'd argue later if he disliked his father's ruling.

And he also realized if Diane could manage to lead them to her, he'd find a way to assure that her rescue team showed up.

CHAPTER 44

Diane dreamt of a woman on a cross, blood pouring from her wound. Time stopped, twisted, and turned, leaving the dreaming prisoner as the burning, bleeding victim.

She called out in her nightmare. "What should I do?"

The misty maiden appeared. "Stop destroying yourself."

Diane recalled her latest attempt to see through the monster's eyes. Encouraged by her two deputy guards, she'd attacked the beast with renewed vigor.

Her mistake had been attacking, and she'd seen nothing. The cost—entrapment in yet another enduring dream.

She'd penetrated deep, earning his rejection and draining her life force. Wishing she'd found a way to heed the French ghost's advice of showing the monster a shred of love, she now languished beyond time and space.

The dreamlike fire and injuries evaporated, leaving Diane with her ghost. "You say I need to love him. I can't!"

"Love is acceptance. Love is patience. Love is kindness. Love is empathy. Love is selflessness. You are capable of all these."

"I can't do any of that trapped here, wherever we are."

"You will have one more chance."

"One chance? I'll do my best."

"To redeem me, you must."

"What do you mean by redeeming you?"

"I died in hatred. Only love can redeem me." The maiden vanished, and Diane awoke on her couch.

Testing her eyes, she blinked and focused on her seated guard. With ramrod alertness, Kim watched over her. "Are you awake?"

"Yeah."

The armed guard raised a phone to her cheek. "She's awake, my lord."

The deputy slid her phone into her jeans.

"What's going on?"

Kim ignored her.

"Answer me."

"I cannot."

Heavy and rapid footsteps banged against the stairs, and the jailor appeared, wearing a shoulder harness with holsters. Jessica, his second armed deputy, followed him as he walked to the room's center and faced Diane from across the coffee table. Kim then stood, flanking him.

He buried angry eyes into her. "Do you command the army that taunts me?"

"I still have no idea what you're talking about."

"I demand to know if you invade my mind."

Instead of lying, Diane tried the ghost's advice, acknowledging that someone exhibiting love would speak the truth. "Yes, I've invaded your mind four times."

"Move this table!"

His sentinels lowered their shotguns and carried the coffee table to the cinderblock wall. Jacob stepped forward and grabbed Diane's jaw. "I can't defile you. I can't damage you. But I can hurt you." He reached into his holster and then jabbed a Taser into her pajama top.

Her world turned white, and her tissues writhed with overloading impulses as she collapsed onto the couch. Her useless and convulsing muscles were stabbing needles. As her convulsions subsided, she stared up at his furious eyes.

But the windows to his spirit also revealed pain. "Why do you taunt me?"

Her facial muscles ignored her as she tried to answer.

"Answer me!"

Kim stepped forward. "She cannot, my lord."

The savage turned and backhanded his sentinel's jaw. "Silence! Your insolence is insufferable."

He looked back to Diane. "Answer me!"

She choked out the words. "To escape."

The murderer smirked. "There is no escape, and I told you if I caught you lying to me, I'd make you suffer." He jabbed the Taser into her stomach again, and then he went back up the stairs with Jessica on his heels. While Diane writhed in agony, Kim sat in her sentinel's seat with perfect posture.

When the incapacitating currents subsided, Diane lay motionless. After several minutes, she gathered her strength and pushed herself upright. She looked at her guard, whose face showed sadness despite its sanguine irises. "Don't blame yourself for helping him. It's not your fault."

"I don't know."

"Forgive yourself."

"I cannot."

"I forgive you."

The sentry's eyes welled with tears. "Thank you."

Her compassion expressed, Diane shifted to her tactical mode. She needed to contact her brother, but first she sought an update from her deputy jailor. "What day is it?"

"May twenty-sixth."

"I was asleep for eleven days?"

"I was... afraid you might never wake up."

Though she'd failed to elicit information from Jessica upon meeting her, she tested Kim's firewalls. "Can you tell me where we are?"

"I cannot."

"What city? What county?"

"I cannot."

"How many bedrooms does this house have?

"I... I cannot."

The firewalls were in place, and Diane tried to get personal. "What do you do for a living? Are you a student?"

"I cannot."

"You know he's going to kill me in four days, right?"

"I... Are you hungry?"

The otherworldly slumber had left Diane ravenous, and she accepted the woman's redirection. "Yes. Can I have a sandwich like last time?"

"I will make you a sandwich." Shotgun in hand, the sentinel walked away.

Alone, Diane sat on her cushion and reached out for her brother. "Josh?"

"Diane?"

"Are you okay?"

"I'm scared for you. You were gone eleven days."

"I tried too hard to see what he saw when I was in his head. I have only one more chance to try it."

"We still have eight days' worth of houses to search."

"Does that make my odds fifty-fifty?"

"Yeah."

"But you feel it. You know you're not going to find me in time unless I help you find me."

"Yeah."

"I'm going into his head one more time."

"No, it's dangerous."

"I need to. I have to save myself. Who else will take care of you if I don't make it out?"

Assuming she'd scared away her brother, she lost the link, and she saw the sentry standing over her. "Where did you go?"

"What do you mean?"

"We're out of ham, and I came back to ask if you wanted turkey instead. But your eyes were closed, and I could tell you weren't here."

"How could you tell?"

"I don't know."

"I don't want to tell you, but it was a happy place for me."

Diane thought she noticed new tears welling in Kim's eyes. "I'm glad you were able to go somewhere happy."

"Turkey's fine, Kim. I appreciate your help."

"I will get your sandwich." Firearm in her hand, the sentry went upstairs.

Alone, Diane recalled the emotions to link to her jailor. Anger. Envy. Haughtiness.

Finding him proved easy as she sensed his reciprocal emotions, but staying within him while avoiding spiritual exhaustion required a new approach. He sickened her, but she called upon her deepest empathies.

Acceptance. "Your name is Jacob. You are human. I accept you."

"Get out of my head, harlot."

Patience. "I have the rest of my life for this."

"I told you to get out."

Kindness. "Express all the anger you want if it makes you feel better."

"You have no right."

Empathy. "I agree. I have no right to invade your mind. I'll leave if you want, but I know you want me to stay."

"How can you know anything?

Selflessness. "I will help you however I can."

"I don't need help."

"Yes, you do. You're alone. You've been alone for centuries. That must be horrible for you."

"You know nothing of real pain."

"I can't imagine what you've been through. It's been horrible, and you can't tell anyone. But now, I'm listening."

His resistance weakened, and she saw a blurry glimpse through his eyes. Whiteness, then nothing. "I am alone. It is my fate."

"You're with me."

"You will leave. Everyone leaves."

She saw through his eyes again, and the vision cleared. He was sitting in the driver's seat of an SUV, probably the one he used to kidnap her. The windshield was an opaque barrier. "Nobody deserves to be alone."

"I do. I murdered my cousin. Then I murdered hundreds."

"Every sin can be forgiven." The windshield became transparent, and she saw the back wall of the vehicle's garage.

From the periphery of his vision, she saw the hood of a dark SUV on one side and a door into the house on the other.

"I am beyond forgiveness. Get out. I expel you."

Her consciousness reappeared within herself, and she opened her eyes.

The sandy blonde sentry held a plate with a sandwich. "You were gone again."

"Yes, I was gone."

"Did you go back to your happy place?"

Diane assessed the outcome of her display of love. "It was a happy place. A really happy place."

CHAPTER 45

Liam burned his eyes on his laptop screen. The three-bedroom house northwest of Cadillac bordered an ancient Chippewa tribal burial ground and garnered his intense interest.

He glanced around the RV for a second opinion but was alone. His father drove into the darkness, seeking a property in Frankfort with a yard touching Lake Michigan. Josh slept on the couch while the ladies shared the bed at the rear of the vehicle.

Leaving the elder hunter to concentrate on the road, he placed the Cadillac property on the list of houses to explore with the hovercraft.

Then the prisoner's brother stirred. "Liam?"

"I'm here, Josh."

"Two-car garage."

The hunter dropped his laptop into the easy chair and darted across the living room. "What?"

Josh pushed himself upward. "Diane talked to me in my sleep."

Liam remembered to be patient with the autism. "That's good, Josh. Is she okay?"

"Yeah."

"You mentioned a two-car garage."

"Yeah."

"Did Diane say the house has a two-car garage?"

"Yeah."

"Are you sure?"

"She saw through his eyes, but this time, she was okay. She came back immediately."

His hands trembling, Liam reran his filters with the new information. As he'd hoped, the remaining population of houses became favorable.

Seven hundred and eighty-two. If the team rallied, they'd find her in time. "Father!"

"Yes?"

"Stop the Winnebago, please."

"Why?"

"The house we're driving towards has no garage, and according to Josh, that's our latest and most useful criteria."

His father pulled the RV to the side of the road, parked, and turned his seat around. "Did Diane contact him?"

"During his sleep. She saw the garage through the wraith's eyes, and she returned immediately to her body this time, apparently with enough energy to contact Josh."

"I assume this changes things?"

Liam's mind raced. "I'm doing the math. We need about twenty-five hours of work. If we start in the morning, we can find her in two days."

The older hunter raised his eyebrows. "I suggest that we all recharge with a good night's sleep and tackle this with zest after a good breakfast."

The next morning, Liam explained the facts while treating the team to a late breakfast at a pancake house. A waitress brought five dishes and set them in front of the rescue team.

As the server departed, the nursing student cut a pile of pancakes with her fork and looked to the young hunter. "What's the great news you wanted to tell us?"

The grandmother qualified the question. "Yeah, why we take the time to eat here? We need to keep looking."

"Agreed, we need to keep looking. And we will. But we now have enough time. Diane spoke to Josh last night and said the house has a two-car garage."

Nana raised an eyebrow. "What's that mean?"

"It just reduced our search time from eight days to two."

"We're going to find my granddaughter?"

"Yes, Nana. I know we will."

The next night, Josh mumbled from the easy chair. "I think I found it."

Liam looked up from the couch. "Josh?"

"Look at my house."

Liam grabbed the remote and toggled to the younger man's computer as the source. Pictures of a cabin appeared that matched the known parameters of Diane's prison. The hunter typed the address into the map on his laptop. "South of Traverse City, forty-two miles away. What do you think, ladies?"

Beside him on the couch, Nana and Judith expressed their optimism, and Josh volunteered his assessment. "I know it's her."

"Okay, then. I'm sending it to the RV's navigation. Father, we have a new destination."

As his father drove, Liam verified the site as an ancient Chippewa burial ground, boosting his optimism.

Parked on the side of a rural road, Liam watched the television. The image showed the hovercraft's perspective as it descended into the target house's backyard.

Dusk was fading into twilight, but as the drone steadied, Liam saw the glass wall of a walkout basement. Behind the transparent façade was darkness.

"The lights are off. Let's try infrared." Liam shifted the view, and the image showed one figure lying on a couch and another on a chair. "Father, have Nana bring it back. I'm going to try something."

Ten minutes later, Liam stood outside the Journey holding the controller of his smaller drone. Without satellite navigation, the small hovercraft needed his steady hand.

He worked two joysticks and watched the craft's perspective rise over the tree line and then descend over the quiet stream.

Following the shoreline, he brought the drone into the house's backyard and steadied it inches from the reflective surface.

Sliding the hovercraft sideways, he moved it slowly. He stopped it at the edge of the glass where he saw dim interior lighting breaking around the end of a curtain.

"Here we go." He drove the craft forward until it hit the glass. The camera spun but steadied again.

Nothing.

Trying again, he took a longer run and crashed the drone into the wall. The camera tumbled, and he released the controls to let the aircraft stabilize itself. Hurrying with the joysticks, he reoriented the lens towards the wall.

Fingers pulled back the curtain, and a young brunette woman looked back at him. By her jeans, the stock of a shotgun was visible, and her irises were blood red.

Liam's heart leapt into his throat, and before he lost his composure, he brought the hovercraft to its highest altitude. Trembling with excitement, he brought the small drone back to his feet, grabbed it, and darted into the RV.

Four curious faces studied him. "That's the house. We found her."

The Chaldean woman raised her arms. "Thank God! What do we do now?"

From the driver's seat, the elder hunter gave an intense stare, reminding Liam of the real possibility of abandoning the prisoner and the slaves to accomplish the mission. Adhering to Connor's desires, the young hunter stopped short of promising a direct assault on the house. "Father and I will evaluate our tactical options, and he will render his final assessment. We have almost twenty-four hours left before the full moon's rise."

Three hours later, penciled floorplans and drawings of the property covered the ottomans. The elder hunter shook his head. "He chose this property well. The short sides are solid walls without access, and the long sides front and back give him elevated positions with clear fields of fire over every approach."

Liam agreed and tried to find an option to storm the cabin. "What about a rear approach?"

"The backyard would be an uphill climb, and we'd be exposed on open grass."

"Okay, then. We can use our RV as a proxy for an armored vehicle and approach from the front."

Again, his father shook his head. "We could make the approach, but we'd be stranded in the driveway."

"From the woods?"

"If we survived the incendiary traps, we'd still be pinned down in open fields of fire."

With midnight approaching, Liam sensed his fatigue anchoring his thoughts. To save Diane, he needed to rest and tackle the problem with a fresh mind. "I concede for the night, Father, but can we tell the others that we're still assessing our options?"

"It would be cruel to give them false hope."

"I know. But can we agree that there's still a chance of saving her?"

"Very well, lad. I won't stop you from hoping while there's still a chance, however remote it may be."

CHAPTER 46

Beside his father, Liam awoke the next morning on the converted couch-ottoman bed in the RV's living room, filled with resignation.

The elder hunter was right.

Storming the house would be foolhardy.

The proper tactic was waiting beside the cabin's access road and ambushing the savage. Tied to the property for the ritual, the beast was tethered. He'd have to drive the route eventually, and with patient surveillance, the hunters could defeat him on their terms.

Surely, Nana and Josh would understand. Perhaps they could even forgive him, because he knew he couldn't forgive himself.

He remained doubly silent, reserved within himself, while tiptoeing to the bathroom to avoid waking his teammates. Glancing out the window, he noticed a solitary car pulling into the empty department store parking lot.

Though he'd spent dozens of nights in the Winnebago in large lots, this morning's routine felt different.

Instead of pondering ways to search faster, compare lists, track maps, and optimize travel times, he was assessing battle options against the savage.

As the paternal wisdom seeped into him, he realized the burden of decision rested upon his father's shoulders. That consolation would mitigate the pain of losing Diane, and years from now, she'd be just another of many victims.

Rolling to the floor, Connor awoke and stood. His normally chipper morning demeanor was off-kilter and pensive. "Liam?"

"Good morning, Father. Did you sleep well?"

"No, I spent many hours thinking, and perhaps that was a good thing."

"Would you like some tea?"

"Yes, thank you."

The young hunter prepared hot water, and he sensed an uncomfortable conversation brewing as his disheveled father approached him before any effort to make himself presentable. "I've come to a conclusion."

"It's okay, Father. I understand."

"I don't think you do. Several days ago, I said I believed we were destined for greatness, but I was mistaken on the method to achieve such a lofty and ambiguous goal. Tactical discipline and self-preservation demand that we forego assaulting the house and establish an ambush."

"Most assuredly, Father. I see why you as the elder hunter are in charge. It's for difficult decisions like this." Thinking they'd reached an agreement, Liam grabbed a cup of hot water and slid it towards his companion.

"A difficult decision, indeed. My life, my son's life, and countless potential innocent victims are at stake. That's why I'm glad my intuition made me focus on the greatness."

"What's that mean?"

"It means we face great danger to save a great woman. We'll draw up the best plan we can manage, and then we'll assault the house before sunset. We're going to save Diane or die trying."

After breakfast and a morning of planning, Liam watched the elder hunter standing in front of the television, briefing the full team. He remained silent to let his father regain authority over the mission. An overhead diagram of the cabin's floorplan overlay the property map on the screen behind the elder hunter.

The nursing student voiced the first objection. "I'm no expert, but this looks like you're at a disadvantage."

"That's correct. We'll have some element of surprise to

mitigate our poor position, but it's certain he knows we mean to attack before moonrise."

"Why can't you just start shooting now and wait for local police to show up?"

"Intentional sloppiness is the same thing as calling for help. It won't be tolerated."

"Let me help you, then. I can shoot a gun. I bet Nana can, too."

"Yes, I can. If you teach Judith to shoot, I shoot a gun, too."

"I can't ask that of you."

Judith glared at Connor. "We're volunteering. Can you deny that extra guns make a difference?"

The nursing student's scowl chilled Liam, and he rescued the elder hunter. "You're not going to win the argument against two ladies, Father. Four guns are better than two, and I have an idea."

Half an hour later, he dropped off his father and the ladies at a car rental site, leaving them to pick up a vehicle, drive to the closest gun range, and teach the new recruits about basic firearms tactics.

With Josh, Liam drove to successive hardware stores until he'd piled three hundred prefilled thirty-pound sandbags into the RV. He parked in the corner of the lot located closest to Diane's prison.

He aimed the windshield towards the trees to allow privacy. "Come on, Josh. Help me out."

"Okay."

"You need to put down your tablet."

"I'm reading about sandbag barriers."

"Well, that's good."

Liam's colleague remained seated with his tablet in his face. "Josh?"

"Yeah."

"Did you learn anything from your reading?"

"Yeah."

"Would you like to tell me?"

"You need to build it like a pyramid with more bags on the lower levels before you build up."

Liam knew the technique, but he appreciated the young man's interest. "That's right, Josh. Can you help me now and then finish your reading later?"

"Okay."

"Josh?"

"Yeah."

"That means you need to put down your tablet and come here to help me."

The young man obeyed and stood near the pile of bags Liam had paid loaders to stack in the vehicle's living room.

"You lift one and give it to me. Then I'll put it in place. Got it?"

"Yeah."

"Okay. I'm ready Josh. Go ahead."

Nothing.

"Josh, would you please hand me a bag?"

The young man grabbed a bag but stopped. "It's heavy."

"I know, Josh. But we need to work hard for Diane."

A frown consumed the young man's face, and he redoubled his efforts to lift the burlap. He managed to balance it against his chest and bring it to the hunter.

"Got it." The Irishman turned and tossed the bag on the couch.

"I can do that, too."

"Okay. We'll both pile bags on the couch. I'll make sure we put them in the right place."

The autistic man caught him off guard with a question. "What should I tell Diane if she contacts me?"

"Tell her when she hears weapons firing to hide in the bathtub and keep her head down."

Two hours later, Liam stood outside the vehicle inspecting his work. With the slide outs retracted, he and Josh had established a sandbag wall covering three quarters of the windshield, rounding the corner into the living room, and continuing over the couch and three quarters of its window.

The top quarters of the windows remained open for shooting and driving.

As a finishing touch, he and Josh had built a small, straight barrier on the RV's roof, canted at forty-five degrees from the vehicle's grill. To reach the higher position, Connor would climb the Journey's far side beyond the reach of retaliatory fire.

As the elder hunter pulled the rental car into the parking lot, Liam hoped his father would be proud of his preparations. But before he could display his barriers, Judith sprang from the car and marched to him. "I shot a rifle, a pistol, and a shotgun. That was like therapy."

The Chaldean grandmother stepped from the vehicle. "That was fun. I wish I'd learned to shoot before now."

Examining the sprawl of sandbags while he walked, the elder hunter caught up to the group. "They're ready to shoot straight enough, and I like what you did with the bags."

"Are we ready, then, Father?"

"Let's make our final checks and suit up."

Behind the bedroom's closed door, Liam helped his father tighten his body armor across his chest. Opened cases covered the bed after the hunters had distributed the weapons between themselves. One open container held foam in the shape of folding bolt cutters, which his father strapped with Velcro onto the back of his vest.

Connor tugged a strap on younger hunter's armor. "I have a present for you."

"Isn't now a bad time for surprises?"

"It's in the living room. Follow me."

He trailed the older hunter out of the bedroom, and Judith greeted the men with enthusiasm. "You guys are the real deal. You look like Navy SEALs."

"I believe I'm older than their official naming as such. But we certainly mean business."

"Why don't we have suits like that?"

"You won't be exposing yourselves."

From the easy chair, Josh looked up. "Remember the dagger. Diane needs it."

As the one who would extract her, Liam checked his vest for a free weapons slot. Then he remembered the knife's magic. "I have room for it, but I can't risk seeing it. I'll tie it to my belt, in its sheath." He grabbed the case from the cabinet and then fastened the lanyard from the bronze knife's sheath around a belt loop at his right hip.

Connor tapped the sheath to test its range of motion. "You'll have to let it bounce while you move. It will seem foreign, but it won't make much noise against the grass and may prove useful if you can get it to Diane."

Liam scanned the living room for the remaining weaponry. The two Heckler and Koch 416 rifles with suppressors, staged by the couch for Nana and Judith, caught his eye. He'd never envisioned leaving the main assault weapons in the hands of a wraith attack survivor and an empath's grandmother.

"It's time for your present." The elder hunter reached into a cabinet and withdrew a locked case with his personal valuables.

"If you hand me your last will and testament, I'll refuse."

"It's nothing like that, I assure you."

Opening the box, his father ogled two identical pieces of jewelry. He lifted them and draped them over his wrist. From each necklace of white gold hung a disk of silver holding a milky iridescent ovular moonstone, which lacey, gothic metal twists surrounded with a sharp point. Examining the silvery structure, Liam thought the stone's setting suggested a dagger underneath a full moon.

"What are these?"

"Amulets. They prevent the wraith from sensing us."

"When I saw him, he appeared like a demon of fire."

"And we suspect that he can see us as something different.

These amulets negate his sensory advantages."

His father put on the first amulet, and then he extended the second necklace, making Liam lower his head. He felt a welcoming energy field surrounding him as the pendant landed on his neck. "Thank you, Father."

"You're quite welcome."

Nana squinted at him. "Where'd you get that?"

"My father gave them to me, and I'm gifting them to Liam. A tradition of our lineage, which Liam is learning in this moment, is that the father separates the amulets before battle with the intent of reuniting with his son after the battle."

With jewelry exposed, the women were upon Liam in seconds. Judith clasped it. "How sweet!"

Nana pointed. "I have one just like it. Diane has it now."

Connor raised his finger for the ladies' attention. "That's splendid. It seems that fate is uniting us on many levels. Now, everyone, remember that we're saving three lives. Judith and Nana, shoot only at the wraith. Liam and I will handle his companions with our non-lethal weapons. Take your places."

Nana moved to the driver's seat, Judith kneeled on the couch, Connor stood over Nana, and Liam grabbed Josh's elbow. "You're going to stay in the rental car, Josh."

"Why?"

"It's dangerous. We need you here where it's safe."

"I want to come."

"Call Nana if Diane contacts you. We'll all be on a conference call with Nana. We'll all be able to hear you."

Liam took Josh to the rental car and left him with his phone and tablet. He returned to the RV. "Let's go."

Nana backed out of the parking spot with her normal caution, but moving forward proved challenging with sandbags in her face. "I can't see."

Standing beside the grandmother, Connor looked over the barrier. "I'll guide you. Forward, slowly. Now brake slowly. Good. You're pulling onto the main road now. Forward slowly while turning right."

Liam joined Judith in helping his father guide Nana. After several miles and five turns, the moment came for the final transformation of the Journey into a war machine.

Outside the RV, Liam heard the evening's first chirping of crickets as he walked to each wheel well and jammed his combat knife into smooth black rubber. Under the Winnebago's weight, each tire deflated in a controlled and equal rate. He moved to the door where his colleagues had gathered with weapons.

A car passed them, its occupants giving strange looks at the armed team. But in a state with deer on its flag, hunting weapons were as common as car starters.

When the rescue team was alone again, Connor borrowed a rifle from Nana and aimed it at the windshield. "Let's have a little test, shall we? Hold your ears."

Rapid bursts cut holes into the glass, and then Connor stepped around the corner to test the side windows.

"Here we go again."

The second volley shattered the side glass. Connor gave the rifle back to Nana and then lifted a shotgun to attack the windshield further. When the safety glass became crumbling spider webs, the older hunter stuck his head into the bus.

"It appears that our sandbags held. We can take it from here, Liam. You must run ahead. I wish you good fortune, my son."

The hunter hugged his father and darted into the trees.

CHAPTER 47

Jacob looked at his vibrating phone and noticed an urgent notification.

An external camera's motion sensor had alarmed.

Calling up the view on his security application, he saw a Winnebago with flat tires driving up his driveway.

With half an hour until moonrise, he hoped to offer Diane as tribute to his Master and return to his predictable killing schedule. But his demonic god had made his demand clear.

This year, there would be no escaping the hunters.

He needed to face them and defeat them.

Yelling to a sentinel in the kitchen, he made sure his voice carried down the stairway to his other guard. "Body armor! Now! They're coming up the driveway."

With most of his gear and weapons laid out in the living room, he jumped up from an easy chair and lifted his vest from the coffee table. As he strapped it on, Jessica entered the room and grabbed her armor.

Her sanguine irises assured him of her spellbound obedience, and he ordered her to a window with her shotgun and a box of extra shells. He tapped the spare cartridges in his armor, lifted the Colt M16A2 assault rifle, and carried it to the wall beside a window facing the front yard.

Squatting beside the glass, he ordered Jessica to remove the hazards of shards. "Shoot out your window and mine."

The sentinel stood, aimed her shotgun, and blew out her glass. As Jacob shielded his face, she turned, fired, and shattered the transparent façade in front of him. "What do we aim for, my lord?"

The question stumped him. The tires were flat, sandbags

protected the occupants, and the engine was mounted out of sight in the rear. But then he had an idea. "Shoot the front wheel. Try to crack it and warp it."

As he spoke, the RV brushed a tree branch, triggering one of his incendiary bombs to crash against a rock. The burst of phosphorus and gasoline charred the vehicle and burned holes through its side panels, but the lumbering six-wheeled nightmare continued towards him.

Rifle bullets and shotgun shells deafened him as he and his sentry fired rounds. He stared at the wheel and saw jagged shadows where the buckshot hit.

He needed more firepower. "Kim! Get up here with your shotgun!"

The shorter sentry arrived at the top of the stairs, stooped, and trotted to a window. "Are we shooting the front rim, my lord?"

"Yes!"

Jessica lowered her weapon. "I need to reload."

"Kim, cover her while she reloads!"

The barista sentry shrugged. "Nobody's shooting at us."

"Shoot the rim, then."

The wraith's fear grew as he realized he'd failed to consider the hunters approaching in a semi-armored vehicle. At least the hunters' weapons remained silent, but that conciliation frightened him further.

Their silence meant they were preparing something terrible.

As the Winnebago rolled closer, the sentinels' shots became more accurate, and their shells more damaging. The wheel became misshapen, the rims jagged, slowing the vehicle.

But the mechanized beast turned, fighting its warping wheel, and showed a quarter profile of its front grill.

"Cease fire! Save your ammo! Reload!"

The sentinels silenced their shotguns, kept their heads below the sills, and reached for spare shells.

The lack of incoming gunfire scared him. "Why are they waiting? What are they doing? They can't rescue her from out there."

Defying his words, his enemies raised rifle barrels over the interior sandbags and sent bullets through the open window frames, compelling the cabin's defenders deeper towards the floor and suppressing any retaliation.

Seconds later, a crack and a whump sounded below and behind Jacob. He registered the attack as a grenade at the downstairs glass wall, and he realized his mistake.

The RV was a diversion, and the real attack was in the basement, with his unguarded prisoner. He issued his enslaved guards a new command. "Shoot anyone you see out there. I'm going downstairs."

As he stood, he saw the torso of a man in body armor rise above the roof's sandbag wall and aim a riot gun. As the weapon sounded, three canisters tumbled into the living room and spewed teargas. "Cease fire! Come downstairs with me!

As he darted to the stairway, his coughing guards hurried through gas clouds, but the hunter showed his grenade skills by landing a weapon in their paths.

Lacking shrapnel, the concussion weapon exploded and sent Jacob's soldiers sideways. The blast hurled him down the stairs, and he landed with a bruising thump against his upper back.

He rolled to his feet and jumped to the door. He slammed it shut, reached in his pocket, and found his key. After locking the deadbolt, he stuffed the key in his pocket and leveled the M16 rifle's barrel ahead of his steps as he descended the stairs.

Reaching the floor, he inspected his potential threats.

Through the checkered section of his cinderblocks, he saw a tattered curtain opened to the evening air. He turned off the overhead lights and aimed his rifle at the solitary lamp. A single round shattered the bulb and shrouded the room in darkness.

He dropped to his knees and crawled behind the couch. Certain nobody could scale his homemade edifice without discernable noise, he controlled his breathing and moved towards the bathroom, listening for the attacker to attempt an ingress.

At the door, he lifted his rifle and scanned outward for an intruder, but there was nobody.

A glance at his watch showed ten minutes until moonrise, and he looked behind him, seeing his prisoner's chains leading into the bathtub.

The otherworldly connection with his Master strengthened in Diane's presence, convincing him that killing her in tribute would lead to his freedom and to the continued enduring life he craved.

He tapped the bronze dagger sheathed in his vest to reassure himself of its presence, and then he breathed a sigh of relief.

His sacrifice-turned-tribute was cornered, he held a strong defensive position, and time was on his side.

CHAPTER 48

Infrared goggles over his eyes, Liam stopped his slithering meters from the shattered glass.

Looking up, he saw a human form in the room's back corner. Unsure who it was, he sought information.

The microphone taped to his neck sent his voice over the cellular network to Nana's phone and to the team in the RV. "Father, its Liam."

The elder hunter's voice played through the speaker in Liam's right ear. "Go ahead, lad."

"I see one person on infrared in the basement."

"There should be two. He made it downstairs. We're approaching the living room up here, but I believe Jessica and Kim are incapacitated."

"I don't have time to wait for backup. Moonrise is coming."

"I'm stepping through the windows up here, now. They're alive but incapacitated. I'm sure Judith and Nana can detain them. Ladies, come to the living room and guard our two prisoners. I'm withdrawing from the house and will circle behind you for backup, Liam. But you need to move. It's three minutes to moonrise."

"I'm going in, Father."

"I know you can do it."

Rising to his knees, the young hunter pulled a concussion grenade from his vest. He reached back and lobbed it towards the gap above the cinderblock wall. Thankful the wraith had left the open space above the edifice for his escape, Liam congratulated himself on an accurate toss–until the metal clanked off the top block and bounced back onto the grass. "Bloody hell."

He rolled away, curled his back against the blast, and pressed his fingers into his ears. Like a wall of metal, compressed air hammered him.

Whining white noise filled his head, and he lost his orientation. A leather-faced angel, his father appeared, kneeling in front of him and screaming. "Get up! Get up!"

The elder hunter pushed the night vision back over Liam's head, letting him see the evening's true colors, and he brought his son to his feet.

"I'm up."

"Get a concussion grenade and flare into that room! I'll cover you, lad."

His father's assurance focused him, and he watched the elder hunter move to the cinderblock wall. Connor aimed a shotgun, loaded with beanbags to prevent friendly deaths, through a crack.

While he pulled the trigger, retaliatory bullets ricocheted off the checkered blocks, sending gray dust into the dusky air. As Liam ran for the wall, he yanked a flare from his vest with one hand and detached a grenade with his other, pulled its pin, and committed himself to a better toss.

He extended his arm over the wall and threw the grenade and then the flare into the basement. Ducking as the weapon exploded, he saw his father crouching and falling, his back against the cinderblocks.

"Father!" Probing the older hunter's clasped hands, he felt blood oozing from a high leg wound.

"Go on, lad. Save her."

"Judith! Get back here with first aid. Father's hit in the leg and bleeding badly."

"I'm on my way."

Grabbing a pistol, Liam climbed the wall and stopped atop its summit. He leveled his weapon, and in the flare's eerie red light, he saw a rifle's barrel behind the couch. Seeing only a clumsy entrance opportunity, he squeezed off two rounds to deter the wraith, slid over the wall, and plummeted down the cinderblock wall's far side.

When his boots hit the floor, quick math ran through his head.

His only lethal weapon, his pistol, held eight more rounds. His enemy's rifle held twice that many. He had a shotgun filled with beanbags strapped over his shoulder, but as the savage stood and took aim, timing restricted Liam to his pistol.

In his eyes, the savage's face was a twisted aberration of sagging and torn skins. Fangs protruded from the slimy mouth towards a long, crooked nose. His inner essence exposed in nakedness, his body appeared as scarred and blighted leather, and at its extreme ends, horns, a pointed tail, and cloven hooves.

Liam aimed at the beast and pulled his trigger, exchanging rounds with his enemy.

Bullets pelted his vest like horse kicks, knocking him down while he fired back at his assailant. The wraith stumbled backwards, but he recovered and moved closer.

More bullets punched Liam, and two hit his free arm, inflicting a searing pain that receded into a tingling coldness. Emptying his clip into the monster delayed the inevitable, but the enemy smirked as he lifted his rifle again.

Unable to move his numbing fractured limb, Liam lay the pistol on his chest and fumbled through his vest pockets for a new magazine. Moving with morbid lethargy, he was trapped.

He said a quick prayer as the savage pointed the rifle at his unprotected face.

Diane screamed as she jumped forward and grabbed the wraith's gun. Her battle cry became a squeal as her right palm burned against the hot barrel.

Remembering the prophecy hidden within the combined tomes, Liam reached for his dagger, unsheathed it, and lobbed it towards Diane.

In mid-flight, the weapon flipped and pointed towards the prior tribute in Flint as Liam's observation imbued it with magic. Judging his toss inaccurate, he thought his eyes tricked him as the dagger's dynamics changed at the apex of its arc.

The natural bronze color receded, and a strong angelic light blue supplanted it, brightening the room. The weapon changed direction and veered into Diane's healthy hand.

His rifle on the ground, the wraith exposed his dagger, ready to overpower his tribute, and Liam expected the pending knife fight to end in the trained killer's favor.

But the azure light rising from Diane's blade offered hope.

Reminding himself to continue reloading his pistol, he missed half the battle, but he saw enough.

By the time he clicked the fresh magazine into his weapon and slammed the bolt forward, Diane, nursing her burned hand against her chest and with her feet bound, wielded the charmed dagger like a superhuman.

She parried a punch, slicing her assailant's forearm. Then she clashed bronze against bronze, and the weapons exchanged a multi-colored bolt of supercharged lightning.

The wraith moved with concise, expert motions, awing Liam with his skill. But a woman possessed, Diane outmaneuvered him, stopping three slashes and two stabbing attempts that would have killed a lesser foe.

As her wide-eyed confidence in her newfound abilities climaxed, she thrust the point towards his exposed neck, and the wraith blocked with his crossguard. Mystical sparks flew as bronze scraped bronze. With a crazed shriek, she pulled her weapon back and then whipped the blade upward with incredible speed, cutting off the wraith's hand.

The cursed dagger hit the ground as the savage howled, clutched his stump, and fell to his knees.

Diane defied the laws of physics again as she reached behind her heels and powered the bronze through her stainless steel toilet tether.

Her chain broken, she stepped to her evil captor. Her voice was a haunting symphony blending the voices of a hundred dead victims.

"I avenge. I free. I redeem."

One handed, she plunged the coppery knife through her enemy's armor and into his heart.

White light cracked though the wraith's skin and clothing, and ghosts wearing milky white dresses emerged from his dying form. Hundreds of apparitions escaped their killer, rose through the house, and ascended beyond sight.

As the final victim flew away, the savage's body turned to dust and bones, crumbling to its proper state of decay for a five-hundred-year old corpse.

CHAPTER 49

After catching her breath during a long stare at the pile of bones, Diane challenged the laws of physics again by slicing the blade's bronze edge through the harder steel of her iron chains. The dagger's magic allowed her freedom, and she enjoyed long strides towards her rescuer.

She recognized him from her past link with Judith. "Liam?"

"Yes."

"You saved my life."

"You saved mine."

"Are you okay?"

"I think my arm's broken, but I'm not bleeding too badly. I'm more worried about my father."

The blade's azure light weakened to a dull glow, and she looked at it. "This is impossible. What just happened?"

"I'm not sure. Maybe you should put it away." He rolled to his knees and extended the sheath.

She slid in the blade, and it assumed its natural color when she released it. "Where's your father?"

"Outside."

She was eager to leap over the cinderblock barrier, run her toes in the grass, and see the stars, but she remembered an important artifact. "What about the other dagger?"

"Don't touch it. Wrap it in a towel and toss it outside. We need to remember it. God willing, it'll remain under guard from his kind until the end of time."

She darted into the bathroom for a towel, rolled the cursed weapon into it, and threw it over the barrier. "The other dagger's outside. Can you get over the top?"

"I'll manage. Ladies first." Despite favoring his injured arm, he offered his shoulder and back to hoist her while she climbed to the edifice's summit.

With blisters forming, her burned hand hurt, but she rolled over the edge and slithered down the other side. Her pajamas crawled up her legs, and the coarse wall abraded her skin, but she reached freedom. In the darkness, she saw the silhouettes of a woman tending to an injured man.

"Diane? I'm Connor. This is Judith."

"Yes, I'm Diane. Are you okay?"

"I should be alright, thanks to the quick work of this skilled nursing student."

Judith had a French accent with a Caribbean vibe. "I did only temporary work. We still need to get you to a hospital, or you're going to lose your leg."

"She's applied a tourniquet. Apparently, a bullet nicked my femoral artery, but I'm more worried about my son. Where's Liam?"

Behind Diane, Liam's boots hit the ground. "How's my father?"

"And there's my son. After all that gunfire, I'd feared the worst."

"I've got a broken arm, but Diane saved me from much worse. The dagger became fierce magic in her hand."

Relieved her Irish rescuers had survived, Diane thought of the other participants. "How are Josh and Nana?"

Liam stepped beside her. "I'm talking to them now. Josh is sitting in a car a few miles from here, and Nana's coming to join us now."

More relief washed over Diane with the affirmation of her family's safety. "What about Jessica and Kim? They couldn't help themselves. They were victims, too."

"I didn't understand your grandmother fully, but I think they're fine. I don't know if they're still threats, though."

Moments later, the silhouettes of three walking women rounded the cabin's corner. Recognizing her grandmother, Diane started towards her, the broken chains of her leg irons jingling.

Before she reached Nana, the two sentries stared at her with moonlit apologetic eyes.

Jessica's sanguine irises were gone. "I'm sorry."

Apologizing with her natural eyes, Kim echoed the sentiment. "So am I. I was trapped inside my own body."

Diane acted upon her urge to hug her former guards. They were both quivering with an overflow of mixed emotions. "I know you were trapped. It's okay."

As Diane released the freed slaves, Jessica reached into her pocket and withdrew the moonstone pendant. "I think this is yours. I found it in the kitchen."

Diane accepted it and put it on. "Why didn't you wear it? It might have broken whatever spell you were under."

"I wanted to, but I couldn't put it on. There were so many things I wanted to say and do, but I couldn't."

The grandmother stepped forward with an assault rifle in her hand. Diane raised her arms and hugged her. "You look great with a gun, Nana."

"I'm so glad you're okay."

The small group encircled the seated elder hunter, who gave commands. "We need to clean up this mess before the authorities arrive. For starters, does anyone need medical attention other than Liam and myself?"

"I can wait, Father. Best that I get treated in Detroit where a gunshot wound won't bring as much attention."

"Good thinking. I, however, need treatment soon. I suggest that Nana, Diane, and I await the authorities. The rest of you should make for the rental car and drive away with Josh as if you were never here."

Liam agreed with his father. "I can take us back on the main road without being seen."

Diane questioned the evolving plan. "Why does anyone need to stay? Why can't we just run?"

"That's a good question I'd love to answer, but first we must sanitize this crime scene. Liam and Judith, run to the garage and get some gasoline. I'm sure there's some there left over from the incendiary devices. You need to start a fire in this house and burn it to the ground, immediately."

As the young rescuers trotted away, Connor continued his explanation. "Since the RV's in my name, I'm tied to the scene of the crime. And since I can't hide the fact that I assaulted this house, I need to admit to having rescued you. That's why you must be here. And with the sandbag setup requiring two people to drive the RV, I must have had at least one helper."

Diane found her grandmother's annoying nod noble as she accepted her risk of criminal guilt. "Me."

"Yes. Nana is my newest partner in crime. I don't expect that the legal system will be too harsh on a grandmother taking up arms to save her granddaughter's life from a madman. And if I understand the nature of their enslavement, Kim and Jessica remember everything they did, but we can't let them confess."

Diane tried to keep pace with the plan. "Is my Nana going to jail?"

"Whatever happens, let's be clear that I killed the murderer, when the authorities ask. And none of you saw how it happened. Come on, now. Help me to my feet."

Diane reached for him and offered leverage while the two former slaves assisted her.

Connor grimaced while moving. "Thank you, ladies. Let's get to the RV."

Paced by the elder hunter's hobbling, the group rounded the house, and the RV came into view. As the entrance to the waterfront cabin became visible, Judith and Liam exited its front door and returned to the vehicle.

Orange flames backlit the handsome young hunter. "It's burning. It'll be an inferno soon enough."

"Lead the others out of here, lad. Diane and Nana, please help an old man into an easy chair, and perhaps we can enjoy some tea while we await the authorities."

CHAPTER 50

Two days later, Diane dreamt of a woman on a cross, blood pouring from her wound.

She called out in her nightmare. "Why are you here again?"

The blood stalled, the cross evaporated, and the unwounded misty maiden appeared. "Help the others."

"I don't understand."

Like a lifting fog, the whiteness drifted from the French sacrifice, revealing a human being. Platinum blonde hair framed a round face with blue eyes. "You helped me. You redeemed all of us whom he killed. But you must do more."

"Why? I killed him. I freed you all."

"You are making a false assumption."

After defeating her enemy, wielding the enchanted dagger, and controlling multiple telepathy connections, Diane embraced her growing power. She braved showing a little moxie in her dream and challenging the visitor. "If you keep up the riddles, I'll cast you out."

The French maiden became translucent. "Please... I will speak eloquently."

Diane allowed the maiden's presence, and the ghost became an opaque apparition. "Go ahead. I'm listening."

"You destroyed one monster, but there are more, and there are many trails of dead victims in need of redemption."

The news startled Diane from her sleep. She awoke on her grandmother's living room couch.

Smelling allspice, garlic, and tomato paste from the pot of beef-and-rice-stuffed grape leaves simmering in the kitchen, she rolled her feet to the floor and stood. "Nana, do you need help making the *dolma*?"

"No, it's okay. You relax."

Joining her grandmother in the kitchen, Diane poured herself a cup of coffee. After she ingested several sips, soft knocks preceded the opening of the internal garage door. Smiling, Judith appeared with the hunters behind her.

The older hunter walked into the kitchen with his white knuckles grasping a cane. His arm in a sling, Liam trailed his father and closed the door behind him.

The Irishmen sat beside Diane at the island and summarized their status. Medical professionals had repaired the arterial damage and had confirmed that the nursing student's field treatment had saved Connor's life.

The events leading to the elder hunter's freedom and that of Nana remained murky in Diane's mind. "I didn't know you were already sprung free from the hospital. I thought they had you chained to a bed."

"Young lady, I'm part of an order that has its ways with the authorities."

"That's it? That's your explanation?"

"Perhaps I'll add a bit more detail during dinner. I'm famished. The hospital food was terrible."

Over dinner, Diane savored the flavors of her culture. The fresh lemon squeezed over the stuffed grape leaves, which she dipped in plain yogurt, helped her forget about her imprisonment.

The group at the dining table skipped small talk and jumped into their meaty topics. In a rare move, Josh started the conversation. "Diane has a secret."

"I do?"

"You had a dream last night."

"What are you, the empath police?"

"I just know. You need to share your dream."

"Okay, I had a dream about something. I wasn't sure how to tell anyone. I wanted to be sure it was real first. The ghost, or whoever she is, told me that there are more wraiths."

A silence fell over the dinner table until Josh broke it. "The new chapter I made from both books didn't specify between two daggers or more daggers."

Fumbling to feed himself with his weak arm, the younger hunter dropped his fork and stuffed grape leaf onto his plate and protested. "We have both daggers now. We have the blessed one and the cursed one."

"That ghost saved my life, and I'm going to believe her until she lies to me. She says there are more wraiths."

Despite the magic he'd seen, the young hunter sounded skeptical. "Dreams. Double-encrypted books. Enchanted daggers. And now multiple wraiths?"

Judith reprised her role as peacemaker. "Calm down. You and Connor knew what you were doing the whole time. I have faith in you guys. You could take on an army of them if you had to."

Connor swallowed his mouthful. "Perhaps I should share a bit more about the secrets of our order."

"I say it's time for you to share everything about the bloody order, Father. You've been mentioning it here and there while keeping it a secret."

Diane sensed a line being crossed. "But you can't share all of it with all of us, can you?"

Connor looked away in thought, glanced at the faces around the table, and then offered a light smile. "Given that we've become a formidable team, we may as well share secrets. If you'd like to hear more about my order, I'd like to oblige." The hunter hesitated while seeming to probe his mind for an ordered list of mysteries to expose.

After her long captivity, Diane's patience was thin. "Well?"

The elder hunter inhaled deeply before answering. "You're right. There are other wraiths, and our order tracks them. We defeated one together, and that was no easy task, but there are more cursed daggers and more wraiths that must be stopped."

Diane voiced one of many questions spinning in her head. "Are there other hunters besides you and Liam?"

"I can't say."

"You don't know, or you can't say?"

"A little of both. I sense that things are changing, thanks to you. It's been a thousand years since a wraith was defeated and the life of his intended sacrifice saved. I must consult the order before I can give you a complete answer."

Hungering for knowledge about the forces that had threatened her, as well as those that had saved her, Diane demanded insight. "Well, can you tell us what you do know?"

"The irony is that I've lived my entire life thinking I know too little about the order, but after battling a wraith, I now fear I may know too much. Events are still arranging themselves within my mind as I take them in and interpret them."

Diane rolled her eyes. "If you don't want to talk about it, just say so."

Connor surprised her by snapping. "No! I mean... I'm sorry. It's just that your survival, your powers, your defeating of a wraith who intended to sacrifice you... this was no isolated incident. This was only the beginning. You're special in the eyes of the order, an enigma, but a welcomed one. A desired one."

"So, I'm their new favorite puzzle?"

The elder hunter furrowed his brow. "Not exactly. It's more like, you're necessary to them, although I'm not sure if that's entirely correct or if they'd agree just yet."

He'd piqued Diane's curiosity. "What wouldn't they agree on?"

"They need to assess your ability to help them defeat other evils."

Wanting to run from the unqualified invitation to danger, Diane overruled her fear. She sensed an obligation to know more. "Did you mean 'other evils' or 'other wraiths'? You hunt wraiths, specifically."

"I meant both. There are evils worse than those monstrous wraiths, evils beyond your imagination that know no bounds. Evils that are older, stronger, wiser, and hungrier for destruction than the wraith who attacked you."

Diane swallowed and gathered her courage. "Tell me, tell us all what you can about the order and what lies ahead."

"Yes, I'll share everything I can. But first, you must promise to take the secrets to your graves and to never, ever share what I'm about to tell you with another living soul."

THE END

Letter to the Reader

Dear Reader,

The wraith is dead.

Well, one of many are.

Diane is just beginning to learn her identity, but she must hurry. A second wraith, the cruelest of the lineage, is surfacing. And she's the only one who can stop his brutal killing.

She must complete her transformation into a selfless empath and arm herself as a psychic. Failure means death to her family, her new friends, and countless innocents.

But she paid her dues escaping the wraith. Why should she risk anything more?

Because she feels destiny calling her.

And she knows she must answer.

Continue your adventure now.

Prophecy of Blood

PROPHECY OF ASHES

www.ingramcontent.com/pod-product-compliance
Lightning Source LLC
Chambersburg PA
CBHW020248200626
46816CB00001BA/188